John Galsworthy was born on August 14, 1867, at Kingston Hill in Surrey, the son of John and Blanche Galsw[...] [...] of four children. John Galsworthy [...], was a successful solicitor in Lon[...] [...] mined to provide privilege and [...] him. By contrast, their mother [...] strict and distant. Galsworthy co[...] ated in me from the start . . . I was so truly and deeply fond of him that I seemed not to have a fair share of love left to give my mother'.

Young Johnny enjoyed the happy secure childhood of a Victorian, upper-middle-class family. Educated at Harrow, he was popular at school and a good sportsman. Holidays were spent with family and friends, moving between their country houses. After finishing school, John went up to New College, Oxford to read law. There he enjoyed the carefree life of a privileged student, not working particularly hard, gambling and becoming known as 'the best dressed man in College'. But he could also be quiet and serious, a contemporary describing how 'He moved among us somewhat withdrawn . . . a sensitive, amused, somewhat cynical spectator of the human scene'.

The period after university was one of indecision for Galsworthy. Although his father wanted him to become a barrister, the law held little appeal. So he decided to get away from it all and travel. It was on a voyage in the South Seas in 1893 that he met Joseph Conrad, and the two became close friends. It was a crucial friendship in Galsworthy's life. Conrad encouraged his love of writing, but Galsworthy attributes his final inspiration to the woman he was falling in love with: Ada.

Ada Nemesis Pearson Cooper married Major Arthur Galsworthy, John's cousin, in 1891. But the marriage was a tragic mistake. Embraced by the entire family, Ada became close friends with John's beloved sisters, Lilian and Mabel, and through them John heard of her increasing misery, fixing in his imagination the pain of an unhappy marriage. Thrown together more and more, John and Ada eventually became lovers in September 1895. They were unafraid of declaring their relationship and facing the consequences, but the only person they couldn't bear to hurt was John's adored father, with his traditional values. And so they endured ten years of secrecy until

Galsworthy's father died in December 1904. By September 1905 Ada's divorce had come through and they were finally able to marry.

It was around this time, in 1906, that Galsworthy's writing career flourished. During the previous decade he had been a man 'in chains', emotionally and professionally, having finally abandoned law in 1894. He struggled to establish himself as an author. But after many false starts and battling a lifelong insecurity about his writing, Galsworthy turned an affectionately satirical eye on the world he knew best and created the indomitable Forsytes, a mirror image of his own relations – old Jolyon: his father; Irene: his beloved Ada, to name but a few. On reading the manuscript, his sister Lilian was alarmed that he could so expose their private lives, but John dismissed her fears saying only herself, Mabel and their mother, 'who perhaps had better not read the book', knew enough to draw comparisons. *The Man of Property*, the first book in *The Forsyte Saga*, was published to instant acclaim; Galsworthy's fame as an author was now sealed.

By the time the first Forsyte trilogy had been completed, with *In Chancery* (1920) and *To Let* (1921), sales of *The Forsyte Saga* had reached one million on both sides of the Atlantic. With the public clambering for more, Galsworthy followed these with six more Forsyte novels, the last of which, *Over The River*, was completed just before his death in 1933. And their appeal endures, immortalised on screen in much-loved adaptations such as the film *That Forsyte Woman* (1949), starring Errol Flynn. The celebrated BBC drama in 1967 with Kenneth Moore and Eric Porter was a phenomenal success, emptying the pubs and churches of Britain on a Sunday evening, and reaching an estimated worldwide audience of 160 million. The recent popular 2002 production starred Damien Lewis, Rupert Graves and Ioan Gruffudd and won a Bafta TV award.

Undoubtedly *The Forsyte Saga* is Galsworthy's most distinguished work, but he was well known, if not more successful in his time, as a dramatist. His inherent compassion meant Galsworthy was always involved in one cause or another, from women's suffrage to a ban on ponies in mines, and his plays very much focus on the social injustices of his day. *The Silver Box* (1906) was his first major success, but *Justice* (1910), a stark depiction of prison life, had an even bigger impact. Winston Churchill was so impressed by it that he immediately arranged for prison reform, reducing the hours of solitary confinement. *The Skin Game* (1920) was another big hit and later adapted into a film, under the same title, by Alfred Hitchcock.

Despite Galsworthy's literary success, his personal life was still troubled. Although he and Ada were deeply in love, the years of uncertainty had taken their toll. They never had children and their marriage reached a crisis in 1910 when Galsworthy formed a close friendship with a young dancer called Margaret Morris while working on one of his plays with her. But John, confused and tortured by the thought of betraying Ada, broke off all contact with Margaret in 1912 and went abroad with his wife. The rest of their lives were spent constantly on the move; travelling in America, Europe, or at home in London, Dartmoor and later Sussex. Numerous trips were made in connection with PEN, the international writers club, after Galsworthy was elected its first president in 1921. Many people have seen the constant travelling as unsettling for Galsworthy and destructive to his writing, but being with Ada was all that mattered to him: 'This is what comes of giving yourself to a woman body and soul. A. paralyses and has always paralysed me. I have never been able to face the idea of being cut off from her.'

By the end of his life, Galsworthy, the man who had railed against poverty and injustice, had become an established, reputable figure in privileged society. Having earlier refused a knighthood, he was presented with an Order of Merit in 1929. And in 1932 he was awarded the Nobel Prize for literature. Although it was fashionable for younger writers to mock the traditional Edwardian authors, Virginia Woolf dismissing Galsworthy as a 'stuffed shirt', J.M. Barrie perceived his contradictory nature: 'A queer fish, like the rest of us. So sincerely weighed down by the out-of-jointness of things socially . . . but outwardly a man-about-town, so neat, so correct – he would go to the stake for his opinions but he would go courteously raising his hat.'

John Galsworthy died on 31 January, 1933, at the age of sixty-five, at Grove Lodge in Hampstead, with Ada by his side. At his request, his ashes were scattered over Bury Hill in Sussex. *The Times* hailed him as the 'mouthpiece' of his age, 'the interpreter in drama, and in fiction of a definite phase in English social history'.

Other Forsyte novels by John Galsworthy and available from Headline Review

The Man Of Property
In Chancery
The White Monkey
The Silver Spoon
Swan Song
Maid In Waiting
Flowering Wilderness
Over The River

The Forsyte Saga

To Let

John Galsworthy

headline
review

First published in Great Britain in 1921

This paperback edition published in 2007 by HEADLINE REVIEW
An imprint of HEADLINE PUBLISHING GROUP

1

ISBN 978 0 7553 4087 3

Typeset in Sabon by
Palimpsest Book Production Limited, Grangemouth, Stirlingshire

Printed and bound in Great Britain by
Clays Ltd, St Ives plc

Headline's policy is to use papers that are natural, renewable
and recyclable products and made from wood grown in
sustainable forests. The logging and manufacturing processes are
expected to conform to the environmental regulations
of the country of origin.

HEADLINE PUBLISHING GROUP
An Hachette Livre UK Company
338 Euston Road
London NW1 3BH

www.reviewbooks.co.uk
www.headline.co.uk

To
My Wife

I dedicate *The Forsyte Saga* in its entirety believing it to be of all my work the least unworthy of one without whose encouragement, sympathy, and critisism I could never have become even such a writer as I am.

FORSYTE FA

b. 1741, JOLYON FORSYTE (Farmer, of Hays, D

b. 1770, Jolyon 'Superior Dossett' (Builder),   Edgar
d. 1850 m. 1798, Ann Pierce, daughter   (In Jute)
of Country Solicitor

(1)   (2)

b. 1799, Ann,   b. 1806, Jolyon 'Old Jolyon' d. 1892
d. 1886   (Tea Merchant 'Forsyte and Treffry'   (Sol
'Aunt Ann'   Chairman of Companies), Stanhope Gate,   a
m. 1846, Edith Moor, d. 1874, daughter of Barrister

b. 1847, Jolyon
'Young Jolyon' (Underwriter and Artist),
St John's Wood and Robin Hill, m. 1880

m. 1868 (1), Frances Crisson (2), Helene Hilmer d. 1894 (Austro-English)   m. 1901 (3), Irene,   m. 1
d. 1880, daughter   daughter of   daug
of Colonel   Professor Heron   He
and divorced wife   d

b. 1869, June   b. 1879, Jolly,   b. 1881, Holly,   of Soames Forsyte
(Engaged to Philip Bosinney,   d. in Transvaal,   m. 1900,
never married)   1900   Val Dartie   b. 1901, Joylon,
'Jon'

★   (5)   (6)   (7)

b. 1813, Roger, d. 1899 (Collector   b. 1814, Julia, d. 1905 'Aunt Juley' m. Septimus   b. 1815, Heste
of House Property), Prince's   Small, of weak constitution, who died   d. 1907 'Aunt He
Gardens, m. 1853, Mary Monk   of it. Reverted to Bayswater Road   Bayswater Ro

b. 1853, Roger   b. 1856,   b. 1858, Francie   b. 1860,   b. 1862,   b. 1849, Nicholas 'Your
'Young Roger'   George   (Composer   Eustace   Thomas   Nicholas' (Insurances
m. Muriel Wake   and poetess)   m. No Offspring   m. No Offspring   m. 1877, Dorothy Boxto
Widower before

b. 1890, Roger   the War   b. 1879, Nicholas   b. 1880,   b. 1
'Very Young Roger',   'Very Young Nicholas',   Blanche
Wounded in the War   (Barrister, O.B.E.) m.

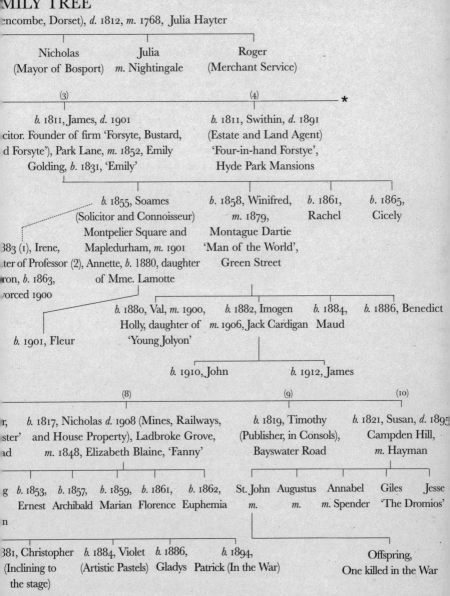

...MILY TREE

...encombe, Dorset), *d.* 1812, *m.* 1768, Julia Hayter

| Nicholas (Mayor of Bosport) | Julia *m.* Nightingale | Roger (Merchant Service) |

(3)   (4)   *

b. 1811, James, *d.* 1901
...citor. Founder of firm 'Forsyte, Bustard,
...d Forsyte'), Park Lane, *m.* 1852, Emily
Golding, *b.* 1831, 'Emily'

b. 1811, Swithin, *d.* 1891
(Estate and Land Agent)
'Four-in-hand Forstye',
Hyde Park Mansions

b. 1855, Soames
(Solicitor and Connoisseur)
Montpelier Square and
Mapledurham, *m.* 1901
(2), Annette, *b.* 1880, daughter
of Mme. Lamotte

...383 (1), Irene,
...ter of Professor
...ron, *b.* 1863,
...orced 1900

b. 1858, Winifred,
m. 1879,
Montague Dartie
'Man of the World',
Green Street

b. 1861, Rachel

b. 1865, Cicely

b. 1880, Val, *m.* 1900,
Holly, daughter of
'Young Jolyon'

b. 1901, Fleur

b. 1882, Imogen
m. 1906, Jack Cardigan

b. 1884, Maud

b. 1886, Benedict

b. 1910, John   *b.* 1912, James

(8)   (9)   (10)

...r, *b.* 1817, Nicholas *d.* 1908 (Mines, Railways,
...ster' and House Property), Ladbroke Grove,
...ad   *m.* 1848, Elizabeth Blaine, 'Fanny'

b. 1819, Timothy
(Publisher, in Consols),
Bayswater Road

b. 1821, Susan, *d.* 1895
Campden Hill,
m. Hayman

...g *b.* 1853, Ernest,   *b.* 1857, Archibald,   *b.* 1859, Marian,   *b.* 1861, Florence,   *b.* 1862, Euphemia
...n

St. John *m.*   Augustus *m.*   Annabel *m.* Spender   Giles   Jesse 'The Dromios'

...381, Christopher
(Inclining to
the stage)

b. 1884, Violet
(Artistic Pastels)

b. 1886, Gladys

b. 1894, Patrick (In the War)

Offspring,
One killed in the War

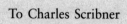

To Charles Scribner

'From out the fatal loins of those two foes
A pair of star-crossed lovers take their life.'

Romeo and Juliet
William Shakespeare

Part I

Chapter One
Encounter

Soames Forsyte emerged from the Knightsbridge Hotel, where he was staying, in the afternoon of 12 May 1920, with the intention of visiting a collection of pictures in a Gallery off Cork Street, and looking into the Future. He walked. Since the War he never took a cab if he could help it. Their drivers were, in his view, an uncivil lot, though now that the War was over and supply beginning to exceed demand again, getting more civil in accordance with the custom of human nature. Still, he had not forgiven them, deeply identifying them with gloomy memories, and now, dimly, like all members of their class, with revolution. The considerable anxiety he had passed through during the War, and the more considerable anxiety he had since undergone in the Peace, had produced psychological consequences in a tenacious nature. He had, mentally, so frequently experienced ruin, that he had ceased to believe in its material probability. Paying away four thousand a year in income and super tax, one could not very well be worse off! A fortune of a quarter of a million, encumbered only by a wife and one daughter, and very diversely invested, afforded substantial guarantee even against that 'wildcat notion': a levy on capital. And as to confiscation of war profits, he was entirely in favour of it, for he had none, and 'serve the beggars right'! The price of pictures, moreover, had, if anything, gone up, and he had done better with his collection since the War began than ever before. Air-raids, also, had acted beneficially on a spirit congenitally cautious, and hardened a character already dogged. To be in danger of being entirely dispersed inclined one to be less apprehensive of the more partial dispersions involved in levies and taxation, while the habit of condemning the impudence of the Germans had led naturally to condemning that of Labour, if not openly at least in the sanctuary of his soul.

He walked. There was, moreover, time to spare, for Fleur was to meet him at the Gallery at four o'clock, and it was as yet but half-past two. It was good for him to walk – his liver was a little constricted, and his nerves rather on edge. His wife was always out when she was in Town, and his daughter *would* flibberty-gibbet all over the place like most young women since the War. Still, he must be thankful that she had been too young to do anything in that War itself. Not, of course, that he had not supported the War from its inception, with all his soul, but between that and supporting it with the bodies of his wife and daughter, there had been a gap fixed by something old-fashioned within him which abhorred emotional extravagance. He had, for instance, strongly objected to Annette, so attractive, and in 1914 only thirty-four, going to her native France, her '*chère patrie*' as, under the stimulus of war, she had begun to call it, to nurse her '*braves poilus*', forsooth! Ruining her health and her looks! As if she were really a nurse! He had put a stopper on it. Let her do needlework for them at home, or knit! She had not gone, therefore, and had never been quite the same woman since. A bad tendency of hers to mock at him, not openly, but in continual little ways, had grown. As for Fleur, the War had resolved the vexed problem whether or not she should go to school. She was better away from her mother in her war mood, from the chance of air-raids, and the impetus to do extravagant things; so he had placed her in a seminary as far west as had seemed to him compatible with excellence, and had missed her horribly. Fleur! He had never regretted the somewhat outlandish name by which at her birth he had decided so suddenly to call her – marked concession though it had been to the French. Fleur! A pretty name – a pretty child! But restless – too restless; and wilful! Knowing her power too over her father! Soames often reflected on the mistake it was to dote on his daughter. To get old and dote! Sixty-five! He was getting on; but he didn't feel it, for, fortunately perhaps, considering Annette's youth and good looks, his second marriage had turned out a cool affair. He had known but one real passion in his life – for that first wife of his – Irene. Yes, and that fellow, his cousin Jolyon, who had gone off with her, was looking very shaky, they said. No wonder, at seventy-two, after twenty years of a third marriage!

Soames paused a moment in his march to lean over the railings of the Row. A suitable spot for reminiscence, half-way between that house in Park Lane which had seen his birth and his parents' deaths, and the little house in Montpelier Square where thirty-five years ago he had enjoyed his first edition of matrimony. Now, after twenty years of his second edition, that old tragedy seemed to him like a previous existence – which had ended when Fleur was born in place of the son he had hoped for. For many years he had ceased regretting, even vaguely, the son who had not been born; Fleur filled the bill in his heart. After all, she bore his name; and he was not looking forward at all to the time when she would change it. Indeed, if he ever thought of such a calamity, it was seasoned by the vague feeling that he could make her rich enough to purchase perhaps and extinguish the name of the fellow who married her – why not, since, as it seemed, women were equal to men nowadays? And Soames, secretly convinced that they were not, passed his curved hand over his face vigorously, till it reached the comfort of his chin.

Thanks to abstemious habits, he had not grown fat and flabby; his nose was pale and thin, his grey moustache close-clipped, his eyesight unimpaired. A slight stoop closened and corrected the expansion given to his face by the heightening of his forehead in the recession of his grey hair. Little change had Time wrought in the 'warmest' of the young Forsytes, as the last of the old Forsytes – Timothy – now in his hundred and first year, would have phrased it.

The shade from the plane-trees fell on his neat Homburg hat; he had given up top hats – it was no use attracting attention to wealth in days like these. Plane-trees! His thoughts travelled sharply to Madrid – the Easter before the War, when, having to make up his mind about that Goya picture, he had taken a voyage of discovery to study the painter on his spot. The fellow had impressed him – great range, real genius! Highly as the chap ranked, he would rank even higher before they had finished with him. The second Goya craze would be greater even than the first; oh, yes! And he had bought. On that visit he had – as never before – commissioned a copy of a fresco painting called *La Vendimia*, wherein was the figure of a girl with an arm akimbo, who had reminded him of his daughter. He had it now in the Gallery at Mapledurham, and rather poor it was – you couldn't copy Goya. He would still look at it, however, if his daughter were not there, for the sake of something irresistibly reminiscent in the light, erect balance of the figure, the width between the arching eyebrows, the eager dreaming of the dark eyes. Curious that Fleur should have dark eyes, when his own were grey – no pure Forsyte had brown eyes – and her mother's blue! But of course her grandmother Lamotte's eyes were dark as treacle!

He began to walk on again toward Hyde Park Corner. No greater change in all England than in the Row! Born almost within hail of it, he could remember it from 1860 on. Brought there as a child between the crinolines to stare at tight-trousered dandies in whiskers, riding with a cavalry seat; to watch the doffing of curly-brimmed and white top hats; the leisurely air of it all, and the little bow-legged man in a long red waistcoat who used to come among the fashion with dogs on several strings, and try to sell one to his mother: King Charles spaniels, Italian greyhounds, affectionate to her crinoline – you never saw them now. You saw no quality of any sort, indeed, just working people sitting in dull rows with nothing to stare at but a few young bouncing females in pot hats, riding astride, or desultory Colonials charging up and down on dismal-looking hacks; with, here and there, little girls on ponies, or old gentlemen jogging their livers, or an orderly trying a great galumphing cavalry horse; no thoroughbreds, no grooms, no bowing, no scraping, no gossip – nothing; only the trees the same – the trees indifferent to the generations and declensions of mankind. A democratic England – dishevelled, hurried, noisy, and seemingly without an apex. And that something fastidious in the soul of Soames turned over within him. Gone forever, the close borough of rank and polish! Wealth there was – oh, yes! wealth – he himself was a richer man than his father had ever been; but manners, flavour, quality, all gone, engulfed in one vast, ugly, shoulder-rubbing, petrol-smelling Cheerio. Little half-beaten pockets of gentility and caste lurking here and there, dispersed and *chétif*, as Annette would say; but nothing ever again firm and coherent to look up to. And into this new hurly-burly of bad manners and loose morals his daughter – flower of his life – was flung! And when those Labour chaps got power – if they ever did – the worst was yet to come.

He passed out under the archway, at last no longer – thank goodness! – disfigured by the gun-grey of its search-light. 'They'd better put a search-light on to where they're all going,' he thought, 'and light up their precious democracy!' And he directed his steps along the Club fronts of Piccadilly. George

Forsyte, of course, would be sitting in the bay window of the Iseeum. The chap was so big now that he was there nearly all his time, like some immovable, sardonic, humorous eye noting the decline of men and things. And Soames hurried, ever constitutionally uneasy beneath his cousin's glance. George, who, as he had heard, had written a letter signed 'Patriot' in the middle of the War, complaining of the Government's hysteria in docking the oats of race-horses. Yes, there he was, tall, ponderous, neat, clean-shaven, with his smooth hair, hardly thinned, smelling, no doubt, of the best hair-wash, and a pink paper in his hand. Well, *he* didn't change! And for perhaps the first time in his life Soames felt a kind of sympathy tapping in his waistcoat for that sardonic kinsman. With his weight, his perfectly parted hair, and bull-like gaze, he was a guarantee that the old order would take some shifting yet. He saw George move the pink paper as if inviting him to ascend – the chap must want to ask something about his property. It was still under Soames's control; for in the adoption of a sleeping partnership at that painful period twenty years back when he had divorced Irene, Soames had found himself almost insensibly retaining control of all purely Forsyte affairs.

Hesitating for just a moment, he nodded and went in. Since the death of his brother-in-law Montague Dartie, in Paris, which no one had quite known what to make of, except that it was certainly not suicide – the Iseeum Club had seemed more respectable to Soames. George, too, he knew, had sown the last of his wild oats, and was committed definitely to the joys of the table, eating only of the very best so as to keep his weight down, and owning, as he said, 'just one or two old screws to give me an interest in life.' He joined his cousin, therefore, in the bay window without the embarrassing sense of indiscretion he had been used to feel up there. George put out a well-kept hand.

'Haven't seen you since the War,' he said. 'How's your wife?'

'Thanks,' said Soames coldly, 'well enough.'

Some hidden jest curved, for a moment, George's fleshy face, and gloated from his eye.

'That Belgian chap, Profond,' he said, 'is a member here now. He's a rum customer.'

'Quite!' muttered Soames. 'What did you want to see me about?'

'Old Timothy; he might go off the hooks at any moment. I suppose he's made his will.'

'Yes.'

'Well, you or somebody ought to give him a look up – last of the old lot; he's a hundred, you know. They say he's like a mummy. Where are you goin' to put him? He ought to have a pyramid by rights.'

Soames shook his head. 'Highgate, the family vault.'

'Well, I suppose the old girls would miss him, if he was anywhere else. They say he still takes an interest in food. He might last on, you know. Don't we *get* anything for the old Forsytes? Ten of them – average age eighty-eight – I worked it out. That ought to be equal to triplets.'

'Is that all?' said Soames. 'I must be getting on.'

'You unsociable devil,' George's eyes seemed to answer. 'Yes, that's all: Look him up in his mausoleum – the old chap might want to prophesy.' The grin died on the rich curves of his face, and he added: 'Haven't you attorneys invented a way yet of dodging this damned income tax? It hits the fixed inherited income like the very deuce. I used to have two thousand five hundred a year; now I've got a beggarly fifteen hundred, and the price of living doubled.'

'Ah!' murmured Soames, 'the turf's in danger.'

Over George's face moved a gleam of sardonic self-defence.

'Well,' he said, 'they brought me up to do nothing, and here I am in the sear and yellow, getting poorer every day. These Labour chaps mean to have the lot before they've done. What are you going to do for a living when it comes? I shall work a six-hour day teaching politicians how to see a joke. Take my tip, Soames; go into Parliament, make sure of your four hundred – and employ me.'

And, as Soames retired, he resumed his seat in the bay window.

Soames moved along Piccadilly deep in reflections excited by his cousin's words. He himself had always been a worker and a saver, George always a drone and a spender; and yet, if confiscation once began, it was he – the worker and the saver – who would be looted! That was the negation of all virtue, the overturning of all Forsyte principles. Could civilisation be built on any other? He did not think so. Well, they wouldn't confiscate his pictures, for they wouldn't know their worth. But what would they be worth, if these maniacs once began to milk capital? A drug on the market. 'I don't care about myself,' he thought; 'I could live on five hundred a year, and never know the difference, at my age.' But Fleur! This fortune, so widely invested, these treasures so carefully chosen and amassed, were all for her. And if it should turn out that he couldn't give or leave them to her – well, life had no meaning, and what was the use of going in to look at this crazy, futuristic stuff with the view of seeing whether it had any future?

Arriving at the Gallery off Cork Street, however, he paid his shilling, picked up a catalogue, and entered. Some ten persons were prowling round. Soames took steps and came on what looked to him like a lamp-post bent by collision with a motor omnibus. It was advanced some three paces from the wall, and was described in his catalogue as 'Jupiter'. He examined it with curiosity, having recently turned some of his attention to sculpture. 'If that's Jupiter,' he thought, 'I wonder what Juno's like.' And suddenly he saw her, opposite. She appeared to him like nothing so much as a pump with two handles, lightly clad in snow. He was still gazing at her, when two of the prowlers halted on his left. '*Épatant*!' he heard one say.

'Jargon!' growled Soames to himself.

The other's boyish voice replied:

'Missed it, old bean; he's pulling your leg. When he created them, he was saying: "I'll see how much these fools will swallow." And they've lapped up the lot.'

'You young duffer! Vospovitch is an innovator. Don't you see that he's brought satire into sculpture? The future of plastic art, of music, painting, and even architecture, has set in satiric. It was bound to. People are tired – the bottom's tumbled out of sentiment.'

'Well, I'm quite equal to taking a little interest in beauty. I was through the War. You've dropped your handkerchief, sir.'

Soames saw a handkerchief held out in front of him. He took it with some natural suspicion, and approached it to his nose. It had the right scent – of distant eau-de-Cologne – and his initials in a corner. Slightly reassured, he raised his eyes to the young man's face. It had rather fawn-like ears, a laughing mouth, with half a toothbrush growing out of it on each side, and small lively eyes, above a normally dressed appearance.

'Thank you,' he said; and moved by a sort of irritation, added: 'Glad to hear you like beauty; that's rare, nowadays.'

'I dote on it,' said the young man; 'but you and I are the last of the old guard, sir.'

Soames smiled.

'If you really care for pictures,' he said, 'here's my card. I can show you some quite good ones any Sunday, if you're down the river and care to look in.'

'Awfully nice of you, sir. I'll drop in like a bird. My name's Mont – Michael.' And he took off his hat.

Soames, already regretting his impulse, raised his own slightly in response, with a downward look at the young man's companion, who had a purple tie, dreadful little sluglike whiskers, and a scornful look – as if he were a poet!

It was the first indiscretion he had committed for so long that he went and sat down in an alcove. What had possessed him to give his card to a rackety young fellow, who went about with a thing like that? And Fleur, always at the back of his thoughts, started out like a filigree figure from a clock when the hour strikes. On the screen opposite the alcove was a large canvas with a great many square tomato-coloured blobs on it, and nothing else, so far as Soames could see from where he sat. He looked at his catalogue: No. 32 *The Future Town* – Paul Post. 'I suppose that's satiric too,' he thought. 'What a thing!' But his second impulse was more cautious. It did not do to condemn hurriedly. There had been those stripey, streaky creations of Monet's, which had turned out such trumps; and then the stippled school; and Gauguin. Why, even since the Post-Impressionists there had been one or two painters not to be sneezed at. During the thirty-eight years of his connoisseur's life, indeed, he had marked so many 'movements', seen the tides of taste and technique so ebb and flow, that there was really no telling anything except that there was money to be made out of every change of fashion. This too might quite well be a case where one must subdue primordial instinct, or lose the market. He got up and stood before the picture, trying hard to see it with the eyes of other people. Above the tomato blobs was what he took to be a sunset, till someone passing said: 'He's got the airplanes wonderfully, don't you think!' Below the tomato blobs was a band of white with vertical black stripes, to which he could assign no meaning whatever, till someone else came by, murmuring: 'What expression he gets with his foreground!' Expression? Of what? Soames went back to his seat. The thing was 'rich', as his father would have said, and he wouldn't give a damn for it. Expression! Ah! they were all Expressionists now, he had heard, on the Continent. So it was coming here too, was it? He remembered the first wave of influenza in 1887 – or '8 – hatched in China, so they said. He wondered where this – this Expressionism had been hatched. The thing was a regular disease!

He had become conscious of a woman and a youth standing between him and the *Future Town*. Their backs were turned; but very suddenly Soames put his catalogue before his face, and drawing his hat forward, gazed through the slit between. No mistaking that back, elegant as ever though the hair above had gone grey. Irene! His divorced wife – Irene! And this, no doubt, was – her son – by that fellow Jolyon Forsyte – their boy, six months older than his own girl! And mumbling over in his mind the bitter days of his divorce, he rose to get out of sight, but quickly sat down again. She had turned her head to speak to her boy; her profile was still so youthful that it made her grey hair seem powdery, as if fancy-dressed; and her lips were smiling as Soames, first possessor of them, had never seen them smile. Grudgingly he admitted her still beautiful and in figure almost as young as ever. And how that boy smiled back at her! Emotion squeezed Soames's heart. The sight infringed his sense of justice. He grudged her that boy's smile – it went beyond what Fleur gave him, and it was undeserved. Their son might have been his son; Fleur might have been her daughter, if she had kept straight! He lowered his catalogue. If she saw him, all the better! A reminder of her conduct in the presence of her son, who probably knew nothing of it, would be a salutary touch from the finger of that Nemesis which surely must soon or late visit her! Then, half-conscious that such a thought was extravagant for a Forsyte of his age, Soames took out his watch. Past four! Fleur was late. She had gone to his niece Imogen Cardigan's, and there they would keep her smoking cigarettes and gossiping, and that. He heard the boy laugh, and say eagerly: 'I say, Mum, is this by one of Auntie June's lame ducks?'

'Paul Post – I believe it is, darling.'

The word produced a little shock in Soames; he had never

heard her use it. And then she saw him. His eyes must have had in them something of George Forsyte's sardonic look; for her gloved hand crisped the folds of her frock, her eyebrows rose, her face went stony. She moved on.

'It *is* a caution,' said the boy, catching her arm again.

Soames stared after them. That boy was good-looking, with a Forsyte chin, and eyes deep-grey, deep in; but with something sunny, like a glass of old sherry spilled over him; his smile perhaps, his hair. Better than they deserved – those two! They passed from his view into the next room, and Soames continued to regard the Future Town, but saw it not. A little smile snarled up his lips. He was despising the vehemence of his own feelings after all these years. Ghosts! And yet as one grew old – was there anything but what was ghost-like left? Yes, there was Fleur! He fixed his eyes on the entrance. She was due; but she would keep him waiting, of course! And suddenly he became aware of a sort of human breeze – a short, slight form clad in a sea-green djibbah with a metal belt and a fillet binding unruly red-gold hair all streaked with grey. She was talking to the Gallery attendants, and something familiar riveted his gaze – in her eyes, her chin, her hair, her spirit – something which suggested a thin Skye terrier just before its dinner. Surely June Forsyte! His cousin June – and coming straight to his recess! She sat down beside him, deep in thought, took out a tablet, and made a pencil note. Soames sat unmoving. A confounded thing, cousinship! 'Disgusting!' he heard her murmur; then, as if resenting the presence of an overhearing stranger, she looked at him. The worst had happened.

'Soames!'

Soames turned his head a very little.

'How are *you*?' he said. 'Haven't seen you for twenty years.'

'No. Whatever made you come here?'

'My sins,' said Soames. 'What stuff!'

'Stuff? Oh, yes – of course; it hasn't *arrived* yet.'

'It never will,' said Soames; 'it must be making a dead loss.'

'Of course it is.'

'How d'you know?'

'It's my Gallery.'

Soames sniffed from sheer surprise.

'Yours? What on earth makes you run a show like this?'

'*I* don't treat Art as if it were grocery.'

Soames pointed to the *Future Town*. 'Look at that! Who's going to live in a town like that, or with it on his walls?'

June contemplated the picture for a moment.

'It's a vision,' she said.

'The deuce!'

There was silence, then June rose. 'Crazy-looking creature!' he thought.

'Well,' he said, 'you'll find your young stepbrother here with a woman I used to know. If you take my advice, you'll close this exhibition.'

June looked back at him. 'Oh! You Forsyte!' she said, and moved on. About her light, fly-away figure, passing so suddenly away, was a look of dangerous decisions. Forsyte! Of course, he was a Forsyte! And so was she! But from the time when, as a mere girl, she brought Bosinney into his life to wreck it, he had never hit it off with June and never would! And here she was, unmarried to this day, owning a Gallery! . . . And suddenly it came to Soames how little he knew now of his own family. The old aunts at Timothy's had been dead so many years; there was no clearing-house for news. What had they all done in the War? Young Roger's boy had been wounded, St John Hayman's second son killed; young Nicholas's eldest had got an O.B.E., or whatever they gave them. They had all joined up somehow, he believed. That boy of Jolyon's and Irene's, he supposed, had been too young; his own generation, of course, too old, though Giles Hayman had driven a car for the Red Cross – and Jesse Hayman been a special constable – those 'Dromios' had always been of a sporting type! As for himself, he had given a motor ambulance, read the papers till he was sick of them, passed through much anxiety, bought no clothes, lost seven pounds in weight; he didn't know what more he could have done at his age. Indeed, thinking it over, it struck him that he and his family had taken this war very differently to that affair with the Boers, which had been supposed to tax all the resources of the Empire. In that old war, of course, his nephew Val Dartie had been wounded, that fellow Jolyon's first son had died of enteric, 'the Dromios' had gone out on horses, and June had been a nurse; but all that had seemed in the nature of a portent, while in *this* war everybody had done 'their bit', so far as he could make out, as a matter of course. It seemed to show the growth of something or other – or perhaps the decline of something else. Had the Forsytes become less individual, or more Imperial, or less provincial? Or was it simply that one hated Germans? . . . Why didn't Fleur come, so that he could get away? He saw those three return together from the other room and pass back along the far side of the screen. The boy was standing before the Juno now. And, suddenly, on the other side of her, Soames saw – his daughter, with eyebrows raised, as well they might be. He could see her eyes glint sideways at the boy, and the boy look back at her. Then Irene slipped her hand through his arm, and drew him on. Soames saw him glancing round, and Fleur looking after them as the three went out.

A voice said cheerfully: 'Bit thick, isn't it, sir?'

The young man who had handed him his handkerchief was again passing. Soames nodded.

'I don't know what we're coming to.'

'Oh! That's all right, sir,' answered the young man cheerfully; 'they don't either.'

Fleur's voice said: 'Hallo, Father! Here you are!' precisely as if he had been keeping her waiting.

The young man, snatching off his hat, passed on.

'Well,' said Soames, looking her up and down, 'you're a punctual sort of young woman!'

This treasured possession of his life was of medium height and colour, with short, dark chestnut hair; her wide-apart brown eyes were set in whites so clear that they glinted when they moved, and yet in repose were almost dreamy under very white, black-lashed lids, held over them in a sort of suspense. She had a charming profile, and nothing of her father in her face save a decided chin. Aware that his expression was softening as he looked at her, Soames frowned to preserve the unemotionalism proper to a Forsyte. He knew she was only too inclined to take advantage of his weakness.

Slipping her hand under his arm, she said:

'Who was that?'

'He picked up my handkerchief. We talked about the pictures.'

'You're not going to buy *that*, Father?'

'No,' said Soames grimly; 'nor that Juno you've been looking at.'

Fleur dragged at his arm. 'Oh! Let's go! It's a ghastly show.'

In the doorway they passed the young man called Mont and his partner. But Soames had hung out a board marked 'Trespassers will be prosecuted', and he barely acknowledged the young fellow's salute.

'Well,' he said in the street, 'whom did you meet at Imogen's?'

'Aunt Winifred, and that Monsieur Profond.'

'Oh!' muttered Soames; 'that chap! What does your aunt see in him?'

'I don't know. He looks pretty deep – mother says she likes him.'

Soames grunted.

'Cousin Val and his wife were there, too.'

'What!' said Soames. 'I thought they were back in South Africa.'

'Oh, no! They've sold their farm. Cousin Val is going to train race-horses on the Sussex Downs. They've got a jolly old manor-house; they asked me down there.'

Soames coughed: the news was distasteful to him. 'What's his wife like now?'

'Very quiet, but nice, I think.'

Soames coughed again. 'He's a rackety chap, your Cousin Val.'

'Oh! no, Father; they're awfully devoted. I promised to go – Saturday to Wednesday next.'

'Training race-horses!' said Soames. It was bad enough, but not the reason for his distaste. Why the deuce couldn't his nephew have stayed out in South Africa? His own divorce had been bad enough, without his nephew's marriage to the daughter of the co-respondent; a half-sister too of June, and of that boy whom Fleur had just been looking at from under the pump-handle. If he didn't look out, she would come to know all about that old disgrace! Unpleasant things! They were round him this afternoon like a swarm of bees!

'I don't like it!' he said.

'I want to see the race-horses,' murmured Fleur; 'and they've promised I shall ride. Cousin Val can't walk much, you know; but he can ride perfectly. He's going to show me their gallops.'

'Racing!' said Soames. 'It's a pity the War didn't knock that on the head. He's taking after his father, I'm afraid.'

'I don't know anything about his father.'

'No,' said Soames, grimly. 'He took an interest in horses and broke his neck in Paris, walking downstairs. Good riddance for your aunt.' He frowned, recollecting the inquiry into those stairs which he had attended in Paris six years ago, because Montague Dartie could not attend it himself – perfectly normal stairs in a house where they played baccarat. Either his winnings or the way he had celebrated them had gone to his brother-in-law's head. The French procedure had been very loose; he had had a lot of trouble with it.

A sound from Fleur distracted his attention. 'Look! The people who were in the Gallery with us.'

'What people?' muttered Soames, who knew perfectly well.

'I think that woman's beautiful.'

'Come into this pastry-cook's,' said Soames abruptly, and tightening his grip on her arm he turned into a confectioner's. It was – for him – a surprising thing to do, and he said rather anxiously: 'What will you have?'

'Oh! I don't want anything. I had a cocktail and a tremendous lunch.'

'We *must* have something now we're here,' muttered Soames, keeping hold of her arm.

'Two teas,' he said; 'and two of those nougat things.'

But no sooner was his body seated than his soul sprang up. Those three – those three were coming in! He heard Irene say something to her boy, and his answer:

'Oh! no, Mum; this place is all right. My stunt.' And the three sat down.

At that moment, most awkward of his existence, crowded with ghosts and shadows from his past, in presence of the only two women he had ever loved – his divorced wife and his daughter by her successor – Soames was not so much afraid of *them* as of his cousin June. She might make a scene – she might introduce those two children – she was capable of anything. He bit too hastily at the nougat, and it stuck to his plate. Working at it with his finger, he glanced at Fleur. She was masticating dreamily, but her eyes were on the boy. The Forsyte in him said: 'Think, feel, and you're done for!' And he wiggled his finger desperately. Plate! Did Jolyon wear a plate? Did that woman wear a plate? Time had been when he had seen her wearing nothing! That was something, anyway, which had never been stolen from him. And she knew it, though she might sit there calm and self-possessed, as if she had never been his wife. An acid humour stirred in his Forsyte blood; a subtle pain divided by hair's breadth from pleasure. If only June did not suddenly bring her hornets about his ears! The boy was talking.

'Of course, Auntie June' – so he called his half-sister 'Auntie' did he? – well, she must be fifty, if she was a day! – 'it's jolly good of you to encourage them. Only – hang it all!' Soames stole a glance. Irene's startled eyes were bent watchfully on her boy. She – she had these devotions – for Bosinney – for that boy's father – for this boy! He touched Fleur's arm, and said:

'Well, have you had enough?'

'One more, Father, please.'

She would be sick! He went to the counter to pay. When he turned round again he saw Fleur standing near the door, holding a handkerchief which the boy had evidently just handed to her.

'F. F.,' he heard her say. 'Fleur Forsyte – it's mine all right. Thank you ever so.'

Good God! She had caught the trick from what he'd told her in the Gallery – monkey!

'Forsyte? Why – that's my name too. Perhaps we're cousins.'

'Really! We must be. There aren't any others. I live at Mapledurham; where do you?'

'Robin Hill.'

Question and answer had been so rapid that all was over before he could lift a finger. He saw Irene's face alive with startled feeling, gave the slightest shake of his head, and slipped his arm through Fleur's.

'Come along!' he said.

She did not move.

'Didn't you hear, Father? Isn't it queer – our name's the same. Are we cousins?'

'What's that?' he said. 'Forsyte? Distant, perhaps.'

'My name's Jolyon, sir. Jon, for short.'

'Oh! Ah!' said Soames. 'Yes. Distant. How are you? Very good of you. Good-bye!'

He moved on.

'Thanks awfully,' Fleur was saying. '*Au revoir!*'

'*Au revoir!*' he heard the boy reply.

Chapter Two

Fine Fleur Forsyte

Emerging from the 'pastry-cook's', Soames' first impulse was to vent his nerves by saying to his daughter: 'Dropping your handkerchief!' to which her reply might well be: 'I picked that up from you!' His second impulse therefore was to let sleeping dogs lie. But she would surely question him. He gave her a sidelong look, and found she was giving him the same. She said softly:

'Why don't you like those cousins, Father?'

Soames lifted the corner of his lip.

'What made you think that?'

'*Cela se voit.*'

'That sees itself!' What a way of putting it! After twenty years of a French wife Soames had still little sympathy with her language; a theatrical affair and connected in his mind with all the refinements of domestic irony.

'How?' he asked.

'You *must* know them; and you didn't make a sign. I saw them looking at you.'

'I've never seen the boy in my life,' replied Soames with perfect truth.

'No; but you've seen the others, dear.'

Soames gave her another look. What had she picked up? Had her Aunt Winifred, or Imogen, or Val Dartie and his wife, been talking? Every breath of the old scandal had been carefully kept from her at home, and Winifred warned many times that he wouldn't have a whisper of it reach her for the world. So far as she ought to know, he had never been married before. But her dark eyes, whose southern glint and clearness often almost frightened him, met his with perfect innocence.

'Well,' he said, 'your grandfather and his brother had a quarrel. The two families don't know each other.'

'How romantic!'

'Now, what does she mean by that?' he thought. The word was to him extravagant and dangerous – it was as if she had said: 'How jolly!'

'And they'll continue not to know each other,' he added, but instantly regretted the challenge in those words. Fleur was smiling. In this age, when young people prided themselves on going their own ways and paying no attention to any sort of decent prejudice, he had said the very thing to excite her wilfulness. Then, recollecting the expression on Irene's face, he breathed again.

'What sort of a quarrel?' he heard Fleur say.

'About a house. It's ancient history for you. Your grandfather died the day you were born. He was ninety.'

'Ninety? Are there many Forsytes besides those in the Red Book?'

'I don't know,' said Soames. 'They're all dispersed now. The old ones are dead, except Timothy.'

Fleur clasped her hands.

'Timothy? Isn't that delicious?'

'Not at all,' said Soames. It offended him that she should think 'Timothy' delicious – a kind of insult to his breed. This new generation mocked at anything solid and tenacious. 'You go and see the old boy. He might want to prophesy.' Ah! If Timothy could see the disquiet England of his great-nephews and great-nieces, he would certainly give tongue. And involuntarily he glanced up at the Iseeum; yes – George was still in the window, with the same pink paper in his hand.

'Where is Robin Hill, Father?'

Robin Hill! Robin Hill, round which all that tragedy had centred! What did she want to know for?

'In Surrey,' he muttered; 'not far from Richmond. Why?'

'Is the house there?'

'What house?'

'That they quarrelled about.'

'Yes. But what's all that to do with you? We're going home to-morrow – you'd better be thinking about your frocks.'

'Bless you! They're all thought about. A family feud? It's like the Bible, or Mark Twain – awfully exciting. What did you do in the feud, Father?'

'Never you mind.'

'Oh! But if I'm to keep it up?'

'Who said you were to keep it up?'

'You, darling.'

'I? I said it had nothing to do with you.'

'Just what *I* think, you know; so that's all right.'

She was too sharp for him; 'fine', as Annette sometimes called her. Nothing for it but to distract her attention.

'There's a bit of rosaline point in here,' he said, stopping before a shop, 'that I thought you might like.'

When he had paid for it and they had resumed their progress, Fleur said:

'Don't you think that boy's mother is the most beautiful woman of her age you've ever seen?'

Soames shivered. Uncanny, the way she stuck to it!

'I don't know that I noticed her.'

'Dear, I saw the corner of your eye.'

'You see everything – and a great deal more, it seems to me!'

'What's her husband like? He must be your first cousin, if your fathers were brothers.'

'Dead, for all I know,' said Soames, with sudden vehemence. 'I haven't seen him for twenty years.'

'What was he?'

'A painter.'

'That's quite jolly.'

The words: 'If you want to please me you'll put those people out of your head,' sprang to Soames's lips, but he choked them back – he must *not* let her see his feelings.

'He once insulted me,' he said.

Her quick eyes rested on his face.

'I see! You didn't avenge it, and it rankles. Poor Father! You let me have a go!'

It was really like lying in the dark with a mosquito hovering above his face. Such pertinacity in Fleur was new to him, and, as they reached the hotel, he said grimly:

'I did my best. And that's enough about these people. I'm going up till dinner.'

'I shall sit here.'

With a parting look at her extended in a chair – a look half-resentful, half-adoring – Soames moved into the lift and was transported to their suite on the fourth floor. He stood by the window of the sitting-room which gave view over Hyde Park, and drummed a finger on its pane. His feelings were confused, tetchy, troubled. The throb of that old wound, scarred over by Time and new interests, was mingled with displeasure and anxiety, and a slight pain in his chest where that nougat stuff had disagreed. Had Annette come in? Not that she was any good to him in such a difficulty. Whenever she had questioned him about his first marriage, he had always shut her up; she knew nothing of it, save that it had been the great passion of his life, and his marriage with herself but domestic makeshift. She had always kept the grudge of that up her sleeve, as it were, and used it commercially. He listened. A sound – the vague murmur of a woman's movements – was coming through the door. She was in. He tapped.

'Who?'

'I,' said Soames.

She had been changing her frock, and was still imperfectly clothed; a striking figure before her glass. There was a certain magnificence about her arms, shoulders, hair, which had darkened since he first knew her, about the turn of her neck, the silkiness of her garments, her dark-lashed, grey-blue eyes – she was certainly as handsome at forty as she had ever been. A fine possession, an excellent housekeeper, a sensible and affectionate enough mother. If only she weren't always so frankly cynical about the relations between them! Soames, who had no more real affection for her than she had for him, suffered from a kind of English grievance in that she had never dropped even the thinnest veil of sentiment over their partnership. Like most of his countrymen and women, he held the view that marriage should be based on mutual love, but that when from a marriage love had disappeared, or, been found never to have really existed – so that it was manifestly not based on love – you must not admit it. There it was, and the love was not – but there you were, and must continue to be! Thus you had it both ways, and were not tarred with cynicism, realism, and immorality like the French. Moreover, it was necessary in the interests of property. He knew that she knew that they both knew there was no love between them, but he still expected her not to admit in words or conduct such a thing, and he could never understand what she meant when she talked of the hypocrisy of the English. He said:

'Whom have you got at "The Shelter" next week?'

Annette went on touching her lips delicately with salve – he always wished she wouldn't do that.

'Your sister Winifred, and the Car-r-digans' – she took up a tiny stick of black – 'and Prosper Profond.'

'That Belgian chap? Why him?'

Annette turned her neck lazily, touched one eyelash, and said:

'He amuses Winifred.'

'I want some one to amuse Fleur; she's restive.'

'R-restive?' repeated Annette. 'Is it the first time you see that, my friend? She was born r-restive, as you call it.'

Would she never get that affected roll out of her r's?

He touched the dress she had taken off, and asked:

'What have you been doing?'

Annette looked at him, reflected in her glass. Her just-brightened lips smiled, rather full, rather ironical.

'Enjoying myself,' she said.

'Oh!' answered Soames glumly. 'Ribbandry, I suppose.'

It was his word for all that incomprehensible running in and out of shops that women went in for. 'Has Fleur got her summer dresses?'

'You don't ask if I have mine.'

'You don't care whether I do or not.'

'Quite right. Well, she has; and I have mine – terribly expensive.'

'H'm!' said Soames. 'What does that chap Profond do in England?'

Annette raised the eyebrows she had just finished.

'He yachts.'

'Ah!' said Soames; 'he's a sleepy chap.'

'Sometimes,' answered Annette, and her face had a sort of quiet enjoyment. 'But sometimes very amusing.'

'He's got a touch of the tar-brush about him.'

Annette stretched herself.

'Tar-brush?' she said. 'What is that? His mother was *Arménienne*.'

'That's it, then,' muttered Soames. 'Does he know anything about pictures?'

'He knows about everything – a man of the world.'

'Well, get someone for Fleur. I want to distract her. She's going off on Saturday to Val Dartie and his wife; I don't like it.'

'Why not?'

Since the reason could not be explained without going into family history, Soames merely answered:

'Racketing about. There's too much of it.'

'I like that little Mrs Val; she is very quiet and clever.'

'I know nothing of her except— This thing's new.' And Soames took up a creation from the bed.

Annette received it from him.

'Would you hook me?' she said.

Soames hooked. Glancing once over her shoulder into the glass, he saw the expression on her face, faintly amused, faintly contemptuous, as much as to say: 'Thanks! You will never learn!' No, thank God, he wasn't a Frenchman! He finished with a jerk, and the words: 'It's too low here.' And he went to the door, with the wish to get away from her and go down to Fleur again.

Annette stayed a powder-puff, and said with startling suddenness:

'*Que tu es grossier!*'

He knew the expression – he had reason to. The first time she had used it he had thought it meant 'What a grocer you are!' and had not known whether to be relieved or not when better informed. He resented the word – he was *not* coarse! If he was coarse, what was that chap in the room beyond his, who made those horrible noises in the morning when he cleared his throat, or those people in the Lounge who thought it well-bred to say nothing but what the whole world could hear at the top of their voices – quacking inanity! Coarse, because he had said her dress was low! Well, so it was! He went out without reply.

Coming into the Lounge from the far end, he at once saw Fleur where he had left her. She sat with crossed knees, slowly balancing a foot in silk stocking and grey shoe, sure sign that she was dreaming. Her eyes showed it too – they went off like that sometimes. And then, in a moment, she would come to life, and be as quick and restless as a monkey. And she knew so much, so self-assured, and not yet nineteen. What was that odious word? Flapper! Dreadful young creatures – squealing and squawking and showing their legs! The worst of them bad dreams, the best of them powdered angels! Fleur was *not* a flapper, *not* one of those slangy, ill-bred young females. And yet she was frighteningly self-willed, and full of life, and determined to enjoy it. Enjoy! The word brought no puritan terror to Soames; but it brought the terror suited to his temperament. He had always been afraid to enjoy to-day for fear he might not enjoy tomorrow so much. And it was terrifying to feel that his daughter was divested of that safeguard. The very way she sat in that chair showed it – lost in her dream. He had never been lost in a dream himself – there was nothing to be had out of it; and where she got it from he did not know! Certainly not from Annette! And yet Annette, as a young girl, when he was hanging about her, had once had a flowery look. Well, she had lost it now!

Fleur rose from her chair – swiftly, restlessly; and flung herself down at a writing-table. Seizing ink and writing paper, she began to write as if she had not time to breathe before she got her letter written. And suddenly she saw him. The air of desperate absorption vanished, she smiled, waved a kiss, made a pretty face as if she were a little puzzled and a little bored.

Ah! She was *'fine'* – *'fine'*!

Chapter Three

At Robin Hill

*J*olyon Forsyte had spent his boy's nineteenth birthday at Robin Hill, quietly going into his affairs. He did everything quietly now, because his heart was in a poor way, and, like all his family, he disliked the idea of dying. He had never realised how much till one day, two years ago, he had gone to his doctor about certain symptoms, and been told:

'At any moment, on any overstrain.'

He had taken it with a smile – the natural Forsyte reaction against an unpleasant truth. But with an increase of symptoms in the train on the way home, he had realised to the full the sentence hanging over him. To leave Irene, his boy, his home, his work – though he did little enough work now! To leave them for unknown darkness, for the unimaginable state, for such nothingness that he would not even be conscious of wind stirring leaves above his grave, nor of the scent of earth and grass. Of such nothingness that, however hard he might try to conceive it, he never could, and must still hover on the hope that he might see again those he loved! To realise this was to endure very poignant spiritual anguish. Before he reached home that day he had determined to keep it from Irene. He would have to be more careful than man had ever been, for the least thing would give it away and make her as wretched as himself, almost. His doctor had passed him sound in other respects, and seventy was nothing of an age – he would last a long time yet, *if he could*.

Such a conclusion, followed out for nearly two years, develops to the full the subtler side of character. Naturally not abrupt, except when nervously excited, Jolyon had become control incarnate. The sad patience of old people who cannot exert themselves was masked by a smile which his lips preserved even in private. He devised continually all manner of cover to conceal his enforced lack of exertion.

Mocking himself for so doing, he counterfeited conversion to the Simple Life; gave up wine and cigars, drank a special kind of coffee with no coffee in it. In short, he made himself as safe as a Forsyte in his condition could, under the rose of his mild irony. Secure from discovery, since his wife and son had gone up to Town, he had spent the fine May day quietly arranging his papers, that he might die to-morrow without inconveniencing anyone, giving in fact a final polish to his terrestrial state. Having docketed and enclosed it in his father's old Chinese cabinet, he put the key into an envelope, wrote the words outside: 'Key of the Chinese cabinet, wherein will be found the exact state of me, J. F.,' and put it in his breast-pocket, where it would be always about him, in case of accident. Then, ringing for tea, he went out to have it under the old oak-tree.

All are under sentence of death; Jolyon, whose sentence was but a little more precise and pressing, had become so used to it that he thought habitually, like other people, of other things. He thought of his son now.

Jon was nineteen that day, and Jon had come of late to a decision. Educated neither at Eton like his father, nor at Harrow, like his dead half-brother, but at one of those establishments which, designed to avoid the evil and contain the good of the Public School system, may or may not contain the evil and avoid the good, Jon had left in April perfectly ignorant of what he wanted to become. The War, which had promised to go on for ever, had ended just as he was about to join the Army, six months before his time. It had taken him ever since to get used to the idea that he could now choose for himself. He had held with his father several discussions, from which, under a cheery show of being ready for anything – except, of course, the Church, Army, Law, Stage, Stock Exchange, Medicine, Business, and Engineering – Jolyon had gathered rather clearly that Jon wanted to go in for nothing. He himself had felt exactly like that at the same age. With him that pleasant vacuity had soon been ended by an early marriage, and its unhappy consequences. Forced to become an underwriter at Lloyd's, he had regained prosperity before his artistic talent had outcropped. But having – as the simple say – 'learned' his boy to draw pigs and other animals, he knew that Jon would never be a painter, and inclined to the conclusion that his aversion from everything else meant that he was going to be a writer. Holding, however, the view that experience was necessary even for that profession, there seemed to Jolyon nothing in the meantime, for Jon, but University, travel, and perhaps the eating of dinners for the Bar. After that one would see, or more probably one would not. In face of these proffered allurements, however, Jon had remained undecided.

Such discussions with his son had confirmed in Jolyon a doubt whether the world had really changed. People said that it was a new age. With the profundity of one not too long for any age, Jolyon perceived that under slightly different surfaces the era was precisely what it had been. Mankind was still divided into two species: The few who had 'speculation' in their souls, and the many who had none, with a belt of hybrids like himself in the middle. Jon appeared to have speculation; it seemed to his father a bad lookout.

With something deeper, therefore, than his usual smile, he had heard the boy say, a fortnight ago: 'I should like to try farming, Dad; if it won't cost you too much. It seems to be about the only sort of life that doesn't hurt anybody; except art, and of course that's out of the question for me.'

Jolyon subdued his smile, and answered:

'All right; you shall skip back to where we were under the first Jolyon in 1760. It'll prove the cycle theory, and incidentally, no doubt, you may grow a better turnip than he did.'

A little dashed, Jon had answered:

'But don't you think it's a good scheme, Dad?'

'Twill serve, my dear; and if you should really take to it, you'll do more good than most men, which is little enough.'

To himself, however, he had said: 'But he won't take to it. I give him four years. Still, it's healthy, and harmless.'

After turning the matter over and consulting with Irene, he wrote to his daughter, Mrs Val Dartie, asking if they knew of a farmer near them on the Downs who would take Jon as an apprentice. Holly's answer had been enthusiastic. There was an excellent man quite close; she and Val would love Jon to live with them.

The boy was due to go to-morrow.

Sipping weak tea with lemon in it, Jolyon gazed through the leaves of the old oak-tree at that view which had appeared to him desirable for thirty-two years. The tree beneath which he sat seemed not a day older! So young, the little leaves of brownish gold; so old, the whitey-grey-green of its thick rough trunk. A tree of memories, which would live on hundreds of years yet, unless some barbarian cut it down – would see old England out at the pace things were going! He remembered a night three years before, when, looking from his window, with his arm close round Irene, he had watched a German aeroplane hovering, it seemed, right over the old tree. Next day they had found a bomb hole in a field on Gage's farm. That was before he knew that he was under sentence of death. He could almost have wished the bomb had finished him. It would have saved a lot of hanging about, many hours of cold fear in the pit of his stomach. He had counted on living to the normal Forsyte age of eighty-five or more, when Irene would be seventy. As it was, she would miss him. Still there was Jon, more important in her life than himself; Jon, who adored his mother.

Under that tree, where old Jolyon – waiting for Irene to come to him across the lawn – had breathed his last, Jolyon wondered, whimsically, whether, having put everything in such perfect order, he had not better close his own eyes and drift away. There was something undignified in parasitically clinging on to the effortless close of a life wherein he regretted two things only – the long division between his father and himself when he was young, and the lateness of his union with Irene.

From where he sat he could see a cluster of apple-trees in blossom. Nothing in Nature moved him so much as fruit-trees in blossom; and his heart ached suddenly because he might never see them flower again. Spring! Decidedly no man ought to have to die while his heart was still young enough to love beauty! Blackbirds sang recklessly in the shrubbery, swallows were flying high, the leaves above him glistened; and over the fields was every imaginable tint of early foliage, burnished by the level sunlight, away to where the distant 'smoke-bush' blue was trailed along the horizon. Irene's flowers in their narrow beds had startling individuality that evening, little deep assertions of gay life. Only Chinese and Japanese painters, and perhaps Leonardo, had known how to get that startling little ego into each painted flower, and bird, and beast – the ego, yet the sense of species, the universality of life as well. They were the fellows! 'I've made nothing that will live!' thought Jolyon; 'I've been an amateur – a mere lover, not a creator. Still, I shall leave Jon behind me when I go.' What luck that the boy had not been caught by that ghastly war! He might so easily have been killed, like poor Jolly twenty years ago out in the Transvaal. Jon would do something some day – if the Age didn't spoil him – an imaginative chap! His whim to take up farming was but a bit of sentiment, and about as likely to last. And just then he saw them coming up the field: Irene and the boy; walking from the station, with their arms linked. And getting up, he strolled down through the new rose garden to meet them . . .

Irene came into his room that night and sat down by the window. She sat there without speaking till he said:

'What is it, my love?'

'We had an encounter to-day.'

'With whom?'

'Soames.'

Soames! He had kept that name out of his thoughts these last two years; conscious that it was bad for him. And, now, his heart moved in a disconcerting manner, as if it had side-slipped within his chest.

Irene went on quietly:

'He and his daughter were in the Gallery, and afterward at the confectioner's where we had tea.'

Jolyon went over and put his hand on her shoulder.

'How did he look?'

'Grey; but otherwise much the same.'

'And the daughter?'

'Pretty. At least, Jon thought so.'

Jolyon's heart side-slipped again. His wife's face had a strained and puzzled look.

'You didn't—?' he began.

'No; but Jon knows their name. The girl dropped her hand-kerchief and he picked it up.'

Jolyon sat down on his bed. An evil chance!

'June was with you. Did she put her foot into it?'

'No; but it was all very queer and strained, and Jon could see it was.'

Jolyon drew a long breath, and said:

'I've often wondered whether we've been right to keep it from him. He'll find out some day.'

'The later the better, Jolyon; the young have such cheap, hard judgment. When you were nineteen what would you have thought of *your* mother if she had done what I have?'

Yes! There it was! Jon worshipped his mother; and knew nothing of the tragedies, the inexorable necessities of life, nothing of the prisoned grief in an unhappy marriage, nothing of jealousy or passion – knew nothing at all, as yet!

'What have you told him?' he said at last.

'That they were relations, but we didn't know them; that you had never cared much for your family, or they for you. I expect he will be asking you.'

Jolyon smiled. 'This promises to take the place of air-raids,' he said. 'After all, one misses them.'

Irene looked up at him.

'We've known it would come some day.'

He answered her with sudden energy:

'I could never stand seeing Jon blame you. He shan't do that, even in thought. He has imagination; and he'll understand if it's put to him properly. I think I had better tell him before he gets to know otherwise.'

'Not yet, Jolyon.'

That was like her – she had no foresight, and never went to meet trouble. Still – who knew? – she might be right. It was ill going against a mother's instinct. It might be well to let the boy go on, if possible, till experience had given him some touchstone by which he could judge the values of that old tragedy; till love, jealousy, longing, had deepened his charity. All the same, one must take precautions – every precaution possible! And, long after Irene had left him, he lay awake turning over those precautions. He must write to Holly, telling her that Jon knew nothing as yet of family history. Holly was discreet, she would make sure of her husband, she would see to it! Jon could take the letter with him when he went to-morrow.

And so the day on which he had put the polish on his material estate died out with the chiming of the stable clock; and another began for Jolyon in the shadow of a spiritual disorder which could not be so rounded off and polished . . .

But Jon, whose room had once been his day nursery, lay awake too, the prey of a sensation disputed by those who have never known it, 'love at first sight'! He had felt it beginning in him with the glint of those dark eyes gazing into his athwart the Juno – a conviction that this was his 'dream'; so that what followed had seemed to him at once natural and miraculous. Fleur! Her name alone was almost enough for one who was terribly susceptible to the charm of words. In a homoeopathic Age, when boys and girls were co-educated, and mixed up in early life till sex was almost abolished, Jon was singularly old-fashioned. His modern school took boys only, and his holidays had been spent at Robin Hill with boy friends, or his parents alone. He had never, therefore, been inoculated against the germs of love by small doses of the poison. And now in the dark his temperature was mounting fast. He lay awake, featuring Fleur – as they called it – recalling her words, especially that '*Au revoir!*' so soft and sprightly.

He was still so wide awake at dawn that he got up, slipped on tennis shoes, trousers, and a sweater, and in silence crept downstairs and out through the study window. It was just light; there was a smell of grass. 'Fleur!' he thought; 'Fleur!' It was mysteriously white out of doors, with nothing awake except the birds just beginning to chirp. 'I'll go down into the coppice,' he thought. He ran down through the fields, reached the pond just as the sun rose, and passed into the coppice. Bluebells carpeted the ground there; among the larch-trees there was mystery – the air, as it were, composed of that romantic quality. Jon sniffed its freshness, and stared at the bluebells in the sharpening light. Fleur! It rhymed with her! And she lived at Mapledurham – a jolly name, too, on the river somewhere. He could find it in the atlas presently. He

would write to her. But would she answer? Oh! She must. She
had said '*Au revoir!*' Not good-bye! What luck that she had
dropped her handkerchief! He would never have known her
but for that. And the more he thought of that handkerchief,
the more amazing his luck seemed. Fleur! It certainly rhymed
with her! Rhythm thronged his head; words jostled to be joined
together; he was on the verge of a poem.

  Jon remained in this condition for more than half an hour,
then returned to the house, and getting a ladder, climbed in
at his bedroom window out of sheer exhilaration. Then,
remembering that the study window was open, he went down
and shut it, first removing the ladder, so as to obliterate all
traces of his feeling. The thing was too deep to be revealed to
mortal soul – even to his mother.

Chapter Four

The Mausoleum

There are houses whose souls have passed into the limbo of Time, leaving their bodies in the limbo of London. Such was not quite the condition of 'Timothy's' on the Bayswater Road, for Timothy's soul still had one foot in Timothy Forsyte's body, and Smither kept the atmosphere unchanging, of camphor and port wine and house whose windows are only opened to air it twice a day.

To Forsyte imagination that house was now a sort of Chinese pill-box, a series of layers in the last of which was Timothy. One did not reach him, or so it was reported by members of the family who, out of old-time habit or absent-mindedness, would drive up once in a blue moon and ask after their surviving uncle. Such were Francie, now quite emancipated from God (she frankly avowed atheism), Euphemia, emancipated from old Nicholas, and Winifred Dartie from her 'man of the world'. But, after all, everybody was emancipated now, or said they were – perhaps not quite the same thing!

When Soames, therefore, took it on his way to Paddington station on the morning after that encounter, it was hardly with the expectation of seeing Timothy in the flesh. His heart made a faint demonstration within him while he stood in full south sunlight on the newly whitened doorstep of that little house where four Forsytes had once lived, and now but one dwelt on like a winter fly; the house into which Soames had come and out of which he had gone times without number, divested of, or burdened with, fardels of family gossip; the house of the 'old people' of another century, another age.

The sight of Smither − still corseted up to the armpits because the new fashion which came in as they were going out about 1903 had never been considered 'nice' by Aunts Juley and Hester − brought a pale friendliness to Soames's lips; Smither, still faithfully arranged to old pattern in every detail, an invaluable servant − none such left − smiling back at him, with the words: 'Why! it's Mr Soames, after all this time! And how are *you*, sir? Mr Timothy will be so pleased to know you've been.'

'How is he?'

'Oh! he keeps fairly bobbish for his age, sir; but of course he's a wonderful man. As I said to Mrs Dartie when she was here last: It *would* please Miss Forsyte and Mrs Juley and Miss Hester to see how he relishes a baked apple still. But he's quite deaf. And a mercy, I always think. For what we should have done with him in the air-raids, I don't know.'

'Ah!' said Soames. 'What *did* you do with him?'

'We just left him in his bed, and had the bell run down into the cellar, so that Cook and I could hear him if he rang. It would never have done to let him know there was a war on. As I said to Cook, "If Mr Timothy rings, they may do what they like − I'm going up. My dear mistresses would have a fit if they could see him ringing and nobody going to him." But he slept through them all beautiful. And the one in the daytime he was having his bath. It *was* a mercy, because he might have noticed the people in the street all looking up − he often looks out of the window.'

'Quite!' murmured Soames. Smither was getting garrulous! 'I just want to look round and see if there's anything to be done.'

'Yes, sir. I don't think there's anything except a smell of mice in the dining-room that we don't know how to get rid of. It's funny they should be there, and not a crumb, since Mr Timothy took to not coming down, just before the War. But they're nasty little things; you never know where they'll take you next.'

'Does he leave his bed?'

'Oh! yes, sir; he takes nice exercise between his bed and the window in the morning, not to risk a change of air. And he's quite comfortable in himself; has his will out every day regular. It's a great consolation to him – that.'

'Well, Smither, I want to see him, if I can; in case he has anything to say to me.'

Smither coloured up above her corsets.

'It *will* be an occasion!' she said. 'Shall I take you round the house, sir, while I send Cook to break it to him?'

'No, you go to him,' said Soames. 'I can go round the house by myself.'

One could not confess to sentiment before another, and Soames felt that he was going to be sentimental nosing round those rooms so saturated with the past. When Smither, creaking with excitement, had left him, Soames entered the dining-room and sniffed. In his opinion it wasn't mice, but incipient wood-rot, and he examined the panelling. Whether it was worth a coat of paint, at Timothy's age, he was not sure. The room had always been the most modern in the house; and only a faint smile curled Soames's lips and nostrils. Walls of a rich green surmounted the oak dado; a heavy metal chandelier hung by a chain from a ceiling divided by imitation beams. The pictures had been bought by Timothy, a bargain, one day at Jobson's sixty years ago – three Snyder 'still lifes', two faintly coloured drawings of a boy and a girl, rather charming, which bore the initials 'J. R.' – Timothy had always believed they might turn out to be Joshua Reynolds, but Soames, who admired them, had discovered that they were only John Robinson; and a doubtful Morland of a white pony being shod. Deep-red plush curtains, ten high-backed dark mahogany chairs with deep-red plush seats, a Turkey carpet, and a mahogany dining-table as large as the room was small, such was an apartment which Soames could remember unchanged in soul or body since he was four years old. He looked especially at the two drawings, and thought: 'I shall buy those at the sale.'

From the dining-room he passed into Timothy's study. He did not remember ever having been in that room. It was lined from floor to ceiling with volumes, and he looked at them with curiosity. One wall seemed devoted to educational books, which Timothy's firm had published two generations back – sometimes as many as twenty copies of one book. Soames read their titles and shuddered. The middle wall had precisely the same books as used to be in the library at his own father's in Park Lane, from which he deduced the fancy that James and his youngest brother had gone out together one day and bought a brace of small libraries. The third wall he approached with more excitement. Here, surely, Timothy's own taste would be found. It was. The books were dummies. The fourth wall was all heavily curtained window. And turned toward it was a large chair with a mahogany reading-stand attached, on which a yellowish and folded copy of *The Times*, dated 6 July 1914, the day Timothy first failed to come down, as if in preparation for the War, seemed waiting for him still. In a corner stood a large globe of that world never visited by Timothy, deeply convinced of the unreality of everything but England, and permanently upset by the sea, on which he had been very sick one Sunday afternoon in 1836, out of a pleasure boat off the pier at Brighton, with Juley and Hester, Swithin and Hatty Chessman; all due to Swithin, who was always taking things into his head, and who, thank goodness, had been sick too. Soames knew all about it, having heard the tale fifty times at least from one or other of them. He went up to the globe, and gave it a spin; it emitted a faint creak and moved about an inch, bringing into his purview a daddy-long-legs which had died on it in latitude 44.

'Mausoleum!' he thought. 'George was right!' And he went out and up the stairs. On the half-landing he stopped before the case of stuffed humming-birds which had delighted his childhood. They looked not a day older, suspended on wires above pampas-grass. If the case were opened the birds would not begin to hum, but the whole thing would crumble, he suspected. It wouldn't be worth putting that into the sale! And suddenly he was caught by a memory of Aunt Ann – dear old Aunt Ann – holding him by the hand in front of that case and saying: 'Look, Soamey! Aren't they bright and pretty, dear little humming-birds!' Soames remembered his own answer: 'They don't hum, Auntie.' He must have been six, in a black velveteen suit with a light-blue collar – he remembered that suit well! Aunt Ann with her ringlets, and her spidery kind hands, and her grave old aquiline smile – a fine old lady, Aunt Ann! He moved on up to the drawing-room door. There on each side of it were the groups of miniatures. Those he would certainly buy in! The miniatures of his four aunts, one of his Uncle Swithin as an adolescent, and one of his Uncle Nicholas as a boy. They had all been painted by a young lady friend of the family at a time, 1830, about, when miniatures were considered very genteel, and lasting too, painted as they were on ivory. Many a time had he heard the tale of that young lady: 'Very talented, my dear; she had quite a weakness for Swithin, and very soon after she went into a consumption and died: so like Keats – we often spoke of it.'

Well, there they were! Ann, Juley, Hester, Susan – quite a small child; Swithin, with sky-blue eyes, pink cheeks, yellow curls, white waistcoat – large as life; and Nicholas, like Cupid with an eye on heaven. Now he came to think of it, Uncle Nick had always been rather like that – a wonderful man to the last. Yes, she must have had talent, and miniatures always had a certain backwatered cachet of their own, little subject to the currents of competition on aesthetic 'Change. Soames opened the drawing-room door. The room was dusted, the furniture uncovered, the curtains drawn back, precisely as if his aunts still dwelt there patiently waiting. And a thought came to him: When Timothy died – why not? Would it not be almost a duty to preserve this house – like Carlyle's – and put up a tablet, and show it? 'Specimen of mid-Victorian abode – entrance, one shilling, with catalogue.' After all, it was the completest thing, and perhaps the deadest in the London of to-day. Perfect in its special taste and culture, if, that is, he took down and carried over to his own collection the four Barbizon pictures he had given them. The still sky-blue walls, tile green curtains patterned with red flowers and ferns; the crewel-worked fire-screen before the cast-iron grate; the mahogany cupboard with glass windows, full of little knick-knacks; the beaded footstools; Keats, Shelley, Southey, Cowper, Coleridge, Byron's *Corsair* (but nothing else), and the Victorian poets in a bookshelf row; the marqueterie cabinet lined with dim red plush, full of family relics: Hester's first fan; the buckles of their mother's father's shoes; three bottled scorpions; and one very yellow elephant's tusk, sent home from India by Great-uncle Edgar Forsyte, who had been in jute; a yellow bit of paper propped up, with spidery writing on it, recording God knew what! And the pictures crowding on the walls – all water-colours save those four Barbizons looking like the foreigners they were, and doubtful customers at that – pictures bright and illustrative, *Telling the Bees*, *Hey for the Ferry!* and two in the style of Frith, all thimblerig and crino-lines, given them by Swithin. Oh! many, many pictures at which Soames had gazed a thousand times in supercilious fascination; a marvellous collection of bright, smooth gilt frames.

And the boudoir-grand piano, beautifully dusted, hermetically sealed as ever; and Aunt Juley's album of pressed seaweed on it. And the gilt-legged chairs, stronger than they looked. And on one side of the fireplace the sofa of crimson silk, where Aunt Ann, and after her Aunt Juley, had been wont to sit, facing the light and bolt upright. And on the other side of the fire the one really easy chair, back to the light, for Aunt Hester. Soames screwed up his eyes; he seemed to see them sitting there. Ah! and the atmosphere – even now, of too many stuffs and washed lace curtains, lavender in bags, and dried bees' wings. 'No,' he thought, 'there's nothing like it left; it ought to be preserved.' And, by George, they might laugh at it, but for a standard of gentle life never departed from, for fastidiousness of skin and eye and nose and feeling, it beat to-day hollow – to-day with its Tubes and cars, its perpetual smoking, its cross-legged, bare-necked girls visible up to the knees and down to the waist if you took the trouble (agreeable to the satyr within each Forsyte but hardly his idea of a lady), with their feet, too, screwed round the legs of their chairs while they ate, and their 'So longs', and their 'Old Beans', and their laughter – girls who gave him the shudders whenever he thought of Fleur in contact with them; and the hard-eyed, capable, older women who managed life and gave him the shudders too. No! his old aunts, if they never opened their minds, their eyes, or very much their windows, at least had manners, and a standard, and reverence for past and future.

With rather a choky feeling he closed the door and went tiptoeing upstairs. He looked in at a place on the way: H'm! in perfect order of the eighties, with a sort of yellow oilskin paper on the walls. At the top of the stairs he hesitated between four doors. Which of them was Timothy's? And he listened. A sound, as of a child slowly dragging a hobby-horse about, came to his ears. That must be Timothy! He tapped, and a door was opened by Smither, very red in the face.

Mr Timothy was taking his walk, and she had not been able to get him to attend. If Mr Soames would come into the back-room, he could see him through the door.

Soames went into the back-room and stood watching.

The last of the old Forsytes was on his feet, moving with the most impressive slowness, and an air of perfect concentration on his own affairs, backward and forward between the foot of his bed and the window, a distance of some twelve feet. The lower part of his square face, no longer clean-shaven, was covered with snowy beard clipped as short as it could be, and his chin looked as broad as his brow where the hair was also quite white, while nose and cheeks and brow were a good yellow. One hand held a stout stick, and the other grasped the skirt of his Jaeger dressing-gown, from under which could be seen his bed-socked ankles and feet thrust into Jaeger slippers. The expression on his face was that of a crossed child, intent on something that he has not got. Each time he turned he stumped the stick, and then dragged it, as if to show that he could do without it:

'He still looks strong,' said Soames under his breath.

'Oh! yes, sir. You should see him take his bath – it's wonderful; he does enjoy it so.'

Those quite loud words gave Soames an insight. Timothy had resumed his babyhood.

'Does he take any interest in things generally?' he said, also loud.

'Oh! yes, sir; his food and his will. It's quite a sight to see him turn it over and over, not to read it, of course; and every now and then he asks the price of Consols, and I write it on a slate for him – very large. Of course, I always write the same, what they were when he last took notice, in 1914. We got the doctor to forbid him to read the paper when the War broke out. Oh! he did take on about that at first. But he soon came round, because he knew it tired him; and he's a wonder to conserve energy as he used to call it when my dear mistresses were alive, bless their hearts! How he did go on at them about that; they were always so active, if you remember, Mr Soames.'

'What would happen if I were to go in?' asked Soames: 'Would he remember me? I made his will, you know, after Miss Hester died in 1907.'

'Oh! that, sir,' replied Smither doubtfully, 'I couldn't take on me to say. I think he might; he really is a wonderful man for his age.'

Soames moved into the doorway, and waiting for Timothy to turn, said in a loud voice: 'Uncle Timothy!'

Timothy trailed back half-way, and halted.

'Eh?' he said.

'Soames,' cried Soames at the top of his voice, holding out his hand, 'Soames Forsyte!'

'No!' said Timothy, and stumping his stick loudly on the floor, he continued his walk.

'It doesn't seem to work,' said Soames.

'No, sir,' replied Smither, rather crestfallen; 'you see, he hasn't finished his walk. It always was one thing at a time with him. I expect he'll ask me this afternoon if you came about the gas, and a pretty job I shall have to make him understand.'

'Do you think he ought to have a man about him?'

Smither held up her hands. 'A man! Oh! no. Cook and me can manage perfectly. A strange man about would send him crazy in no time. And my mistresses wouldn't like the idea of a man in the house. Besides, we're so proud of him.'

'I suppose the doctor comes?'

'Every morning. He makes special terms for such a quantity, and Mr Timothy's so used, he doesn't take a bit of notice, except to put out his tongue.'

'Well,' said Soames, turning away, 'it's rather sad and painful to me.'

'Oh! sir,' returned Smither anxiously, 'you mustn't think that. Now that he can't worry about things, he quite enjoys his life, really he does. As I say to Cook, Mr Timothy is more of a man than he ever was. You see, when he's not walkin', or takin' his bath, he's eatin', and when he's not eatin', he's sleepin'; and there it is. There isn't an ache or a care about him anywhere.'

'Well,' said Soames, 'there's something in that. I'll go down. By the way, let me see his will.'

'I should have to take my time about that, sir; he keeps it under his pillow, and he'd see me, while he's active.'

'I only want to know if it's the one I made,' said Soames; 'you take a look at its date some time, and let me know.'

'Yes, sir; but I'm sure it's the same, because me and Cook witnessed, you remember, and there's our names on it still, and we've only done it once.'

'Quite,' said Soames. He did remember. Smither and Jane had been proper witnesses, having been left nothing in the Will that they might have no interest in Timothy's death. It had been – he fully admitted – an almost improper precaution, but Timothy had wished it, and, after all, Aunt Hester had provided for them amply.

'Very well,' he said; 'good-bye, Smither. Look after him, and if he should say anything at any time, put it down, and let me know.'

'Oh! yes, Mr Soames; I'll be sure to do that. It's been such a pleasant change to see you. Cook will be quite excited when I tell her.'

Soames shook her hand and went downstairs. He stood for fully two minutes by the hat-stand whereon he had hung his hat so many times. 'So it all passes,' he was thinking; 'passes and begins again. Poor old chap!' And he listened, if perchance the sound of Timothy trailing his hobby-horse might come down the well of the stairs; or some ghost of an old face show over the banisters, and an old voice say: 'Why, it's dear Soames, and we were only saying that we hadn't seen him for a week!'

Nothing – nothing! Just the scent of camphor, and dust-motes in a sunbeam through the fanlight over the door. The little old house! A mausoleum! And, turning on his heel, he went out, and caught his train.

Chapter Five

The Native Heath

'His foot's upon his native heath,
His name's – *Val Dartie*.'

*W*ith some such feeling did Val Dartie, in the fortieth year of his age, set out that same Thursday morning very early from the old manor-house he had taken on the north side of the Sussex Downs. His destination was Newmarket, and he had not been there since the autumn of 1899, when he stole over from Oxford for the Cambridgeshire. He paused at the door to give his wife a kiss, and put a flask of port into his pocket.

'Don't overtire your leg, Val, and don't bet too much.'

With the pressure of her chest against his own, and her eyes looking into his, Val felt both leg and pocket safe. He should be moderate; Holly was always right – she had a natural aptitude. It did not seem so remarkable to him, perhaps, as it might to others, that – half Dartie as he was – he should have been perfectly faithful to his young first cousin during the twenty years since he married her romantically out in the Boer War; and faithful without any feeling of sacrifice or boredom – she was so quick, so slyly always a little in front of his mood. Being first cousins they had decided, or rather Holly had, to have no children; and, though a little sallower, she had kept her looks, her slimness, and the colour of her dark hair.

Val particularly admired the life of her own she carried on, besides carrying on his, and riding better every year. She kept up her music, she read an awful lot – novels, poetry, all sorts of stuff. Out on their farm in Cape colony she had looked after all the 'nigger' babies and women in a miraculous manner. She was, in fact, clever; yet made no fuss about it, and had no 'side'. Though not remarkable for humility, Val had come to have the feeling that she was his superior, and he did not grudge it – a great tribute. It might be noted that he never looked at Holly without her knowing of it, but that she looked at him sometimes unawares.

He had kissed her in the porch because he should not be doing so on the platform, though she was going to the station with him, to drive the car back. Tanned and wrinkled by Colonial weather and the wiles inseparable from horses, and handicapped by the leg which, weakened in the Boer War, had probably saved his life in the War just past, Val was still much as he had been in the days of his courtship; his smile as wide and charming, his eyelashes, if anything, thicker and darker, his eyes screwed up under them, as bright a grey, his freckles rather deeper, his hair a little grizzled at the sides. He gave the impression of one who has lived actively with horses in a sunny climate.

Twisting the car sharp round at the gate, he said:

'When is young Jon coming?'

'To-day.'

'Is there anything you want for him? I could bring it down on Saturday.'

'No; but you might come by the same train as Fleur – one-forty.'

Val gave the Ford full rein; he still drove like a man in a new country on bad roads, who refuses to compromise, and expects heaven at every hole.

'That's a young woman who knows her way about,' he said. 'I say, has it struck you?'

'Yes,' said Holly.

'Uncle Soames and your Dad – bit awkward, isn't it?'

'She won't know, and he won't know, and nothing must be said, of course. It's only for five days, Val.'

'Stable secret! Righto!' If Holly thought it safe, it was. Glancing slyly round at him, she said: 'Did you notice how beautifully she asked herself?'

'No!'

'Well, she did. What do you think of her, Val?'

'Pretty and clever; but she might run out at any corner if she got her monkey up, I should say.'

'I'm wondering,' Holly murmured, 'whether she is the modern young woman. One feels at sea coming home into all this.'

'You? You get the hang of things so quick.'

Holly slid her hand into his coat-pocket.

'You keep one in the know,' said Val, encouraged. 'What do you think of that Belgian fellow, Profond?'

'I think he's rather "a good devil".'

Val grinned.

'He seems to me a queer fish for a friend of our family. In fact, our family is in pretty queer waters, with Uncle Soames marrying a Frenchwoman, and your Dad marrying Soames's first. Our grandfathers would have had fits!'

'So would anybody's, my dear.'

'This car,' Val said suddenly, 'wants rousing; she doesn't get her hind legs under her uphill. I shall have to give her her head on the slope if I'm to catch that train.'

There was that about horses which had prevented him from ever really sympathising with a car, and the running of the Ford under his guidance compared with its running under that of Holly was always noticeable. He caught the train.

'Take care going home; she'll throw you down if she can. Good-bye, darling.'

'Good-bye,' called Holly, and kissed her hand.

In the train, after quarter of an hour's indecision between thoughts of Holly, his morning paper, the look of the bright day, and his dim memory of Newmarket, Val plunged into the recesses of a small square book, all names, pedigrees, tap-roots, and notes about the make and shape of horses. The Forsyte in him was bent on the acquisition of a certain strain of blood, and he was subduing resolutely as yet the Dartie hankering for a flutter. On getting back to England, after the profitable sale of his South African farm and stud, and observing that the sun seldom shone, Val had said to himself: 'I've absolutely got to have an interest in life, or this country will give me the blues. Hunting's not enough, I'll breed and I'll train.' With just that extra pinch of shrewdness and deci-sion imparted by long residence in a new country, Val had seen the weak point of modern breeding. They were all hypno-tised by fashion and high price. He should buy for looks, and let names go hang! And here he was already, hypnotised by the prestige of a certain strain of blood! Half-consciously, he thought: 'There's something in this damned climate which makes one go round in a ring. All the same, I must have a strain of Mayfly blood.'

In this mood he reached the Mecca of his hopes. It was one of those quiet meetings favourable to such as wish to look into horses, rather than into the mouths of bookmakers; and Val clung to the paddock. His twenty years of Colonial life, divesting him of the dandyism in which he had been bred, had left him the essential neatness of the horseman, and given him a queer and rather blighting eye over what he called 'the silly haw-haw' of some Englishmen, the 'flapping cockatoory' of some Englishwomen – Holly had none of that and Holly was his model. Observant, quick, resourceful, Val went straight to the heart of a transaction, a horse, a drink; and he was on his way to the heart of a Mayfly filly, when a slow voice said at his elbow:

'Mr Val Dartie? How's Mrs Val Dartie? She's well, I hope.'

And he saw beside him the Belgian he had met at his sister Imogen's.

'Prosper Profond – I met you at lunch,' said the voice.

'How are you?' murmured Val.

'I'm very well,' replied Monsieur Profond, smiling with a certain inimitable slowness. 'A good devil' Holly had called him. Well! He looked a little like a devil, with his dark, clipped, pointed beard; a sleepy one though, and good-humoured, with fine eyes, unexpectedly intelligent.

'Here's a gentleman wants to know you – cousin of yours – Mr George Forsyte.'

Val saw a large form, and a face clean-shaven, bull-like, a little lowering, with sardonic humour bubbling behind a full grey eye; he remembered it dimly from old days when he would dine with his father at the Iseeum Club.

'I used to go racing with your father,' George was saying: 'How's the stud? Like to buy one of my screws?'

Val grinned, to hide the sudden feeling that the bottom had fallen out of breeding. They believed in nothing over here, not even in horses. George Forsyte, Prosper Profond! The devil himself was not more disillusioned than those two.

'Didn't know you were a racing man,' he said to Monsieur Profond.

'I'm not. I don't care for it. I'm a yachtin' man. I don't care for yachtin' either, but I like to see my friends. I've got some lunch, Mr Val Dartie, just a small lunch, if you'd like to 'ave some; not much – just a small one – in my car.'

'Thanks,' said Val; 'very good of you. I'll come along in about quarter of an hour.'

'Over there. Mr Forsyde's comin',' and Monsieur Profond 'poinded' with a yellow-gloved finger; 'small car, with a small lunch'; he moved on, groomed, sleepy, and remote, George Forsyte following, neat, huge, and with his jesting air.

Val remained gazing at the Mayfly filly. George Forsyte, of course, was an old chap, but this Profond might be about his own age; Val felt extremely young, as if the Mayfly filly were a toy at which those two had laughed. The animal had lost reality.

'That "small" mare' – he seemed to hear the voice of Monsieur Profond – 'what do you see in her? – we must all die!'

And George Forsyte, crony of his father, racing still! The Mayfly strain – was it any better than any other? He might just as well have a flutter with his money instead.

'No, by gum!' he muttered suddenly, 'if it's no good breeding horses, it's no good doing anything. What did I come for? I'll buy her.'

He stood back and watched the ebb of the paddock visitors toward the stand. Natty old chips, shrewd portly fellows, Jews, trainers looking as if they had never been guilty of seeing a horse in their lives; tall, flapping, languid women, or brisk, loud-voiced women; young men with an air as if trying to take it seriously – two or three of them with only one arm.

'Life over here's a game!' thought Val. 'Muffin bell rings, horses run, money changes hands; ring again, run again, money changes back.'

But, alarmed at his own philosophy, he went to the paddock gate to watch the Mayfly filly canter down. She moved well; and he made his way over to the 'small' car. The 'small' lunch was the sort a man dreams of but seldom gets; and when it was concluded Monsieur Profond walked back with him to the paddock.

'Your wife's a nice woman,' was his surprising remark.

'Nicest woman I know,' returned Val drily.

'Yes,' said Monsieur Profond; 'she has a nice face. I admire nice women.'

Val looked at him suspiciously, but something kindly and direct in the heavy diabolism of his companion disarmed him for the moment.

'Any time you like to come on my yacht, I'll give her a small cruise.'

'Thanks,' said Val, in arms again, 'she hates the sea.'

'So do I,' said Monsieur Profond.

'Then why do you yacht?'

The Belgian's eyes smiled. 'Oh! I don't know. I've done everything; it's the last thing I'm doin'.'

'It must be d—d expensive. I should want more reason than that.'

Monsieur Prosper Profond raised his eyebrows, and puffed out a heavy lower lip.

'I'm an easy-goin' man,' he said.

'Were you in the War?' asked Val.

'Ye-es. I've done that too. I was gassed; it was a small bit unpleasant.' He smiled with a deep and sleepy air of prosperity, as if he had caught it from his name.

Whether his saying 'small' when he ought to have said 'little' was genuine mistake or affectation Val could not decide; the fellow was evidently capable of anything.

Among the ring of buyers round the Mayfly filly who had won her race, Monsieur Profond said:

'You goin' to bid?'

Val nodded. With this sleepy Satan at his elbow, he felt in need of faith. Though placed above the ultimate blows of Providence by the forethought of a grand-father who had tied him up a thousand a year to which was added the thousand a year tied up for Holly by *her* grandfather, Val was not flush of capital that he could touch, having spent most of what he had realised from his South African farm on his establishment in Sussex. And very soon he was thinking: 'Dash it! she's going beyond me!' His limit – six hundred – was exceeded; he dropped out of the bidding. The Mayfly filly passed under the hammer at seven hundred and fifty guineas. He was turning away vexed when the slow voice of Monsieur Profond said in his ear:

'Well, I've bought that small filly, but I don't want her; you take her and give her to your wife.'

Val looked at the fellow with renewed suspicion, but the good humour in his eyes was such that he really could not take offence.

'I made a small lot of money in the War,' began Monsieur Profond in answer to that look. 'I 'ad armament shares. I like to give it away. I'm always makin' money. I want very small lot myself. I like my friends to 'ave it.'

'I'll buy her off you at the price you gave,' said Val with sudden resolution.

'No,' said Monsieur Profond. 'You take her. I don' want her.'

'Hang it! one doesn't—'

'Why not?' smiled Monsieur Profond. 'I'm a friend of your family.'

'Seven hundred and fifty guineas is not a box of cigars,' said Val impatiently.

'All right; you keep her for me till I want her, and do what you like with her.'

'So long as she's yours,' said Val. 'I don't mind that.'

'That's all right,' murmured Monsieur Profond, and moved away.

Val watched; he might be 'a good devil', but then again he might not. He saw him rejoin George Forsyte, and thereafter saw him no more.

He spent those nights after racing at his mother's house in Green Street.

Winifred Dartie at sixty-two was marvellously preserved, considering the three-and-thirty years during which she had put up with Montague Dartie, till almost happily released by a French staircase. It was to her a vehement satisfaction to have her favourite son back from South Africa after all this time, to feel him so little changed, and to have taken a fancy to his wife. Winifred, who in the late seventies, before her marriage, had been in the vanguard of freedom, pleasure, and fashion, confessed her youth outclassed by the donzellas of the day. They seemed, for instance, to regard marriage as an incident, and Winifred sometimes regretted that she had not done the same; a second, third, fourth incident might have secured her a partner of less dazzling inebriety; though, after all, he had left her Val, Imogen, Maud, Benedict (almost a colonel and unharmed by the War) – none of whom had been divorced as yet. The steadiness of her children often amazed one who remembered their father; but, as she was fond of believing, they were really all Forsytes, favouring herself, with the exception, perhaps, of Imogen. Her brother's 'little girl' Fleur frankly puzzled Winifred. The child was as restless as any of these modern young women – 'She's a small flame in a draught,' Prosper Profond had said one day after dinner – but she did not flop, or talk at the top of her voice. The steady Forsyteism in Winifred's own character instinctively resented the feeling in the air, the modern girl's habits and her motto: 'All's much of a muchness! Spend, to-morrow we shall be poor!' She found it a saving grace in Fleur that, having set her heart on a thing, she had no change of heart until she got it – though what happened after, Fleur was, of course, too young to have made evident. The child was a 'very pretty little thing', too, and quite a credit to take about, with her mother's French taste and gift for wearing clothes; everybody turned to look at Fleur – great consideration to Winifred, a lover of the style and distinction which had so cruelly deceived her in the case of Montague Dartie.

In discussing her with Val, at breakfast on Saturday morning, Winifred dwelt on the family skeleton.

'That little affair of your father-in-law and your Aunt Irene, Val – it's old as the hills, of course, Fleur need know nothing about it – making a fuss. Your Uncle Soames is very particular about that. So you'll be careful.'

'Yes! But it's dashed awkward – Holly's young half-brother

is coming to live with us while he learns farming. He's there already.'

'Oh!' said Winifred. 'That is a gaff! What is he like?'

'Only saw him once – at Robin Hill, when we were home in 1909; he was naked and painted blue and yellow in stripes – a jolly little chap.'

Winifred thought that 'rather nice', and added comfortably: 'Well, Holly's sensible; she'll know how to deal with it. I shan't tell your uncle. It'll only bother him. It's a great comfort to have you back, my dear boy, now that I'm getting on.'

'Getting on! Why! you're as young as ever. That chap Profond, Mother, is he all right?'

'Prosper Profond! Oh! the most amusing man I know.'

Val grunted, and recounted the story of the Mayfly filly.

'That's so like him,' murmured Winifred. 'He does all sorts of things.'

'Well,' said Val shrewdly, 'our family haven't been too lucky with that kind of cattle; they're too light-hearted for us.'

It was true, and Winifred's blue study lasted a full minute before she answered:

'Oh! well! He's a foreigner, Val; one must make allowances.'

'All right, I'll use his filly and make it up to him, somehow.'

And soon after he gave her his blessing, received a kiss, and left her for his bookmaker's, the Iseeum Club, and Victoria station.

Chapter Six

Jon

*M*rs Val Dartie, after twenty years of South Africa, had fallen deeply in love, fortunately with something of her own, for the object of her passion was the prospect in front of her windows, the cool clear light on the green Downs. It was England again, at last! England more beautiful than she had dreamed. Chance had, in fact, guided the Val Darties to a spot where the South Downs had real charm when the sun shone. Holly had enough of her father's eye to apprehend the rare quality of their outlines and chalky radiance; to go up there by the ravine-like lane and wander along toward Chanctonbury or Amberley, was still a delight which she hardly attempted to share with Val, whose admiration of Nature was confused by a Forsyte's instinct for getting something out of it, such as the condition of the turf for his horses' exercise.

Driving the Ford home with a certain humouring, smoothness, she promised herself that the first use she would make of Jon would be to take him up there, and show him 'the view' under this May-day sky.

She was looking forward to her young half-brother with a motherliness not exhausted by Val. A three-day visit to Robin Hill, soon after their arrival home, had yielded no sight of him – he was still at school; so that her recollection, like Val's, was of a little sunny-haired boy, striped blue and yellow, down by the pond.

Those three days at Robin Hill had been exciting, sad, embarrassing. Memories of her dead brother, memories of Val's courtship; the ageing of her father, not seen for twenty years, something funereal in his ironic gentleness which did not escape one who had much subtle instinct; above all, the presence of her stepmother, whom she could still vaguely remember as the 'lady in grey' of days when she was little and grandfather alive and Mademoiselle Beauce so cross because that intruder gave her music lessons – all these confused and tantalised a spirit which had longed to find Robin Hill untroubled. But Holly was adept at keeping things to herself, and all had seemed to go quite well.

Her father had kissed her when she left him, with lips which she was sure had trembled.

'Well, my dear,' he said, 'the War hasn't changed Robin Hill, has it? If only you could have brought Jolly back with you! I say, can you stand this spiritualistic racket? When the oak-tree dies, it dies, I'm afraid.'

From the warmth of her embrace he probably divined that he had let the cat out of the bag, for he rode off at once on irony.

'Spiritualism – queer word, when the more they manifest the more they prove that they've got hold of matter.'

'How?' said Holly.

'Why! Look at their photographs of auric presences. You must have something material for light and shade to fall on before you can take a photograph. No, it'll end in our calling all matter spirit, or all spirit matter – I don't know which.'

'But don't you believe in survival, Dad?'

Jolyon had looked at her, and the sad whimsicality of his face impressed her deeply.

'Well, my dear, I should like to get something out of death. I've been looking into it a bit. But for the life of me I can't find anything that telepathy, sub-consciousness, and emanation from the storehouse of this world can't account for just as well. Wish I could! Wishes father thought but they don't breed evidence.' Holly had pressed her lips again to his forehead with the feeling that it confirmed his theory that all matter was becoming spirit – his brow felt, somehow, so insubstantial.

But the most poignant memory of that little visit had been watching, unobserved, her stepmother reading to herself a letter from Jon. It was – she decided – the prettiest sight she had ever seen. Irene, lost as it were in the letter of her boy, stood at a window where the light fell on her face and her fine grey hair; her lips were moving, smiling, her dark eyes laughing, dancing, and the hand which did not hold the letter was pressed against her breast. Holly withdrew as from a vision of perfect love, convinced that Jon must be nice.

When she saw him coming out of the station with a kit-bag in either hand, she was confirmed in her predisposition. He was a little like Jolly, that long-lost idol of her childhood, but eager-looking and less formal, with deeper eyes and brighter-coloured hair, for he wore no hat; altogether a very interesting 'little' brother!

His tentative politeness charmed one who was accustomed to assurance in the youthful manner; he was disturbed because she was to drive him home, instead of his driving her. Shouldn't he have a shot? They hadn't a car at Robin Hill since the War, of course, and he had only driven once, and landed up a bank, so she oughtn't to mind his trying. His laugh, soft and infectious, was very attractive, though that word, she had heard, was now quite old-fashioned. When they reached the house he pulled out a crumpled letter which she read while he was washing – a quite short letter, which must have cost her father many a pang to write.

My Dear,
You and Val will not forget, I trust, that Jon knows

nothing of family history. His mother and I think he is too young at present. The boy is very dear, and the apple of her eye. *Verbum sapientibus.*
Your loving father,
J. F.

That was all; but it renewed in Holly an uneasy regret that Fleur was coming.

After tea she fulfilled that promise to herself and took Jon up the hill. They had a long talk, sitting above an old chalk-pit grown over with brambles and goosepenny. Milkwort and liverwort starred the green slope, the larks sang, and thrushes in the brake, and now and then a gull flighting inland would wheel very white against the paling sky, where the vague moon was coming up. Delicious fragrance came to them, as if little invisible creatures were running and treading scent out of the blades of grass.

Jon, who had fallen silent, said rather suddenly:

'I say, this is wonderful! There's no fat on it at all. Gull's flight and sheep-bells.'

'"Gull's flight and sheep-bells"! You're a poet, my dear!'

Jon sighed.

'Oh, Holly! No go!'

'Try! I used to at your age.'

'Did you? Mother says "try" too; but I'm so rotten. Have you any of yours for me to see?'

'My dear,' Holly murmured, 'I've been married nineteen years. I only wrote verses when I wanted to be.'

'Oh!' said Jon, and turned over on his face: the one cheek she could see was a charming colour. Was Jon 'touched in the wind', then, as Val would have called it? Already? But, if so, all the better, he would take no notice of young Fleur. Besides, on Monday he would begin his farming. And she smiled. Was it Burns who followed the plough, or only Piers Plowman? Nearly every young man and most young women seemed to be poets now, judging from the number of their books she had read out in South Africa, importing them from Hatchus and Bumphards; and quite good – oh! quite; much better than she had been herself! But then poetry had only really come in since her day – with motor-cars. Another long talk after dinner over a wood fire in the low hall, and there seemed little left to know about Jon except anything of real importance. Holly parted from him at his bedroom door, having seen twice over that he had everything, with the conviction that she would love him, and Val would like him. He was eager, but did not gush; he was a splendid listener, sympathetic, reticent about himself. He evidently loved their father, and adored his mother. He liked riding, rowing, and fencing better than games. He saved moths from candles, and couldn't bear spiders, but put them out of doors in screws of paper sooner than kill them. In a word, he was amiable. She went to sleep, thinking that he would suffer horribly if anybody hurt him; but who would hurt him?

Jon, on the other hand, sat awake at his window with a bit of paper and a pencil, writing his first 'real poem' by the light of a candle because there was not enough moon to see by, only enough to make the night seem fluttery and as if engraved on silver. Just the night for Fleur to walk, and turn her eyes, and lead on – over the hills and far away. And Jon, deeply furrowed in his ingenuous brow, made marks on the paper and rubbed them out and wrote them in again, and did all that was necessary for the completion of a work of art; and he had a feeling such as the winds of spring must have, trying their first songs among the coming blossom. Jon was one of those boys (not many) in whom a home-trained love of beauty had survived school life. He had had to keep it to himself, of course, so that not even the drawing-master knew of it; but it was there, fastidious and clear within him. And his poem seemed to him as lame and stilted as the night was winged.

But he kept it, all the same. It was a 'beast', but better than nothing as an expression of the inexpressible. And he thought with a sort of discomfiture: 'I shan't be able to show it to Mother.' He slept terribly well, when he did sleep, over-whelmed by novelty.

Chapter Seven

Fleur

*T*o avoid the awkwardness of questions which could not be answered, all that had been told Jon was:

'There's a girl coming down with Val for the week-end.'

For the same reason, all that had been told Fleur was: 'We've got a youngster staying with us.'

The two yearlings, as Val called them in his thoughts, met therefore in a manner which for unpreparedness left nothing to be desired. They were thus introduced by Holly:

'This is Jon, my little brother; Fleur's a cousin of ours, Jon.'

Jon, who was coming in through a French window out of strong sunlight, was so confounded by the providential nature of this miracle, that he had time to hear Fleur say calmly: 'Oh, how do you do?' as if he had never seen her, and to understand dimly from the quickest imaginable little movement of her head that he never *had* seen her. He bowed therefore over her hand in an intoxicated manner, and became more silent than the grave. He knew better than to speak. Once in his early life, surprised reading by a nightlight, he had said fatuously: 'I was just turning over the leaves, Mum,' and his mother had replied: 'Jon, never tell stories, because of your face – nobody will ever believe them.'

The saying had permanently undermined the confidence necessary to the success of spoken untruth. He listened therefore to Fleur's swift and rapt allusions to the jolliness of everything, plied her with scones and jam, and got away as soon as might be. They say that in delirium tremens you see a fixed object, preferably dark, which suddenly changes shape and position. Jon saw the fixed object; it had dark eyes and passably dark hair, and changed its position, but never its shape. The knowledge that between him and that object there was already a secret understanding (however impossible to understand) thrilled him so that he waited feverishly, and began to copy out his poem – which of course he would never dare to show her – till the sound of horses' hoofs roused him, and, leaning from his window, he saw her riding forth with Val. It was clear that she wasted no time, but the sight filled him with grief. He wasted his. If he had not bolted, in his fearful ecstasy, he might have been asked to go too. And from his window he sat and watched them disappear, appear again in the chine of the road, vanish, and emerge once more for a minute clear on the outline of the Down. 'Silly brute!' he thought; 'I always miss my chances.'

Why couldn't he be self-confident and ready? And, leaning his chin on his hands, he imagined the ride he might have had with her. A week-end was but a week-end, and he had missed three hours of it. Did he know anyone except himself who would have been such a flat? He did not.

He dressed for dinner early, and was first down. He would miss no more. But he missed Fleur, who came down last. He sat opposite her at dinner, and it was terrible – impossible to say anything for fear of saying the wrong thing, impossible to keep his eyes fixed on her in the only natural way; in sum, impossible to treat normally one with whom in fancy he had already been over the hills and far away; conscious, too, all the time, that he must seem to her, to all of them, a dumb gawk. Yes, it was terrible! And she was talking so well – swooping with swift wing this way and that. Wonderful how she had learned an art which he found so disgustingly difficult. She must think him hopeless indeed!

His sister's eyes, fixed on him with a certain astonishment, obliged him at last to look at Fleur; but instantly her eyes, very wide and eager, seeming to say, 'Oh! for goodness' sake!' obliged him to look at Val, where a grin obliged him to look at his cutlet – that, at least, had no eyes, and no grin, and he ate it hastily.

'Jon is going to be a farmer,' he heard Holly say; 'a farmer and a poet.'

He glanced up reproachfully, caught the comic lift of her eyebrow just like their father's, laughed, and felt better.

Val recounted the incident of Monsieur Prosper Profond; nothing could have been more favourable, for, in relating it, he regarded Holly, who in turn regarded him, while Fleur seemed to be regarding with a slight frown some thought of her own, and Jon was really free to look at her at last. She had on a white frock, very simple and well made; her arms were bare, and her hair had a white rose in it. In just that swift moment of free vision, after such intense discomfort, Jon saw her sublimated, as one sees in the dark a slender white fruit-tree; caught her like a verse of poetry flashed before the eyes of the mind, or a tune which floats out in the distance and dies. He wondered giddily how old she was – she seemed so much more self-possessed and experienced than himself. Why mustn't he say they had met? He remembered suddenly his mother's face; puzzled, hurt-looking, when she answered: 'Yes, they're relations, but we don't know them.' Impossible that his mother, who loved beauty, should not admire Fleur if she did know her.

Alone with Val after dinner, he sipped port deferentially and answered the advances of this new-found brother-in-law. As to riding (always the first consideration with Val) he could have the young chestnut, saddle and unsaddle it himself, and generally look after it when he brought it in. Jon said he was accustomed to all that at home, and saw that he had gone up one in his host's estimation.

'Fleur,' said Val, 'can't ride much yet, but she's keen. Of course, her father doesn't know a horse from a cart-wheel. Does your dad ride?'

'He used to; but now he's – you know, he's—' He stopped, so hating the word 'old'. His father was old, and yet not old; no – never!

'Quite,' muttered Val. 'I used to know your brother up at Oxford, ages ago, the one who died in the Boer War. We had a fight in New College Gardens. That was a queer business,' he added, musing; 'a good deal came out of it.'

Jon's eyes opened wide; all was pushing him toward historical research, when his sister's voice said gently from the doorway:

'Come along, you two,' and he rose, his heart pushing him toward something far more modern.

Fleur having declared that it was 'simply too wonderful to stay indoors,' they all went out. Moonlight was frosting the dew, and an old sundial threw a long shadow. Two box hedges at right angles, dark and square, barred off the orchard. Fleur turned through that angled opening.

'Come on!' she called. Jon glanced at the others, and followed. She was running among the trees like a ghost. All was lovely and foamlike above her, and there was a scent of old trunks, and of nettles. She vanished. He thought he had lost her, then almost ran into her standing quite still.

'Isn't it jolly?' she cried, and Jon answered:

'Rather!'

She reached up, twisted off a blossom and, twirling it in her fingers. said:

'I suppose I can call you Jon?'

'I should think so just.'

'All right! But you know there's a feud between our families?'

Jon stammered: 'Feud? Why?'

'It's ever so romantic and silly. That's why I pretended we

hadn't met. Shall we get up early to-morrow morning and go for a walk before breakfast and have it out? I hate being slow about things, don't you?'

Jon murmured a rapturous assent.

'Six o'clock, then. I think your mother's beautiful.'

Jon said fervently: 'Yes, she is.'

'I love all kinds of beauty,' went on Fleur, 'when it's exciting. I don't like Greek things a bit.'

'What! Not Euripides?'

'Euripides? Oh! no, I can't bear Greek plays; they're so long. I think beauty's always swift. I like to look at one picture, for instance, and then run off. I can't bear a lot of things together. Look!' She held up her blossom in the moonlight. 'That's better than all the orchard, I think.'

And, suddenly, with her other hand she caught Jon's.

'Of all things in the world, don't you think caution's the most awful? Smell the moonlight!'

She thrust the blossom against his face; Jon agreed giddily that of all things in the world caution was the worst, and bending over, kissed the hand which held his.

'That's nice and old-fashioned,' said Fleur calmly. 'You're frightfully silent, Jon. Still I like silence when it's swift.' She let go his hand. 'Did you think I dropped my handkerchief on purpose?'

'No!' cried Jon, intensely shocked.

'Well, I did, of course. Let's get back, or they'll think we're doing this on purpose too.' And again she ran like a ghost among the trees. Jon followed, with love in his heart, Spring in his heart, and over all the moonlit white unearthly blossom. They came out where they had gone in, Fleur walking demurely.

'It's quite wonderful in there,' she said dreamily to Holly.

Jon preserved silence, hoping against hope that she might be thinking it swift.

She bade him a casual and demure good-night, which made him think he had been dreaming . . .

In her bedroom Fleur had flung off her gown, and, wrapped in a shapeless garment, with the white flower still in her hair, she looked like a *mousmé*, sitting cross-legged on her bed, writing by candlelight.

Dearest Cherry,
I believe I'm in love. I've got it in the neck, only the feeling is really lower down. He's a second cousin – such a child, about six months older and ten years younger than I am. Boys always fall in love with their seniors, and girls with their juniors or with old men of forty. Don't laugh, but his eyes are the truest things I ever saw; and he's quite divinely silent! We had a most romantic first meeting in London under the Vospovitch Juno. And now he's sleeping in the next room and the moonlight's on the blossom; and to-morrow morning, before anybody's awake, we're going to walk off into Down fairyland. There's a feud between our families, which makes it really exciting. Yes! and I may have to use subterfuge and come on you for invitations – if so, you'll know why! My father doesn't want us to know each other, but I can't help that. Life's too short. He's got the most beautiful mother, with lovely silvery hair and a young face with dark eyes. I'm staying with his sister – who married my cousin; it's all mixed up, but I mean to pump her to-morrow. We've often talked about love being a spoil-sport; well, that's all tosh, it's the beginning of sport, and the sooner you feel it, my dear, the better for you.

'Jon (not simplified spelling, but short for Jolyon, which is a name in my family, they say) is the sort that lights up and goes out; about five feet ten, still growing, and I believe he's going to be a poet. If you laugh at me I've done with you forever. I perceive all sorts of difficulties, but you know when I really want a thing I get it. One of the chief effects of love is that you see the air sort of inhabited, like seeing a face in the moon; and you feel – you feel dancey and soft at the same time, with a funny sensation – like a continual first sniff of orange-blossom – just above your stays. This is my first, and I feel as if it were going to be my last, which is absurd, of course, by all the laws of Nature and morality. If you mock me I will smite you, and if you tell anybody I will never forgive you. So much so, that I almost don't think I'll send this letter. Anyway, I'll sleep over it. So goodnight, my Cherry-oh!

Your,

Fleur

Chapter Eight

Idyll on Grass

When those two young Forsytes emerged from the chine lane, and set their faces east toward the sun, there was not a cloud in heaven, and the Downs were dewy. They had come at a good bat up the slope and were a little out of breath; if they had anything to say they did not say it, but marched in the early awkwardness of unbreakfasted morning under the songs of the larks. The stealing out had been fun, but with the freedom of the tops the sense of conspiracy ceased, and gave place to dumbness.

'We've made one blooming error,' said Fleur, when they had gone half a mile. 'I'm hungry.'

Jon produced a stick of chocolate. They shared it and their tongues were loosened. They discussed the nature of their homes and previous existences, which had a kind of fascinating unreality up on that lonely height. There remained but one thing solid in Jon's past – his mother; but one thing solid in Fleur's – her father; and of these figures, as though seen in the distance with disapproving faces, they spoke little.

The Down dipped and rose again toward Chanctonbury Ring; a sparkle of far sea came into view, a sparrow-hawk hovered in the sun's eye so that the blood-nourished brown of his wings gleamed nearly red. Jon had a passion for birds, and an aptitude for sitting very still to watch them; keen-sighted, and with a memory for what interested him, on birds he was almost worth listening to. But in Chanctonbury Ring there were none – its great beech temple was empty of life, and almost chilly at this early hour; they came out willingly again into the sun on the far side. It was Fleur's turn now. She spoke of dogs, and the way people treated them. It was wicked to keep them on chains! She would like to flog people who did that. Jon was astonished to find her so humanitarian. She knew a dog, it seemed, which some farmer near her home kept chained up at the end of his chicken run, in all weathers, till it had almost lost its voice from barking!

'And the misery is,' she said vehemently, 'that if the poor thing didn't bark at everyone who passes it wouldn't be kept there. I do think men are cunning brutes. I've let it go twice, on the sly; it's nearly bitten me both times, and then it goes simply mad with joy; but it always runs back home at last, and they chain it up again. If I had my way, I'd chain that man up.' Jon saw her teeth and her eyes gleam. 'I'd brand him on his forehead with the word "Brute"; that would teach him!'

Jon agreed that it would be a good remedy.

'It's their sense of property,' he said, 'which makes people chain things. The last generation thought of nothing but property; and that's why there was the War.'

'Oh!' said Fleur, 'I never thought of that. Your people and mine quarrelled about property. And anyway we've all got it – at least, I suppose your people have.'

'Oh! yes, luckily; I don't suppose I shall be any good at making money.'

'If you were, I don't believe I should like you.'

Jon slipped his hand tremulously under her arm. Fleur looked straight before her and chanted:

'Jon, Jon, the farmer's son,
Stole a pig, and away he run!'

Jon's arm crept round her waist.

'This is rather sudden,' said Fleur calmly; 'do you often do it?'

Jon dropped his arm. But when she laughed his arm stole back again; and Fleur began to sing:

> 'O who will o'er the downs so free,
>   O who will with me ride?
>   O who will up and follow me—'

'Sing, Jon!'

Jon sang. The larks joined in, sheep-bells, and an early morning church far away over in Steyning. They went on from tune to tune, till Fleur said:

'My God! I am hungry now!'

'Oh! I *am* sorry!'

She looked round into his face.

'Jon, you're rather a darling.'

And she pressed his hand against her waist. Jon almost reeled from happiness. A yellow-and-white dog coursing a hare startled them apart. They watched the two vanish down the slope, till Fleur said with a sigh: 'He'll never catch it, thank goodness! What's the time? Mine's stopped. I never wound it.'

Jon looked at his watch. 'By Jove!' he said, 'mine's stopped; too.'

They walked on again, but only hand in hand.

'If the grass is dry,' said Fleur, 'let's sit down for half a minute.'

Jon took off his coat, and they shared it.

'Smell! Actually wild thyme!'

With his arm round her waist again, they sat some minutes in silence.

'We are goats!' cried Fleur, jumping up; 'we shall be most fearfully late, and look so silly, and put them on their guard. Look here, Jon! We only came out to get an appetite for breakfast, and lost our way. See?'

'Yes,' said Jon.

'It's serious; there'll be a stopper put on us. Are you a good liar?'

'I believe not very; but I can try.'

Fleur frowned.

'You know,' she said, 'I realise that they don't mean us to be friends.'

'Why not?'

'I told you why.'

'But that's silly.'

'Yes; but you don't know my father!'

'I suppose he's fearfully fond of you.'

'You see, I'm an only child. And so are you – of your mother. Isn't it a bore? There's so much expected of one. By the time they've done expecting, one's as good as dead.'

'Yes,' muttered Jon, 'life's beastly short. One wants to live forever, and know everything.'

'And love everybody?'

'No,' cried Jon; 'I only want to love once – you.'

'Indeed! You're coming on! Oh! Look! There's the chalk-pit; we can't be very far now. Let's run.'

Jon followed, wondering fearfully if he had offended her.

The chalk-pit was full of sunshine and the murmuration of bees. Fleur flung back her hair.

'Well,' she said, 'in case of accidents, you may give me one kiss, Jon,' and she pushed her cheek forward. With ecstasy he kissed that hot soft cheek.

'Now, remember! We lost our way; and leave it to me as much as you can. I'm going to be rather beastly to you; it's safer; try and be beastly to me!'

Jon shook his head. 'That's impossible.'

'Just to please me; till five o'clock, at all events.'

'Anybody will be able to see through it,' said Jon gloomily.

'Well, do your best. Look! There they are! Wave your hat! Oh! you haven't got one. Well, I'll cooee! Get a little away from me, and look sulky.'

Five minutes later, entering the house and doing his utmost to look sulky, Jon heard her clear voice in the dining-room:

'Oh! I'm simply ravenous! He's going to be a farmer – and he loses his way! The boy's an idiot!'

Chapter Nine

Goya

Lunch was over and Soames mounted to the picture-gallery in his house near Mapledurham. He had what Annette called 'a grief'. Fleur was not yet home. She had been expected on Wednesday; had wired that it would be Friday; and again on Friday that it would be Sunday after-noon; and here were her aunt, and her cousins the Cardigans, and this fellow Profond, and everything flat as a pancake for the want of her. He stood before his Gauguin – sorest point of his collection. He had bought the ugly great thing with two early Matisses before the War, because there was such a fuss about those Post-Impressionist chaps. He was wondering whether Profond would take them off his hands – the fellow seemed not to know what to do with his money – when he heard his sister's voice say: 'I think that's a horrid thing, Soames,' and saw that Winifred had followed him up.

'Oh you *do*?' he said drily; 'I gave five hundred for it.'

'Fancy! Women aren't made like that even if they are black.'

Soames uttered a glum laugh. 'You didn't come up to tell me that.'

'No. Do you know that Jolyon's boy is staying with Val and his wife?'

Soames spun round.

'What?'

'Yes,' drawled Winifred; 'he's gone to live with them there while he learns farming.'

Soames had turned away, but her voice pursued him as he walked up and down. 'I warned Val that neither of them was to be spoken to about old matters.'

'Why didn't you tell me before?'

Winifred shrugged her substantial shoulders.

'Fleur does what she likes. You've always spoiled her. Besides, my dear boy, what's the harm?'

'The harm!' muttered Soames. 'Why, she—' he checked himself. The Juno, the handkerchief, Fleur's eyes, her questions, and now this delay in her return – the symptoms seemed to him so sinister that, faithful to his nature, he could not part with them.

'I think you take too much care,' said Winifred. 'If I were you, I should tell her of that old matter. It's no good thinking that girls in these days are as they used to be. Where they pick up their knowledge I can't tell, but they seem to know everything.'

Over Soames's face, closely composed, passed a sort of spasm, and Winifred added hastily:

'If you don't like to speak of it, I could for you.'

Soames shook his head. Unless there was absolute necessity the thought that his adored daughter should learn of that old scandal hurt his pride too much.

'No,' he said, 'not yet. Never if I can help it.'

'Nonsense, my dear. Think what people are!'

'Twenty years is a long time,' muttered Soames. 'Outside our family, who's likely to remember?'

Winifred was silenced. She inclined more and more to that peace and quietness of which Montague Dartie had deprived her in her youth. And, since pictures always depressed her, she soon went down again.

Soames passed into the corner where, side by side, hung his real Goya and the copy of the fresco *La Vendimia*. His acquisition of the real Goya rather beautifully illustrated the cobweb of vested interests and passions which mesh the bright-winged fly of human life. The real Goya's noble owner's ancestor had come into possession of it during some Spanish war – it was in a word loot. The noble owner had remained in ignorance of its value until in the nineties an enterprising critic discovered that a Spanish painter named Goya was a genius. It was only a fair Goya, but almost unique in England, and the noble owner became a marked man. Having many possessions and that aristocratic culture which, independent of mere sensuous enjoyment, is founded on the sounder principle that one must know everything and be fearfully interested in life, he had fully intended to keep an article which contributed to his reputation while he was alive, and to leave it to the nation after he was dead. Fortunately for Soames, the House of Lords was violently attacked in 1909, and the noble owner became alarmed and angry. 'If,' he said to himself, 'they think they can have it both ways they are very much mistaken. So long as they leave me in quiet enjoyment the nation can have some of my pictures at my death. But if the nation is going to bait me, and rob me like this, I'm damned if I won't sell the lot. They can't have my private property and my public spirit – both.' He brooded in this fashion for several months till one morning, after reading the speech of a certain statesman, he telegraphed to his agent to come down and bring Bodkin. On going over the collection Bodkin, than whose opinion on market values none was more sought, pronounced that with a free hand to sell to America, Germany, and other places where there was an interest in art, a lot more money could be made than by selling in England. The noble owner's public spirit – he said – was well known but the pictures were unique. The noble owner put this opinion in his pipe and smoked it for a year. At the end of that time he read another speech by the same statesman, and telegraphed to his agents: 'Give Bodkin a free hand.' It was at this juncture that Bodkin conceived the idea which salved the Goya and two other unique pictures for the native country of the noble owner. With one hand Bodkin proffered the pictures to the foreign market, with the other he formed a list of private British collectors. Having obtained what he considered the highest possible bids from across the seas, he submitted pictures and bids to the private British collectors, and invited them, of their public spirit, to outbid. In three instances (including the Goya) out of twenty-one he was successful. And why? One of the private collectors made buttons – he had made so many that he desired that his wife should be called Lady 'Buttons'. He therefore bought a unique picture at great cost, and gave it to the nation. It was 'part,' his friends said, 'of his general game.' The second of the private collectors was an Americophobe, and bought an unique picture to 'spite the damned Yanks'. The third of the private collectors was Soames, who – more sober than either of the others – bought after a visit to Madrid, because he was certain that Goya was still on the up grade. Goya was not booming at the moment, but he would come again; and, looking at that portrait, Hogarthian, Manetesque in its directness, but with its own queer sharp beauty of paint, he was perfectly satisfied still that he had made no error, heavy though the price had been – heaviest he had ever paid. And next to it was hanging the copy of *La Vendimia*. There she was – the little wretch – looking back at him in her dreamy mood, the mood he loved best because he felt so much safer when she looked like that.

He was still gazing when the scent of a cigar impinged on his nostrils, and a voice said:

'Well, Mr Forsyde, what you goin' to do with this small lot?'

That Belgian chap, whose mother – as if Flemish blood were not enough – had been Armenian! Subduing a natural irritation, he said:

'Are you a judge of pictures?'

'Well, I've got a few myself.'

'Any Post-Impressionists?'

'Ye-es, I rather like them.'

'What do you think of this?' said Soames, pointing to the Gauguin.

Monsieur Profond protruded his lower lip and short pointed beard.

'Rather fine, I think,' he said; 'do you want to sell it?'

Soames checked his instinctive 'Not particularly' – he would not chaffer with this alien.

'Yes,' he said.

'What do you want for it?'

'What I gave.'

'All right,' said Monsieur Profond. 'I'll be glad to take that small picture. Post-Impressionists – they're awful dead, but they're amusin'. I don't care for pictures much, but I've got some, just a small lot.'

'What do you care for?'

Monsieur Profond shrugged his shoulders.

'Life's awful like a lot of monkeys scramblin' for empty nuts.'

'You're young,' said Soames. If the fellow must make a generalisation, he needn't suggest that the forms of property lacked solidity!

'I don't worry,' replied Monsieur Profond smiling; 'we're born, and we die. Half the world's starvin'. I feed a small lot of babies out in my mother's country; but what's the use? Might as well throw my money in the river.'

Soames looked at him, and turned back toward his Goya. He didn't know what the fellow wanted.

'What shall I make my cheque for?' pursued Monsieur Profond.

'Five hundred,' said Soames shortly; 'but I don't want you to take it if you don't care for it more than that.'

'That's all right,' said Monsieur Profond; 'I'll be 'appy to 'ave that picture.'

He wrote a cheque with a fountain-pen heavily chased with gold. Soames watched the process uneasily. How on earth had the fellow known that he wanted to sell that picture? Monsieur Profond held out the cheque.

'The English are awful funny about pictures,' he said. 'So are the French, so are my people. They're all awful funny.'

'I don't understand you,' said Soames stiffly.

'It's like hats,' said Monsieur Profond enigmatically, 'small or large, turnin' up or down – just the fashion. Awful funny.' And, smiling, he drifted out of the gallery again, blue and solid like the smoke of his excellent cigar.

Soames had taken the cheque, feeling as if the intrinsic value of ownership had been called in question. 'He's a cosmopolitan,' he thought, watching Profond emerge from under the verandah with Annette, and saunter down the lawn toward the river. What his wife saw in the fellow he didn't know, unless it was that he could speak her language; and there passed in Soames what Monsieur Profond would have called a 'small doubt' whether Annette was not too handsome to be walking with any one so 'cosmopolitan'. Even at that distance he could see the blue fumes from Profond's cigar wreath out in the quiet sunlight; and his grey buckskin shoes, and his grey hat – the fellow was a dandy! And he could see the quick turn of his wife's head, so very straight on her desirable neck and shoulders. That turn of her neck always seemed to him a little too showy, and in the 'Queen of all I survey' manner – not quite distinguished. He watched them walk along the path at the bottom of the garden. A young man in flannels joined them down there – a Sunday caller no doubt, from up the river. He went back to his Goya. He was still staring at that replica of Fleur, and worrying over Winifred's news, when his wife's voice said:

'Mr Michael Mont, Soames. You invited him to see your pictures.'

There was the cheerful young man of the Gallery off Cork Street!

'Turned up, you see, sir; I live only four miles from Pangbourne. Jolly day, isn't it?'

Confronted with the results of his expansiveness, Soames scrutinised his visitor. The young man's mouth was excessively large and curly – he seemed always grinning. Why didn't he grow the rest of those idiotic little moustaches, which made him look like a music-hall buffoon? What on earth were young men about, deliberately lowering their class with these tooth-brushes, or little slug whiskers? Ugh! Affected young idiots! In other respects he was presentable, and his flannels very clean.

'Happy to see you!' he said.

The young man, who had been turning his head from side to side, became transfixed. 'I say!' he said, '"some" picture!'

Soames saw, with mixed sensations, that he had addressed the remark to the Goya copy.

'Yes,' he said drily, 'that's not a Goya. It's a copy. I had it painted because it reminded me of my daughter.'

'By Jove! I thought I knew the face, sir. Is she here?'

The frankness of his interest almost disarmed Soames.

'She'll be in after tea,' he said. 'Shall we go round the pictures?'

And Soames began that round which never tired him. He had not anticipated much intelligence from one who had mistaken a copy for an original, but as they passed from section to section, period to period, he was startled by the young man's frank and relevant remarks. Natively shrewd himself, and even sensuous beneath his mask, Soames had not spent thirty-eight years over his one hobby without knowing something more about pictures than their market values. He was, as it were, the missing link between the artist and the commercial public. Art for art's sake and all that, of course, was cant. But aesthetics and good taste were necessary. The appreciation of enough persons of good taste was what gave a work of art its permanent market value, or in other words made it

'a work of art'. There was no real cleavage. And he was sufficiently accustomed to sheep-like and unseeing visitors, to be
intrigued by one who did not hesitate to say of Mauve: 'Good
old haystacks!' or of James Maris: 'Didn't he just paint and
paper 'em! Mathew was the real swell, sir; you could dig into
his surfaces!' It was after the young man had whistled before
a Whistler, with the words, 'D'you think he ever really saw a
naked woman, sir?' that Soames remarked:

'What *are* you, Mr Mont, if I may ask?'

'I, sir? I was going to be a painter, but the War knocked
that. Then in the trenches, you know, I used to dream of the
Stock Exchange, snug and warm and just noisy enough. But
the Peace knocked that, shares seem off, don't they? I've only
been demobbed about a year. What do you recommend, sir?'

'Have you got money?'

'Well,' answered the young man, 'I've got a father; I kept
him alive during the War, so he's bound to keep me alive now.
Though, of course, there's the question whether he ought to
be allowed to hang on to his property. What do you think
about that, sir?'

Soames, pale and defensive, smiled.

'The old man has fits when I tell him he may have to work
yet. He's got land, you know; it's a fatal disease.'

'This is my real Goya,' said Soames drily.

'By George! He *was* a swell. I saw a Goya in Munich once
that bowled me middle stump. A most evil-looking old woman
in the most gorgeous lace. He made no compromise with the
public taste. That old boy was "some" explosive; he must have
smashed up a lot of convention in his day. Couldn't he just
paint! He makes Velasquez stiff, don't you think?'

'I have no Velasquez,' said Soames.

The young man stared. 'No,' he said; 'only nations or profiteers can afford him, I suppose. I say, why shouldn't all the
bankrupt nations sell their Velasquez and Titians and other
swells to the profiteers by force, and then pass a law that any

one who holds a picture by an Old Master – see schedule – must hang it in a public gallery? There seems something in that.'

'Shall we go down to tea?' said Soames.

The young man's ears seemed to droop on his skull. 'He's not dense,' thought Soames, following him off the premises.

Goya, with his satiric and surpassing precision, his original 'line', and the daring of his light and shade, could have reproduced to admiration the group assembled round Annette's tea-tray in the inglenook below. He alone, perhaps, of painters would have done justice to the sunlight filtering through a screen of creeper, to the lovely pallor of brass, the old cut glasses, the thin slices of lemon in pale amber tea; justice to Annette in her black lacey dress; there was something of the fair Spaniard in her beauty, though it lacked the spirituality of that rare type; to Winifred's grey-haired, corseted solidity; to Soames, of a certain grey and flat-cheeked distinction; to the vivacious Michael Mont, pointed in ear and eye; to Imogen, dark, luscious of glance, growing a little stout; to Prosper Profond, with his expression as who should say, 'Well, Mr Goya, what's the use of paintin' this small party?' finally, to Jack Cardigan, with his shining stare and tanned sanguinity betraying the moving principle: 'I'm English, and I live to be fit.'

Curious, by the way, that Imogen, who as a girl had declared solemnly one day at Timothy's that she would never marry a good man – they were so dull – should have married Jack Cardigan, in whom health had so destroyed all traces of orig-inal sin, that she might have retired to rest with ten thousand other Englishmen without knowing the difference from the one she had chosen to repose beside. 'Oh!' she would say of him, in her 'amusing' way, 'Jack keeps himself so fearfully fit; he's never had a day's illness in his life. He went right through the War without a finger-ache. You really can't imagine how fit he is!' Indeed, he was so 'fit' that he couldn't see when she was flirting, which was such a comfort in a way. All the same she was quite fond of him, so far as one could be of a sports-machine, and of the two little Cardigans made after his pattern. Her eyes just then were comparing him maliciously with Prosper Profond. There was no 'small' sport or game which Monsieur Profond had not played at too, it seemed, from skittles to tarpon-fishing, and worn out every one. Imogen would sometimes wish that they had worn out Jack, who continued to play at them and talk of them with the simple zeal of a school-girl learning hockey; at the age of Great-uncle Timothy she well knew that Jack would be playing carpet golf in her bedroom, and 'wiping somebody's eye'.

He was telling them now how he had 'pipped the pro – a charmin' fellow, playin' a very good game,' at the last hole this morning; and how he had pulled down to Caversham since lunch, and trying to incite Prosper Profond to play him a set of tennis after tea – do him good – 'keep him fit'.

'But what's the use of keepin' fit?' said Monsieur Profond.

'Yes, sir,' murmured Michael Mont, 'what do you keep fit for?'

'Jack,' cried Imogen, enchanted, 'what *do* you keep fit for?'

Jack Cardigan stared with all his health. The questions were like the buzz of a mosquito, and he put up his hand to wipe them away. During the War, of course, he had kept fit to kill Germans; now that it was over he either did not know, or shrank in delicacy from explanation of his moving principle.

'But he's right,' said Monsieur Profond unexpectedly, 'there's nothin' left but keepin' fit.'

The saying, too deep for Sunday afternoon, would have passed unanswered, but for the mercurial nature of young Mont.

'Good!' he cried. 'That's the great discovery of the War. We all thought we were progressing – now we know we're only changing.'

'For the worse,' said Monsieur Profond genially.

'How you are cheerful, Prosper!' murmured Annette.

'You come and play tennis!' said Jack Cardigan; 'you've got the hump. We'll soon take that down. D'you play, Mr Mont?'

'I hit the ball about, sir.'

At this juncture Soames rose, ruffled in that deep instinct of preparation for the future which guided his existence.

'When Fleur comes—' he heard Jack Cardigan say.

Ah! and why didn't she come? He passed through drawing-room, hall, and porch out on to the drive, and stood there listening for the car. All was still and Sundayfied; the lilacs in full flower scented the air. There were white clouds, like the feathers of ducks gilded by the sunlight. Memory of the day when Fleur was born, and he had waited in such agony with her life and her mother's balanced in his hands, came to him sharply. He had saved her then, to be the flower of his life. And now! was she going to give him trouble – pain – give him trouble? He did not like the look of things! A blackbird broke in on his reverie with an evening song – a great big fellow up in that acacia-tree. Soames had taken quite an interest in his birds of late years; he and Fleur would walk round and watch them; her eyes were sharp as needles, and she knew every nest. He saw her dog, a retriever, lying on the drive in a patch of sunlight, and called to him. 'Hallo, old fellow – waiting for her too?' The dog came slowly with a grudging tail, and Soames mechanically laid a pat on his head. The dog, the bird, the lilac, all were part of Fleur for him; no more, no less. 'Too fond of her!' he thought, 'too fond!' He was like a man uninsured, with his ships at sea. Uninsured again – as in that other time, so long ago, when he would wander dumb and jealous in the wilderness of London, longing for that woman – his first wife – the mother of this infernal boy. Ah! There was the car at last! It drew up, it had luggage, but no Fleur.

'Miss Fleur is walking up, sir, by the towing-path.'

Walking all those miles? Soames stared. The man's face had the beginning of a smile on it. What was he grinning at? And very quickly he turned, saying, 'All right, Sims!' and went into the house. He mounted to the picture-gallery once more. He had from there a view of the river bank, and stood with his eyes fixed on it, oblivious of the fact that it would be an hour at least before her figure showed there. Walking up! And that fellow's grin! The boy— ! He turned abruptly from the window. He couldn't spy on her. If she wanted to keep things from him – she must; he could not spy on her. His heart felt empty, and bitterness mounted from it into his very mouth. The staccato shouts of Jack Cardigan pursuing the ball, the laugh of young Mont rose in the stillness and came in. He hoped they were making that chap Profond run. And the girl in *La Vendimia* stood with her arm akimbo and her dreamy eyes looking past him. 'I've done all I could for you,' he thought, 'since you were no higher than my knee. You aren't going to – to – hurt me, are you?'

But the Goya copy answered not, brilliant in colour just beginning to tone down. 'There's no real life in it,' thought Soames. 'Why doesn't she come?'

Chapter Ten

Trio

*A*mong those four Forsytes of the third, and, as one might say, fourth generation, at Wansdon under the Downs, a weekend prolonged unto the ninth day had stretched the crossing threads of tenacity almost to snapping-point. Never had Fleur been so 'fine', Holly so watchful, Val so stable-secretive, Jon so silent and disturbed. What he learned of farming in that week might have been balanced on the point of a penknife and puffed off. He, whose nature was essentially averse from intrigue, and whose adoration of Fleur disposed him to think that any need for concealing it was 'skittles', chafed and fretted, yet obeyed, taking what relief he could in the few moments when they were alone. On Thursday, while they were standing in the bay window of the drawing-room, dressed for dinner, she said to him:

'Jon, I'm going home on Sunday by the 3.40 from Paddington; if you were to go home on *Saturday* you could come up on Sunday and take me down, and just get back here by the last train, after. You *were* going home anyway, weren't you?'

Jon nodded.

'Anything to be with you,' he said; 'only why need I pretend—'

Fleur slipped her little finger into his palm:

'You have no instinct, Jon; you *must* leave things to me.

It's serious about our people. We've simply got to be secret at present, if we want to be together.' The door was opened, and she added loudly: 'You *are* a duffer, Jon.'

Something turned over within Jon; he could not bear this subterfuge about a feeling so natural, so overwhelming, and so sweet.

On Friday night about eleven he had packed his bag, and was leaning out of his window, half miserable, and half lost in a dream of Paddington station, when he heard a tiny sound, as of a finger-nail tapping on his door. He rushed to it and listened. Again the sound. It *was* a nail. He opened. Oh! What a lovely thing came in!

'I wanted to show you my fancy dress,' it said, and struck an attitude at the foot of his bed.

Jon drew a long breath and leaned against the door. The apparition wore white muslin on its head, a fichu round its bare neck over a wine-coloured dress, fulled out below its slender waist. It held one arm akimbo, and the other raised, right-angled, holding a fan which touched its head.

'This ought to be a basket of grapes,' it whispered, 'but I haven't got it here. It's my Goya dress. And this is the attitude in the picture. Do you like it?'

'It's a dream.'

The apparition pirouetted. 'Touch it, and see.'

Jon knelt down and took the skirt reverently.

'Grape colour,' came the whisper, 'all grapes – La Vendimia – the vintage.'

Jon's fingers scarcely touched each side of the waist; he looked up, with adoring eyes.

'Oh! Jon,' it whispered; bent, kissed his forehead, pirouetted again, and, gliding out, was gone.

Jon stayed on his knees, and his head fell forward against the bed. How long he stayed like that he did not know. The little noises – of the tapping nail, the feet, the skirts rustling – as in a dream – went on about him; and before his closed eyes the figure stood and smiled and whispered, a faint perfume of narcissus lingering in the air. And his forehead where it had been kissed had a little cool place between the brows, like the imprint of a flower. Love filled his soul, that love of boy for girl which knows so little, hopes so much, would not brush the down off for the world, and must become in time a fragrant memory – a searing passion – a humdrum mateship – or, once in many times, vintage full and sweet with sunset colour on the grapes.

Enough has been said about Jon Forsyte here and in another place to show what long marches lay between him and his great-great-grandfather, the first Jolyon, in Dorset down by the sea. Jon was sensitive as a girl, more sensitive than nine out of ten girls of the day; imaginative as one of his half-sister June's 'lame duck' painters; affectionate as a son of his father and his mother naturally would be. And yet, in his inner tissue, there was something of the old founder of his family, a secret tenacity of soul, a dread of showing his feelings, a determination not to know when he was beaten. Sensitive, imaginative, affectionate boys get a bad time at school, but Jon had instinctively kept his nature dark, and been but normally unhappy there. Only with his mother had he, up till then, been absolutely frank and natural; and when he went home to Robin Hill that Saturday his heart was heavy because Fleur had said that he must not be frank and natural with her from whom he had never yet kept anything, must not even tell her that they had met again, unless he found that she knew already. So intolerable did this seem to him that he was very near to telegraphing an excuse and staying up in London. And the first thing his mother said to him was:

'So you've had our little friend of the confectioner's there, Jon. What is she like on second thoughts?'

With relief, and a high colour, Jon answered:

'Oh! awfully jolly, Mum.'

Her arm pressed his.

Jon had never loved her so much as in that minute which seemed to falsify Fleur's fears and to release his soul. He turned to look at her, but something in her smiling face – something which only he perhaps would have caught – stopped the words bubbling up in him. Could fear go with a smile? If so, there was fear in her face. And out of Jon tumbled quite other words, about farming, Holly, and the Downs. Talking fast, he waited for her to come back to Fleur. But she did not. Nor did his father mention her, though of course he, too, must know. What deprivation, and killing of reality was in this silence about Fleur – when he was so full of her; when his mother was so full of Jon, and his father so full of his mother! And so the trio spent the evening of that Saturday.

After dinner his mother played; she seemed to play all the things he liked best, and he sat with one knee clasped, and his hair standing up where his fingers had run through it. He gazed at his mother while she played, but he saw Fleur – Fleur in the moonlit orchard, Fleur in the sunlit gravel-pit, Fleur in that fancy dress, swaying, whispering, stooping, kissing his forehead. Once, while he listened, he forgot himself and glanced at his father in that other easy chair. What was Dad looking like that for? The expression on his face was so sad and puzzling. It filled him with a sort of remorse, so that he got up and went and sat on the arm of his father's chair. From there he could not see his face; and again he saw Fleur – in his mother's hands, slim and white on the keys, in the profile of her face and her powdery hair; and down the long room in the open window where the May night walked outside.

When he went up to bed his mother came into his room. She stood at the window, and said:

'Those cypresses your grandfather planted down there have done wonderfully. I always think they look beautiful under a dropping moon. I wish you had known your grandfather, Jon.'

'Were you married to father when he was alive?' asked Jon suddenly.

'No, dear; he died in '92 – very old – eighty-five, I think.'

'Is Father like him?'

'A little, but more subtle, and not quite so solid.'

'I know, from Grandfather's portrait; who painted that?'

'One of June's "lame ducks". But it's quite good.'

Jon slipped his hand through his mother's arm. 'Tell me about the family quarrel, Mum.'

He felt her arm quivering. 'No, dear; that's for your Father some day, if he thinks fit.'

'Then it *was* serious,' said Jon, with a catch in his breath.

'Yes.' And there was a silence, during which neither knew whether the arm or the hand within it were quivering most.

'Some people,' said Irene softly, 'think the moon on her back is evil; to me she's always lovely. Look at those cypress shadows! Jon, Father says we may go to Italy, you and I, for two months. Would you like?'

Jon took his hand from under her arm; his sensation was so sharp and so confused. Italy with his mother! A fortnight ago it would have been perfection; now it filled him with dismay; he felt that the sudden suggestion had to do with Fleur. He stammered out:

'Oh! yes; only – I don't know. Ought I – now I've just begun? I'd like to think it over.'

Her voice answered, cool and gentle:

'Yes, dear; think it over. But better now than when you've begun farming seriously. Italy with you! It would be nice!'

Jon put his arm round her waist, still slim and firm as a girl's.

'Do you think you ought to leave Father?' he said feebly, feeling very mean.

'Father suggested it; he thinks you ought to see Italy at least before you settle down to anything.'

The sense of meanness died in Jon; he knew, yes – he

knew – that his father and his mother were not speaking frankly, no more than he himself. They wanted to keep him from Fleur. His heart hardened. And, as if she felt that process going on, his mother said:

'Good-night, darling. Have a good sleep and think it over. But it would be lovely!'

She pressed him to her so quickly that he did not see her face. Jon stood feeling exactly as he used to when he was a naughty little boy; sore because he was not loving, and because he was justified in his own eyes.

But Irene, after she had stood a moment in her own room, passed through the dressing-room between it and her husband's.

'Well?'

'He will think it over, Jolyon.'

Watching her lips that wore a little drawn smile, Jolyon said quietly:

'You had better let me tell him, and have done with it. After all, Jon has the instincts of a gentleman. He has only to under-stand—'

'Only! He can't understand; that's impossible.'

'I believe I could have at his age.'

Irene caught his hand. 'You were always more of a realist than Jon; and never so innocent.'

'That's true,' said Jolyon. 'It's queer, isn't it? You and I would tell our stories to the world without a particle of shame; but our own boy stumps us.'

'We've never cared whether the world approves or not.'

'Jon would not disapprove of *us*!'

'Oh! Jolyon, yes. He's in love, I feel he's in love. And he'd say: "My mother once married *without* love! How could she have!" It'll seem to him a crime! And so it was!'

Jolyon took her hand, and said with a wry smile:

'Ah! why on earth are we born young? Now, if only we were born old and grew younger year by year, we should understand how things happen, and drop all our cursed intolerance. But you know if the boy is really in love, he won't forget, even if he goes to Italy. We're a tenacious breed; and he'll know by instinct why he's being sent. Nothing will really cure him but the shock of being told.'

'Let me try, anyway.'

Jolyon stood a moment without speaking. Between this devil and this deep sea – the pain of a dreaded disclosure and the grief of losing his wife for two months – he secretly hoped for the devil; yet if she wished for the deep sea he must put up with it. After all, it would be training for that departure from which there would be no return. And, taking her in his arms, he kissed her eyes, and said:

'As you will, my love.'

Chapter Eleven

Duet

That 'small' emotion, love, grows amazingly when threatened with extinction. Jon reached Paddington station half an hour before his time and a full week after, as it seemed to him. He stood at the appointed book-stall, amid a crowd of Sunday travellers, in a Harris tweed suit exhaling, as it were, the emotion of his thumping heart. He read the names of the novels on the book-stall, and bought one at last, to avoid being regarded with suspicion by the book-stall clerk. It was called *The Heart of the Trail* which must mean something, though it did not seem to. He also bought *The Lady's Mirror* and *The Landsman*. Every minute was an hour long, and full of horrid imaginings. After nineteen had passed, he saw her with a bag and a porter wheeling her luggage. She came swiftly; she came cool. She greeted him as if he were a brother.

'First class,' she said to the porter, 'corner seats; opposite.'

Jon admired her frightful self-possession.

'Can't we get a carriage to ourselves,' he whispered.

'No good; it's a stopping train. After Maidenhead perhaps. Look natural, Jon.'

Jon screwed his features into a scowl. They got in – with two other beasts! – oh! heaven! He tipped the porter unnaturally, in his confusion. The brute deserved nothing for putting them in there, and looking as if he knew all about it into the bargain.

Fleur hid herself behind *The Lady's Mirror*. Jon imitated her behind *The Landsman*. The train started. Fleur let *The Lady's Mirror* fall and leaned forward.

'Well?' she said.

'It's seemed about fifteen days.'

She nodded, and Jon's face lighted up at once.

'Look natural,' murmured Fleur, and went off into a bubble of laughter. It hurt him. How could he look natural with Italy hanging over him? He had meant to break it to her gently, but now he blurted it out.

'They want me to go to Italy with Mother for two months.'

Fleur drooped her eyelids; turned a little pale, and bit her lips. 'Oh!' she said. It was all, but it was much.

That 'Oh!' was like the quick drawback of the wrist in fencing ready for riposte. It came.

'You must go!'

'Go?' said Jon in a strangled voice.

'Of course.'

'But – two months— it's ghastly.'

'No,' said Fleur, 'six weeks. You'll have forgotten me by then. We'll meet in the National Gallery the day after you get back.'

Jon laughed.

'But suppose you've forgotten me,' he muttered into the noise of the train.

Fleur shook her head.

'Some other beast—' murmured Jon.

Her foot touched his.

'No other beast,' she said, lifting *The Lady's Mirror*.

The train stopped; two passengers got out, and one got in.

'I shall die,' thought Jon, 'if we're not alone at all.'

The train went on; and again Fleur leaned forward.

'I never let go,' she said; 'do you?'

Jon shook his head vehemently.

'Never!' he said. 'Will you write to me?'

'No; but *you* can – to my Club.'

She had a Club; she was wonderful!

'Did you pump Holly?' he muttered.

'Yes, but I got nothing. I didn't dare pump hard.'

'What can it be?' cried Jon.

'I shall find out all right.'

A long silence followed till Fleur said: 'This is Maidenhead; stand by, Jon!'

The train stopped. The remaining passenger got out. Fleur drew down her blind.

'Quick!' she cried. 'Hang out! Look as much of a beast as you can.'

Jon blew his nose, and scowled; never in all his life had he scowled like that! An old lady recoiled, a young one tried the handle. It turned, but the door would not open. The train moved, the young lady darted to another carriage.

'What luck!' cried Jon. 'It jammed.'

'Yes,' said Fleur; 'I was holding it.'

The train moved out, and Jon fell on his knees.

'Look out for the corridor,' she whispered; 'and – quick!'

Her lips met his. And though their kiss only lasted perhaps ten seconds, Jon's soul left his body and went so far beyond, that, when he was again sitting opposite that demure figure, he was pale as death. He heard her sigh, and the sound seemed to him the most precious he had ever heard – an exquisite declaration that he meant something to her.

'Six weeks isn't really long,' she said; 'and you can easily make it six if you keep your head out there, and never seem to think of me.'

Jon gasped.

'This is just what's really wanted, Jon, to convince them, don't you see? If we're just as bad when you come back they'll stop being ridiculous about it. Only, I'm sorry it's not Spain; there's a girl in a Goya picture at Madrid who's like me, Father says. Only she isn't – we've got a copy of her.'

It was to Jon like a ray of sunshine piercing through a fog.

'I'll make it Spain,' he said, 'Mother won't mind; she's never been there. And my Father thinks a lot of Goya.'

'Oh! yes, he's a painter – isn't he?'

'Only water-colour,' said Jon, with honesty.

'When we come to Reading, Jon, get out first and go down to Caversham lock and wait for me. I'll send the car home and we'll walk by the towing-path.'

Jon seized her hand in gratitude, and they sat silent, with the world well lost, and one eye on the corridor. But the train seemed to run twice as fast now, and its sound was almost lost in that of Jon's sighing.

'We're getting near,' said Fleur; 'the towing-path's awfully exposed. One more! Oh! Jon, don't forget me.'

Jon answered with his kiss. And very soon, a flushed, distracted-looking youth could have been seen – as they say – leaping from the train and hurrying along the platform, searching his pockets for his ticket.

When at last she rejoined him on the towing-path a little beyond Caversham lock he had made an effort, and regained some measure of equanimity. If they had to part, he would not make a scene! A breeze by the bright river threw the white side of the willow leaves up into the sunlight, and followed those two with its faint rustle.

'I told our chauffeur that I was train-giddy,' said Fleur. 'Did you look pretty natural as you went out?'

'I don't know. What is natural?'

'It's natural to you to look seriously happy. When I first saw you I thought you weren't a bit like other people.'

'Exactly what I thought when I saw you. I knew at once I should never love anybody else.'

Fleur laughed.

'We're absurdly young. And love's young dream is out of date, Jon. Besides, it's awfully wasteful. Think of all the fun you might have. You haven't begun, even; it's a shame, really. And there's me. I wonder!'

Confusion came on Jon's spirit. How could she say such things just as they were going to part?

'If you feel like that,' he said, 'I can't go. I shall tell Mother that I ought to try and work. There's always the condition of the world!'

'The condition of the world!'

Jon thrust his hands deep into his pockets.

'But there is,' he said; 'think of the people starving!'

Fleur shook her head. 'No, no, I never, never will make myself miserable for nothing.'

'Nothing! But there's an awful state of things, and of course one ought to help.'

'Oh! yes, I know all that. But you can't help people, Jon; they're hopeless. When you pull them out they only get into another hole. Look at them, still fighting and plotting and struggling, though they're dying in heaps all the time. Idiots!'

'Aren't you sorry for them?'

'Oh! sorry – yes, but I'm not going to make myself unhappy about it; that's no good.'

And they were silent, disturbed by this first glimpse of each other's natures.

'I think people are brutes and idiots,' said Fleur stubbornly.

'I think they're poor wretches,' said Jon. It was as if they had quarrelled – and at this supreme and awful moment, with parting visible out there in that last gap of the willows!

'Well, go and help your poor wretches, and don't think of me.'

Jon stood still. Sweat broke out on his forehead, and his limbs trembled. Fleur too had stopped, and was frowning at the river.

'I *must* believe in things,' said Jon with a sort of agony; 'we're all meant to enjoy life.'

Fleur laughed. 'Yes; and that's what you won't do, if you don't take care. But perhaps your idea of enjoyment is to make yourself wretched. There are lots of people like that, of course.'

She was pale, her eyes had darkened, her lips had thinned. Was it Fleur thus staring at the water? Jon had an unreal feeling as if he were passing through the scene in a book where the lover has to choose between love and duty. But just then she looked round at him. Never was anything so intoxicating as that vivacious look. It acted on him exactly as the tug of a chain acts on a dog – brought him up to her with his tail wagging and his tongue out.

'Don't let's be silly,' she said, 'time's too short. Look, Jon, you can just see where I've got to cross the river. There, round the bend, where the woods begin.'

Jon saw a gable, a chimney or two, a patch of wall through the trees – and felt his heart sink.

'I mustn't dawdle any more. It's no good going beyond the next hedge, it gets all open. Let's get on to it and say good-bye.'

They went side by side, hand in hand, silently toward the hedge, where the may-flower, both pink and white, was in full bloom.

'My Club's the "Talisman", Stratton Street, Piccadilly. Letters there will be quite safe, and I'm almost always up once a week.'

Jon nodded. His face had become extremely set, his eyes stared straight before him.

'To-day's the twenty-third of May,' said Fleur; 'on the ninth of July I shall be in front of the *Bacchus and Ariadne* at three o'clock; will you?'

'I will.'

'If you feel as bad as I it's all right. Let those people pass!'

A man and woman airing their children went by strung out in Sunday fashion.

The last of them passed the wicket gate.

'Domesticity!' said Fleur, and blotted herself against the hawthorn hedge. The blossom sprayed out above her head, and one pink cluster brushed her cheek. Jon put up his hand jealously to keep it off.

'Good-bye, Jon.' For a second they stood with hands hard clasped. Then their lips met for the third time, and when they parted Fleur broke away and fled through the wicket gate. Jon stood where she had left him, with his forehead against that pink cluster. Gone! For an eternity – for seven weeks all but two days! And here he was, wasting the last sight of her! He rushed to the gate. She was walking swiftly on the heels of the straggling children. She turned her head, he saw her hand make a little flitting gesture; then she sped on, and the trailing family blotted her out from his view.

The words of a comic song –

> Paddington groan – worst ever known
> He gave a sepulchral Paddington groan –

came into his head, and he sped incontinently back to Reading station. All the way up to London and down to Wansdon he sat with *The Heart of the Trail* open on his knee, knitting in his head a poem so full of feeling that it would not rhyme.

Chapter Twelve

Caprice

Fleur sped on. She had need of rapid motion; she was late, and wanted all her wits about her when she got in. She passed the islands, the station, and hotel, and was about to take the ferry, when she saw a skiff with a young man standing up in it, and holding to the bushes.

'Miss Forsyte,' he said; 'let me put you across. I've come on purpose.'

She looked at him in blank amazement.

'It's all right, I've been having tea with your people. I thought I'd save you the last bit. It's on my way, I'm just off back to Pangbourne. My name's Mont. I saw you at the picture-gallery – you remember – when your father invited me to see his pictures.'

'Oh!' said Fleur; 'yes – the handkerchief.'

To this young man she owed Jon; and, taking his hand, she stepped down into the skiff. Still emotional, and a little out of breath, she sat silent; not so the young man. She had never heard anyone say so much in so short a time. He told her his age, twenty-four; his weight, ten stone eleven; his place of residence, not far away; described his sensations under fire, and what it felt like to be gassed; criticised the Juno, mentioned his own conception of that goddess; commented on the Goya copy, said Fleur was not too awfully like it; sketched in rapidly the condition of England; spoke of Monsieur Profond – or whatever his name was – as 'an awful sport'; thought her father had some 'ripping' pictures and some rather 'dug-up'; hoped he might row down again and take her on the river because he was quite trustworthy; inquired her opinion of Tchekov, gave her his own; wished they could go to the Russian ballet together some time – considered the name Fleur Forsyte simply topping; cursed his people for giving him the name of Michael on the top of Mont; outlined his father, and said that if she wanted a good book she should read 'Job'; his father was rather like Job while Job still had land.

'But Job didn't have land,' Fleur murmured; 'he only had flocks and herds and moved on.'

'Ah!' answered Michael Mont, 'I wish my gov'nor would move on. Not that I want his land. Land's an awful bore these days, don't you think?'

'We never have it in my family,' said Fleur. 'We have everything else. I believe one of my great-uncles once had a sentimental farm in Dorset, because we came from there originally, but it cost him more than it made him happy.'

'Did he sell it?'

'No; he kept it.'

'Why?'

'Because nobody would buy it.'

'Good for the old boy!'

'No, it wasn't good for him. Father says it soured him. His name was Swithin.'

'What a corking name!'

'Do you know that we're getting farther off, not nearer? This river flows.'

'Splendid!' cried Mont, dipping his sculls vaguely; 'it's good to meet a girl who's got wit.'

'But better to meet a young man who's got it in the plural.'

Young Mont raised a hand to tear his hair.

'Look out!' cried Fleur. 'Your scull!'

'All right! It's thick enough to bear a scratch.'

'Do you mind *sculling*?' said Fleur severely. 'I want to get in.'

'Ah!' said Mont; 'but when you get in, you see, I shan't see you any more to-day. *Fini*, as the French girl said when she jumped on her bed after saying her prayers. Don't you bless the day that gave you a French mother, and a name like yours?'

'I like my name, but Father gave it me. Mother wanted me called Marguerite.'

'Which is absurd. Do you mind calling me M. M. and letting me call you F. F.? It's in the spirit of the age.'

'I don't mind anything, so long as I get in.'

Mont caught a little crab, and answered: 'That was a nasty one!'

'Please row.'

'I am.' And he did for several strokes, looking at her with rueful eagerness. 'Of course, you know,' he ejaculated, pausing, 'that I came to see you, not your father's pictures.'

Fleur rose.

'If you don't row, I shall get out and swim.'

'Really and truly? Then I could come in after you.'

'Mr Mont, I'm late and tired; please put me on shore at once.'

When she stepped out on to the garden landing-stage he rose, and grasping his hair with both hands, looked at her.

Fleur smiled.

'Don't!' cried the irrepressible Mont. 'I know you're going to say: "Out, damnèd hair!"'

Fleur whisked round, threw him a wave of her hand. 'Good-bye, Mr M.M.!' she called, and was gone among the rose-trees. She looked at her wrist-watch and the windows of the house. It struck her as curiously uninhabited. Past six! The pigeons were just gathering to roost, and sunlight slanted on the dovecot, on their snowy feathers, and beyond in a shower on the top boughs of the woods. The click of billiard-balls came from the ingle-nook – Jack Cardigan, no doubt; a faint rustling, too, from a eucalyptus-tree, startling Southerner in this old English garden. She reached the verandah and was passing in, but stopped at the sound of voices from the drawing-room to her left. Mother! Monsieur Profond! From behind the verandah screen which fenced the ingle-nook she heard these words:

'I don't, Annette.'

Did Father know that he called her mother 'Annette'? Always on the side of her Father – as children are ever on one side or the other in houses where relations are a little strained – she stood, uncertain. Her mother was speaking in her low, pleasing, slightly metallic voice – one word she caught: '*Demain.*' And Profond's answer: 'All right.' Fleur frowned. A little sound came out into the stillness. Then Profond's voice: 'I'm takin' a small stroll.'

Fleur darted through the window into the morning-room. There he came from the drawing-room, crossing the verandah, down the lawn; and the click of billiard-balls which, in listening for other sounds, she had ceased to hear, began again. She shook herself, passed into the hall, and opened the drawing-room door. Her mother was sitting on the sofa between the windows, her knees crossed, her head resting on a cushion, her lips half parted, her eyes half closed. She looked extraordinarily handsome.

'Ah! Here you are, Fleur! Your father is beginning to fuss.'

'Where is he?'

'In the picture-gallery. Go up!'

'What are you going to do to-morrow, Mother?'

'To-morrow? I go up to London with your aunt.'

'I thought you might be. Will you get me a quite plain parasol?'

'What colour?'

'Green. They're all going back, I suppose.'

'Yes, all; you will console your father. Kiss me, then.'

Fleur crossed the room, stooped, received a kiss on her

forehead, and went out past the impress of a form on the sofa-cushions in the other corner. She ran upstairs.

Fleur was by no means the old-fashioned daughter who demands the regulation of her parents' lives in accordance with the standard imposed upon herself. She claimed to regulate her own life, not those of others; besides, an unerring instinct for what was likely to advantage her own case was already at work. In a disturbed domestic atmosphere the heart she had set on Jon would have a better chance. None the less was she offended, as a flower by a crisping wind. If that man had really been kissing her mother it was – serious, and her father ought to know. '*Demain*!' 'All right!' And her mother going up to Town! She turned into her bedroom and hung out of the window to cool her face, which had suddenly grown very hot. Jon must be at the station by now! What did her father know about Jon? Probably everything – pretty nearly!

She changed her dress, so as to look as if she had been in some time, and ran up to the gallery.

Soames was standing stubbornly still before his Alfred Stevens – the picture he loved best. He did not turn at the sound of the door, but she knew he had heard, and she knew he was hurt. She came up softly behind him, put her arms round his neck, and poked her face over his shoulder till her cheek lay against his. It was an advance which had never yet failed, but it failed her now, and she augured the worst.

'Well,' he said stonily, 'so you've come!'

'Is that all,' murmured Fleur, 'from a bad parent?' And she rubbed her cheek against his.

Soames shook his head so far as that was possible.

'Why do you keep me on tenterhooks like this, putting me off and off?'

'Darling, it was very harmless.'

'Harmless! Much you know what's harmless and what isn't.'

Fleur dropped her arms.

'Well, then, dear, suppose you tell me; and be quite frank about it.'

And she went over to the window-seat.

Her father had turned from his picture, and was staring at his feet. He looked very grey. 'He has nice small feet,' she thought, catching his eye, at once averted from her.

'You're my only comfort,' said Soames suddenly, 'and you go on like this.'

Fleur's heart began to beat.

'Like what, dear?'

Again Soames gave her a look which, but for the affection in it, might have been called furtive.

'You know what I told you,' he said. 'I don't choose to have anything to do with that branch of our family.'

'Yes, ducky, but I don't know why *I* shouldn't.'

Soames turned on his heel.

'I'm not going into the reasons,' he said; 'you ought to trust me, Fleur!'

The way he spoke those words affected Fleur, but she thought of Jon, and was silent, tapping her foot against the wainscot. Unconsciously she had assumed a modern attitude, with one leg twisted in and out of the other, with her chin on one bent wrist, her other arm across her chest, and its hand hugging her elbow; there was not a line of her that was not involuted, and yet – in spite of all – she retained a certain grace.

'You knew my wishes,' Soames went on, 'and yet you stayed on there four days. And I suppose that boy came with you to-day.'

Fleur kept her eyes on him.

'I don't ask you anything,' said Soames; 'I make no inquisition where you're concerned.'

Fleur suddenly stood up, leaning out at the window with her chin on her hands. The sun had sunk behind trees, the pigeons were perched, quite still, on the edge of the dovecot;

the click of the billiard-balls mounted, and a faint radiance shone out below where Jack Cardigan had turned the light up.

'Will it make you any happier,' she said suddenly, 'if I promise you not to see him for say – the next six weeks?' She was not prepared for a sort of tremble in the blankness of his voice.

'Six weeks? Six years – sixty years more like. Don't delude yourself, Fleur; don't delude yourself!'

Fleur turned in alarm.

'Father, what is it?'

Soames came close enough to see her face.

'Don't tell me,' he said, 'that you're foolish enough to have any feeling beyond caprice. That would be too much!' And he laughed.

Fleur, who had never heard him laugh like that, thought: 'Then it *is* deep! Oh! what is it?' And putting her hand through his arm she said lightly:

'No, of course; caprice. Only, I like my caprices and I don't like yours, dear.'

'Mine!' said Soames bitterly, and turned away.

The light outside had chilled, and threw a chalky whiteness on the river. The trees had lost all gaiety of colour. She felt a sudden hunger for Jon's face, for his hands, and the feel of his lips again on hers. And pressing her arms tight across her breast she forced out a little light laugh.

'*O la! la!* What a small fuss! as Profond would say. Father, I don't like that man.'

She saw him stop, and take something out of his breast pocket.

'You don't?' he said. 'Why?'

'Nothing,' murmured Fleur; 'just caprice!'

'No,' said Soames; 'not caprice!' And he tore what was in his hands across. 'You're right. *I* don't like him either!'

'Look!' said Fleur softly. 'There he goes! I hate his shoes; they don't make any noise.'

Down in the failing light Prosper Profond moved, his hands in his side pockets, whistling softly in his beard; he stopped, and glanced up at the sky, as if saying: 'I don't think much of that small moon.'

Fleur drew back. 'Isn't he a great cat?' she whispered; and the sharp click of the billiard-balls rose, as if Jack Cardigan had capped the cat, the moon, caprice, and tragedy with: 'In off the red!'

Monsieur Profond had resumed his stroll, to a teasing little tune in his beard. What was it? Oh! yes, from *Rigoletto*: *Donna é mobile*. Just what he *would* think! She squeezed her father's arm.

'Prowling!' she muttered, as he turned the corner of the house. It was past that disillusioned moment which divides the day and night – still and lingering and warm, with hawthorn scent and lilac scent clinging on the riverside air. A blackbird suddenly burst out. Jon would be in London by now; in the Park perhaps, crossing the Serpentine, thinking of her! A little sound beside her made her turn her eyes; her father was again tearing the paper in his hands. Fleur saw it was a cheque.

'I shan't sell him my Gauguin,' he said. 'I don't know what your aunt and Imogen see in him.'

'Or Mother.'

'Your mother!' said Soames.

'Poor Father!' she thought. 'He never looks happy – not really happy. I don't want to make him worse, but of course I shall have to, when Jon comes back. Oh! well, sufficient unto the night!'

'I'm going to dress,' she said.

In her room she had a fancy to put on her 'freak' dress. It was of gold tissue with little trousers of the same, tightly drawn in at the ankles, a page's cape slung from the shoulders, little gold shoes, and a gold-winged Mercury helmet; and all over her were tiny gold bells, especially on the helmet; so that if she shook her head she pealed. When she was dressed she felt quite sick because Jon could not see her; it even seemed a pity that the sprightly young man Michael Mont would not have a view. But the gong had sounded, and she went down.

She made a sensation in the drawing-room. Winifred thought it 'Most amusing'. Imogen was enraptured. Jack Cardigan called it 'stunning', 'ripping', 'topping', and 'corking'. Monsieur Profond, smiling with his eyes, said: 'That's a nice small dress!' Her mother, very handsome in black, sat looking at her, and said nothing. It remained for her father to apply the test of common sense. 'What did you put on that thing for? You're not going to dance.'

Fleur spun round, and the bells pealed.

'Caprice!'

Soames stared at her, and, turning away, gave his arm to Winifred. Jack Cardigan took her mother. Prosper Profond took Imogen. Fleur went in by herself, with her bells jingling . . .

The 'small' moon had soon dropped down, and May night had fallen soft and warm, enwrapping with its grape-bloom colour and its scents the billion caprices, intrigues, passions, longings, and regrets of men and women. Happy was Jack Cardigan who snored into Imogen's white shoulder, fit as a flea; or Timothy in his 'mausoleum', too old for anything but baby's slumber. For so many lay awake, or dreamed, teased by the criss-cross of the world.

The dew fell and the flowers closed; cattle grazed on in the river meadows, feeling with their tongues for the grass they could not see; and the sheep on the Downs lay quiet as stones. Pheasants in the tall trees of the Pangbourne woods, larks on their grassy nests above the gravel-pit at Wansdon, swallows in the eaves at Robin Hill, and the sparrows of Mayfair, all made a dreamless night of it, soothed by the lack of wind. The Mayfly filly, hardly accustomed to her new quarters, scraped at her straw a little; and the few night-flitting things – bats, moths, owls – were vigorous in the warm darkness; but the peace of night lay in the brain of all day-time Nature, colourless and still. Men and women, alone, riding the hobby-horses of anxiety or love, burned their wavering tapers of dream and thought into the lonely hours.

Fleur, leaning out of her window, heard the hall clock's muffled chime of twelve, the tiny splash of a fish, the sudden shaking of an aspen's leaves in the puffs of breeze that rose along the river, the distant rumble of a night train, and time and again the sounds which none can put a name to in the darkness, soft obscure expressions of uncatalogued emotions from man and beast, bird and machine, or, maybe, from departed Forsytes, Darties, Cardigans, taking night strolls back into a world which had once suited their embodied spirits. But Fleur heeded not these sounds; her spirit, far from disembodied, fled with swift wing from railway-carriage to flowery hedge, straining after Jon, tenacious of his forbidden image, and the sound of his voice, which was taboo. And she crinkled her nose, retrieving from the perfume of the riverside night that moment when his hand slipped between the mayflowers and her cheek. Long she leaned out in her freak dress, keen to burn her wings at life's candle; while the moths brushed her cheeks on their pilgrimage to the lamp on her dressing-table, ignorant that in a Forsyte's house there is no open flame. But at last even she felt sleepy, and, forgetting her bells, drew quickly in.

Through the open window of his room, alongside Annette's, Soames, wakeful too, heard their thin faint tinkle, as it might be shaken from stars, or the dewdrops falling from a flower, if one could hear such sounds.

'Caprice!' he thought. 'I can't tell. She's wilful. What shall I do? Fleur!'

And long into the 'small' night he brooded.

Part II

Chapter One
Mother and Son

To say that Jon Forsyte accompanied his mother to Spain unwillingly would scarcely have been adequate. He went as a well-natured dog goes for a walk with its mistress, leaving a choice mutton-bone on the lawn. He went looking back at it. Forsytes deprived of their mutton-bones are wont to sulk. But Jon had little sulkiness in his composition. He adored his mother, and it was his first travel. Spain had become Italy by his simply saying: 'I'd rather go to Spain, Mum; you've been to Italy so many times; I'd like it new to both of us.'

The fellow was subtle besides being naive. He never forgot that he was going to shorten the proposed two months into six weeks, and must therefore show no sign of wishing to do so. For one with so enticing a mutton-bone and so fixed an idea, he made a good enough travelling companion, indifferent to where or when he arrived, superior to food, and thoroughly appreciative of a country strange to the most travelled Englishman. Fleur's wisdom in refusing to write to him was profound, for he reached each new place entirely without hope or fever, and could concentrate immediate attention on the donkeys and tumbling bells, the priests, patios, beggars, children, crowing cocks, sombreros, cactus-hedges, old high white villages, goats, olive-trees, greening plains, singing birds in tiny cages, watersellers, sunsets, melons, mules, great churches, pictures, and swimming grey-brown mountains of a fascinating land.

It was already hot, and they enjoyed an absence of their compatriots. Jon, who, so far as he knew, had no blood in him which was not English, was often innately unhappy in the presence of his own countrymen. He felt they had no nonsense about them, and took a more practical view of things than himself. He confided to his mother that he must be an unsociable beast – it was jolly to be away from everybody who could talk about the things people did talk about. To which Irene had replied simply:

'Yes, Jon, I know.'

In this isolation he had unparalleled opportunities of appreciating what few sons can apprehend, the whole-heartedness of a mother's love. Knowledge of something kept from her made him, no doubt, unduly sensitive; and a Southern people stimulated his admiration for her type of beauty, which he had been accustomed to hear called Spanish, but which he now perceived to be no such thing. Her beauty was neither English, French, Spanish, nor Italian – it was special! He appreciated, too, as never before, his mother's subtlety of instinct. He could not tell, for instance, whether she had noticed his absorption in that Goya picture, *La Vendimia*, or whether she knew that he had slipped back there after lunch and again next morning, to stand before it full half an hour, a second and third time. It was not Fleur, of course, but like enough to give him heartache – so dear to lovers – remembering her standing at the foot of his bed with her hand held above her head. To keep a postcard reproduction of this picture in his pocket and slip it out to look at became for Jon one of those bad habits which soon or late disclose themselves to eyes sharpened by love, fear, or jealousy. And his mother's were sharpened by all three. In Granada he was fairly caught, sitting on a sun-warmed stone bench in a little battlemented garden on the Alhambra hill, whence he ought to have been looking at the view. His mother, he had thought, was examining the potted stocks between the polled acacias, when her voice said:

'Is that your favourite Goya, Jon?'

He checked, too late, a movement such as he might have made at school to conceal some surreptitious document, and answered: 'Yes.'

'It certainly is most charming; but I think I prefer the *Quitasol*. Your father would go crazy about Goya; I don't believe he saw them when he was in Spain in '92.'

In '92 – nine years before he had been born! What had been the previous existences of his father and his mother? If they had a right to share in his future, surely he had a right to share in their pasts. He looked up at her. But something in her face – a look of life hard-lived, the mysterious impress of emotions, experience, and suffering – seemed, with its incalculable depth, its purchased sanctity, to make curiosity impertinent. His mother must have had a wonderfully interesting life; she was so beautiful, and so – so – but he could not frame what he felt about her. He got up, and stood gazing down at the town, at the plain all green with crops, and the ring of mountains glamorous in sinking sunlight. Her life was like the past of this old Moorish city, full, deep, remote – his own life as yet such a baby of a thing, hopelessly ignorant and innocent! They said that in those mountains to the West, which rose sheer from the blue-green plain, as if out of a sea, Phoenicians had dwelt – a dark, strange, secret race, above the land! His mother's life was as unknown to him, as secret, as that Phoenician past was to the town down there, whose cocks crowed and whose children played and clamoured so gaily, day in, day out. He felt aggrieved that she should know all about him and he nothing about her except that she loved him and his father, and was beautiful. His callow ignorance – he had not even had the advantage of the War, like nearly everybody else! – made him small in his own eyes.

That night, from the balcony of his bedroom, he gazed down on the roof of the town – as if inlaid with honeycomb of jet, ivory, and gold; and, long after, he lay awake, listening

to the cry of the sentry as the hours struck, and forming in
his head these lines:

Voice in the night crying, down in the old sleeping
Spanish city darkened under her white stars!

What says the voice – its clear – lingering anguish?
Just the watchman, telling his dateless tale of safety?
Just a road-man, flinging to the moon his song?

No! Tis one deprived, whose lover's heart is weeping,
Just his cry: 'How long?'

The word 'deprived' seemed to him cold and unsatisfactory,
but 'bereaved' was too final, and no other word of two sylla-
bles short-long came to him, which would enable him to keep
'whose lover's heart is weeping'. It was past two by the time
he had finished it, and past three before he went to sleep,
having said it over to himself at least twenty-four times. Next
day he wrote it out and enclosed it in one of those letters to
Fleur which he always finished before he went down, so as to
have his mind free and companionable.

About noon that same day, on the tiled terrace of their
hotel, he felt a sudden dull pain in the back of his head, a
queer sensation in the eyes, and sickness. The sun had touched
him too affectionately. The next three days were passed in
semi-darkness, and a dulled, aching indifference to all except
the feel of ice on his forehead and his mother's smile. She
never moved from his room, never relaxed her noiseless vigi-
lance, which seemed to Jon angelic. But there were moments
when he was extremely sorry for himself, and wished terribly
that Fleur could see him. Several times he took a poignant
imaginary leave of her and of the earth, tears oozing out of
his eyes. He even prepared the message he would send to her
by his mother – who would regret to her dying day that she

had ever sought to separate them – his poor mother! He was not slow, however, in perceiving that he had now his excuse for going home.

Toward half-past six each evening came a '*gasgacha*' of bells – a cascade of tumbling chimes, mounting from the city below and falling back chime on chime. After listening to them on the fourth day he said suddenly:

'I'd like to be back in England, Mum, the sun's too hot.'

'Very well, darling. As soon as you're fit to travel.' And at once he felt better, and – meaner.

They had been out five weeks when they turned toward home. Jon's head was restored to its pristine clarity, but he was confined to a hat lined by his mother with many layers of orange and green silk and he still walked from choice in the shade. As the long struggle of discretion between them drew to its close, he wondered more and more whether she could see his eagerness to get back to that which she had brought him away from. Condemned by Spanish Providence to spend a day in Madrid between their trains, it was but natural to go again to the Prado. Jon was elaborately casual this time before his Goya girl. Now that he was going back to her, he could afford a lesser scrutiny. It was his mother who lingered before the picture, saying:

'The face and the figure of the girl are exquisite.'

Jon heard her uneasily. Did she understand? But he felt once more that he was no match for her in self-control and subtlety. She could, in some supersensitive way, of which he had not the secret, feel the pulse of his thoughts; she knew by instinct what he hoped and feared and wished. It made him terribly uncomfortable and guilty, having, beyond most boys, a conscience. He wished she would be frank with him, he almost hoped for an open struggle. But none came, and steadily, silently, they travelled north. Thus did he first learn how much better than men women play a waiting game. In Paris they had again to pause for a day. Jon was grieved because it lasted two, owing to certain matters in connection with a dressmaker; as if his mother, who looked beautiful in anything, had any need of dresses! The happiest moment of his travel was that when he stepped on to the Folkestone boat.

Standing by the bulwark rail, with her arm in his, she said:

'I'm afraid you haven't enjoyed it much, Jon. But you've been very sweet to me.'

Jon squeezed her arm.

'Oh! yes, I've enjoyed it awfully – except for my head lately.'

And now that the end had come, he really had, feeling a sort of glamour over the past weeks – a kind of painful pleasure, such as he had tried to screw into those lines about the voice in the night crying; a feeling such as he had known as a small boy listening avidly to Chopin, yet wanting to cry. And he wondered why it was that he couldn't say to her quite simply what she had said to him:

'You were very sweet to me.' Odd – one never could be nice and natural like that! He substituted the words: 'I expect we shall be sick.'

They were, and reached London somewhat attenuated, having been away six weeks and two days, without a single allusion to the subject which had hardly ever ceased to occupy their minds.

Chapter Two

Fathers and Daughters

Deprived of his wife and son by the Spanish adventure, Jolyon found the solitude at Robin Hill intolerable. A philosopher when he has all that he wants is different from a philosopher when he has not. Accustomed, however, to the idea, if not to the reality of resignation, he would perhaps have faced it out but for his daughter June. He was a 'lame duck' now, and on her conscience. Having achieved – momentarily – the rescue of an etcher in low circumstances, which she happened to have in hand, she appeared at Robin Hill a fortnight after Irene and Jon had gone. June was living now in a tiny house with a big studio at Chiswick. A Forsyte of the best period, so far as the lack of responsibility was concerned, she had overcome the difficulty of a reduced income in a manner satisfactory to herself and her father. The rent of the Gallery off Cork Street which he had bought for her and her increased income tax happening to balance, it had been quite simple – she no longer paid him the rent. The Gallery might be expected now at any time, after eighteen years of barren usufruct, to pay its way, so that she was sure her father would not feel it. Through this device she still had twelve hundred a year, and by reducing what she ate, and, in place of two Belgians in a poor way, employing one Austrian in a poorer, practically the same surplus for the relief of genius. After three days at Robin Hill she carried her father back with

her to Town. In those three days she had stumbled on the
secret he had kept for two years, and had instantly decided
to cure him. She knew, in fact, the very man. He had done
wonders with Paul Post – that painter a little in advance of
Futurism; and she was impatient with her father because his
eyebrows would go up, and because he had heard of neither.
Of course, if he hadn't 'faith' he would never get well! It was
absurd not to have faith in the man who had healed Paul Post
so that he had only just relapsed, from having overworked,
or overlived, himself again. The great thing about this healer
was that he relied on Nature. He had made a special study of
the symptoms of Nature – when his patient failed in any natural
symptom he supplied the poison which caused it – and there
you were! She was extremely hopeful. Her father had clearly
not been living a natural life at Robin Hill, and she intended
to provide the symptoms. He was – she felt – out of touch
with the times, which was not natural; his heart wanted stimulating. In the little Chiswick house she and the Austrian – a
grateful soul, so devoted to June for rescuing her that she was
in danger of decease from overwork – stimulated Jolyon in all
sorts of ways, preparing him for his cure. But they could not
keep his eyebrows down; as, for example, when the Austrian
woke him at eight o'clock just as he was going to sleep, or
June took *The Times* away from him, because it was unnatural to read 'that stuff' when he ought to be taking an interest
in 'life'. He never failed, indeed, to be astonished at her
resource, especially in the evenings. For his benefit, as she
declared, though he suspected that she also got something out
of it, she assembled the Age so far as it was satellite to genius;
and with some solemnity it would move up and down the
studio before him in the foxtrot, and that more mental form
of dancing – the one-step – which so pulled against the music,
that Jolyon's eyebrows would be almost lost in his hair from
wonder at the strain it must impose on the dancers' will-power.
Aware that, hung on the line in the Water Colour Society, he

was a back number to those with any pretension to be called artists, he would sit in the darkest corner he could find, and wonder about rhythm, on which so long ago he had been raised. And when June brought some girl or young man up to him, he would rise humbly to their level so far as that was possible, and think: 'Dear me! This is very dull for them!' Having his father's perennial sympathy with Youth, he used to get very tired from entering into their points of view. But it was all stimulating, and he never failed in admiration of his daughter's indomitable spirit. Even genius itself attended these gatherings now and then, with its nose on one side; and June always introduced it to her father. This, she felt, was exceptionally good for him, for genius was a natural symptom he had never had – fond as she was of him.

Certain as a man can be that she was his own daughter, he often wondered whence she got herself – her red-gold hair, now greyed into a special colour; her direct, spirited face, so different from his own rather folded and subtilised countenance, her little lithe figure, when he and most of the Forsytes were tall. And he would dwell on the origin of species, and debate whether she might be Danish or Celtic. Celtic, he thought, from her pugnacity, and her taste in fillets and djibbahs. It was not too much to say that he preferred her to the Age with which she was surrounded, youthful though, for the greater part, it was. She took, however, too much interest in his teeth, for he still had some of those natural symptoms. Her dentist at once found 'Staphylococcus aureus present in pure culture' (which might cause boils, of course), and wanted to take out all the teeth he had and supply him with two complete sets of unnatural symptoms. Jolyon's native tenacity was roused, and in the studio that evening he developed his objections. He had never had any boils, and his own teeth would last his time. Of course – June admitted – they would last his time if he didn't have them out! But if he had more teeth he would have a better heart and his time would be longer. His recalcitrance – she said – was a symptom of his whole attitude; he was taking it lying down. He ought to be fighting. When was he going to see the man who had cured Paul Post? Jolyon was very sorry, but the fact was he was not going to see him. June chafed. Pondridge – she said – the healer, was such a fine man, and he had such difficulty in making two ends meet, and getting his theories recognised. It was just such indifference and prejudice as her father manifested which was keeping him back. It would be so splendid for both of them!

'I perceive,' said Jolyon, 'that you are trying to kill two birds with one stone.'

'To cure, you mean!' cried June.

'My dear, it's the same thing.'

June protested. It was unfair to say that without a trial.

Jolyon thought he might not have the chance, of saying it after.

'Dad!' cried June, 'you're hopeless.'

'That,' said Jolyon, 'is a fact, but I wish to remain hopeless as long as possible. I shall let sleeping dogs lie, my child. They are quiet at present.'

'That's not giving science a chance,' cried June. 'You've no idea how devoted Pondridge is. He puts his science before everything.'

'Just,' replied Jolyon, puffing the mild cigarette to which he was reduced, 'as Mr Paul Post puts his art, eh? Art for Art's sake – Science for the sake of Science. I know those enthusiastic egomaniac gentry. They vivisect you without blinking. I'm enough of a Forsyte to give them the go-by, June.'

'Dad,' said June, 'if you only knew how old-fashioned that sounds! Nobody can afford to be half-hearted nowadays.'

'I'm afraid,' murmured Jolyon, with his smile, 'that's the only natural symptom with which Mr Pondridge need not supply me. We are born to be extreme or to be moderate, my dear; though, if you'll forgive my saying so, half the people nowadays who believe they're extreme are really very moderate. I'm getting on as well as I can expect, and I must leave it at that.'

June was silent, having experienced in her time the inexorable character of her father's amiable obstinacy so far as his own freedom of action was concerned.

How he came to let her know why Irene had taken Jon to Spain puzzled Jolyon, for he had little confidence in her discretion. After she had brooded on the news, it brought a rather sharp discussion, during which he perceived to the full the fundamental opposition between her active temperament and his wife's passivity. He even gathered that a little soreness still remained from that generation-old struggle between them over the body of Philip Bosinney, in which the passive had so signally triumphed over the active principle.

According to June, it was foolish and even cowardly to hide the past from Jon. Sheer opportunism, she called it.

'Which,' Jolyon put in mildly, 'is the working principle of real life, my dear.'

'Oh!' cried June, '*you* don't really defend her for not telling Jon, Dad. If it were left to you, you would.'

'I might, but simply because I know he must find out, which will be worse than if we told him.'

'Then why *don't* you tell him? It's just sleeping dogs again.'

'My dear,' said Jolyon, 'I wouldn't for the world go against Irene's instinct. He's her boy.'

'Yours too,' cried June.

'What is a man's instinct compared with a mother's?'

'Well, I think it's very weak of you.'

'I dare say,' said Jolyon, 'I dare say.'

And that was all she got from him; but the matter rankled in her brain. She could not bear sleeping dogs. And there stirred in her a tortuous impulse to push the matter toward decision. Jon ought to be told, so that either his feeling might be nipped in the bud, or, flowering in spite of the past, come to fruition. And she determined to see Fleur, and judge for herself. When June determined on anything, delicacy became a somewhat minor consideration. After all, she was Soames's cousin, and they were both interested in pictures. She would go and tell him that he ought to buy a Paul Post, or perhaps a piece of sculpture by Boris Strumolowski, and of course she would say nothing to her father. She went on the following Sunday, looking so determined that she had some difficulty in getting a cab at Reading station. The river country was lovely in those days of her own month, and June ached at its loveliness. She who had passed through this life without knowing what union was had a love of natural beauty which was almost madness. And when she came to that choice spot where Soames had pitched his tent, she dismissed her cab, because, business over, she wanted to revel in the bright water and the woods. She appeared at his front door, therefore, as a mere pedestrian, and sent in her card. It was in June's character to know that when her nerves were fluttering she was doing something worth while. If one's nerves did not flutter, she was taking the line of least resistance, and knew that nobleness was not obliging her. She was conducted to a drawing-room, which, though not in her style, showed every mark of fastidious elegance. Thinking, 'Too much taste – too many knick-knacks,' she saw in an old lacquer-framed mirror the figure of a girl coming in from the verandah. Clothed in white, and holding some white roses in her hand, she had, reflected in that silvery-grey pool of glass, a vision-like appearance, as if a pretty ghost had come out of the green garden.

'How do you do?' said June, turning round. 'I'm a cousin of your father's.'

'Oh, yes; I saw you in that confectioner's.'

'With my young stepbrother. Is your father in?'

'He will be directly. He's only gone for a little walk.'

June slightly narrowed her blue eyes, and lifted her decided chin.

'Your name's Fleur, isn't it? I've heard of you from Holly. What do you think of Jon?'

The girl lifted the roses in her hand, looked at them, and answered calmly:

'He's quite a nice boy.'

'Not a bit like Holly or me, is he?'

'Not a bit.'

'She's cool,' thought June.

And suddenly the girl said: 'I wish you'd tell me why our families don't get on?'

Confronted with the question she had advised her father to answer, June was silent; whether because this girl was trying to get something out of her, or simply because what one would do theoretically is not always what one will do when it comes to the point.

'You know,' said the girl, 'the surest way to make people find out the worst is to keep them ignorant. My father's told me it was a quarrel about property. But I don't believe it; we've both got heaps. They wouldn't have been so *bourgeois* as all that.'

June flushed. The word applied to her grandfather and father offended her.

'My grandfather,' she said, 'was very generous, and my father is, too; neither of them was in the least *bourgeois*.'

'Well, what was it then?' repeated the girl. Conscious that this young Forsyte meant having what she wanted, June at once determined to prevent her, and to get something for herself instead.

'Why do you want to know?'

The girl smelled at her roses. 'I only want to know because they won't tell me.'

'Well, it was about property, but there's more than one kind.'

'That makes it worse. Now I really *must* know.'

June's small and resolute face quivered. She was wearing a

round cap, and her hair had fluffed out under it. She looked quite young at that moment, rejuvenated by encounter.

'You know,' she said, 'I saw you drop your handkerchief. Is there anything between you and Jon? Because, if so, you'd better drop that too.'

The girl grew paler, but she smiled.

'If there were, that isn't the way to make me.'

At the gallantry of that reply, June held out her hand.

'I like you; but I don't like your father; I never have. We may as well be frank.'

'Did you come down to tell him that?'

June laughed. 'No; I came down to see you.'

'How delightful of you.'

This girl could fence.

'I'm two and a half times your age,' said June, 'but I quite sympathise. It's horrid not to have one's own way.'

The girl smiled again. 'I really think you might tell me.'

How the child stuck to her point

'It's not my secret. But I'll see what I can do, because I think both you and Jon ought to be told. And now I'll say good-bye.'

'Won't you wait and see Father?'

June shook her head. 'How can I get over to the other side?'

'I'll row you across.'

'Look!' said June impulsively, 'next time you're in London, come and see me. This is where I live. I generally have young people in the evening. But I shouldn't tell your father that you're coming.'

The girl nodded.

Watching her scull the skiff across, June thought: 'She's awfully pretty and well made. I never thought Soames would have a daughter as pretty as this. She and Jon would make a lovely couple.

The instinct to couple, starved within herself, was always at work in June. She stood watching Fleur row back; the girl took her hand off a scull to wave farewell, and June walked languidly on between the meadows and the river, with an ache in her heart. Youth to youth, like the dragon-flies chasing each other, and love like the sun warming them through and through. Her youth! So long ago – when Phil and she – And since? Nothing – no one had been quite what she had wanted. And so she had missed it all. But what a coil was round those two young things, if they really were in love, as Holly would have it – as her father, and Irene, and Soames himself seemed to dread. What a coil, and what a barrier! And the itch for the future, the contempt, as it were, for what was overpast, which forms the active principle, moved in the heart of one who ever believed that what one wanted was more important than what other people did not want. From the bank, awhile, in the warm summer stillness, she watched the water-lily plants and willow leaves, the fishes rising; sniffed the scent of grass and meadow-sweet, wondering how she could force everybody to be happy. Jon and Fleur! Two little lame ducks – charming callow yellow little ducks! A great pity! Surely something could be done! One must not take such situations lying down. She walked on, and reached a station, hot and cross.

That evening, faithful to the impulse toward direct action, which made many people avoid her, she said to her father:

'Dad, I've been down to see young Fleur. I think she's very attractive. It's no good hiding our heads under our wings, is it?'

The startled Jolyon set down his barley-water, and began crumbling his bread.

'It's what you appear to be doing,' he said. 'Do you realise whose daughter she is?'

'Can't the dead past bury its dead?'

Jolyon rose.

'Certain things can never be buried.'

'I disagree,' said June. 'It's that which stands in the way of all happiness and progress. You don't understand the Age,

Dad. It's got no use for outgrown things. Why do you think it matters so terribly that Jon should know about his mother? Who pays any attention to that sort of thing now? The marriage laws are just as they were when Soames and Irene couldn't get a divorce, and you had to come in. We've moved, and they haven't. So nobody cares. Marriage without a decent chance of relief is only a sort of slave-owning; people oughtn't to own each other. Everybody sees that now. If Irene broke such laws, what does it matter?'

'It's not for me to disagree there,' said Jolyon; 'but that's all quite beside the mark. This is a matter of human feeling.'

'Of course it is,' cried June, 'the human feeling of those two young things.'

'My dear,' said Jolyon with gentle exasperation; 'you're talking nonsense.'

'I'm not. If they prove to be really fond of each other, why should they be made unhappy because of the past?'

'*You* haven't lived that past. I have – through the feelings of my wife; through my own nerves and my imagination, as only one who is devoted can.'

June, too, rose, and began to wander restlessly.

'If,' she said suddenly, 'she were the daughter of Philip Bosinney, I could understand you better. Irene loved him, she never loved Soames.'

Jolyon uttered a deep sound – the sort of noise an Italian peasant woman utters to her mule. His heart had begun beating furiously, but he paid no attention to it, quite carried away by his feelings.

'That shows how little you understand. Neither I nor Jon, if I know him, would mind a love-past. It's the brutality of a union without love. This girl is the daughter of the man who once owned Jon's mother as a negro-slave was owned. You can't lay that ghost; don't try to, June! It's asking us to see Jon joined to the flesh and blood of the man who possessed Jon's mother against her will. It's no good mincing words; I want it clear once for all. And now I mustn't talk any more, or I shall have to sit up with this all night.' And, putting his hand over his heart, Jolyon turned his back on his daughter and stood looking at the river Thames.

June, who by nature never saw a hornet's nest until she had put her head into it, was seriously alarmed. She came and slipped her arm through his. Not convinced that he was right, and she herself wrong, because that was not natural to her, she was yet profoundly impressed by the obvious fact that the subject was very bad for him. She rubbed her cheek against his shoulder, and said nothing.

After taking her elderly cousin across, Fleur did not land at once, but pulled in among the reeds, into the sunshine. The peaceful beauty of the afternoon seduced for a little one not much given to the vague and poetic. In the field beyond the bank where her skiff lay up, a machine drawn by a grey horse was turning an early field of hay. She watched the grass cascading over and behind the light wheels with fascination – it looked so cool and fresh. The click and swish blended with the rustle of the willows and the poplars, and the cooing of a wood-pigeon, in a true river song. Alongside, in the deep green water, weeds, like yellow snakes, were writhing and nosing with the current; pied cattle on the farther side stood in the shade lazily swishing their tails. It was an afternoon to dream. And she took out Jon's letters – not flowery effusions, but haunted in their recital of things seen and done by a longing very agreeable to her, and all ending 'Your devoted J.' Fleur was not sentimental, her desires were ever concrete and concentrated, but what poetry there was in the daughter of Soames and Annette had certainly in those weeks of waiting gathered round her memories of Jon. They all belonged to grass and blossom, flowers and running water. She enjoyed him in the scents absorbed by her crinkling nose. The stars could persuade her that she was standing beside him in the centre of the map of Spain; and of an early morning the dewy cobwebs, the hazy sparkle and promise of the day down in the garden, were Jon personified to her.

Two white swans came majestically by, while she was reading his letters, followed by their brood of six young swans in a line, with just so much water between each tail and head, a flotilla of grey destroyers. Fleur thrust her letters back, got out her sculls, and pulled up to the landing-stage. Crossing the lawn, she wondered whether she should tell her father of June's visit. If he learned of it from the butler, he might think it odd if she did not. It gave her, too, another chance to startle out of him the reason of the feud. She went, therefore, up the road to meet him.

Soames had gone to look at a patch of ground on which the Local Authorities were proposing to erect a Sanatorium for people with weak lungs. Faithful to his native individualism, he took no part in local affairs, content to pay the rates which were always going up. He could not, however, remain indifferent to this new and dangerous scheme. The site was not half a mile from his own house. He was quite of opinion that the country should stamp out tuberculosis; but this was not the place. It should be done farther away. He took, indeed, an attitude common to all true Forsytes, that disability of any sort in other people was not his affair, and the State should do its business without prejudicing in any way the natural advantages which he had acquired or inherited. Francie, the most free-spirited Forsyte of his generation (except perhaps that fellow Jolyon) had once asked him in her malicious way: 'Did you ever see the name Forsyte in a subscription list, Soames?' That was as it might be, but a Sanatorium would depreciate the neighbourhood, and he should certainly sign the petition which was being got up against it. Returning with this decision fresh within him, he saw Fleur coming.

She was showing him more affection of late, and the quiet time down here with her in this summer weather had been making him feel quite young; Annette was always running up to Town for one thing or another, so that he had Fleur to himself almost as much as he could wish. To be sure, young Mont had formed a habit of appearing on his motor-cycle almost every other day. Thank goodness, the young fellow had shaved off his half-toothbrushes, and no longer looked like a mountebank! With a girl friend of Fleur's who was staying in the house, and a neighbouring youth or so, they made two couples after dinner, in the hall, to the music of the electric pianola, which performed foxtrots unassisted, with a surprised shine on its expressive surface. Annette, even, now and then passed gracefully up and down in the arms of one or other of the young men. And Soames, coming to the drawing-room door, would lift his nose a little sideways, and watch them, waiting to catch a smile from Fleur; then move back to his chair by the drawing-room hearth, to peruse *The Times* or some other collector's price list. To his ever-anxious eyes Fleur showed no signs of remembering that caprice of hers.

When she reached him on the dusty road, he slipped his hand within her arm.

'Who, do you think, has been to see you, Dad? She couldn't wait! Guess!'

'I never guess,' said Soames uneasily. 'Who?'

'Your cousin, June Forsyte.'

Quite unconsciously Soames gripped her arm. 'What did she want?'

'I don't know. But it was rather breaking through the feud, wasn't it?'

'Feud? What feud?'

'The one that exists in your imagination, dear.'

Soames dropped her arm. Was she mocking, or trying to draw him on?

'I suppose she wanted me to buy a picture,' he said at last.

'I don't think so. Perhaps it was just family affection.'

'She's only a first cousin once removed,' muttered Soames.

'And the daughter of your enemy.'

'What d'you mean by that?'

'I beg your pardon, dear; I thought he was.'

'Enemy!' repeated Soames. 'It's ancient history. I don't know where you get your notions.'

'From June Forsyte.'

It had come to her as an inspiration that if he thought she knew, or were on the edge of knowledge, he would tell her.

Soames was startled, but she had underrated his caution and tenacity.

'If you know,' he said coldly, 'why do you plague me?'

Fleur saw that she had overreached herself.

'I don't want to plague you, darling. As you say, why want to know more? Why want to know anything of that "small" mystery – *Je m'en fiche*, as Profond says?'

'That chap!' said Soames profoundly.

That chap, indeed, played a considerable, if invisible, part this summer – for he had not turned up again. Ever since the Sunday when Fleur had drawn attention to him prowling on the lawn, Soames had thought of him a good deal, and always in connection with Annette, for no reason, except that she was looking handsomer than for some time past. His possessive instinct, subtle, less formal, more elastic since the War, kept all misgiving underground. As one looks on some American river, quiet and pleasant, knowing that an alligator perhaps is lying in the mud with his snout just raised and indistinguishable from a snag of wood – so Soames looked on the river of his own existence, subconscious of Monsieur Profond, refusing to see more than the suspicion of his snout. He had at this epoch in his life practically all he wanted, and was as nearly happy as his nature would permit. His senses were at rest; his affections found all the vent they needed in his daughter; his collection was well known, his money well invested; his health excellent, save for a touch of liver now and again; he had not yet begun to worry seriously about what would happen after death, inclining to think that nothing would happen. He resembled one of his own gilt-edged securities, and to knock the gilt off by seeing anything he could avoid seeing would be, he felt instinctively, perverse and retrogressive. Those two crumpled rose-leaves, Fleur's caprice and Monsieur Profond's snout, would level away if he lay on them industriously.

That evening Chance, which visits the lives of even the best-invested Forsytes, put a clue into Fleur's hands. Her father came down to dinner without a handkerchief, and had occasion to blow his nose.

'I'll get you one, dear,' she had said, and ran upstairs. In the sachet where she sought for it – an old sachet of very faded silk – there were two compartments: one held handkerchiefs; the other was buttoned, and contained something flat and hard. By some childish impulse Fleur unbuttoned it. There was a frame and in it a photograph of herself as a little girl. She gazed at it, fascinated, as one is by one's own presentment. It slipped under her fidgeting thumb, and she saw that another photograph was behind. She pressed her own down further, and perceived a face, which she seemed to know, of a young woman, very good-looking, in a very old style of evening dress. Slipping her own photograph up over it again, she took out a handkerchief and went down. Only on the stairs did she identify that face. Surely – surely Jon's mother! The conviction came as a shock. And she stood still in a flurry of thought. Why, of course! Jon's father had married the woman her father had wanted to marry, had cheated him out of her, perhaps. Then, afraid of showing by her manner that she had lighted on his secret, she refused to think further, and, shaking out the silk handkerchief, entered the dining-room.

'I chose the softest, Father.'

'H'm!' said Soames; 'I only use those after a cold. Never mind!'

That evening passed for Fleur in putting two and two together; recalling the look on her father's face in the confectioner's shop – a look strange and coldly intimate, a queer look. He must have loved that woman very much to have kept her photograph all this time, in spite of having lost her. Unsparing and matter-of-fact, her mind darted to his relations with her own mother. Had he ever really loved her? She thought not. Jon was the son of the woman he had really loved. Surely, then, he ought not to mind his daughter loving him; it only wanted getting used to. And a sigh of sheer relief was caught in the folds of her nightgown slipping over her head.

Chapter Three

Meetings

*Y*outh only recognises Age by fits and starts. Jon, for one, had never really seen his father's age till he came back from Spain. The face of the fourth Jolyon, worn by waiting, gave him quite a shock – it looked so wan and old. His father's mask had been forced awry by the emotion of the meeting, so that the boy suddenly realised how much he must have felt their absence. He summoned to his aid the thought: 'Well, I didn't want to go!' It was out of date for Youth to defer to Age. But Jon was by no means typically modern. His father had always been 'so jolly' to him, and to feel that one meant to begin again at once the conduct which his father had suffered six weeks' loneliness to cure was not agreeable.

At the question, 'Well, old man, how did the great Goya strike you?' his conscience pricked him badly. The great Goya only existed because he had created a face which resembled Fleur's.

On the night of their return, he went to bed full of compunction; but awoke full of anticipation. It was only the fifth of July, and no meeting was fixed with Fleur until the ninth. He was to have three days at home before going back to farm. Somehow he must contrive to see her!

In the lives of men an inexorable rhythm, caused by the need for trousers, not even the fondest parents can deny. On the second day, therefore, Jon went to Town, and having satisfied his conscience by ordering what was indispensable in Conduit Street, turned his face toward Piccadilly. Stratton Street, where her Club was, adjoined Devonshire House. It would be the merest chance that she should be at her Club. But he dawdled down Bond Street with a beating heart, noticing the superiority of all other young men to himself. They wore their clothes with such an air; they had assurance; they were *old*. He was suddenly overwhelmed by the conviction that Fleur must have forgotten him. Absorbed in his own feeling for her all these weeks, he had mislaid that possibility. The corners of his mouth drooped, his hands felt clammy. Fleur with the pick of youth at the beck of her smile – Fleur incomparable! It was an evil moment. Jon, however, had a great idea that one must be able to face anything. And he braced himself with that dour reflection in front of a bric-à-brac shop. At this high-water mark of what was once the London season, there was nothing to mark it out from any other except a grey top hat or two, and the sun. Jon moved on, and turning the corner into Piccadilly, ran into Val Dartie moving toward the Iseeum Club, to which he had just been elected.

'Hallo! young man! Where are you off to?'

Jon flushed. 'I've just been to my tailor's.'

Val looked him up and down. 'That's good! I'm going in here to order some cigarettes; then come and have some lunch.'

Jon thanked him. He might get news of *her* from Val!

The condition of England, that nightmare of its Press and Public men, was seen in different perspective within the tobacconist's which they now entered.

'Yes, sir; precisely the cigarette I used to supply your father with. Bless me! Mr Montague Dartie was a customer here from – let me see – the year Melton won the Derby. One of my very best customers he was.' A faint smile illumined the tobacconist's face. 'Many's the tip he's given me, to be sure! I suppose he took a couple of hundred of these every week, year in, year out, and never changed his cigarette. Very affable gentleman, brought me a lot of custom. I was sorry he met with that accident. One misses an old customer like him.'

Val smiled. His father's decease had closed an account which had been running longer, probably, than any other; and in a ring of smoke puffed out from that time-honoured cigarette he seemed to see again his father's face, dark, good-looking, moustachioed, a little puffy, in the only halo it had earned. His father had his fame here, anyway – a man who smoked two hundred cigarettes a week, who could give tips, and run accounts for ever! To his tobacconist a hero! Even that was some distinction to inherit!

'I pay cash,' he said; 'how much?'

'To his son, sir, and cash – ten and six. I shall never forget Mr Montague Dartie. I've known him stand talkin' to me half an hour. We don't get many like him now, with everybody in such a hurry. The War was bad for manners, sir – it was bad for manners. You were in it, I see.'

'No,' said Val, tapping his knee, 'I got this in the war before. Saved my life, I expect. Do you want any cigarettes, Jon?'

Rather ashamed, Jon murmured, 'I don't smoke, you know,' and saw the tobacconist's lips twisted, as if uncertain whether to say 'Good God!' or 'Now's your chance, sir!'

'That's right,' said Val; 'keep off it while you can. You'll want it when you take a knock. This is really the same tobacco, then?'

'Identical, sir; a little dearer, that's all. Wonderful staying power – the British Empire, I always say.'

'Send me down a hundred a week to this address, and invoice it monthly. Come on, Jon.'

Jon entered the Iseeum with curiosity. Except to lunch now and then at the Hotch-Potch with his father, he had never been in a London Club. The Iseeum, comfortable and unpretentious, did not move, could not, so long as George Forsyte sat on its Committee, where his culinary acumen was almost the controlling force. The Club had made a stand against the newly rich, and it had taken all George Forsyte's prestige, and praise of him as a 'good sportsman', to bring in Prosper Profond.

The two were lunching together when the half-brothers-in-law entered the dining-room, and attracted by George's fore-finger, sat down at their table, Val with his shrewd eyes and charming smile, Jon with solemn lips and an attractive shyness in his glance. There was an air of privilege around that corner table, as though past masters were eating there. Jon was fascinated by the hypnotic atmosphere. The waiter, lean in the chaps, pervaded with such free-masonical deference. He seemed to hang on George Forsyte's lips, to watch the gloat in his eye with a kind of sympathy, to follow the movements of the heavy club-marked silver fondly. His liveried arm and confidential voice alarmed Jon, they came so secretly over his shoulder.

Except for George's 'Your grandfather tipped me once; he was a deuced good judge of a cigar!' neither he nor the other past master took any notice of him, and he was grateful for this. The talk was all about the breeding, points, and prices of horses, and he listened to it vaguely at first, wondering how it was possible to retain so much knowledge in a head. He could not take his eyes off the dark past master – what he said was so deliberate and discouraging – such heavy, queer, smiled-out words. Jon was thinking of butterflies, when he heard him say:

'I want to see Mr Soames Forsyde take an interest in 'orses.'

'Old Soames! He's too dry a file!'

With all his might Jon tried not to grow red, while the dark past master went on.

'His daughter's an attractive small girl. Mr Soames Forsyde is a bit old-fashioned. I want to see him have a pleasure some day.' George Forsyte grinned.

'Don't you worry; he's not so miserable as he looks. He'll never show he's enjoying anything – they might try and take it from him. Old Soames! Once bit, twice shy!'

'Well, Jon,' said Val, hastily, 'if you've finished, we'll go and have coffee.'

'Who were those?' Jon asked, on the stairs. 'I didn't quite—'

'Old George Forsyte is a first cousin of your father's and of my Uncle Soames. He's always been here. The other chap, Profond, is a queer fish. I think he's hanging round Soames's wife, if you ask me!'

Jon looked at him, startled. 'But that's awful,' he said: 'I mean – for Fleur.'

'Don't suppose Fleur cares very much; she's very up-to-date.'

'Her mother!'

'You're very green, Jon.'

Jon grew red. 'Mothers,' he stammered angrily, 'are different.'

'You're right,' said Val suddenly; 'but things aren't what they were when I was your age. There's a "To-morrow we die" feeling. That's what old George meant about my Uncle Soames. He doesn't mean to die to-morrow.'

Jon said, quickly: 'What's the matter between him and my father?'

'Stable secret, Jon. Take my advice, and bottle up. You'll do no good by knowing. Have a liqueur?'

Jon shook his head.

'I hate the way people keep things from one,' he muttered, 'and then sneer at one for being green.'

'Well, you can ask Holly. If *she* won't tell you, you'll believe it's for your own good, I suppose.'

Jon got up. 'I must go now; thanks awfully for the lunch.'

Val smiled up at him half-sorry, and yet amused. The boy looked so upset.

'All right! See you on Friday.'

'I don't know,' murmured Jon.

And he did not. This conspiracy of silence made him

desperate. It was humiliating to be treated like a child! He retraced his moody steps to Stratton Street. But he would go to her Club now, and find out the worst! To his enquiry the reply was that Miss Forsyte was not in the Club. She might be in perhaps later. She was often in on Monday – they could not say. Jon said he would call again, and, crossing into the Green Park, flung himself down under a tree. The sun was bright, and a breeze fluttered the leaves of the young lime-tree beneath which he lay; but his heart ached. Such darkness seemed gathered round his happiness. He heard Big Ben chime 'Three' above the traffic. The sound moved something in him, and, taking out a piece of paper, he began to scribble on it with a pencil. He had jotted a stanza, and was searching the grass for another verse, when something hard touched his shoulder – a green parasol. There above him stood Fleur!

'They told me you'd been, and were coming back. So I thought you might be out here; and you are – it's rather wonderful!'

'Oh, Fleur! I thought you'd have forgotten me.'

'When I told you that I shouldn't!'

Jon seized her arm.

'It's too much luck! Let's get away from this side.' He almost dragged her on through that too thoughtfully regulated Park, to find some cover where they could sit and hold each other's hands.

'Hasn't anybody cut in?' he said, gazing round at her lashes, in suspense above her cheeks.

'There is a young idiot, but he doesn't count.'

Jon felt a twitch of compassion for the – young idiot.

'You know I've had sunstroke; I didn't tell you.'

'Really! Was it interesting?'

'No. Mother was an angel. Has anything happened to you?'

'Nothing. Except that I think I've found out what's wrong between our families, Jon.'

His heart began beating very fast.

'I believe my father wanted to marry your mother, and your father got her instead.'

'Oh!'

'I came on a photo of her; it was in a frame behind a photo of me. Of course, if he was very fond of her, that would have made him pretty mad, wouldn't it?'

Jon thought for a minute. 'Not if she loved my father best.'

'But suppose they were engaged?'

'If we were engaged, and you found you loved somebody better, I might go cracked, but I shouldn't grudge it you.'

'I should. You mustn't ever do that with me, Jon.'

'My God! Not much!'

'I don't believe that he's ever really cared for my mother.'

Jon was silent. Val's words – the two past masters in the Club!

'You see, we don't know,' went on Fleur; 'it may have been a great shock. She may have behaved badly to him. People do.'

'My mother wouldn't.'

Fleur shrugged her shoulders. 'I don't think we know much about our fathers and mothers. We just see them in the light of the way they treat *us*; but they've treated other people, you know, before we were born – plenty, I expect. You see, they're both old. Look at your father, with three separate families!'

'Isn't there any place,' cried Jon, 'in all this beastly London where we can be alone?'

'Only a taxi.'

'Let's get one, then.'

When they were installed, Fleur asked suddenly: 'Are you going back to Robin Hill? I should like to see where you live, Jon. I'm staying with my aunt for the night, but I could get back in time for dinner. I wouldn't come to the house, of course.'

Jon gazed at her enraptured.

'Splendid! I can show it you from the copse, we shan't meet anybody. There's a train at four.'

The god of property and his Forsytes great and small, leisured, official, commercial, or professional, like the working classes, still worked their seven hours a day, so that those two of the fourth generation travelled down to Robin Hill in an empty first-class carriage, dusty and sun-warmed, of that too early train. They travelled in blissful silence, holding each other's hands.

At the station they saw no one except porters, and a villager or two unknown to Jon, and walked out up the lane, which smelled of dust and honeysuckle.

For Jon – sure of her now, and without separation before him – it was a miraculous dawdle, more wonderful than those on the Downs, or along the river Thames. It was love-in-a-mist – one of those illumined pages of Life, where every word and smile, and every light touch they gave each other were as little gold and red and blue butterflies and flowers and birds scrolled in among the text – a happy communing, without afterthought, which lasted thirty-seven minutes. They reached the coppice at the milking hour. Jon would not take her as far as the farmyard; only to where she could see the field leading up to the gardens, and the house beyond. They turned in among the larches, and suddenly, at the winding of the path, came on Irene, sitting on an old log seat.

There are various kinds of shocks: to the vertebrae; to the nerves; to moral sensibility; and, more potent and permanent, to personal dignity. This last was the shock Jon received, coming thus on his mother. He became suddenly conscious that he was doing an indelicate thing. To have brought Fleur down openly – yes! But to sneak her in like this! Consumed with shame, he put on a front as brazen as his nature would permit.

Fleur was smiling, a little defiantly; his mother's startled face was changing quickly to the impersonal and gracious. It was she who uttered the first words:

'I'm very glad to see you. It was nice of Jon to think of bringing you down to us.'

'We weren't coming to the house,' Jon blurted out. 'I just wanted Fleur to see where I lived.'

His mother said quietly:

'Won't you come up and have tea?'

Feeling that he had but aggravated his breach of breeding, he heard Fleur answer:

'Thanks very much; I have to get back to dinner. I met Jon by accident, and we thought it would be rather jolly just to see his home.'

How self-possessed she was!

'Of course; but you *must* have tea. We'll send you down to the station. My husband will enjoy seeing you.'

The expression of his mother's eyes, resting on him for a moment, cast Jon down level with the ground – a true worm. Then she led on, and Fleur followed her. He felt like a child, trailing after those two, who were talking so easily about Spain and Wansdon, and the house up there beyond the trees and the grassy slope. He watched the fencing of their eyes, taking each other in – the two beings he loved most in the world.

He could see his father sitting under the oak tree; and suffered in advance all the loss of caste he must go through in the eyes of that tranquil figure, with his knees crossed, thin, old, and elegant; already he could feel the faint irony which would come into his voice and smile.

'This is Fleur Forsyte, Jolyon; Jon brought her down to see the house. Let's have tea at once – she has to catch a train. Jon, tell them, dear, and telephone to the Dragon for a car.'

To leave her alone with them was strange, and yet, as no doubt his mother had foreseen, the least of evils at the moment; so he ran up into the house. Now he would not see Fleur alone again – not for a minute, and they had arranged no further meeting! When he returned under cover of the maids and teapots, there was not a trace of awkwardness beneath the tree; it was all within himself, but not the less for that. They were talking of the Gallery off Cork Street.

'We back numbers,' his father was saying, 'are awfully anxious to find out why we can't appreciate the new stuff; you and Jon must tell us.'

'It's supposed to be satiric, isn't it?' said Fleur.

He saw his father's smile.

'Satiric? Oh! I think it's more than that. What do you say, Jon?'

'I don't know at all,' stammered Jon. His father's face had a sudden grimness.

'The young are tired of us, our gods and our ideals. Off with their heads, they say – smash their idols! And let's get back to – nothing! And, by Jove, they've done it! Jon's a poet. He'll be going in, too, and stamping on what's left of us. Property, beauty, sentiment – all smoke. We mustn't own anything nowadays, not even our feelings. They stand in the way of – nothing.'

Jon listened, bewildered, almost outraged by his father's words, behind which he felt a meaning that he could not reach. He didn't want to stamp on anything!

'Nothing's the god of to-day,' continued Jolyon; 'we're back where the Russians were sixty years ago, when they started Nihilism.'

'No, Dad,' cried Jon suddenly, 'we only want to *live*, and we don't know how, because of the Past – that's all!'

'By George!' said Jolyon, 'that's profound, Jon. Is it your own? The Past! Old ownerships, old passions, and their aftermath. Let's have cigarettes.'

Conscious that his mother had lifted her hand to her lips, quickly, as if to hush something, Jon handed the cigarettes. He lighted his father's and Fleur's, then one for himself. Had he taken the knock that Val had spoken of? The smoke was blue when he had not puffed, grey when he had; he liked the sensation in his nose, and the sense of equality it gave him.

He was glad no one said: 'So you've begun!' He felt less young.

Fleur looked at her watch, and rose. His mother went with her into the house. Jon stayed with his father, puffing at the cigarette.

'See her into the car, old man,' said Jolyon; 'and when she's gone, ask your mother to come back to me.'

Jon went. He waited in the hall. He saw her into the car. There was no chance for any word; hardly for a pressure of the hand. He waited all that evening for something to be said to him. Nothing was said. Nothing might have happened. He went up to bed, and in the mirror on his dressing-table met himself. He did not speak, nor did the image; but both looked as if they thought the more.

Chapter Four

In Green Street

$\mathcal{U}$ncertain whether the impression that Prosper Profond was dangerous should be traced to his attempt to give Val the Mayfly filly; to a remark of Fleur's: 'He's like the hosts of Midian – he prowls and prowls around'; to his preposterous inquiry of Jack Cardigan: 'What's the use of keepin' fit?' or, more simply, to the fact that he was a foreigner, or alien as it was now called. Certain, that Annette was looking particularly handsome, and that Soames had sold him a Gauguin and then torn up the cheque, so that Monsieur Profond himself had said: 'I didn't get that small picture I bought from Mr Forsyde.'

However suspiciously regarded, he still frequented Winifred's evergreen little house in Green Street, with a good-natured obtuseness which no one mistook for naivete, a word hardly applicable to Monsieur Prosper Profond. Winifred still found him 'amusing', and would write him little notes saying: 'Come and have a "jolly" with us' – it was breath of life to her to keep up with the phrases of the day.

The mystery, with which all felt him to be surrounded, was due to his having done, seen, heard, and known everything, and found nothing in it – which was unnatural. The English type of disillusionment was familiar enough to Winifred, who had always moved in fashionable circles. It gave a certain cachet or distinction, so that one got something out of it. But to see nothing in anything, not as a pose, but because there was nothing in anything, was not English; and that which was not English one could not help secretly feeling dangerous, if not precisely bad form. It was like having the mood which the War had left, seated – dark, heavy, smiling, indifferent – in your Empire chair; it was like listening to that mood talking through thick pink lips above a little diabolic beard. It was, as Jack Cardigan expressed it – for the English character at large – 'a bit too thick' – for if nothing was really worth getting excited about, there were always games, and one could make it so! Even Winifred, ever a Forsyte at heart, felt that there was nothing to be had out of such a mood of disillusionment, so that it really ought not to be there. Monsieur Profond, in fact, made the mood too plain in a country which decently veiled such realities.

When Fleur, after her hurried return from Robin Hill, came down to dinner that evening, the mood was standing at the window of Winifred's little drawing-room, looking out into Green Street, with an air of seeing nothing in it. And Fleur gazed promptly into the fireplace with an air of seeing a fire which was not there.

Monsieur Profond came from the window. He was in full fig, with a white waistcoat and a white flower in his button-hole.

'Well, Miss Forsyde,' he said, 'I'm awful pleased to see you. Mr Forsyde well? I was sayin' to-day I want to see him have some pleasure. He worries.'

'You think so?' said Fleur shortly.

'Worries,' repeated Monsieur Profond, burring the r's.

Fleur spun round. 'Shall I tell you,' she said, 'what would give him pleasure?' But the words, 'To hear that you had cleared out,' died at the expression on his face. All his fine white teeth were showing.

'I was hearin' at the Club to-day about his old trouble.'

Fleur opened her eyes. 'What do you mean?'

Monsieur Profond moved his sleek head as if to minimise his statement.

'Before you were born,' he said; 'that small business.'

Though conscious that he had cleverly diverted her from his own share in her father's worry, Fleur was unable to withstand a rush of nervous curiosity. 'Tell me what you heard.'

'Why!' murmured Monsieur Profond, 'you know all that.'

'I expect I do. But I should like to know that you haven't heard it all wrong.'

'His first wife,' murmured Monsieur Profond.

Choking back the words, 'He was never married before,' she said: 'Well, what about her?'

'Mr George Forsyde was tellin' me about your father's first wife marryin' his cousin Jolyon afterward. It was a small bit unpleasant, I should think. I saw their boy – nice boy!'

Fleur looked up. Monsieur Profond was swimming, heavily diabolical, before her. That – the reason! With the most heroic effort of her life so far, she managed to arrest that swimming figure. She could not tell whether he had noticed. And just then Winifred came in.

'Oh! here you both are already; Imogen and I have had the most amusing afternoon at the Babies' bazaar.'

'What babies?' said Fleur mechanically.

'The "Save the Babies". I got such a bargain, my dear. A piece of old Armenian work – from before the Flood. I want your opinion on it, Prosper.'

'Auntie,' whispered Fleur suddenly.

At the tone in the girl's voice Winifred closed in on her.

'What's the matter? Aren't you well?'

Monsieur Profond had withdrawn into the window, where he was practically out of hearing.

'Auntie, he – he told me that Father has been married before.

Is it true that he divorced her, and she married Jon Forsyte's father?'

Never in all the life of the mother of four little Darties had Winifred felt more seriously embarrassed. Her niece's face was so pale, her eyes so dark, her voice so whispery and strained.

'Your father didn't wish you to hear,' she said, with all the aplomb she could muster. 'These things will happen. I've often told him he ought to let you know.'

'Oh!' said Fleur, and that was all, but it made Winifred pat her shoulder – a firm little shoulder, nice and white! She never could help an appraising eye and touch in the matter of her niece, who would have to be married, of course – though not to that boy Jon.

'We've forgotten all about it years and years ago,' she said comfortably. 'Come and have dinner!'

'No, Auntie. I don't feel very well. May I go upstairs?'

'My dear!' murmured Winifred, concerned, 'you're not taking this to heart? Why, you haven't properly come out yet! That boy's a child!'

'What boy? I've only got a headache. But I can't stand that man to-night.'

'Well, well,' said Winifred, 'go and lie down. I'll send you some bromide, and I shall talk to Prosper Profond. What business had he to gossip? Though I must say I think it's much better you should know.'

Fleur smiled. 'Yes,' she said, and slipped from the room.

She went up with her head whirling, a dry sensation in her throat, a fluttered, frightened feeling in her breast. Never in her life as yet had she suffered from even momentary fear that she would not get what she had set her heart on. The sensations of the afternoon had been full and poignant, and this gruesome discovery coming on the top of them had really made her head ache. No wonder her father had hidden that photograph so secretly behind her own – ashamed of having kept it! But could he hate Jon's mother and yet keep her photograph? She pressed her hands over her forehead, trying to see things clearly. Had they told Jon – had her visit to Robin Hill forced them to tell him? Everything now turned on that! She knew, they all knew, except – perhaps – Jon!

She walked up and down, biting her lip and thinking desperately hard. Jon loved his mother. If they had told him, what would he do? She could not tell. But if they had not told him, should she not – could she not get him for herself – get married to him, before he knew? She searched her memories of Robin Hill. His mother's face so passive – with its dark eyes and as if powdered hair, its reserve, its smile – baffled her; and his father's – kindly, sunken, ironic. Instinctively she felt they would shrink from telling Jon, even now, shrink from hurting him – for of course it would hurt him awfully to know!

Her aunt must be made not to tell her father that she knew. So long as neither she herself nor Jon were supposed to know, there was still a chance – freedom to cover one's tracks, and get what her heart was set on. But she was almost overwhelmed by her isolation. Everyone's hand was against her – everyone's! It was as Jon had said – he and she just wanted to live and the past was in their way, a past they hadn't shared in, and didn't understand! Oh! What a shame! And suddenly she thought of June. Would she help them? For somehow June had left on her the impression that she would be sympathetic with their love, impatient of obstacle. Then, instinctively, she thought: 'I won't give anything away, though, even to her. I daren't. I mean to have Jon; against them all.'

Soup was brought up to her, and one of Winifred's pet headache cachets. She swallowed both. Then Winifred herself appeared. Fleur opened her campaign with the words:

'You know, Auntie, I do wish people wouldn't think I'm in love with that boy. Why, I've hardly seen him!'

Winifred, though experienced, was not 'fine'. She accepted

the remark with considerable relief. Of course, it was not pleasant for the girl to hear of the family scandal, and she set herself to minimise the matter, a task for which she was eminently qualified, 'raised' fashionably under a comfortable mother and a father whose nerves might not be shaken, and for many years the wife of Montague Dartie. Her description was a masterpiece of understatement. Fleur's father's first wife had been very foolish. There had been a young man who had got run over, and she had left Fleur's father. Then, years after, when it might all have come right again, she had taken up with their cousin Jolyon; and, of course, her father had been obliged to have a divorce. Nobody remembered anything of it now, except just the family. And, perhaps, it had all turned out for the best; her father had Fleur; and Jolyon and Irene had been quite happy, they said, and their boy was a nice boy. 'Val having Holly, too, is a sort of plaster, don't you know?' With these soothing words, Winifred patted her niece's shoulder; thought: 'She's a nice, plump little thing!' and went back to Prosper Profond, who, in spite of his indiscretion, was very 'amusing' this evening.

For some minutes after her aunt had gone Fleur remained under influence of bromide material and spiritual. But then reality came back. Her aunt had left out all that mattered – all the feeling, the hate, the love, the unforgivingness of passionate hearts. She, who knew so little of life, and had touched only the fringe of love, was yet aware by instinct that words have as little relation to fact and feeling as coin to the bread it buys. 'Poor Father!' she thought. 'Poor me! Poor Jon! But I don't care, I mean to have him!' From the window of her darkened room she saw 'that man' issue from the door below and 'prowl' away. If he and her mother – how would that affect her chance? Surely it must make her father cling to her more closely, so that he would consent in the end to anything she wanted, or become reconciled the sooner to what she did without his knowledge.

She took some earth from the flower-box in the window, and with all her might flung it after that disappearing figure. It fell short, but the action did her good.

And a little puff of air came up from Green Street, smelling of petrol, not sweet.

Chapter Five

Purely Forsyte Affairs

Soames, coming up to the City, with the intention of calling in at Green Street at the end of his day and taking Fleur back home with him, suffered from rumination. Sleeping partner that he was, he seldom visited the City now, but he still had a room of his own at Cuthcott, Kingson, and Forsyte's, and one special clerk and a half assigned to the management of purely Forsyte affairs. They were somewhat in flux just now – an auspicious moment for the disposal of house property. And Soames was unloading the estates of his father and Uncle Roger, and to some extent of his Uncle Nicholas. His shrewd and matter-of-course probity in all money concerns had made him something of an autocrat in connection with these trusts. If Soames thought this or thought that, one had better save oneself the bother of thinking too. He guaranteed, as it were, irresponsibility to numerous Forsytes of the third and fourth generations. His fellow trustees, such as his cousins Roger or Nicholas, his cousins-in-law Tweetyman and Spender, or his sister Cicely's husband, all trusted him; he signed first, and where he signed first they signed after, and nobody was a penny the worse. Just now they were all a good many pennies the better, and Soames was beginning to see the close of certain trusts, except for distribution of the income from securities as gilt-edged as was compatible with the period.

Passing the more feverish parts of the City toward the most perfect backwater in London, he ruminated. Money was extraordinarily tight; and morality extraordinarily loose! The War had done it. Banks were not lending; people breaking contracts all over the place. There was a feeling in the air and a look on faces that he did not like. The country seemed in for a spell of gambling and bankruptcies. There was satisfaction in the thought that neither he nor his trusts had an investment which could be affected by anything less maniacal than national repudiation or a levy on capital. If Soames had faith, it was in what he called 'English common sense' – or the power to have things, if not one way then another. He might – like his father James before him – say he didn't know what things were coming to, but he never in his heart believed they were. If it rested with him, they wouldn't – and, after all, he was only an Englishman like any other, so quietly tenacious of what he had that he knew he would never really part with it without something more or less equivalent in exchange. His mind was essentially equilibristic in material matters, and his way of putting the national situation difficult to refute in a world composed of human beings. Take his own case, for example! He was well off. Did that do anybody harm? He did not eat ten meals a day; he ate no more than, perhaps not so much as, a poor man. He spent no money on vice; breathed no more air, used no more water to speak of than the mechanic or the porter. He certainly had pretty things about him, but they had given employment in the making, and somebody must use them. He bought pictures, but Art must be encouraged. He was, in fact, an accidental channel through which money flowed, employing labour. What was there objectionable in that? In his charge money was in quicker and more useful flux than it would be in charge of the State and a lot of slow-fly money-sucking officials. And as to what he saved each year – it was just as much in flux as what he didn't save, going into Water Board or Council Stocks, or something sound and useful.

The State paid him no salary for being trustee of his own or other people's money – *he did all that for nothing*. Therein lay the whole case against nationalisation – owners of private property were unpaid, and yet had every incentive to quicken up the flux. Under nationalisation – just the opposite! In a country smarting from officialism he felt that he had a strong case.

It particularly annoyed him, entering that backwater of perfect peace, to think that a lot of unscrupulous Trusts and Combinations had been cornering the market in goods of all kinds, and keeping prices at an artificial height. Such abusers of the individualistic system were the ruffians who caused all the trouble, and it was some satisfaction to see them getting into a stew at last lest the whole thing might come down with a run – and land them in the soup.

The offices of Cuthcott, Kingson, and Forsyte occupied the ground and first floors of a house on the right-hand side; and, ascending to his room, Soames thought: 'Time we had a coat of paint.'

His old clerk Gradman was seated, where he always was, at a huge bureau with countless pigeonholes. Half-the-clerk stood beside him, with a broker's note recording investment of the proceeds from sale of the Bryanston Square house, in Roger Forsyte's estate. Soames took it, and said:

'Vancouver City Stock. H'm. It's down today!'

With a sort of grating ingratiation old Gradman answered him:

'Ye-es; but everything's down, Mr Soames.' And half-the-clerk withdrew.

Soames skewered the document on to a number of other papers and hung up his hat.

'I want to look at my will and marriage settlement, Gradman.'

Old Gradman, moving to the limit of his swivel chair, drew out two drafts from the bottom left-hand drawer. Recovering his body, he raised his grizzle-haired face, very red from stooping.

'Copies, sir.'

Soames took them. It struck him suddenly how like Gradman was to the stout brindled yard dog they had been wont to keep on his chain at The Shelter, till one day Fleur had come and insisted it should be let loose, so that it had at once bitten the cook and been destroyed. If you let Gradman off his chain, would he bite the cook?

Checking this frivolous fancy, Soames unfolded his marriage settlement. He had not looked at it for over eighteen years, not since he remade his will when his father died and Fleur was born. He wanted to see whether the words 'during coverture' were in. Yes, they were – odd expression, when you thought of it, and derived perhaps from horse-breeding! Interest on fifteen thousand pounds (which he paid her without deducting income tax) so long as she remained his wife, and afterward during widowhood '*dum casta*' – old-fashioned and rather pointed words, put in to insure the conduct of Fleur's mother. His will made it up to an annuity of a thousand under the same conditions. All right! He returned the copies to Gradman, who took them without looking up, swung the chair, restored the papers to their drawer, and went on casting up.

'Gradman! I don't like the condition of the country; there are a lot of people about without any common sense. I want to find a way by which I can safeguard Miss Fleur against anything which might arise.'

Gradman wrote the figure '2' on his blotting-paper.

'Ye-es,' he said; 'there's a nahsty spirit.'

'The ordinary restraint against anticipation doesn't meet the case.'

'Nao,' said Gradman.

'Suppose those Labour fellows come in, or worse! It's these people with fixed ideas who are the danger. Look at Ireland!'

'Ah!' said Gradman.

'Suppose I were to make a settlement on her at once with myself as beneficiary for life, they couldn't take anything but the interest from me, unless of course they alter the law.'

Gradman moved his head and smiled.

'Ah!' he said, 'they wouldn't do tha-at!'

'I don't know,' muttered Soames; 'I don't trust them.'

'It'll take two years, sir, to be valid against death duties.'

Soames sniffed. Two years! He was only sixty-five!

'That's not the point. Draw a form of settlement that passes all my property to Miss Fleur's children in equal shares, with antecedent life-interests first to myself and then to her without power of anticipation, and add a clause that in the event of anything happening to divert her life-interest, that interest passes to the trustees, to apply for her benefit, in their absolute discretion.'

Gradman grated: 'Rather extreme at your age, sir; you lose control.'

'That's my business,' said Soames sharply.

Gradman wrote on a piece of paper: 'Life-interest – anticipation – divert interest – absolute discretion . . .' and said:

'What trustees? There's young Mr Kingson; he's a nice steady young fellow.'

'Yes, he might do for one. I must have three. There isn't a Forsyte now who appeals to me.'

'Not young Mr Nicholas? He's at the Bar. We've given 'im briefs.'

'He'll never set the Thames on fire,' said Soames.

A smile oozed out on Gradman's face, greasy from countless mutton-chops, the smile of a man who sits all day.

'You can't expect it, at his age, Mr Soames.'

'Why? What is he? Forty?'

'Ye-es, quite a young fellow.'

'Well, put him in; but I want somebody who'll take a personal interest. There's no one that I can see.'

'What about Mr Valerius, now he's come home?'

'Val Dartie? With that father?'

'We-ell,' murmured Gradman, 'he's been dead seven years – the Statute runs against him.'

'No,' said Soames. 'I don't like the connection.' He rose. Gradman said suddenly:

'If they were makin' a levy on capital, they could come on the trustees, sir. So there you'd be just the same. I'd think it over, if I were you.'

'That's true,' said Soames. 'I will. What have you done about that dilapidation notice in Vere Street?'

'I 'aven't served it yet. The party's very old. She won't want to go out at her age.'

'I don't know. This spirit of unrest touches everyone.'

'Still, I'm lookin' at things broadly, sir. She's eighty-one.'

'Better serve it,' said Soames, 'and see what she says. Oh! and Mr Timothy? Is everything in order in case of—'

'I've got the inventory of his estate all ready; had the furniture and pictures valued so that we know what reserves to put on. I shall be sorry when he goes, though. Dear me! It is a time since I first saw Mr Timothy!'

'We can't live for ever,' said Soames, taking down his hat.

'Nao,' said Gradman; 'but it'll be a pity – the last of the old family! Shall I take up the matter of that nuisance in Old Compton Street? Those organs – they're nahsty things.'

'Do. I must call for Miss Fleur and catch the four o'clock. Good-day, Gradman.'

'Good-day, Mr Soames. I hope Miss Fleur—'

'Well enough, but gads about too much.'

'Ye-es,' grated Gradman; 'she's young.'

Soames went out, musing: 'Old Gradman! If he were younger I'd put him in the trust. There's nobody I can depend on to take a real interest.'

Leaving the bilious and mathematical exactitude, the preposterous peace of that backwater, he thought suddenly: 'During coverture! Why can't they exclude fellows like

Profond, instead of a lot of hard-working Germans?' and was surprised at the depth of uneasiness which could provoke so unpatriotic a thought. But there it was! One never got a moment of real peace. There was always something at the back of everything! And he made his way toward Green Street.

Two hours later by his watch, Thomas Gradman, stirring in his swivel chair, closed the last drawer of his bureau, and putting into his waistcoat pocket a bunch of keys so fat that they gave him a protuberance on the liver side, brushed his old top hat round with his sleeve, took his umbrella, and descended. Thick, short, and buttoned closely into his old frock coat, he walked toward Covent Garden market. He never missed that daily promenade to the Tube for Highgate, and seldom some critical transaction on the way in connection with vegetables and fruit. Generations might be born, and hats might change, wars be fought, and Forsytes fade away, but Thomas Gradman, faithful and grey, would take his daily walk and buy his daily vegetable. Times were not what they were, and his son had lost a leg, and they never gave him those nice little plaited baskets to carry the stuff in now, and these Tubes were convenient things – still he mustn't complain; his health was good considering his time of life, and after fifty-four years in the Law he was getting a round eight hundred a year and a little worried of late, because it was mostly collector's commission on the rents, and with all this conversion of Forsyte property going on, it looked like drying up, and the price of living still so high; but it was no good worrying – 'The good God made us all' – as he was in the habit of saying; still, house property in London – he didn't know what Mr Roger or Mr James would say if they could see it being sold like this – seemed to show a lack of faith; but Mr Soames – he worried. Life and lives in being and twenty-one years after – beyond that you couldn't go; still, he kept his health wonderfully – and Miss Fleur was a pretty little thing – she was; she'd marry; but lots of people had no children nowadays – he had had his first child at twenty-two; and Mr Jolyon, married while he was at Cambridge, had his child the same year – gracious Peter! That was back in '69, a long time before old Mr Jolyon – fine judge of property – had taken his will away from Mr James – dear, yes! Those were the days when they were buyin' property right and left, and none of this khaki and fallin' over one another to get out of things; and cucumbers at twopence; and a melon – the old melons, that made your mouth water! Fifty years since he went into Mr James's office, and Mr James had said to him: 'Now, Gradman, you're only a shaver – you pay attention, and you'll make your five hundred a year before you've done.' And he had, and feared God, and served the Forsytes, and kept a vegetable diet at night. And, buying a copy of *John Bull* – not that he approved of it, an extravagant affair – he entered the Tube elevator with his mere brown-paper parcel, and was borne down into the bowels of the earth.

Chapter Six

Soames's Private Life

*O*n his way to Green Street it occurred to Soames that he ought to go into Dumetrius's in Suffolk Street about the possibility of the Bolderby Old Crome. Almost worth while to have fought the war to have the Bolderby Old Crome, as it were, in flux! Old Bolderby had died, his son and grandson had been killed – a cousin was coming into the estate, who meant to sell it, some said because of the condition of England, others said because he had asthma.

If Dumetrius once got hold of it the price would become prohibitive; it was necessary for Soames to find out whether Dumetrius had got it, before he tried to get it himself. He therefore confined himself to discussing with Dumetrius whether Monticellis would come again now that it was the fashion for a picture to be anything except a picture; and the future of Johns, with a side-slip into Buxton Knights. It was only when leaving that he added: 'So they're not selling the Bolderby Old Crome, after all?' In sheer pride of racial superiority, as he had calculated would be the case, Dumetrius replied:

'Oh! I shall get it, Mr Forsyte, sir!'

The flutter of his eyelid fortified Soames in a resolution to write direct to the new Bolderby, suggesting that the only dignified way of dealing with an Old Crome was to avoid dealers. He therefore said, 'Well, good-day!' and went, leaving Dumetrius the wiser.

At Green Street he found that Fleur was out and would be all the evening; she was staying one more night in London. He cabbed on dejectedly, and caught his train.

He reached his house about six o'clock. The air was heavy, midges biting, thunder about. Taking his letters he went up to his dressing-room to cleanse himself of London.

An uninteresting post. A receipt, a bill for purchases on behalf of Fleur. A circular about an exhibition of etchings. A letter beginning:

Sir,
I feel it my duty . . .

That would be an appeal or something unpleasant. He looked at once for the signature. There was none! Incredulously he turned the page over and examined each corner. Not being a public man, Soames had never yet had an anonymous letter, and his first impulse was to tear it up, as a dangerous thing; his second to read it, as a thing still more dangerous.

Sir,
I feel it my duty to inform you that having no interest
in the matter your lady is carrying on with a
foreigner –

Reaching that word Soames stopped mechanically and examined the postmark. So far as he could pierce the impenetrable disguise in which the Post Office had wrapped it, there was something with a 'sea' at the end and a 't' in it. Chelsea? No! Battersea? Perhaps! He read on.

These foreigners are all the same. Sack the lot. This
one meets your lady twice a week. I know it of my
own knowledge – and to see an Englishman put on
goes against the grain. You watch it and see if what I

say isn't true. I shouldn't meddle if it wasn't a dirty
foreigner that's in it. Yours obedient.

The sensation with which Soames dropped the letter was
similar to that he would have had entering his bedroom
and finding it full of black-beetles. The meanness of
anonymity gave a shuddering obscenity to the moment. And
the worst of it was that this shadow had been at the back
of his mind ever since the Sunday evening when Fleur had
pointed down at Prosper Profond strolling on the lawn, and
said: 'Prowling cat!' Had he not in connection therewith,
this very day, perused his will and marriage settlement? And
now this anonymous ruffian, with nothing to gain, appar-
ently, save the venting of his spite against foreigners, had
wrenched it out of the obscurity in which he had hoped
and wished it would remain. To have such knowledge forced
on him, at his time of life, about Fleur's mother! He picked
the letter up from the carpet, tore it across, and then, when
it hung together by just the fold at the back, stopped tearing,
and reread it. He was taking at that moment one of the
decisive resolutions of his life. He would *not* be forced into
another scandal. No! However he decided to deal with this
matter – and it required the most far-sighted and careful
consideration – he would do nothing that might injure Fleur.
That resolution taken, his mind answered the helm again,
and he made his ablutions. His hands trembled as he dried
them. Scandal he would not have, but something must be
done to stop this sort of thing! He went into his wife's room
and stood looking around him. The idea of searching for
anything which would incriminate, and entitle him to hold
a menace over her, did not even come to him. There would
be nothing – she was much too practical. The idea of having
her watched had been dismissed before it came – too well
he remembered his previous experience of that. No! He had
nothing but this torn-up letter from some anonymous ruffian,

whose impudent intrusion into his private life he so violently resented. It was repugnant to him to make use of it, but he might have to. What a mercy Fleur was not at home to-night! A tap on the door broke up his painful cogitations.

'Mr Michael Mont, sir, is in the drawing-room. Will you see him?'

'No,' said Soames; 'yes. I'll come down.'

Anything that would take his mind off for a few minutes! Michael Mont in flannels stood on the verandah smoking a cigarette. He threw it away as Soames came up, and ran his hand through his hair.

Soames's feeling toward this young man was singular. He was no doubt a rackety, irresponsible young fellow according to old standards, yet somehow likeable, with his extraordinarily cheerful way of blurting out his opinions.

'Come in,' he said; 'have you had tea?'

Mont came in.

'I thought Fleur would have been back, sir; but I'm glad she isn't. The fact is, I – I'm fearfully gone on her; so fearfully gone that I thought you'd better know. It's old-fashioned, of course, coming to fathers first, but I thought you'd forgive that. I went to my own dad, and he says if I settle down he'll see me through. He rather cottons to the idea, in fact. I told him about your Goya.'

'Oh!' said Soames, inexpressibly dry. 'He rather cottons?'

'Yes, sir; do you?'

Soames smiled faintly.

'You see,' resumed Mont, twiddling his straw hat, while his hair, ears, eyebrows, all seemed to stand up from excitement, 'when you've been through the War you can't help being in a hurry.'

'To get married; and unmarried afterward,' said Soames slowly.

'Not from Fleur, sir. Imagine, if you were me!'

Soames cleared his throat. That way of putting it was forcible enough.

'Fleur's too young,' he said.

'Oh! no, sir. We're awfully old nowadays. My dad seems to me a perfect babe; his thinking apparatus hasn't turned a hair. But he's a Baronight, of course; that keeps him back.'

'Baronight,' repeated Soames; 'what may that be?'

'Bart, sir. I shall be a Bart some day. But I shall live it down, you know.'

'Go away and live this down,' said Soames.

Young Mont said imploringly: 'Oh! no, sir. I simply must hang around, or I shouldn't have a dog's chance. You'll let Fleur do what she likes, I suppose, anyway. Madame passes me.'

'Indeed!' said Soames frigidly.

'You don't really bar me, do you?' and the young man looked so doleful that Soames smiled.

'You may think you're very old,' he said; 'but you strike me as extremely young. To rattle ahead of everything is not a proof of maturity.'

'All right, sir; I give you our age. But to show you I mean business – I've got a job.'

'Glad to hear it.'

'Joined a publisher; my governor is putting up the stakes.'

Soames put his hand over his mouth – he had so very nearly said: 'God help the publisher!' His grey eyes scrutinised the agitated young man.

'I don't dislike you, Mr Mont, but Fleur is everything to me. Everything – do you understand?'

'Yes, sir, I know; but so she is to me.'

'That's as may be. I'm glad you've told me, however. And now I think there's nothing more to be said.'

'I know it rests with her, sir.'

'It will rest with her a long time, I hope.'

'You aren't cheering,' said Mont suddenly.

'No,' said Soames, 'my experience of life has not made me anxious to couple people in a hurry. Good-night, Mr Mont. I shan't tell Fleur what you've said.'

'Oh!' murmured Mont blankly; 'I really could knock my brains out for want of her. She knows that perfectly well.'

'I dare say.' And Soames held out his hand. A distracted squeeze, a heavy sigh, and soon after sounds from the young man's motor-cycle called up visions of flying dust and broken bones.

'The younger generation!' he thought heavily, and went out on to the lawn. The gardeners had been mowing, and there was still the smell of fresh-cut grass – the thundery air kept all scents close to earth. The sky was of a purplish hue – the poplars black. Two or three boats passed on the river, scuttling, as it were, for shelter before the storm. 'Three days' fine weather,' thought Soames, 'and then a storm!' Where was Annette? With that chap, for all he knew – she was a young woman! Impressed with the queer charity of that thought, he entered the summerhouse and sat down. The fact was – and he admitted it – Fleur was so much to him that his wife was very little – very little; French – had never been much more than a mistress, and he was getting indifferent to that side of things! It was odd how, with all this ingrained care for moderation and secure investment, Soames ever put his emotional eggs into one basket. First Irene – now Fleur. He was dimly conscious of it, sitting there, conscious of its odd dangerousness. It had brought him to wreck and scandal once, but now – now it should save him! He cared so much for Fleur that he would have no further scandal. If only he could get at that anonymous letter-writer, he would teach him not to meddle and stir up mud at the bottom of water which he wished should remain stagnant! ... A distant flash, a low rumble, and large drops of rain spattered on the thatch above him. He remained indifferent, tracing a pattern with his finger on the dusty surface of a little rustic table. Fleur's future! 'I want fair sailing for her,' he thought. 'Nothing else matters at my time of life.' A lonely business – life! What you had you never could keep to yourself! As you warned one off, you let another in. One could make sure of nothing! He reached up and pulled a red rambler rose from a cluster which blocked the window. Flowers grew and dropped – Nature was a queer thing! The thunder rumbled and crashed, travelling east along a river, the paling flashes flicked his eyes; the poplar tops showed sharp and dense against the sky, a heavy shower rustled and rattled and veiled in the little house wherein he sat, indifferent, thinking.

When the storm was over, he left his retreat and went down the wet path to the river bank.

Two swans had come, sheltering in among the reeds. He knew the birds well, and stood watching the dignity in the curve of those white necks and formidable snake-like heads. 'Not dignified – what I have to do!' he thought. And yet it must be tackled, lest worse befell. Annette must be back by now from wherever she had gone, for it was nearly dinnertime, and as the moment for seeing her approached, the difficulty of knowing what to say and how to say it had increased. A new and scaring thought occurred to him. Suppose she wanted her liberty to marry this fellow! Well, if she did, she couldn't have it. He had not married her for that. The image of Prosper Profond dawdled before him reassuringly. Not a marrying man! No, no! Anger replaced that momentary scare. 'He had better not come my way,' he thought. The mongrel represented— ! But what did Prosper Profond represent? Nothing that mattered surely. And yet something real enough in the world – unmorality let off its chain, disillusionment on the prowl! That expression Annette had caught from him: '*Je m'en fiche!*' A fatalistic chap! A continental – a cosmopolitan – a product of the age! If there were condemnation more complete, Soames felt that he did not know it.

The swans had turned their heads, and were looking past

him into some distance of their own. One of them uttered a little hiss, wagged its tail, turned as if answering to a rudder, and swam away. The other followed. Their white bodies, their stately necks, passed out of his sight, and he went toward the house.

Annette was in the drawing-room, dressed for dinner, and he thought as he went upstairs: 'Handsome is as handsome does.' Handsome! Except for remarks about the curtains in the drawing-room, and the storm, there was practically no conversation during a meal distinguished by exactitude of quantity and perfection of quality. Soames drank nothing. He followed her into the drawing-room afterward, and found her smoking a cigarette on the sofa between the two French windows. She was leaning back, almost upright, in a low black frock, with her knees crossed and her blue eyes half-closed; grey-blue smoke issued from her red, rather full lips, a fillet bound her chestnut hair, she wore the thinnest silk stockings, and shoes with very high heels showing off her instep. A fine piece in any room! Soames, who held that torn letter in a hand thrust deep into the side-pocket of his dinner-jacket, said:

'I'm going to shut the window; the damp's lifting in.'

He did so, and stood looking at a David Cox adorning the cream-panelled wall close by.

What was she thinking of? He had never understood a woman in his life – except Fleur – and Fleur not always! His heart beat fast. But if he meant to do it, now was the moment. Turning from the David Cox, he took out the torn letter.

'I've had this.'

Her eyes widened, stared at him, and hardened.

Soames handed her the letter.

'It's torn, but you can read it.' And he turned back to the David Cox – a sea-piece, of good tone – but without movement enough. 'I wonder what that chap's doing at this moment?' he thought. 'I'll astonish him yet.' Out of the corner of his eye he saw Annette holding the letter rigidly; her eyes moved from side to side under her darkened lashes and frowning, darkened eyes. She dropped the letter, gave a little shiver, smiled, and said:

'Dirrty!'

'I quite agree,' said Soames; 'degrading. Is it true?'

A tooth fastened on her red lower lip. 'And what if it were?'

She was brazen!

'Is that all you have to say?'

'No.'

'Well, speak out!'

'What is the good of talking?'

Soames said icily: 'So you admit it?'

'I admit nothing. You are a fool to ask. A man like you should not ask. It is dangerous.'

Soames made a tour of the room, to subdue his rising anger.

'Do you remember,' he said, halting in front of her, 'what you were when I married you? Working at accounts in a restaurant.'

'Do you remember that I was not half your age?'

Soames broke off the hard encounter of their eyes, and went back to the David Cox.

'I am not going to bandy words. I require you to give up this – friendship. I think of the matter entirely as it affects Fleur.'

'Ah! – Fleur!'

'Yes,' said Soames stubbornly; 'Fleur. She is your child as well as mine.'

'It is kind to admit that!'

'Are you going to do what I say?'

'I refuse to tell you.'

'Then I must make you.'

Annette smiled.

'No, Soames,' she said. 'You are helpless. Do not say things that you will regret.'

Anger swelled the veins on his forehead. He opened his

mouth to vent that emotion, and could not. Annette went on:

'There shall be no more such letters, I promise you. That is enough.'

Soames writhed. He had a sense of being treated like a child by this woman who had deserved he did not know what.

'When two people have married, and lived like us, Soames, they had better be quiet about each other. There are things one does not drag up into the light for people to laugh at. You will be quiet, then; not for my sake but for your own. You are getting old; I am not, yet. You have made me ver-ry practical.'

Soames, who had passed through all the sensations of being choked, repeated dully:

'I require you to give up this friendship.'

'And if I do not?'

'Then – then I will cut you out of my will.'

Somehow it did not seem to meet the case. Annette laughed.

'You will live a long time, Soames.'

'You – you are a bad woman,' said Soames suddenly.

Annette shrugged her shoulders.

'I do not think so. Living with you has killed things in me, it is true; but I am not a bad woman. I am sensible – that is all. And so will you be when you have thought it over.'

'I shall see this man,' said Soames sullenly, 'and warn him off.'

'*Mon cher*, you are funny. You do not want me, you have as much of me as you want; and you wish the rest of me to be dead. I admit nothing, but I am not going to be dead, Soames, at my age; so you had better be quiet, I tell you. I myself will make no scandal; none. Now, I am not saying any more, whatever you do.'

She reached out, took a French novel off a little table, and opened it. Soames watched her, silenced by the tumult of his feelings. The thought of that man was almost making him want her, and this was a revelation of their relationship, startling to one little given to introspective philosophy. Without saying another word he went out and up to the picture-gallery. This came of marrying a Frenchwoman! And yet, without her there would have been no Fleur! She had served her purpose.

'She's right,' he thought; 'I can do nothing. I don't even know that there's anything in it.' The instinct of self-preservation warned him to batten down his hatches, to smother the fire with want of air. Unless one believed there was something in a thing, there wasn't.

That night he went into her room. She received him in the most matter-of-fact way, as if there had been no scene between them. And he returned to his own room with a curious sense of peace. If one didn't choose to see, one needn't. And he did not choose – in future he did not choose. There was nothing to be gained by it – nothing! Opening the drawer he took from the sachet a handkerchief, and the framed photograph of Fleur. When he had looked at it a little he slipped it down, and there was that other one – that old one of Irene. An owl hooted while he stood in his window gazing at it. The owl hooted, the red climbing roses seemed to deepen in colour, there came a scent of lime-blossom. God! That had been a different thing! Passion – Memory! Dust!

Chapter Seven

June Takes a Hand

*O*ne who was a sculptor, a Slav, a sometime resident in New York, an egoist, and impecunious, was to be found of an evening in June Forsyte's studio on the bank of the Thames at Chiswick. On the evening of 6 July, Boris Strumolowski – several of whose works were on show there because they were as yet too advanced to be on show anywhere else – had begun well, with that aloof and rather Christ-like silence which admirably suited his youthful, round, broad cheek-boned countenance framed in bright hair banged like a girl's. June had known him three weeks, and he still seemed to her the principal embodiment of genius, and hope of the future; a sort of Star of the East which had strayed into an unappreciative West. Until that evening he had conversationally confined himself to recording his impressions of the United States, whose dust he had just shaken from off his feet – a country, in his opinion, so barbarous in every way that he had sold practically nothing there, and become an object of suspicion to the police; a country, as he said, without a race of its own, without liberty, equality, or fraternity, without principles, traditions, taste, without – in a word – a soul. He had left it for his own good, and come to the only other country where he could live well. June had dwelt unhappily on him in her lonely moments, standing before his creations – frightening, but powerful and symbolic once they had been explained! That he, haloed by bright hair like an early Italian painting, and absorbed in his genius to the exclusion of all else – the only sign of course by which real genius could be told – should still be a 'lame duck' agitated her warm heart almost to the exclusion of Paul Post. And she had begun to take steps to clear her Gallery, in order to fill it with Strumolowski masterpieces. She had at once encountered trouble. Paul Post had kicked; Vospovitch had stung. With all the emphasis of a genius which she did not as yet deny them, they had demanded another six weeks at least of her Gallery. The American stream, still flowing in, would soon be flowing out. The American stream was their right, their only hope, their salvation – since nobody in this 'beastly' country cared for Art. June had yielded to the demonstration. After all Boris would not mind their having the full benefit of an American stream, which he himself so violently despised.

This evening she had put that to Boris with nobody else present, except Hannah Hobdey, the mediaeval black-and-whitist, and Jimmy Portugal, editor of the *Neo-Artist*. She had put it to him with that sudden confidence which continual contact with the neo-artistic world had never been able to dry up in her warm and generous nature. He had not broken his Christ-like silence, however, for more than two minutes before she began to move her blue eyes from side to side, as a cat moves its tail. This – he said – was characteristic of England, the most selfish country in the world; the country which sucked the blood of other countries; destroyed the brains and hearts of Irishmen, Hindus, Egyptians, Boers, and Burmese, all the best races in the world; bullying, hypocritical England! This was what he had expected, coming to such a country, where the climate was all fog, and the people all tradesmen perfectly blind to Art, and sunk in profiteering and the grossest materialism. Conscious that Hannah Hobdey was murmuring, 'Hear, hear!' and Jimmy Portugal sniggering, June grew crimson, and suddenly rapped out:

'Then why did you ever come? We didn't ask you.'

The remark was so singularly at variance with all she had led him to expect from her, that Strumolowski stretched out his hand and took a cigarette.

'England never wants an idealist,' he said.

But in June something primitively English was thoroughly upset; old Jolyon's sense of justice had risen, as it were, from bed. 'You come and sponge on us,' she said, 'and then abuse us. If you think that's playing the game, I don't.'

She now discovered that which others had discovered before her – the thickness of hide beneath which the sensibility of genius is sometimes veiled. Strumolowski's young and ingenuous face became the incarnation of a sneer.

'Sponge, one does not sponge, one takes what is owing – a tenth part of what is owing. You will repent to say that, Miss Forsyte.'

'Oh, no,' said June, 'I shan't.'

'Ah! We know very well, we artists – you take us to get what you can out of us. I want nothing from you' – and he blew out a cloud of June's smoke.

Decision rose in an icy puff from the turmoil of insulted shame within her. 'Very well, then, you can take your things away.'

And, almost in the same moment, she thought: 'Poor boy! He's only got a garret, and probably not a taxi fare. In front of these people, too; it's positively disgusting!'

Young Strumolowski shook his head violently; his hair, thick, smooth, close as a golden plate, did not fall off.

'I can live on nothing,' he said shrilly; 'I have often had to for the sake of my Art. It is you bourgeois who force us to spend money.'

The words hit June like a pebble, in the ribs. After all she had done for Art, all her identification with its troubles and lame ducks. She was struggling for adequate words when the door was opened, and her Austrian murmured:

'A young lady, *gnädiges Fräulein*.'

'Where?'

'In the little meal-room.'

With a glance at Boris Strumolowski, at Hannah Hobdey, at Jimmy Portugal, June said nothing, and went out, devoid of equanimity. Entering the 'little meal-room,' she perceived the young lady to be Fleur – looking very pretty, if pale. At this disenchanted moment a little lame duck of her own breed was welcome to June, so homoeopathic by instinct.

The girl must have come, of course, because of Jon; or, if not, at least to get something out of her. And June felt just then that to assist somebody was the only bearable thing.

'So you've remembered to come,' she said.

'Yes. What a jolly little duck of a house! But please don't let me bother you, if you've got people.'

'Not at all,' said June. 'I want to let them stew in their own juice for a bit. Have you come about Jon?'

'You said you thought we ought to be told. Well, I've found out.'

'Oh!' said June blankly. 'Not nice, is it?'

They were standing one on each side of the little bare table at which June took her meals. A vase on it was full of Iceland poppies; the girl raised her hand and touched them with a gloved finger. To her new-fangled dress, frilly about the hips and tight below the knees, June took a sudden liking – a charming colour, flax-blue.

'She makes a picture,' thought June. Her little room, with its whitewashed walls, its floor and hearth of old pink brick, its black paint, and latticed window athwart which the last of the sunlight was shining, had never looked so charming, set off by this young figure, with the creamy, slightly frowning face. She remembered with sudden vividness how nice she herself had looked in those old days when her heart was set on Philip Bosinney, that dead lover, who had broken from her to destroy for ever Irene's allegiance to this girl's father. Did Fleur know of that, too?

'Well,' she said, 'what are you going to do?'

It was some seconds before Fleur answered.

'I don't want Jon to suffer. I must see him once more to put an end to it.'

'You're going to put an end to it!'

'What else is there to do?'

The girl seemed to June, suddenly, intolerably spiritless.

'I suppose you're right,' she muttered. 'I know my father thinks so; but – I should never have done it myself. I can't take things lying down.'

How poised and watchful that girl looked; how unemotional her voice sounded!

'People *will* assume that I'm in love.'

'Well, aren't you?'

Fleur shrugged her shoulders. 'I might have known it,' thought June; 'she's Soames's daughter – fish! And yet – he!'

'What do you want *me* to do then?' she said with a sort of disgust.

'Could I see Jon here to-morrow on his way down to Holly's? He'd come if you sent him a line to-night. And perhaps afterward you'd let them know quietly at Robin Hill that it's all over, and that they needn't tell Jon about his mother.'

'All right!' said June abruptly. 'I'll write now, and you can post it. Half-past two tomorrow. I shan't be in, myself.'

She sat down at the tiny bureau which filled one corner. When she looked round with the finished note Fleur was still touching the poppies with her gloved finger.

June licked a stamp. 'Well, here it is. If you're not in love, of course, there's no more to be said. Jon's lucky.'

Fleur took the note. 'Thanks awfully!'

'Cold-blooded little baggage!' thought June. Jon, son of her father, to love, and not to be loved by the daughter of – Soames! It was humiliating!

'Is that all?'

Fleur nodded; her frills shook and trembled as she swayed toward the door.

'Good-bye!'

'Good-bye! . . . Little piece of fashion!' muttered June, closing the door. 'That family!' And she marched back toward her studio. Boris Strumolowski had regained his Christ-like silence and Jimmy Portugal was damning everybody, except the group in whose behalf he ran the *Neo-Artist*. Among the condemned were Eric Cobbley, and several other 'lame-duck' genii who at one time or another had held first place in the repertoire of June's aid and adoration. She experienced a sense of futility and disgust, and went to the window to let the river-wind blow those squeaky words away.

But when at length Jimmy Portugal had finished, and gone with Hannah Hobdey, she sat down and mothered young Strumolowski for half an hour, promising him a month, at least, of the American stream; so that he went away with his halo in perfect order. 'In spite of all,' June thought, 'Boris is wonderful.'

Chapter Eight

The Bit Between the Teeth

To know that your hand is against everyone's is – for some natures – to experience a sense of moral release. Fleur felt no remorse when she left June's house. Reading condemnatory resentment in her little kinswoman's blue eyes – she was glad that she had fooled her, despising June because that elderly idealist had not seen what she was after.

End it, forsooth! She would soon show them all that she was only just beginning. And she smiled to herself on the top of the bus which carried her back to Mayfair. But the smile died, squeezed out by spasms of anticipation and anxiety. Would she be able to manage Jon? She had taken the bit between her teeth, but could she make him take it too? She knew the truth and the real danger of delay – he knew neither; therein lay all the difference in the world.

'Suppose I tell him,' she thought; 'wouldn't it really be safer?' This hideous luck had no right to spoil their love; he must see that! They could not let it! People always accepted an accomplished fact in time! From that piece of philosophy – profound enough at her age – she passed to another consideration less philosophic. If she persuaded Jon to a quick and secret marriage, and he found out afterward that she had known the truth. What then? Jon hated subterfuge. Again, then, would it not be better to tell him? But the memory of his mother's face kept intruding on that impulse. Fleur was afraid. His mother had power over him; more power perhaps than she herself. Who could tell? It was too great a risk. Deepsunk in these instinctive calculations she was carried on past Green Street as far as the Ritz Hotel. She got down there, and walked back on the Green Park side. The storm had washed every tree; they still dripped. Heavy drops fell on to her frills, and to avoid them she crossed over under the eyes of the Iseeum Club. Chancing to look up she saw Monsieur Profond with a tall stout man in the bay window. Turning into Green Street she heard her name called, and saw 'that prowler' coming up. He took off his hat – a glossy 'bowler' such as she particularly detested.

'Good evenin'! Miss Forsyde. Isn't there a small thing I can do for you?'

'Yes, pass by on the other side.'

'I say! Why do you dislike me?'

'Do I?'

'It looks like it.'

'Well, then, because you make me feel life isn't worth living.'

Monsieur Profond smiled.

'Look here, Miss Forsyde, don't worry. It'll be all right. Nothing lasts.'

'Things do last,' cried Fleur; 'with me anyhow – especially likes and dislikes.'

'Well, that makes me a bit un'appy.'

'I should have thought nothing could ever make you happy or unhappy.'

'I don't like to annoy other people. I'm goin' on my yacht.'

Fleur looked at him, startled.

'Where?'

'Small voyage to the South Seas or somewhere,' said Monsieur Profond.

Fleur suffered relief and a sense of insult. Clearly he meant to convey that he was breaking with her mother. How dared he have anything to break, and yet how dared he break it?

'Good-night, Miss Forsyde! Remember me to Mrs Dartie. I'm not so bad really. Good-night!' Fleur left him standing there with his hat raised. Stealing a look round, she saw him stroll – immaculate and heavy – back toward his Club.

'He can't even love with conviction,' she thought. 'What will Mother do?'

Her dreams that night were endless and uneasy; she rose heavy and unrested, and went at once to the study of Whitaker's Almanac. A Forsyte is instinctively aware that facts are the real crux of any situation. She might conquer Jon's prejudice, but without exact machinery to complete their desperate resolve, nothing would happen. From the invaluable tome she learned that they must each be twenty-one; or someone's consent would be necessary, which of course was unobtainable; then she became lost in directions concerning licenses, certificates, notices, districts, coming finally to the word 'perjury'. But that was nonsense! Who would really mind their giving wrong ages in order to be married for love! She ate hardly any breakfast, and went back to Whitaker. The more she studied the less sure she became; till, idly turning the pages, she came to Scotland. People could be married there without any of this nonsense. She had only to go and stay there twenty-one days, then Jon could come, and in front of two people they could declare themselves married. And what was more – they would be! It was far the best way; and at once she ran over her schoolfellows. There was Mary Lambe who lived in Edinburgh and was 'quite a sport'! She had a brother too. She could stay with Mary Lambe, who with her brother would serve for witnesses. She well knew that some girls would think all this unnecessary, and that all she and Jon need do was to go away together for a weekend and then say to their people: 'We are married by Nature, we must now be married by Law.' But Fleur was Forsyte enough to feel such a proceeding dubious, and to dread her father's face when he heard of it. Besides, she did not believe that Jon would do it; he had an opinion of her such as she could not bear to diminish. No! Mary Lambe was preferable, and it was just the time of year to go to Scotland. More at ease now she packed, avoided her aunt, and took a bus to Chiswick. She was too early, and went on to Kew Gardens. She found no peace among its flower-beds, labelled trees, and broad green spaces, and having lunched off anchovy-paste sandwiches and coffee, returned to Chiswick and rang June's bell. The Austrian admitted her to the 'little meal-room'. Now that she knew what she and Jon were up against, her longing for him had increased tenfold, as if he were a toy with sharp edges or dangerous paint such as they had tried to take from her as a child. If she could not have her way, and get Jon for good and all, she felt like dying of privation. By hook or crook she must and would get him! A round dim mirror of very old glass hung over the pink brick hearth. She stood looking at herself reflected in it, pale, and rather dark under the eyes; little shudders kept passing through her nerves. Then she heard the bell ring, and, stealing to the window, saw him standing on the doorstep smoothing his hair and lips, as if he too were trying to subdue the fluttering of his nerves.

She was sitting on one of the two rush-seated chairs, with her back to the door, when he came in, and she said at once:

'Sit down, Jon, I want to talk seriously.'

Jon sat on the table by her side, and without looking at him she went on:

'If you don't want to lose me, we must get married.'

Jon gasped.

'Why? Is there anything new?'

'No, but I felt it at Robin Hill, and among my people.'

'But –' stammered Jon, 'at Robin Hill – it was all smooth – and they've said nothing to me.'

'But they mean to stop us. Your mother's face was enough. And my father's.'

'Have you seen him since?'

Fleur nodded. What mattered a few supplementary lies?

'But,' said Jon eagerly, 'I can't see how they can feel like that after all these years.'

Fleur looked up at him.

'Perhaps you don't love me enough.'

'Not love you enough! Why – I'

'Then make sure of me.'

'Without telling them?'

'Not till after.'

Jon was silent. How much older he looked than on that day, barely two months ago, when she first saw him – quite two years older!

'It would hurt Mother awfully,' he said.

Fleur drew her hand away.

'You've got to choose.'

Jon slid off the table on to his knees.

'But why not tell them? They can't really stop us, Fleur!'

'They can! I tell you, they can.'

'How?'

'We're utterly dependent – by putting money pressure, and all sorts of other pressure. I'm not patient, Jon.'

'But it's deceiving them.'

Fleur got up.

'You can't really love me, or you wouldn't hesitate. "He either fears his fate too much—"!'

Lifting his hands to her waist, Jon forced her to sit down again. She hurried on:

'I've planned it all out. We've only to go to Scotland. When we're married they'll soon come round. People always come round to facts. Don't you see, Jon?'

'But to hurt them so awfully!'

So he would rather hurt her than those people of his! 'All right, then; let me go!'

Jon got up and put his back against the door.

'I expect you're right,' he said slowly; 'but I want to think it over.'

She could see that he was seething with feelings he wanted to express; but she did not mean to help him. She hated herself at this moment and almost hated him. Why had she to do all the work to secure their love? It wasn't fair. And then she saw his eyes, adoring and distressed.

'Don't look like that! I only don't want to lose you, Jon.'

'You can't lose me so long as you want me.'

'Oh, yes, I can.'

Jon put his hands on her shoulders.

'Fleur, do you know anything you haven't told me?'

It was the point-blank question she had dreaded. She looked straight at him, and answered: 'No.' She had burned her boats; but what did it matter, if she got him? He would forgive her. And throwing her arms round his neck, she kissed him on the lips. She was winning! She felt it in the beating of his heart against her, in the closing of his eyes. 'I want to make sure! I want to make sure!' she whispered. 'Promise!'

Jon did not answer. His face had the stillness of extreme trouble. At last he said:

'It's like hitting them. I must think a little, Fleur. I really must.'

Fleur slipped out of his arms.

'Oh! Very well!' And suddenly she burst into tears of disappointment, shame, and overstrain. Followed five minutes of acute misery. Jon's remorse and tenderness knew no bounds; but he did not promise. Despite her will to cry, 'Very well, then, if you don't love me enough – goodbye!' she dared not. From birth accustomed to her own way, this check from one so young, so tender, so devoted, baffled and surprised her. She wanted to push him away from her, to try what anger and coldness would do, and again she dared not. The knowledge that she was scheming to rush him blindfold into the irrevocable weakened everything – weakened the sincerity of pique, and the sincerity of passion; even her kisses had not the lure she wished for them. That stormy little meeting ended inconclusively.

'Will you some tea, *gnädiges Fräulein*?'

Pushing Jon from her, she cried out:

'No – no, thank you! I'm just going.'

And before he could prevent her she was gone.

She went stealthily, mopping her flushed, stained cheeks, frightened, angry, very miserable. She had stirred Jon up so fearfully, yet nothing definite was promised or arranged! But the more uncertain and hazardous the future, the more 'the will to have' worked its tentacles into the flesh of her heart – like some burrowing tick!

No one was at Green Street. Winifred had gone with Imogen to see a play which some said was allegorical, and others 'very exciting, don't you know'. It was because of what others said that Winifred and Imogen had gone. Fleur went on to Paddington. Through the carriage the air from the brick-kilns of West Drayton and the late hayfields fanned her still flushed cheeks. Flowers had seemed to be had for the picking; now they were all thorned and prickled. But the golden flower within the crown of spikes seemed to her tenacious spirit all the fairer and more desirable.

Chapter Nine

The Fat in the Fire

On reaching home Fleur found an atmosphere so peculiar that it penetrated even the perplexed aura of her own private life. Her mother was inaccessibly entrenched in a brown study; her father contemplating fate in the vinery. Neither of them had a word to throw to a dog. 'Is it because of me?' thought Fleur. 'Or because of Profond?' To her mother she said:

'What's the matter with Father?'

Her mother answered with a shrug of her shoulders.

To her father:

'What's the matter with Mother?'

Her father answered:

'Matter? What should be the matter?' and gave her a sharp look.

'By the way,' murmured Fleur, 'Monsieur Profond is going on a "small" voyage on his yacht, to the South Seas.'

Soames examined a branch on which no grapes were growing.

'This vine's a failure,' he said. 'I've had young Mont here. He asked me something about you.'

'Oh! How do you like him, Father?'

'He – he's a product – like all these young people.'

'What were you at his age, dear?'

Soames smiled grimly.

'We went to work, and didn't play about – flying and motoring, and making love.'

'Didn't you ever make love?'

She avoided looking at him while she said that, but she saw him well enough. His pale face had reddened, his eyebrows, where darkness was still mingled with the grey, had come close together.

'I had no time or inclination to philander.'

'Perhaps you had a grand passion.'

Soames looked at her intently.

'Yes – if you want to know – and much good it did me.' He moved away, along by the hot-water pipes. Fleur tiptoed silently after him.

'Tell me about it, Father!'

Soames became very still.

'What should you want to know about such things, at your age?'

'Is she alive?'

He nodded.

'And married?'

'Yes.'

'It's Jon Forsyte's mother, isn't it? And she was your wife first.'

It was said in a flash of intuition. Surely his opposition came from his anxiety that she should not know of that old wound to his pride. But she was startled. To see someone so old and calm wince as if struck, to hear so sharp a note of pain in his voice!

'Who told you that? If your aunt—! I can't bear the affair talked of.'

'But, darling,' said Fleur, softly, 'it's so long ago.'

'Long ago or not, I—'

Fleur stood stroking his arm.

'I've tried to forget,' he said suddenly; 'I don't wish to be reminded.' And then, as if venting some long and secret irritation, he added: 'In these days people don't understand. Grand passion, indeed! No one knows what it is.'

'I do,' said Fleur, almost in a whisper.

Soames, who had turned his back on her, spun round.

'What are you talking of – a child like you!'

'Perhaps I've inherited it, Father.'

'What?'

'For her son, you see.'

He was pale as a sheet, and she knew that she was as bad. They stood staring at each other in the steamy heat, redolent of the mushy scent of earth, of potted geranium, and of vines coming along fast.

'This is crazy,' said Soames at last, between dry lips.

Scarcely moving her own, she murmured:

'Don't be angry, Father. I can't help it.'

But she could see he wasn't angry; only scared, deeply scared.

'I thought that foolishness,' he stammered, 'was all forgotten.'

'Oh, no! It's ten times what it was.'

Soames kicked at the hot-water pipe. The hapless movement touched her, who had no fear of her father – none.

'Dearest!' she said. 'What must be, must, you know.'

'Must!' repeated Soames. 'You don't know what you're talking of. Has that boy been told?'

The blood rushed into her cheeks.

'Not yet.'

He had turned from her again, and, with one shoulder a little raised, stood staring fixedly at a joint in the pipes.

'It's most distasteful to me,' he said suddenly; 'nothing could be more so. Son of that fellow! It's – it's – perverse!'

She had noted, almost unconsciously, that he did not say 'son of that woman', and again her intuition began working.

Did the ghost of that grand passion linger in some corner of his heart?

She slipped her hand under his arm.

'Jon's father is quite ill and old; I saw him.'

'You—?'

'Yes, I went there with Jon; I saw them both.'

'Well, and what did they say to you?'

'Nothing. They were very polite.'

'They would be.' He resumed his contemplation of the pipe-joint, and then said suddenly:

'I must think this over – I'll speak to you again to-night.'

She knew this was final for the moment, and stole away, leaving him still looking at the pipe-joint. She wandered into the fruit-garden, among the raspberry and currant bushes, without impetus to pick and eat. Two months ago – she was light-hearted! Even two days ago – light-hearted, before Prosper Profond told her. Now she felt tangled in a web – of passions, vested rights, oppressions and revolts, the ties of love and hate. At this dark moment of discouragement there seemed, even to her hold-fast nature, no way out. How deal with it – how sway and bend things to her will, and get her heart's desire? And, suddenly, round the corner of the high box hedge, she came plump on her mother, walking swiftly, with an open letter in her hand. Her bosom was heaving, her eyes dilated, her cheeks flushed. Instantly Fleur thought: 'The yacht! Poor Mother!'

Annette gave her a wide startled look, and said:

'*J'ai la migraine.*'

'I'm awfully sorry, Mother.'

'Oh, yes! you and your father – sorry!'

'But, Mother – I am. I know what it feels like.'

Annette's startled eyes grew wide, till the whites showed above them.

'Poor innocent!' she said.

Her mother – so self-possessed, and common-sensical – to look and speak like this! It was all frightening! Her father, her mother, herself! And only two months back they had seemed to have everything they wanted in this world.

Annette crumpled the letter in her hand. Fleur knew that she must ignore the sight.

'Can't I do anything for your head, Mother?'

Annette shook that head and walked on, swaying her hips.

'It's cruel,' thought Fleur, 'and I was glad! That man! What do men come prowling for, disturbing everything! I suppose he's tired of her. What business has he to be tired of my mother? What business!' And at that thought, so natural and so peculiar, she uttered a little choked laugh.

She ought, of course, to be delighted, but what was there to be delighted at? Her father didn't really care! Her mother did, perhaps? She entered the orchard, and sat down under a cherry-tree. A breeze sighed in the higher boughs; the sky seen through their green was very blue and very white in cloud – those heavy white clouds almost always present in river landscape. Bees, sheltering out of the wind, hummed softly, and over the lush grass fell the thick shade from those fruit-trees planted by her father five-and-twenty years ago. Birds were almost silent, the cuckoos had ceased to sing, but wood-pigeons were cooing. The breath and drone and cooing of high summer were not for long a sedative to her excited nerves. Crouched over her knees she began to scheme. Her father must be made to back her up. Why should he mind so long as she was happy? She had not lived for nearly nineteen years without knowing that her future was all he really cared about. She had, then, only to convince him that her future could not be happy without Jon. He thought it a mad fancy. How foolish the old were, thinking they could tell what the young felt! Had not he confessed that he – when young – had loved with a grand passion? He ought to understand! 'He piles up his money for me,' she thought; 'but what's the use, if I'm not going to be happy?' Money, and all it bought, did not bring happiness. Love only brought that. The ox-eyed daisies in this orchard, which gave it such a moony look sometimes, grew wild and happy, and had their hour. 'They oughtn't to have called me

Fleur,' she mused, 'if they didn't mean me to have my hour, and be happy while it lasts.' Nothing real stood in the way, like poverty, or disease – sentiment only, a ghost from the unhappy past! Jon was right. They wouldn't let you live, these old people! They made mistakes, committed crimes, and wanted their children to go on paying! The breeze died away; midges began to bite. She got up, plucked a piece of honey-suckle, and went in.

It was hot that night. Both she and her mother had put on thin, pale low frocks. The dinner flowers were pale. Fleur was struck with the pale look of everything; her father's face, her mother's shoulders; the pale panelled walls, the pale grey velvety carpet, the lamp-shade, even the soup was pale. There was not one spot of colour in the room, not even wine in the pale glasses, for no one drank it. What was not pale was black – her father's clothes, the butler's clothes, her retriever stretched out exhausted in the window, the curtains black with a cream pattern. A moth came in, and that was pale. And silent was that half-mourning dinner in the heat.

Her father called her back as she was following her mother out.

She sat down beside him at the table, and, unpinning the pale honeysuckle, put it to her nose.

'I've been thinking,' he said.

'Yes, dear?'

'It's extremely painful for me to talk, but there's no help for it. I don't know if you understand how much you are to me I've never spoken of it, I didn't think it necessary; but – but you're everything. Your mother—' he paused, staring at his finger-bowl of Venetian glass.

'Yes?'

'I've only you to look to. I've never had – never wanted anything else, since you were born.'

'I know,' Fleur murmured.

Soames moistened his lips.

'You may think this a matter I can smooth over and arrange for you. You're mistaken. I'm helpless.'

Fleur did not speak.

'Quite apart from my own feelings,' went on Soames with more resolution, 'those two are not amenable to anything I can say. They – they hate me, as people always hate those whom they have injured.'

'But he – Jon—'

'He's their flesh and blood, her only child. Probably he means to her what you mean to me. It's a deadlock.'

'No,' cried Fleur, 'no, Father!'

Soames leaned back, the image of pale patience, as if resolved on the betrayal of no emotion.

'Listen!' he said. 'You're putting the feelings of two months – two months – against the feelings of thirty-five years! What chance do you think you have? Two months – your very first love affair, a matter of half a dozen meetings, a few walks and talks, a few kisses – against, against what you can't imagine, what no one could who hasn't been through it. Come, be reasonable, Fleur! It's midsummer madness!'

Fleur tore the honeysuckle into little, slow bits.

'The madness is in letting the past spoil it all. What do we care about the past? It's our lives, not yours.'

Soames raised his hand to his forehead, where suddenly she saw moisture shining.

'Whose child are you?' he said. 'Whose child is he? The present is linked with the past, the future with both. There's no getting away from that.'

She had never heard philosophy pass those lips before. Impressed even in her agitation, she leaned her elbows on the table, her chin on her hands.

'But, Father, consider it practically. We want each other. There's ever so much money, and nothing whatever in the way but sentiment. Let's bury the past, Father.'

His answer was a sigh.

'Besides,' said Fleur gently, 'you can't prevent us.'

'I don't suppose,' said Soames, 'that if left to myself I should try to prevent you; I must put up with things, I know, to keep your affection. But it's not I who control this matter. That's what I want you to realise before it's too late. If you go on thinking you can get your way and encourage this feeling, the blow will be much heavier when you find you can't.'

'Oh!' cried Fleur, 'help me, Father; you can help me, you know.'

Soames made a startled movement of negation. 'I?' he said bitterly. 'Help? I am the impediment – the just cause and impediment – isn't that the jargon? You have my blood in your veins.'

He rose.

'Well, the fat's in the fire. If you persist in your wilfulness you'll have yourself to blame. Come! Don't be foolish, my child – my only child!'

Fleur laid her forehead against his shoulder.

All was in such turmoil within her. But no good to show it! No good at all! She broke away from him, and went out into the twilight, distraught, but unconvinced. All was indeterminate and vague within her, like the shapes and shadows in the garden, except – her will to have. A poplar pierced up into the dark-blue sky and touched a white star there. The dew wetted her shoes, and chilled her bare shoulders. She went down to the river bank, and stood gazing at a moonstreak on the darkening water. Suddenly she smelled tobacco smoke, and a white figure emerged as if created by the moon. It was young Mont in flannels, standing in his boat. She heard the tiny hiss of his cigarette extinguished in the water.

'Fleur,' came his voice, 'don't be hard on a poor devil! I've been waiting hours.'

'For what?'

'Come in my boat!'

'Not I.'

'Why not?'

'I'm not a water-nymph.'

'Haven't you *any* romance in you? Don't be modern, Fleur!' He appeared on the path within a yard of her.

'Go away!'

'Fleur, I love you. Fleur!'

Fleur uttered a short laugh.

'Come again,' she said, 'when I haven't got my wish.'

'What is your wish?'

'Ask another.'

'Fleur,' said Mont, and his voice sounded strange, 'don't mock me! Even vivisected dogs are worth decent treatment before they're cut up for good.'

Fleur shook her head; but her lips were trembling.

'Well, you shouldn't make me jump. Give me a cigarette.'

Mont gave her one, lighted it, and another for himself.

'I don't want to talk rot,' he said, 'but please imagine all the rot that all the lovers that ever were have talked, and all my special rot thrown in.'

'Thank you, I have imagined it. Good-night!' They stood for a moment facing each other in the shadow of an acacia-tree with very moonlit blossoms, and the smoke from their cigarettes mingled in the air between them.

'Also ran: "Michael Mont"?' he said. Fleur turned abruptly toward the house. On the lawn she stopped to look back. Michael Mont was whirling his arms above him; she could see them dashing at his head; then waving at the moonlit blossoms of the acacia. His voice just reached her. 'Jolly-jolly!' Fleur shook herself. She couldn't help him, she had too much trouble of her own! On the verandah she stopped very suddenly again. Her mother was sitting in the drawing-room at her writing bureau, quite alone. There was nothing remarkable in the expression of her face except its utter immobility. But she looked desolate! Fleur went upstairs. At the door of her room she paused. She could hear her father walking up and down, up and down the picture-gallery.

'Yes,' she thought, 'jolly! Oh, Jon!'

Chapter Ten

Decision

*W*hen Fleur left him Jon stared at the Austrian. She was a thin woman with a dark face and the concerned expression of one who has watched every little good that life once had slip from her, one by one. 'No tea?' she said.

Susceptible to the disappointment in her voice, Jon murmured:

'No, really; thanks.'

'A lil cup – it ready. A lil cup and cigarette.'

Fleur was gone! Hours of remorse and indecision lay before him! And with a heavy sense of disproportion he smiled, and said:

'Well – thank you!'

She brought in a little pot of tea with two little cups, and a silver box of cigarettes on a little tray.

'Sugar? Miss Forsyte has much sugar – she buy my sugar, my friend's sugar also. Miss Forsyte is a veree kind lady. I am happy to serve her. You her brother?'

'Yes,' said Jon, beginning to puff the second cigarette of his life.

'Very young brother,' said the Austrian, with a little anxious smile, which reminded him of the wag of a dog's tail.

'May I give you some?' he said. 'And won't you sit down, please?'

The Austrian shook her head.

'Your father a very nice old man – the most nice old man
I ever see. Miss Forsyte tell me all about him. Is he better?'

Her words fell on Jon like a reproach. 'Oh! Yes, I think
he's all right.'

'I like to see him again,' said the Austrian, putting a hand
on her heart; 'he have veree kind heart.'

'Yes,' said Jon. And again her words seemed to him a
reproach.

'He never give no trouble to no one, and smile so gentle.'

'Yes, doesn't he?'

'He look at Miss Forsyte so funny sometimes. I tell him all
my story; he so *sympátisch*. Your mother – she nice and well?'

'Yes, very.'

'He have her photograph on his dressing-table. Veree beautiful.'

Jon gulped down his tea. This woman, with her concerned
face and her reminding words, was like the first and second
murderers.

'Thank you,' he said; 'I must go now. May – may I leave
this with you?'

He put a ten-shilling note on the tray with a doubting hand
and gained the door. He heard the Austrian gasp, and hurried
out. He had just time to catch his train, and all the way to
Victoria looked at every face that passed, as lovers will, hoping
against hope. On reaching Worthing he put his luggage into
the local train, and set out across the Downs for Wansdon,
trying to walk off his aching irresolution. So long as he went
full bat, he could enjoy the beauty of those green slopes, stopping now and again to sprawl on the grass, admire the perfection of a wild rose or listen to a lark's song. But the war of
motives within him was but postponed – the longing for Fleur,
and the hatred of deception. He came to the old chalk-pit
above Wansdon with his mind no more made up than when
he started. To see both sides of a question vigorously was at
once Jon's strength and weakness. He tramped in, just as the

first dinner-bell rang. His things had already been brought up. He had a hurried bath and came down to find Holly alone – Val had gone to Town and would not be back till the last train.

Since Val's advice to him to ask his sister what was the matter between the two families, so much had happened – Fleur's disclosure in the Green Park, her visit to Robin Hill, to-day's meeting – that there seemed nothing to ask. He talked of Spain, his sunstroke, Val's horses, their father's health. Holly startled him by saying that she thought their father not at all well. She had been twice to Robin Hill for the week-end. He had seemed fearfully languid, sometimes even in pain, but had always refused to talk about himself.

'He's awfully dear and unselfish – don't you think, Jon?'

Feeling far from dear and unselfish himself, Jon answered: 'Rather!'

'I think, he's been a simply perfect father, so long as I can remember.'

'Yes,' answered Jon, very subdued.

'He's never interfered, and he's always seemed to understand. I shall never forget his letting me go to South Africa in the Boer War when I was in love with Val.'

'That was before he married Mother, wasn't it?' said Jon suddenly.

'Yes. Why?'

'Oh! Nothing. Only, wasn't she engaged to Fleur's father first?'

Holly put down the spoon she was using, and raised her eyes. Her stare was circumspect. What did the boy know? Enough to make it better to tell him? She could not decide. He looked strained and worried, altogether older, but that might be the sunstroke.

'There *was* something,' she said. 'Of course we were out there, and got no news of anything.' She could not take the risk.

It was not her secret. Besides, she was in the dark about his feelings now. Before Spain she had made sure he was in love; but boys were boys; that was seven weeks ago, and all Spain between.

She saw that he knew she was putting him off, and added: 'Have you heard anything of Fleur?'

'Yes.'

His face told her, then, more than the most elaborate explanations. So he had not forgotten!

She said very quietly: 'Fleur is awfully attractive, Jon, but you know – Val and I don't really like her very much.'

'Why?'

'We think she's got rather a "having" nature.'

'"Having"? I don't know what you mean. She – she—' he pushed his dessert plate away, got up, and went to the window.

Holly, too, got up, and put her arm round his waist.

'Don't be angry, Jon dear. We can't all see people in the same light, can we? You know, I believe each of us only has about one or two people who can see the best that's in us, and bring it out. For you I think it's your mother. I once saw her looking at a letter of yours; it was wonderful to see her face. I think she's the most beautiful woman I ever saw – Age doesn't seem to touch her.'

Jon's face softened; then again became tense. Everybody – everybody was against him and Fleur! It all strengthened the appeal of her words: 'Make sure of me – marry me, Jon!'

Here, where he had passed that wonderful week with her – the tug of her enchantment, the ache in his heart increased with every minute that she was not there to make the room, the garden, the very air magical. Would he ever be able to live down here, not seeing her? And he closed up utterly, going early to bed. It would not make him healthy, wealthy, and wise, but it closeted him with memory of Fleur in her fancy frock. He heard Val's arrival – the Ford discharging cargo, then the stillness of the summer night stole back – with only the bleating of very distant sheep, and a night-jar's harsh purring. He leaned far out. Cold moon – warm air – the Downs like silver! Small wings, a stream bubbling, the rambler roses! God – how empty all of it without her! In the Bible it was written: Thou shall leave father and mother and cleave to – Fleur!

Let him have pluck, and go and tell them! They couldn't stop him marrying her – they wouldn't want to stop him when they knew how he felt. Yes! He would go! Bold and open – Fleur was wrong!

The night-jar ceased, the sheep were silent; the only sound in the darkness was the bubbling of the stream. And Jon in his bed slept, freed from the worst of life's evils – indecision.

Chapter Eleven

Timothy Prophesies

*O*n the day of the cancelled meeting at the National Gallery began the second anniversary of the resurrection of England's pride and glory – or, more shortly, the top hat. 'Lord's' – that festival which the War had driven from the field – raised its light and dark blue flags for the second time, displaying almost every feature of a glorious past. Here, in the luncheon interval, were all species of female and one species of male hat, protecting the multiple types of face associated with 'the classes'. The observing Forsyte might discern in the free or unconsidered seats a certain number of the squash-hatted, but they hardly ventured on the grass; the old school – or schools – could still rejoice that the proletariat was not yet paying the necessary half-crown. Here was still a close borough, the only one left on a large scale – for the papers were about to estimate the attendance at ten thousand. And the ten thousand, all animated by one hope, were asking each other one question: 'Where are you lunching?' Something wonderfully uplifting and reassuring in that query and the sight of so many people like themselves voicing it! What reserve power in the British realm – enough pigeons, lobsters, lamb, salmon mayonnaise, strawberries, and bottles of champagne to feed the lot! No miracle in prospect – no case of seven loaves and a few fishes – faith rested on surer foundations. Six thousand top hats, four thousand parasols would be doffed and furled, ten thousand mouths all speaking the same English would be filled. There was life in the old dog yet! Tradition! And again Tradition! How strong and how elastic! Wars might rage, taxation prey, Trades Unions take toll, and Europe perish of starvation; but the ten thousand would be fed; and, within their ring fence, stroll upon green turf, wear their top hats, and meet – themselves. The heart was sound, the pulse still regular. E-ton! E-ton! Har-r-o-o-o-w!

Among the many Forsytes present on a hunting-ground theirs, by personal prescriptive right, or proxy, was Soames with his wife and daughter. He had not been at either school, he took no interest in cricket, but he wanted Fleur to show her frock, and he wanted to wear his top hat – parade it again in peace and plenty among his peers. He walked sedately with Fleur between him and Annette. No women equalled them, so far as he could see. They could walk, and hold themselves up; there was substance in their good looks; the modern woman had no build, no chest, no anything! He remembered suddenly with what intoxication of pride he had walked round with Irene in the first years of his first marriage. And how they used to lunch on the drag which his mother *would* make his father have, because it was so 'chic' – all drags and carriages in those days, not these lumbering great Stands! And how consistently Montague Dartie had drunk too much. He supposed that people drank too much still, but there was not the scope for it there used to be. He remembered George Forsyte – whose brothers Roger and Eustace had been at Harrow and Eton – towering up on the top of the drag waving a light-blue flag with one hand and a dark-blue flag with the other, and shouting 'Etroow – Harrton!' Just when everybody was silent, like the buffoon he had always been; and Eustace got up to the nines below, too dandified to wear any colour or take any notice. H'm! Old days, and Irene in grey silk shot with palest green. He looked, sideways, at Fleur's face. Rather

colourless – no light, no eagerness! That love affair was preying
on her – a bad business! He looked beyond, at his wife's face,
rather more touched up than usual, a little disdainful – not
that she had any business to disdain, so far as he could see.
She was taking Profond's defection with curious quietude; or
was his 'small' voyage just a blind? If so, he should refuse to
see it! Having promenaded round the pitch and in front of
the pavilion, they sought Winifred's table in the Bedouin Club
tent. This Club – a new 'cock and hen' – had been founded
in the interests of travel, and of a gentleman with an old
Scottish name, whose father had somewhat strangely been
called Levi. Winifred had joined, not because she had travelled, but because instinct told her that a Club with such a
name and such a founder was bound to go far; if one didn't
join at once one might never have the chance. Its tent, with a
text from the Koran on an orange ground, and a small green
camel embroidered over the entrance, was the most striking
on the ground. Outside it they found Jack Cardigan in a dark
blue tie (he had once played for Harrow), batting with a
Malacca cane to show how that fellow ought to have hit that
ball. He piloted them in. Assembled in Winifred's corner were
Imogen, Benedict with his young wife, Val Dartie without
Holly, Maud and her husband, and, after Soames and his two
were seated, one empty place.

'I'm expecting Prosper,' said Winifred, 'but he's so busy
with his yacht.'

Soames stole a glance. No movement in his wife's face!
Whether that fellow were coming or not, she evidently knew
all about it. It did not escape him that Fleur, too, looked at
her mother. If Annette didn't respect his feelings, she might
think of Fleur's! The conversation, very desultory, was synco-
pated by Jack Cardigan talking about 'mid-off'. He cited all
the 'great mid-offs' from the beginning of time, as if they
had been a definite racial entity in the composition of the
British people. Soames had finished his lobster, and was

beginning on pigeon-pie, when he heard the words, 'I'm a small bit late, Mrs Dartie,' and saw that there was no longer any empty place. *That fellow* was sitting between Annette and Imogen. Soames ate steadily on, with an occasional word to Maud and Winifred. Conversation buzzed around him. He heard the voice of Profond say:

'I think you're mistaken, Mrs Forsyde; I'll – I'll bet Miss Forsyde agrees with me.'

'In what?' came Fleur's clear voice across the table.

'I was sayin', young gurls are much the same as they always were – there's very small difference.'

'Do you know so much about them?'

That sharp reply caught the ears of all, and Soames moved uneasily on his thin green chair.

'Well, I don't know, I think they want their own small way, and I think they always did.'

'Indeed!'

'Oh, but – Prosper,' Winifred interjected comfortably, 'the girls in the streets – the girls who've been in munitions, the little flappers in the shops; their manners now really quite hit you in the eye.'

At the word 'hit' Jack Cardigan stopped his disquisition; and in the silence Monsieur Profond said:

'It was inside before, now it's outside; that's all.'

'But their morals!' cried Imogen.

'Just as moral as they ever were, Mrs Cardigan, but they've got more opportunity.'

The saying, so cryptically cynical, received a little laugh from Imogen, a slight opening of Jack Cardigan's mouth, and a creak from Soames's chair.

Winifred said: 'That's too bad, Prosper.'

'What do you say, Mrs Forsyde; don't you think human nature's always the same?'

Soames subdued a sudden longing to get up and kick the fellow. He heard his wife reply:

'Human nature is not the same in England as anywhere else.' That was her confounded mockery!

'Well, I don't know much about this small country' – 'No, thank God!' thought Soames – 'but I should say the pot was boilin' under the lid everywhere. We all want pleasure, and we always did.'

Damn the fellow! His cynicism was – was outrageous!

When lunch was over they broke up into couples for the digestive promenade. Too proud to notice, Soames knew perfectly that Annette and that fellow had gone prowling round together. Fleur was with Val; she had chosen him, no doubt, because he knew that boy. He himself had Winifred for partner. They walked in the bright, circling stream, a little flushed and sated, for some minutes, till Winifred sighed:

'I wish we were back forty years, old boy!'

Before the eyes of her spirit an interminable procession of her own 'Lord's' frocks was passing, paid for with the money of her father, to save a recurrent crisis. 'It's been very amusing, after all. Sometimes I even wish Monty was back. What do you think of people nowadays, Soames?'

'Precious little style. The thing began to go to pieces with bicycles and motor-cars; the War has finished it.'

'I wonder what's coming?' said Winifred in a voice dreamy from pigeon-pie. 'I'm not at all sure we shan't go back to crinolines and pegtops. Look at that dress!'

Soames shook his head.

'There's money, but no faith in things. We don't lay by for the future. These youngsters – it's all a short life and a merry one with them.'

'There's a hat!' said Winifred. 'I don't know – when you come to think of the people killed and all that in the War, it's rather wonderful, I think. There's no other country – Prosper says the rest are all bankrupt, except America; and of course her men always took their style in dress from us.'

'Is that chap,' said Soames, 'really going to the South Seas?'

'Oh! one never knows where Prosper's going!'

'*He's* a sign of the times,' muttered Soames, 'if you like.'

Winifred's hand gripped his arm.

'Don't turn your head,' she said in a low voice, 'but look to your right in the front row of the Stand.'

Soames looked as best he could under that limitation. A man in a grey top hat, grey-bearded, with thin brown, folded cheeks, and a certain elegance of posture, sat there with a woman in a lawn-coloured frock, whose dark eyes were fixed on himself. Soames looked quickly at his feet. How funnily feet moved, one after the other like that! Winifred's voice said in his ear:

'Jolyon looks very ill; but he always had style. She doesn't change – except her hair.'

'Why did you tell Fleur about that business?'

'I didn't; she picked it up. I always knew she would.'

'Well, it's a mess. She's set her heart upon their boy.'

'The little wretch,' murmured Winifred. 'She tried to take me in about that. What shall you do, Soames?'

'Be guided by events.'

They moved on, silent, in the almost solid crowd.

'Really,' said Winifred suddenly; 'it almost seems like Fate. Only that's so old-fashioned. Look! there are George and Eustace!'

George Forsyte's lofty bulk had halted before them.

'Hallo, Soames!' he said. 'Just met Profond and your wife. You'll catch 'em if you put on pace. Did you ever go to see old Timothy?'

Soames nodded, and the streams forced them apart.

'I always liked old George,' said Winifred. 'He's so droll.'

'I never did,' said Soames. 'Where's your seat? I shall go to mine. Fleur may be back there.'

Having seen Winifred to her seat, he regained his own,

conscious of small, white, distant figures running, the click of the bat, the cheers and counter-cheers. No Fleur, and no Annette! You could expect nothing of women nowadays! They had the vote. They were 'emancipated', and much good it was doing them! So Winifred would go back, would she, and put up with Dartie all over again? To have the past once more – to be sitting here as he had sat in '83 and '84, before he was certain that his marriage with Irene had gone all wrong, before her antagonism had become so glaring that with the best will in the world he could not overlook it. The sight of her with that fellow had brought all memory back. Even now he could not understand why she had been so impracticable. She could love other men; she had it in her! To himself, the one person she ought to have loved, she had chosen to refuse her heart. It seemed to him, fantastically, as he looked back, that all this modern relaxation of marriage – though its forms and laws were the same as when he married her – that all this modern looseness had come out of her revolt; it seemed to him, fantastically, that she had started it, till all decent ownership of anything had gone, or was on the point of going. All came from her! And now – a pretty state of things! Homes! How could you have them without mutual ownership? Not that he had ever had a real home! But had that been his fault? He had done his best. And his rewards were – those two sitting in that Stand, and this affair of Fleur's!

And overcome by loneliness he thought: 'Shan't wait any longer! They must find their own way back to the hotel – if they mean to come!' Hailing a cab outside the ground, he said:

'Drive me to the Bayswater Road.' His old aunts had never failed him. To them he had meant an ever-welcome visitor. Though they were gone, there, still, was Timothy!

Smither was standing in the open doorway.

'Mr Soames! I was just taking the air. Cook will be so pleased.'

'How is Mr Timothy?'

'Not himself at all these last few days, sir; he's been talking a great deal. Only this morning he was saying: 'My brother James, he's getting old.' His mind wanders, Mr Soames, and then he will talk of them. He troubles about their investments. The other day he said: 'There's my brother Jolyon won't look at Consols' – he seemed quite down about it. Come in, Mr Soames, come in! It's such a pleasant change!'

'Well,' said Soames, 'just for a few minutes.'

'No,' murmured Smither in the hall, where the air had the singular freshness of the outside day, 'we haven't been very satisfied with him, not all this week. He's always been one to leave a titbit to the end; but ever since Monday he's been eating it first. If you notice a dog, Mr Soames, at its dinner, it eats the meat first. We've always thought it such a good sign of Mr Timothy at his age to leave it to the last, but now he seems to have lost all his self-control; and, of course, it makes him leave the rest. The doctor doesn't make anything of it, but' – Smither shook her head – 'he seems to think he's got to eat it first, in case he shouldn't get to it. That and his talking makes us anxious.'

'Has he said anything important?'

'I shouldn't like to say that, Mr Soames; but he's turned against his will. He gets quite pettish – and after having had it out every morning for years, it does seem funny. He said the other day: "They want my money." It gave me such a turn, because, as I said to him, nobody wants his money, I'm sure. And it does seem a pity he should be thinking about money at his time of life. I took my courage in my 'ands. "You know, Mr Timothy," I said, "my dear mistress" – that's Miss Forsyte, Mr Soames, Miss Ann that trained me – "*she* never thought about money," I said, "it was all *character* with her." He looked at me, I can't tell you how funny, and he said quite dry: "Nobody wants my character." Think of his saying a thing like that! But sometimes he'll say something as sharp and sensible as anything.'

Soames, who had been staring at an old print by the hat-rack, thinking, 'That's got value!' murmured: 'I'll go up and see him, Smither.'

'Cook's with him,' answered Smither above her corsets; 'she will be pleased to see you.'

He mounted slowly, with the thought: 'Shan't care to live to be that age.'

On the second floor, he paused, and tapped. The door was opened, and he saw the round homely face of a woman about sixty.

'Mr Soames!' she said: 'Why! Mr Soames!'

Soames nodded. 'All right, Cook!' and entered.

Timothy was propped up in bed, with his hands joined before his chest, and his eyes fixed on the ceiling, where a fly was standing upside down. Soames stood at the foot of the bed, facing him.

'Uncle Timothy,' he said, raising his voice. 'Uncle Timothy!'

Timothy's eyes left the fly, and levelled themselves on his visitor. Soames could see his pale tongue passing over his darkish lips.

'Uncle Timothy,' he said again, 'is there anything I can do for you? Is there anything you'd like to say?'

'Ha!' said Timothy.

'I've come to look you up and see that everything's all right.'

Timothy nodded. He seemed trying to get used to the apparition before him.

'Have you got everything you want?'

'No,' said Timothy.

'Can I get you anything?'

'No,' said Timothy.

'I'm Soames, you know; your nephew, Soames Forsyte. Your brother James's son.'

Timothy nodded.

'I shall be delighted to do anything I can for you.'

Timothy beckoned. Soames went close to him:

'You—' said Timothy in a voice which seemed to have outlived tone, 'you tell them all from me – you tell them all—' and his finger tapped on Soames's arm, 'to hold on – hold on – Consols are goin' up,' and he nodded thrice.

'All right!' said Soames; 'I will.'

'Yes,' said Timothy, and, fixing his eyes again on the ceiling, he added: 'That fly!'

Strangely moved, Soames looked at the Cook's pleasant fattish face, all little puckers from staring at fires.

'That'll do him a world of good, sir,' she said.

A mutter came from Timothy, but he was clearly speaking to himself, and Soames went out with the cook.

'I wish I could make you a pink cream, Mr Soames, like in old days; you did so relish them. Good-bye, sir; it *has* been a pleasure.'

'Take care of him, Cook, he *is* old.'

And, shaking her crumpled hand, he went downstairs. Smither was still taking the air in the doorway.

'What do you think of him, Mr Soames?'

'H'm!' Soames murmured: 'He's lost touch.'

'Yes,' said Smither, 'I was afraid you'd think that coming fresh out of the world to see him like.'

'Smither,' said Soames, 'we're all indebted to you.'

'Oh, no, Mr Soames, don't say that! It's a pleasure – he's such a wonderful man.'

'Well, good-bye!' said Soames, and got into his taxi.

'Going up!' he thought; 'going up!'

Reaching the hotel at Knightsbridge he went to their sitting-room, and rang for tea. Neither of them were in. And again that sense of loneliness came over him. These hotels. What monstrous great places they were now! He could remember when there was nothing bigger than Long's or Brown's, Morley's or the Tavistock, and the heads that were

shaken over the Langham and the Grand. Hotels and Clubs
– Clubs and Hotels; no end to them now! And Soames, who
had just been watching at Lord's a miracle of tradition and
continuity, fell into reverie over the changes in that London
where he had been born five-and-sixty years before. Whether
Consols were going up or not, London had become a terrific
property. No such property in the world, unless it were New
York! There was a lot of hysteria in the papers nowadays;
but anyone who, like himself, could remember London sixty
years ago, and see it now, realised the fecundity and elas-
ticity of wealth. They had only to keep their heads, and go
at it steadily. Why! he remembered cobblestones, and stinking
straw on the floor of your cab. And old Timothy – what
could *he* not have told them, if he had kept his memory!
Things were unsettled, people in a funk or in a hurry, but
here were London and the Thames, and out there the British
Empire, and the ends of the earth. 'Consols are goin' up!'
He shouldn't be a bit surprised. It was the breed that counted.
And all that was bull-dogged in Soames stared for a moment
out of his grey eyes, till diverted by the print of a Victorian
picture on the walls. The hotel had bought three dozen of
that little lot! The old hunting or *Rake's Progress* prints in
the old inns were worth looking at – but this sentimental
stuff – well, Victorianism had gone! 'Tell them to hold on!'
old Timothy had said. But to what were they to hold on in
this modern welter of the 'democratic principle'? Why, even
privacy was threatened! And at the thought that privacy
might perish, Soames pushed back his teacup and went to
the window. Fancy owning no more of Nature than the crowd
out there owned of the flowers and trees and waters of Hyde
Park! No, no! Private possession underlay everything worth
having. The world had slipped its sanity a bit, as dogs now
and again at full moon slipped theirs and went off for a
night's rabbiting; but the world, like the dog, knew where
its bread was buttered and its bed warm, and would come

back sure enough to the only home worth having – to private ownership. The world was in its second childhood for the moment, like old Timothy – eating its titbit first!

He heard a sound behind him, and saw that his wife and daughter had come in.

'So you're back!' he said.

Fleur did not answer; she stood for a moment looking at him and her mother, then passed into her bedroom. Annette poured herself out a cup of tea.

'I am going to Paris, to my mother, Soames.'

'Oh! To your mother?'

'Yes.'

'For how long?'

'I do not know.'

'And when are you going?'

'On Monday.'

Was she really going to her mother? Odd, how indifferent he felt! Odd, how clearly she had perceived the indifference he would feel so long as there was no scandal. And suddenly between her and himself he saw distinctly the face he had seen that afternoon – Irene's.

'Will you want money?'

'Thank you; I have enough.'

'Very well. Let us know when you are coming back.'

Annette put down the cake she was fingering, and, looking up through darkened lashes, said:

'Shall I give *Maman* any message?'

'My regards.'

Annette stretched herself, her hands on her waist, and said in French:

'What luck that you have never loved me, Soames!' Then rising, she too left the room. Soames was glad she had spoken it in French – it seemed to require no dealing with. Again that other face – pale, dark-eyed, beautiful still! And there stirred far down within him the ghost of warmth, as from sparks lingering beneath a mound of flaky ash. And Fleur infatuated with *her* boy! Queer chance! Yet, was there such a thing as chance? A man went down a street, a brick fell on his head. Ah! that was chance, no doubt. But this! 'Inherited,' his girl had said. She – she was 'holding on'!

Part III

Chapter One

Old Jolyon Walks

wofold impulse had made Jolyon say to his wife at breakfast: 'Let's go up to Lord's!'

'Wanted' – something to abate the anxiety in which those two had lived during the sixty hours since Jon had brought Fleur down. 'Wanted' – too, that which might assuage the pangs of memory in one who knew he might lose them any day!

Fifty-eight years ago Jolyon had become an Eton boy, for old Jolyon's whim had been that he should be canonised at the greatest possible expense. Year after year he had gone to Lord's from Stanhope Gate with a father whose youth in the eighteen-twenties had been passed without polish in the game of cricket. Old Jolyon would speak quite openly of swipes, full tosses, half and three-quarter balls; and young Jolyon with the guileless snobbery of youth had trembled lest his sire should be overheard. Only in this supreme matter of cricket he had been nervous, for his father – in Crimean whiskers then – had ever impressed him as the beau idéal. Though never canonised himself, old Jolyon's natural fastidiousness and balance had saved him from the errors of the vulgar. How delicious, after howling in a top hat and a sweltering heat, to go home with his father in a hansom cab, bathe, dress, and forth to the 'Disunion' Club, to dine off whitebait, cutlets, and a tart, and go – two 'swells', old and young, in lavender kid gloves – to the opera or play. And on Sunday, when the match was over, and his top hat duly broken, down with his father in a special hansom to the 'Crown and Sceptre', and the terrace above the river – the golden sixties when the world was simple, dandies glamorous, Democracy not born, and the books of Whyte Melville coming thick and fast.

A generation later, with his own boy, Jolly, Harrowbuttonholed with corn-flowers – by old Jolyon's whim his grandson had been canonised at a trifle less expense – again Jolyon had experienced the heat and counter-passions of the day, and come back to the cool and the strawberry beds of Robin Hill, and billiards after dinner, his boy making the most heart-breaking flukes and trying to seem languid and grown-up. Those two days each year he and his son had been alone together in the world, one on each side – and Democracy just born!

And so, he had unearthed a grey top hat, borrowed a tiny bit of light-blue ribbon from Irene, and gingerly, keeping cool, by car and train and taxi, had reached Lord's Ground. There, beside her in a lawn-coloured frock with narrow black edges, he had watched the game, and felt the old thrill stir within him.

When Soames passed, the day was spoiled. Irene's face was distorted by compression of the lips. No good to go on sitting here with Soames or perhaps his daughter recurring in front of them, like decimals. And he said:

'Well, dear, if you've had enough – let's go!'

That evening Jolyon felt exhausted. Not wanting her to see him thus, he waited till she had begun to play, and stole off to the little study. He opened the long window for air, and the door, that he might still hear her music drifting in; and, settled in his father's old armchair, closed his eyes, with his head against the worn brown leather. Like that passage of the César Franck sonata – so had been his life with her, a divine third movement. And now this business of Jon's – this bad business! Drifted to the edge of consciousness, he hardly knew if it were in sleep that he smelled the scent of a cigar, and seemed to see his father in the blackness before his closed eyes. That shape formed, went, and formed again; as if in the very chair where he himself was sitting, he saw his father, black-coated, with knees crossed, glasses balanced between thumb and finger; saw the big white moustaches, and the deep eyes looking up below a dome of forehead and seeming to search his own, seeming to speak. 'Are you facing it, Jo? It's for you to decide. She's only a woman!' Ah! how well he knew his father in that phrase; how all the Victorian Age came up with it! And his answer 'No, I've funked it – funked hurting her and Jon and myself. I've got a heart; I've funked it.' But the old eyes, so much older, so much younger than his own, kept at it; 'It's your wife, your son; your past. Tackle it, my boy!' Was it a message from a walking spirit; or but the instinct of his sire living on within him? And again came that scent of cigar smoke – from the old saturated leather. Well! he would tackle it, write to Jon, and put the whole thing down in black and white! And suddenly he breathed with difficulty, with a sense of suffocation, as if his heart were swollen. He got up and went out into the air. The stars were very bright. He passed along the terrace round the corner of the house, till, through the window of the music-room, he could see Irene at the piano, with lamp-light falling on her powdery hair; withdrawn into herself she seemed, her dark eyes staring straight before her, her hands idle. Jolyon saw her raise those hands and clasp them over her breast. 'It's Jon, with her,' he thought; 'all Jon! I'm dying out of her – it's natural!'

And, careful not to be seen, he stole back.

Next day, after a bad night, he sat down to his task. He wrote with difficulty and many erasures.

My Dearest Boy,
You are old enough to understand how very
difficult it is for elders to give themselves away to
their young. Especially when – like your mother and
myself, though I shall never think of her as anything
but young – their hearts are altogether set on him to
whom they must confess. I cannot say we are
conscious of having sinned exactly – people in real life
very seldom are, I believe – but most persons would
say we had, and at all events our conduct, righteous
or not, has found us out. The truth is, my dear, we
both have pasts, which it is now my task to make
known to you, because they so grievously and deeply
affect your future. Many, very many years ago, as far
back indeed as 1883, when she was only twenty, your
mother had the great and lasting misfortune to make
an unhappy marriage – no, not with me, Jon. Without
money of her own, and with only a stepmother –
closely related to Jezebel – she was very unhappy in
her home life. It was Fleur's father that she married,
my cousin Soames Forsyte. He had pursued her very
tenaciously and to do him justice was deeply in love
with her. Within a week she knew the fearful mistake
she had made. It was not his fault; it was her error of
judgment – her misfortune.

So far Jolyon had kept some semblance of irony, but now
his subject carried him away.

Jon, I want to explain to you if I can – and it's
very hard – how it is that an unhappy marriage such
as this can so easily come about. You will of course
say: 'If she didn't really love him how could she ever
have married him?' You would be right if it were
not for one or two rather terrible considerations.
From this initial mistake of hers all the subsequent

trouble, sorrow, and tragedy have come, and so I must make it clear to you if I can. You see, Jon, in those days and even to this day – indeed, I don't see, for all the talk of enlightenment, how it can well be otherwise – most girls are married ignorant of the sexual side of life. Even if they know what it means they have not *experienced* it. That's the crux. It is this actual lack of experience, whatever verbal knowledge they have, which makes all the difference and all the trouble. In a vast number of marriages – and your mother's was one – girls are not and cannot be certain whether they love the man they marry or not; they do not know until after that act of union which makes the reality of marriage. Now, in many, perhaps in most doubtful cases, this act cements and strengthens the attachment, but in other cases, and your mother's was one, it is a revelation of mistakes, a destruction of such attraction as there was. There is nothing more tragic in a woman's life than such a revelation, growing daily, nightly clearer. Coarse-grained and unthinking people are apt to laugh at such a mistake, and say, 'What a fuss about nothing!' Narrow and self-righteous people, only capable of judging the lives of others by their own, are apt to condemn those who make this tragic error, to condemn them for life to the dungeons they have made for themselves. You know the expression: 'She has made her bed, she must lie on it!' It is a hard-mouthed saying, quite unworthy of a gentleman or lady in the best sense of those words; and I can use no stronger condemnation. I have not been what is called a moral man, but I wish to use no words to you, my dear, which will make you think lightly of ties or contracts into which you enter. Heaven forbid! But with the experience of a life behind me I

do say that those who condemn the victims of these
tragic mistakes, condemn them and hold out no
hands to help them, are inhuman, or rather they
would be if they had the understanding to know
what they are doing. But they haven't! Let them go!
They are as much anathema to me as I, no doubt,
am to them. I have had to say all this, because I am
going to put you into a position to judge your
mother, and you are very young, without experience
of what life is. To go on with the story. After three
years of effort to subdue her shrinking – I was going
to say her loathing and it's not too strong a word,
for shrinking soon becomes loathing under such
circumstances – three years of what to a sensitive,
beauty-loving nature like your mother's, Jon, was
torment, she met a young man who fell in love with
her. He was the architect of this very house that we
live in now, he was building it for her and Fleur's
father to live in, a new prison to hold her, in place
of the one she inhabited with him in London.
Perhaps that fact played some part in what came of
it. But in any case she, too, fell in love with him. I
know it's not necessary to explain to you that one
does not precisely choose with whom one will fall in
love. It comes. Very well! It came. I can imagine –
though she never said much to me about it – the
struggle that then took place in her, because, Jon,
she was brought up strictly and was not light in her
ideas – not at all. However, this was an overwhelming feeling, and it came to pass that they
loved in deed as well as in thought. Then came a
fearful tragedy. I must tell you of it because if I
don't you will never understand the real situation
that you have now to face. The man whom she had
married – Soames Forsyte, the father of Fleur – one

night, at the height of her passion for this young man, forcibly reasserted his rights over her. The next day she met her lover and told him of it. Whether he committed suicide or whether he was accidentally run over in his distraction, we never knew; but so it was. Think of your mother as she was that evening when she heard of his death. I happened to see her. Your grandfather sent me to help her if I could. I only just saw her, before the door was shut against me by her husband. But I have never forgotten her face, I can see it now. I was not in love with her then, not for twelve years after, but I have never forgotten. My dear boy – it is not easy to write like this. But you see, I must. Your mother is wrapped up in you, utterly, devotedly. I don't wish to write harshly of Soames Forsyte. I don't think harshly of him. I have long been sorry for him; perhaps I was sorry even then. As the world judges she was in error, he within his rights. He loved her – in his way. *She was his property.* That is the view he holds of life – of human feelings and hearts – property. It's not his fault – so was he born. To me it is a view that has always been abhorrent – so was I born! Knowing you as I do, I feel it cannot be otherwise than abhorrent to you. Let me go on with the story. Your mother fled from his house that night; for twelve years she lived quietly alone without companionship of any sort, until in 1899 her husband – you see, he was still her husband, for he did not attempt to divorce her, and she of course had no right to divorce him – became conscious, it seems, of the want of children, and commenced a long attempt to induce her to go back to him and give him a child. I was her trustee then, under your grandfather's will, and I watched this going on. While watching, I became attached to her, devotedly attached. His pressure increased, till one day she came to me here and practically put herself under my protection. Her husband, who was kept informed of all her movements, attempted to force us apart by bringing a divorce suit, or possibly he really meant it, I don't know; but anyway our names were publicly joined. That decided us, and we became united in fact. She was divorced, married me, and you were born. We have lived in perfect happiness, at least I have, and I believe your mother also. Soames, soon after the divorce, married Fleur's mother, and she was born. That is the story, Jon. I have told it you, because by the affection which we see you have formed for this man's daughter you are blindly moving toward what must utterly destroy your mother's happiness, if not your own. I don't wish to speak of myself, because at my age there's no use supposing I shall cumber the ground much longer, besides, what I should suffer would be mainly on her account, and on yours. But what I want you to realise is that feelings of horror and aversion such as those can never be buried or forgotten. They are alive in her to-day. Only yesterday at Lord's we happened to see Soames Forsyte. Her face, if you had seen it, would have convinced you. The idea that you should marry his daughter is a nightmare to her, Jon. I have nothing to say against Fleur save that she *is* his daughter. But your children, if you married her, would be the grandchildren of Soames, as much as of your mother, of a man who once owned your mother as a man might own a slave. Think what that would mean. By such a marriage you enter the camp which held your mother prisoner and wherein she ate her heart out. You are just on the threshold of life, you

have only known this girl two months, and however
deeply you think you love her, I appeal to you to
break it off at once. Don't give your mother this
rankling pain and humiliation during the rest of her
life. Young though she will always seem to me, she
is fifty-seven. Except for us two she has no one in
the world. She will soon have only you. Pluck up
your spirit, Jon, and break away. Don't put this
cloud and barrier between you. Don't break her
heart! Bless you, my dear boy, and again forgive me
for all the pain this letter must bring you – we tried
to spare it you, but Spain – it seems – was no good.
Ever your devoted father,
Jolyon Forsyte.

Having finished his confession, Jolyon sat with a thin cheek
on his hand, re-reading. There were things in it which hurt
him so much, when he thought of Jon reading them, that
he nearly tore the letter up. To speak of such things at all
to a boy – his own boy – to speak of them in relation to
his own wife and the boy's own mother, seemed dreadful to
the reticence of his Forsyte soul. And yet without speaking
of them how make Jon understand the reality, the deep
cleavage, the ineffaceable scar? Without them, how justify
this stifling of the boy's love? He might just as well not
write at all!

He folded the confession, and put it in his pocket. It was
– thank Heaven! – Saturday; he had till Sunday evening to
think it over; for even if posted now it could not reach Jon
till Monday. He felt a curious relief at this delay, and at the
fact that, whether sent or not, it was written.

In the rose garden, which had taken the place of the old
fernery, he could see Irene snipping and pruning, with a little
basket on her arm. She was never idle, it seemed to him,
and he envied her now that he himself was idle nearly all

his time. He went down to her. She held up a stained glove and smiled. A piece of lace tied under her chin concealed her hair, and her oval face with its still dark brows looked very young.

'The green-fly are awful this year, and yet it's cold. You look tired, Jolyon.'

Jolyon took the confession from his pocket. 'I've been writing this. I think you ought to see it.'

'To Jon?' Her whole face had changed, in that instant, becoming almost haggard.

'Yes; the murder's out.'

He gave it to her, and walked away among the roses. Presently, seeing that she had finished reading and was standing quite still with the sheets of the letter against her skirt, he came back to her.

'Well?'

'It's wonderfully put. I don't see how it could be put better. Thank you, dear.'

'Is there anything you would like left out?'

She shook her head.

'No; he must know all, if he's to understand.'

'That's what I thought, but – I hate it!'

He had the feeling that he hated it more than she – to him sex was so much easier to mention between man and woman than between man and man; and she had always been more natural and frank, not deeply secretive like his Forsyte self.

'I wonder if he will understand, even now, Jolyon? He's so young; and he shrinks from the physical.'

'He gets that shrinking from my father, he was as fastidious as a girl in all such matters. Would it be better to rewrite the whole thing, and just say you hated Soames?'

Irene shook her head.

'Hate's only a word. It conveys nothing. No, better as it is.'

'Very well. It shall go to-morrow.'

She raised her face to his, and in sight of the big house's many creepered windows, he kissed her.

Chapter Two

Confession

Late that same afternoon, Jolyon had a nap in the old armchair. Face down on his knee was La Rôtisserie de la Reine Pédauque, and just before he fell asleep he had been thinking: 'As a people shall we ever really like the French? Will they ever really like us!' He himself had always liked the French, feeling at home with their wit, their taste, their cooking. Irene and he had paid many visits to France before the War, when Jon had been at his private school. His romance with her had begun in Paris – his last and most enduring romance. But the French – no Englishman could like them who could not see them in some sort with the detached aesthetic eye! And with that melancholy conclusion he had nodded off.

When he woke he saw Jon standing between him and the window. The boy had evidently come in from the garden and was waiting for him to wake. Jolyon smiled, still half asleep. How nice the chap looked – sensitive, affectionate, straight! Then his heart gave a nasty jump; and a quaking sensation overcame him. Jon! That confession! He controlled himself with an effort. 'Why, Jon, where did you spring from?'

Jon bent over and kissed his forehead.

Only then he noticed the look on the boy's face.

'I came home to tell you something, Dad.'

With all his might Jolyon tried to get the better of the jumping, gurgling sensations within his chest.

'Well, sit down, old man. Have you seen your mother?'

'No.' The boy's flushed look gave place to pallor; he sat down on the arm of the old chair, as, in old days, Jolyon himself used to sit beside his own father, installed in its recesses. Right up to the time of the rupture in their relations he had been wont to perch there – had he now reached such a moment with his own son? All his life he had hated scenes like poison, avoided rows, gone on his own way quietly and let others go on theirs. But now – it seemed – at the very end of things, he had a scene before him more painful than any he had avoided. He drew a visor down over his emotion, and waited for his son to speak.

'Father,' said Jon slowly, 'Fleur and I are engaged.'

'Exactly!' thought Jolyon, breathing with difficulty.

'I know that you and Mother don't like the idea. Fleur says that Mother was engaged to her father before you married her. Of course I don't know what happened, but it must be ages ago. I'm devoted to her, Dad, and she says she is to me.'

Jolyon uttered a queer sound, half laugh, half groan.

'You are nineteen, Jon, and I am seventy-two. How are we to understand each other in a matter like this, eh?'

'You love Mother, Dad; you must know what we feel. It isn't fair to us to let old things spoil our happiness, is it?'

Brought face to face with his confession, Jolyon resolved to do without it if by any means he could. He laid his hand on the boy's arm.

'Look, Jon! I might put you off with talk about your both being too young and not knowing your own minds, and all that, but you wouldn't listen, besides, it doesn't meet the case – Youth, unfortunately, cures itself. You talk lightly about "old things like that", knowing nothing – as you say truly – of what happened. Now, have I ever given you reason to doubt my love for you, or my word?'

At a less anxious moment he might have been amused by the conflict his words aroused – the boy's eager clasp, to reassure him on these points, the dread on his face of what that reassurance would bring forth; but he could only feel grateful for the squeeze.

'Very well, you can believe what I tell you. If you don't give up this love affair, you will make Mother wretched to the end of her days. Believe me, my dear, the past, whatever it was, can't be buried – it can't indeed.'

Jon got off the arm of the chair.

'The girl' – thought Jolyon – 'there she goes – starting up before him – life itself – eager, pretty, loving!'

'I can't, Father; how can I – just because you say that? Of course I can't!'

'Jon, if you knew the story you would give this up without hesitation; you would have to! Can't you believe me?'

'How can you tell what I should think? Father, I love her better than anything in the world.'

Jolyon's face twitched, and he said with painful slowness: 'Better than your mother, Jon?'

From the boy's face, and his clenched fists Jolyon realised the stress and struggle he was going through.

'I don't know,' he burst out, 'I don't know! But to give Fleur up for nothing – for something I don't understand, for something that I don't believe can really matter half so much, will make me – make me—'

'Make you feel us unjust, put a barrier – yes. But that's better than going on with this.'

'I can't. Fleur loves me, and I love her. You want me to trust you; why don't you trust *me*, Father? We wouldn't want to know anything – we wouldn't let it make any difference. It'll only make us both love you and Mother all the more.'

Jolyon put his hand into his breast pocket, but brought it out again empty, and sat, clucking his tongue against his teeth.

'Think what your mother's been to you, Jon! She has nothing but you; I shan't last much longer.'

'Why not? It isn't fair to— Why not?'

'Well,' said Jolyon, rather coldly, 'because the doctors tell me I shan't; that's all.'

'Oh, Dad!' cried Jon, and burst into tears.

This downbreak of his son, whom he had not seen cry since he was ten, moved Jolyon terribly. He recognised to the full how fearfully soft the boy's heart was, how much he would suffer in this business, and in life generally. And he reached out his hand helplessly – not wishing, indeed not daring to get up.

'Dear man,' he said, 'don't – or you'll make me!'

Jon smothered down his paroxysm, and stood with face averted, very still.

'What now?' thought Jolyon. 'What can I say to move him?'

'By the way, don't speak of that to Mother,' he said; 'she has enough to frighten her with this affair of yours. I know how you feel. But, Jon, you know her and me well enough to be sure we wouldn't wish to spoil your happiness lightly. Why, my dear boy, we don't care for anything but your happiness – at least, with me it's just yours and Mother's and with her just yours. It's all the future for you both that's at stake.'

Jon turned. His face was deadly pale; his eyes, deep in his head, seemed to burn.

'What is it? *What is it*? Don't keep me like this!'

Jolyon, who knew that he was beaten, thrust his hand again into his breast pocket, and sat for a full minute, breathing with difficulty, his eyes closed. The thought passed through his mind: 'I've had a good long innings – some pretty bitter moments – this is the worst!' Then he brought his hand out with the letter, and said with a sort of fatigue: 'Well, Jon, if you hadn't come to-day, I was going to send you this. I wanted to spare you – I wanted to spare your mother and myself, but I see it's no good. Read it, and I think I'll go into the garden.' He reached forward to get up.

Jon, who had taken the letter, said quickly, 'No, I'll go'; and was gone.

Jolyon sank back in his chair. A blue-bottle chose that moment to come buzzing round him with a sort of fury; the sound was homely, better than nothing . . . Where had the boy gone to read his letter? The wretched letter – the wretched story! A cruel business – cruel to her – to Soames – to those two children – to himself! . . . His heart thumped and pained him. Life – its loves – its work – its beauty – its aching, and – its end! A good time; a fine time in spite of all; until – you regretted that you had ever been born. Life – it wore you down, yet did not make you want to die – that was the cunning evil! Mistake to have a heart! Again the blue-bottle came buzzing – bringing in all the heat and hum and scent of summer – yes, even the scent – as of ripe fruits, dried grasses, sappy shrubs, and the vanilla breath of cows. And out there somewhere in the fragrance Jon would be reading that letter, turning and twisting its pages in his trouble, his bewilderment and trouble – breaking his heart about it! The thought made Jolyon acutely miserable. Jon was such a tender-hearted chap, affectionate to his bones, and conscientious, too – it was so unfair, so damned unfair! He remembered Irene saying to him once: 'Never was anyone born more loving and lovable than Jon.' Poor little Jon! His world gone up the spout, all of a summer afternoon! Youth took things so hard! And stirred, tormented by that vision of Youth taking things hard, Jolyon got out of his chair, and went to the window. The boy was nowhere visible. And he passed out. If one could take any help to him now – one must!

He traversed the shrubbery, glanced into the walled garden – no Jon! Nor where the peaches and the apricots were beginning to swell and colour. He passed the Cupressus trees, dark and spiral, into the meadow. Where had the boy got to? Had he rushed down to the coppice – his old hunting-ground? Jolyon crossed the rows of hay. They would cock it on Monday and be carrying the day after, if rain held off. Often they had crossed this field together – hand in hand, when Jon was a little chap. Dash it! The golden age was over by the time one was ten! He came to the pond, where flies and gnats were dancing over a bright reedy surface; and on into the coppice. It was cool there, fragrant of larches. Still no Jon! He called. No answer! On the log seat he sat down, nervous, anxious, forgetting his own physical sensations. He had been wrong to let the boy get away with that letter; he ought to have kept him under his eye from the start! Greatly troubled, he got up to retrace his steps. At the farm-buildings he called again, and looked into the dark cow-house. There in the cool, and the scent of vanilla and ammonia, away from flies, the three Alderneys were chewing the quiet cud; just milked, waiting for evening, to be turned out again into the lower field. One turned a lazy head, a lustrous eye; Jolyon could see the slobber on its grey lower lip. He saw everything with passionate clearness, in the agitation of his nerves – all that in his time he had adored and tried to paint – wonder of light and shade and colour. No wonder the legend put Christ into a manger – what more devotional than the eyes and moon-white horns of a chewing cow in the warm dusk! He called again. No answer! And he hurried away out of the coppice, past the pond, up the hill. Oddly ironical – now he came to think of it – if Jon had taken the gruel of his discovery down in the coppice where his mother and Bosinney in those old days had made the plunge of acknowledging their love. Where he himself, on the log seat the Sunday morning he came back from Paris, had realised to the full that Irene had become the world to him. That would have been the place for Irony to tear the veil from before the eyes of Irene's boy! But he was not here! Where had he got to? One must find the poor chap!

A gleam of sun had come, sharpening to his hurrying senses all the beauty of the afternoon, of the tall trees and lengthening shadows, of the blue, and the white clouds, the scent of the hay, and the cooing of the pigeons; and the flower shapes standing tall. He came to the rosery, and the beauty of the roses in that sudden sunlight seemed to him unearthly. 'Rose, you Spaniard!' Wonderful three words! There she had stood by that bush of dark red roses; had stood to read and decide that Jon must know it all! He knew all now! Had she chosen wrong? He bent and sniffed a rose, its petals brushed his nose and trembling lips; nothing so soft as a rose-leaf's velvet, except her neck – Irene! On across the lawn he went, up the slope, to the oak-tree. Its top alone was glistening, for the sudden sun was away over the house; the lower shade was thick, blessedly cool – he was greatly overheated. He paused a minute with his hand on the rope of the swing – Jolly, Holly – Jon! The old swing! And suddenly, he felt horribly – deadly ill. 'I've overdone it!' he thought: 'by Jove! I've overdone it – after all!' He staggered up toward the terrace, dragged himself up the steps, and fell against the wall of the house. He leaned there gasping, his face buried in the honey-suckle that he and she had taken such trouble with that it might sweeten the air which drifted in. Its fragrance mingled with awful pain. 'My love!' he thought; 'the boy!' And with a great effort he tottered in through the long window, and sank into old Jolyon's chair. The book was there, a pencil in it; he caught it up, scribbled a word on the open page . . . His hand dropped . . . So it was like this – was it? . . .

There was a great wrench; and darkness . . .

Chapter Three

Irene

When Jon rushed away with the letter in his hand, he ran along the terrace and round the corner of the house, in fear and confusion. Leaning against the creepered wall he tore open the letter. It was long – very long! This added to his fear, and he began reading. When he came to the words: 'It was Fleur's father that she married,' everything seemed to spin before him. He was close to a window, and entering by it, he passed, through music-room and hall, up to his bedroom. Dipping his face in cold water, he sat on his bed, and went on reading, dropping each finished page on the bed beside him. His father's writing was easy to read – he knew it so well, though he had never had a letter from him one quarter so long. He read with a dull feeling – imagination only half at work. He best grasped, on that first reading, the pain his father must have had in writing such a letter. He let the last sheet fall, and in a sort of mental, moral helplessness began to read the first again. It all seemed to him disgusting – dead and disgusting. Then, suddenly, a hot wave of horrified emotion tingled through him. He buried his face in his hands. His mother! Fleur's father! He took up the letter again, and read on mechanically. And again came the feeling that it was all dead and disgusting; his own love so different! This letter said his mother – and her father! An awful letter!

Property! Could there be men who looked on women as

their property? Faces seen in street and countryside came thronging up before him – red, stock-fish faces; hard, dull faces; prim, dry faces; violent faces; hundreds, thousands of them! How could he know what men who had such faces thought and did? He held his head in his hands and groaned. His mother! He caught up the letter and read on again: 'horror and aversion – alive in her to-day . . . your children . . . grand-children . . . of a man who once owned your mother as a man might own a slave . . .' He got up from his bed. This cruel shadowy past, lurking there to murder his love and Fleur's, was true, or his father could never have written it. 'Why didn't they tell me the first thing,' he thought, 'the day I first saw Fleur? They knew I'd seen her. They were afraid, and – now – I've – got it!' Overcome by misery too acute for thought or reason, he crept into a dusky corner of the room and sat down on the floor. He sat there, like some unhappy little animal. There was comfort in dusk, and the floor – as if he were back in those days when he played his battles sprawling all over it. He sat there huddled, his hair ruffled, his hands clasped round his knees, for how long he did not know. He was wrenched from his blank wretchedness by the sound of the door opening from his mother's room. The blinds were down over the windows of his room, shut up in his absence, and from where he sat he could only hear a rustle, her footsteps crossing, till beyond the bed he saw her standing before his dressing-table. She had something in her hand. He hardly breathed, hoping she would not see him, and go away. He saw her touch things on the table as if they had some virtue in them, then face the window – grey from head to foot like a ghost. The least turn of her head, and she must see him! Her lips moved: 'Oh! Jon!' She was speaking to herself; the tone of her voice troubled Jon's heart. He saw in her hand a little photograph. She held it toward the light, looking at it – very small. He knew it – one of himself as a tiny boy, which she always kept in her bag. His heart beat fast. And, suddenly as if she had heard it, she turned her eyes and saw him. At the gasp she gave, and the movement of her hands pressing the photograph against her breast, he said:

'Yes, it's me.'

She moved over to the bed, and sat down on it, quite close to him, her hands still clasping her breast, her feet among the sheets of the letter which had slipped to the floor. She saw them, and her hands grasped the edge of the bed. She sat very upright, her dark eyes fixed on him. At last she spoke.

'Well, Jon, you know, I see.'

'Yes.'

'You've seen Father?'

'Yes.'

There was a long silence, till she said:

'Oh! my darling!'

'It's all right.' The emotions in him were so violent and so mixed that he dared not move – resentment, despair, and yet a strange yearning for the comfort of her hand on his forehead.

'What are you going to do?'

'I don't know.'

There was another long silence, then she got up. She stood a moment, very still, made a little movement with her hand, and said: 'My darling boy, my most darling boy, don't think of me – think of yourself,' and, passing round the foot of the bed, went back into her room.

Jon turned – curled into a sort of ball, as might a hedgehog – into the corner made by the two walls.

He must have been twenty minutes there before a cry roused him. It came from the terrace below. He got up, scared. Again came the cry: 'Jon!' His mother was calling! He ran out and down the stairs, through the empty dining-room into the study. She was kneeling before the old armchair, and his father was lying back quite white, his head on his breast, one of his hands resting on an open book, with a pencil clutched in it – more strangely still than anything he had ever seen. She looked round wildly, and said:

'Oh! Jon – he's dead – he's dead!'

Jon flung himself down, and reaching over the arm of the chair, where he had lately been sitting, put his lips to the forehead. Icy cold! How could – how could Dad be dead, when only an hour ago—! His mother's arms were round the knees; pressing her breast against them. 'Why – why wasn't I with him?' he heard her whisper. Then he saw the tottering word 'Irene' pencilled on the open page, and broke down himself. It was his first sight of human death, and its unutterable stillness blotted from him all other emotion; all else, then, was but preliminary to this! All love and life, and joy, anxiety, and sorrow, all movement, light and beauty, but a beginning to this terrible white stillness. It made a dreadful mark on him; all seemed suddenly little, futile, short. He mastered himself at last, got up, and raised her.

'Mother! don't cry – Mother!'

Some hours later, when all was done that had to be, and his mother was lying down, he saw his father alone, on the bed, covered with a white sheet. He stood for a long time gazing at that face which had never looked angry – always whimsical, and kind. 'To be kind and keep your end up – there's nothing else in it,' he had once heard his father say. How wonderfully Dad had acted up to that philosophy! He understood now that his father had known for a long time past that this would come suddenly – known, and not said a word. He gazed with an awed and passionate reverence. The loneliness of it – just to spare his mother and himself! His own trouble seemed small while he was looking at that face. The word scribbled on the page! The farewell word! Now his mother had no one but himself! He went up close to the dead face – not changed at all, and yet completely changed. He had heard his father say once that he did not believe in consciousness surviving death, or that if it did it might be just survival till the natural age limit of the body had been reached – the natural term of its inherent vitality; so that if the body were broken by accident, excess, violent disease, consciousness might still persist till, in the course of Nature uninterfered with, it would naturally have faded out. It had struck him because he had never heard anyone else suggest it. When the heart failed like this – surely it was not quite natural! Perhaps his father's consciousness was in the room with him. Above the bed hung a picture of his father's father. Perhaps *his* consciousness, too, was still alive; and his brother's – his half-brother, who had died in the Transvaal. Were they all gathered round this bed? Jon kissed the forehead, and stole back to his own room. The door between it and his mother's was ajar; she had evidently been in – everything was ready for him, even some biscuits and hot milk, and the letter no longer on the floor. He ate and drank, watching the last light fade. He did not try to see into the future – just stared at the dark branches of the oak-tree, level with his window, and felt as if life had stopped. Once in the night, turning in his heavy sleep, he was conscious of something white and still, beside his bed, and started up.

His mother's voice said:

'It's only I, Jon dear!' Her hand pressed his forehead gently back; her white figure disappeared.

Alone! He fell heavily asleep again, and dreamed he saw his mother's name crawling on his bed.

Chapter Four

Soames Cogitates

The announcement in *The Times* of his cousin Jolyon's death affected Soames quite simply. So that chap was gone! There had never been a time in their two lives when love had not been lost between them. That quick-blooded sentiment hatred had run its course long since in Soames's heart, and he had refused to allow any recrudescence, but he considered this early decease a piece of poetic justice. For twenty years the fellow had enjoyed the reversion of his wife and house, and – he was dead! The obituary notice, which appeared a little later, paid Jolyon – he thought – too much attention. It spoke of that 'diligent and agreeable painter whose work we have come to look on as typical of the best late-Victorian water-colour art.' Soames, who had almost mechanically preferred Mole, Morpin, and Caswell Baye, and had always sniffed quite audibly when he came to one of his cousin's on the line, turned *The Times* with a crackle.

He had to go up to Town that morning on Forsyte affairs, and was fully conscious of Gradman's glance sidelong over his spectacles. The old clerk had about him an aura of regretful congratulation. He smelled, as it were, of old days. One could almost hear him thinking: 'Mr Jolyon, ye-es – just my age, and gone – dear, dear! I dare say she feels it. She was a naice-lookin' woman. Flesh is flesh! They've given 'im a notice in the papers. Fancy!' His atmosphere in fact caused Soames to handle certain leases and conversions with exceptional swiftness.

'About that settlement on Miss Fleur, Mr Soames?'

'I've thought better of that,' answered Soames shortly.

'Ah! I'm glad of that. I thought you were a little hasty. The times do change.'

How this death would affect Fleur had begun to trouble Soames. He was not certain that she knew of it – she seldom looked at the paper, never at the births, marriages, and deaths.

He pressed matters on, and made his way to Green Street for lunch. Winifred was almost doleful. Jack Cardigan had broken a splashboard, so far as one could make out, and would not be 'fit' for some time. She could not get used to the idea.

'Did Profond ever get off?' he said suddenly.

'He got off,' replied Winifred, 'but where – I don't know.'

Yes, there it was – impossible to tell anything! Not that he wanted to know. Letters from Annette were coming from Dieppe, where she and her mother were staying.

'You saw that fellow's death, I suppose?'

'Yes,' said Winifred. 'I'm sorry for – for his children. He was very amiable.' Soames uttered a rather queer sound. A suspicion of the old deep truth – that men were judged in this world rather by what they *were* than by what they *did* – crept and knocked resentfully at the back doors of his mind.

'I know there was a superstition to that effect,' he muttered.

'One must do him justice now he's dead.'

'I should like to have done him justice before,' said Soames; 'but I never had the chance. Have you got a *Baronetage* here?'

'Yes; in that bottom row.'

Soames took out a fat red book, and ran over the leaves.

'Mont – Sir Lawrence, 9th Bt., cr. 1620, e. s. of Geoffrey, 8th Bt., and Lavinia, daur. of Sir Charles Muskham, Bt., of Muskham Hall, Shrops: marr. 1890 Emily, daur. of Conway Charwell, Esq., of Condaford Grange, co. Oxon; 1 son, heir Michael Conway, b. 1895, 2 daurs. Residence: Lippinghall

Manor, Folwell, Bucks. Clubs: Snooks': Coffee House: Aeroplane. See Bidlicott.'

'H'm!' he said. 'Did you ever know a publisher?'

'Uncle Timothy.'

'Alive, I mean.'

'Monty knew one at his Club. He brought him here to dinner once. Monty was always thinking of writing a book, you know, about how to make money on the turf. He tried to interest that man.'

'Well?'

'He put him on to a horse – for the Two Thousand. We didn't see him again. He was rather smart, if I remember.'

'Did it win?'

'No; it ran last, I think. You know Monty really was quite clever in his way.'

'Was he?' said Soames. 'Can you see any connection between a sucking baronet and publishing?'

'People do all sorts of things nowadays,' replied Winifred. 'The great stunt seems not to be idle – so different from our time. To do nothing was the thing then. But I suppose it'll come again.'

'This young Mont that I'm speaking of is very sweet on Fleur. If it would put an end to that other affair I might encourage it.'

'Has he got style?' asked Winifred.

'He's no beauty; pleasant enough, with some scattered brains. There's a good deal of land, I believe. He seems genuinely attached. But I don't know.'

'No,' murmured Winifred; 'it's very difficult. I always found it best to do nothing. It is such a bore about Jack; now we shan't get away till after Bank Holiday. Well, the people are always amusing, I shall go into the Park and watch them.'

'If I were you,' said Soames, 'I should have a country cottage, and be out of the way of holidays and strikes when you want.'

'The country bores me,' answered Winifred, 'and I found the railway strike quite exciting.'

Winifred had always been noted for sang-froid.

Soames took his leave. All the way down to Reading he debated whether he should tell Fleur of that boy's father's death. It did not alter the situation except that he would be independent now, and only have his mother's opposition to encounter. He would come into a lot of money, no doubt, and perhaps the house – the house built for Irene and himself – the house whose architect had wrought his domestic ruin. His daughter – mistress of that house! That would be poetic justice! Soames uttered a little mirthless laugh. He had designed that house to re-establish his failing union, meant it for the seat of his descendants, if he could have induced Irene to give him one! Her son and Fleur! Their children would be, in some sort, offspring of the union between himself and her!

The theatricality in that thought was repulsive to his sober sense. And yet – it would be the easiest and wealthiest way out of the impasse, now that Jolyon was gone. The juncture of two Forsyte fortunes had a kind of conservative charm. And she – Irene – would be linked to him once more. Nonsense! Absurd! He put the notion from his head.

On arriving home he heard the click of billiard-balls, and through the window saw young Mont sprawling over the table. Fleur, with her cue akimbo, was watching with a smile. How pretty she looked! No wonder that young fellow was out of his mind about her. A title – land! There was little enough in land, these days; perhaps less in a title. The old Forsytes had always had a kind of contempt for titles, rather remote and artificial things – not worth the money they cost, and having to do with the Court. They had all had that feeling in differing measure – Soames remembered. Swithin, indeed, in his most expansive days had once attended a Levee. He had come away saying he shouldn't go again – 'all that small fry'. It was suspected that he had looked too big in knee-breeches. Soames remembered how his own mother had wished to be presented because of the fashionable nature of the performance, and how his father had put his foot down with unwonted decision. What did she want with that peacocking – wasting time and money; there was nothing in it!

The instinct which had made and kept the English Commons the chief power in the State, a feeling that their own world was good enough and a little better than any other because it was *their* world, had kept the old Forsytes singularly free of 'flummery', as Nicholas had been wont to call it when he had the gout. Soames's generation, more self-conscious and iron- ical, had been saved by a sense of Swithin in knee-breeches. While the third and the fourth generation, as it seemed to him, laughed at everything.

However, there was no harm in the young fellow's being heir to a title and estate – a thing one couldn't help. He entered quietly, as Mont missed his shot. He noted the young man's eyes, fixed on Fleur bending over in her turn; and the adoration in them almost touched him.

She paused with the cue poised on the bridge of her slim hand, and shook her crop of short dark chestnut hair.

'I shall never do it.'

'"Nothing venture."'

'All right.' The cue struck, the ball rolled. 'There!'

'Bad luck! Never mind!'

Then they saw him, and Soames said:

'I'll mark for you.'

He sat down on the raised seat beneath the marker, trim and tired, furtively studying those two young faces. When the game was over Mont came up to him.

'I've started in, sir. Rum game, business, isn't it? I suppose you saw a lot of human nature as a solicitor.'

'I did.'

'Shall I tell you what I've noticed: People are quite on the wrong tack in offering less than they can afford to give; they ought to offer more, and work backward.'

Soames raised his eyebrows.

'Suppose the more is accepted?'

'That doesn't matter a little bit,' said Mont; 'it's much more paying to abate a price than to increase it. For instance, say we offer an author good terms – he naturally takes them. Then we go into it, find we can't publish at a decent profit and tell him so. He's got confidence in us because we've been generous to him, and he comes down like a lamb, and bears us no malice. But if we offer him poor terms at the start, he doesn't take them, so we have to advance them to get him, and he thinks us damned screws into the bargain.'

'Try buying pictures on that system,' said Soames; 'an offer accepted is a contract – haven't you learned that?'

Young Mont turned his head to where Fleur was standing in the window.

'No,' he said, 'I wish I had. Then there's another thing. Always let a man off a bargain if he wants to be let off.'

'As advertisement?' said Soames drily.

'Of course it *is*; but I meant on principle.'

'Does your firm work on those lines?'

'Not yet,' said Mont, 'but it'll come.'

'And they will go.'

'No, really, sir. I'm making any number of observations, and they all confirm my theory. Human nature is consistently underrated in business, people do themselves out of an awful lot of pleasure and profit by that. Of course, you must be perfectly genuine and open, but that's easy if you feel it. The more human and generous you are the better chance you've got in business.'

Soames rose.

'Are you a partner?'

'Not for six months, yet.'

'The rest of the firm had better make haste and retire.'

Mont laughed.

'You'll see,' he said. 'There's going to be a big change. The possessive principle has got its shutters up.'

'What?' said Soames.

'The house is to let! Good-bye, sir; I'm off now.'

Soames watched his daughter give her hand, saw her wince at the squeeze it received, and distinctly heard the young man's sigh as he passed out. Then she came from the window, trailing her finger along the mahogany edge of the billiard-table. Watching her, Soames knew that she was going to ask him something. Her finger felt round the last pocket, and she looked up.

'Have you done anything to stop Jon writing to me, Father?'

Soames shook his head.

'You haven't seen, then?' he said. 'His father died just a week ago to-day.'

'Oh!'

In her startled, frowning face he saw the instant struggle to apprehend what this would mean.

'Poor Jon! Why didn't you tell me, Father?'

'I never know!' said Soames slowly; 'you don't confide in me.'

'I would, if you'd help me, dear.'

'Perhaps I shall.'

Fleur clasped her hands. 'Oh! darling – when one wants a thing fearfully, one doesn't think of other people. Don't be angry with me.'

Soames put out his hand, as if pushing away an aspersion.

'I'm cogitating,' he said. What on earth had made him use a word like that! 'Has young Mont been bothering you again?'

Fleur smiled. 'Oh! Michael! He's always bothering; but he's such a good sort – I don't mind him.'

'Well,' said Soames, 'I'm tired; I shall go and have a nap before dinner.'

He went up to his picture-gallery, lay down on the couch there, and closed his eyes. A terrible responsibility this girl of his – whose mother was – ah! what was she? A terrible responsibility! Help her – how could he help her? He could not alter the fact that he was her father. Or that Irene—! What was it young Mont had said – some nonsense about the possessive instinct – shutters up – To let? Silly!

The sultry air, charged with a scent of meadow-sweet, of river and roses, closed on his senses, drowsing them.

Chapter Five

The Fixed Idea

' The fixed idea,' which has outrun more constables than any other form of human disorder, has never more speed and stamina than when it takes the avid guise of love. To hedges and ditches, and doors, to humans without ideas fixed or otherwise, to perambulators and the contents sucking their fixed ideas, even to the other sufferers from this fast malady – the fixed idea of love pays no attention. It runs with eyes turned inward to its own light, oblivious of all other stars. Those with the fixed ideas that human happiness depends on their art, on vivisecting dogs, on hating foreigners, on paying supertax, on remaining Ministers, on making wheels go round, on preventing their neighbours from being divorced, on conscientious objection, Greek roots, Church dogma, paradox and superiority to everybody else, with other forms of ego-mania – all are unstable compared with him or her whose fixed idea is the possession of some her or him. And though Fleur, those chilly summer days, pursued the scattered life of a little Forsyte whose frocks are paid for, and whose business is pleasure, she was – as Winifred would have said in the latest fashion of speech – 'honest to God' indifferent to it all. She wished and wished for the moon, which sailed in cold skies above the river or the Green Park when she went to Town. She even kept Jon's letters, covered with pink silk, on her heart, than which in days when corsets were so low, sentiment so despised, and chests so out of fashion, there could, perhaps, have been no greater proof of the fixity of her idea.

After hearing of his father's death, she wrote to Jon, and received his answer three days later on her return from a river picnic. It was his first letter since their meeting at June's. She opened it with misgiving, and read it with dismay.

'Since I saw you I've heard everything about the past. I won't tell it you – I think you knew when we met at June's. She says you did. If you did, Fleur, you ought to have told me. I expect you only heard your father's side of it. I have heard my mother's.

'It's dreadful. Now that she's so sad I can't do anything to hurt her more. Of course, I long for you all day, but I don't believe now that we shall ever come together – there's something too strong pulling us apart.'

So! Her deception had found her out. But Jon – she felt – had forgiven that. It was what he said of his mother which caused the fluttering in her heart and the weak sensation in her legs.

Her first impulse was to reply – her second, not to reply. These impulses were constantly renewed in the days which followed, while desperation grew within her. She was not her father's child for nothing. The tenacity which had at once made and undone Soames was her backbone, too, frilled and embroidered by French grace and quickness. Instinctively she conjugated the verb 'to have' always with the pronoun 'I'. She concealed, however, all signs of her growing desperation, and pursued such river pleasures as the winds and rain of a disagreeable July permitted, as if she had no care in the world; nor did any 'sucking baronet' ever neglect the business of a publisher more consistently than her attendant spirit, Michael Mont.

To Soames she was a puzzle. He was almost deceived by this careless gaiety. Almost – because he did not fail to mark her eyes often fixed on nothing, and the film of light shining from her bedroom window late at night. What was she thinking and brooding over into small hours when she ought to have been asleep? But he dared not ask what was in her mind; and, since that one little talk in the billiard-room, she said nothing to him.

In this taciturn condition of affairs it chanced that Winifred invited them to lunch and to go afterward to 'a most amusing little play, *The Beggar's Opera*' and would they bring a man to make four? Soames, whose attitude toward theatres was to go to nothing, accepted, because Fleur's attitude was to go to everything. They motored up, taking Michael Mont, who, being in his seventh heaven, was found by Winifred 'very amusing'. *The Beggar's Opera* puzzled Soames. The people were very unpleasant, the whole thing very cynical. Winifred was 'intrigued' – by the dresses. The music, too, did not displease her. At the Opera, the night before, she had arrived too early for the Russian Ballet, and found the stage occupied by singers, for a whole hour pale or apoplectic from terror lest by some dreadful inadvertence they might drop into a tune. Michael Mont was enraptured with the whole thing. And all three wondered what Fleur was thinking of it. But Fleur was not thinking of it. Her fixed idea stood on the stage and sang with Polly Peachum, mimed with Filch, danced with Jenny Diver, postured with Lucy Lockit, kissed, trolled, and cuddled with Macheath. Her lips might smile, her hands applaud, but the comic old masterpiece made no more impression on her than if it had been pathetic, like a modern 'Revue'. When they embarked in the car to return, she ached because Jon was not sitting next to her instead of Michael Mont. When, at some jolt, the young man's arm touched hers as if by accident, she only thought: 'If that were Jon's arm!' When his cheerful voice, tempered by her proximity, murmured above the sound of the car's progress, she smiled and answered, thinking: 'If that were Jon's voice!' and when once he said, 'Fleur, you look a perfect angel in that dress!' she answered, 'Oh, do you like it?' thinking, 'If only Jon could see it!'

During this drive she took a resolution. She would go to Robin Hill and see him – alone; she would take the car, without word beforehand to him or to her father. It was nine days since his letter, and she could wait no longer. On Monday she would go! The decision made her well disposed toward young Mont. With something to look forward to she could afford to tolerate and respond. He might stay to dinner; propose to her as usual; dance with her, press her hand, sigh – do what he liked. He was only a nuisance when he interfered with her fixed idea. She was even sorry for him so far as it was possible to be sorry for anybody but herself just now. At dinner he seemed to talk more wildly than usual about what he called 'the death of the close borough' – she paid little attention, but her father seemed paying a good deal, with the smile on his face which meant opposition, if not anger.

'The younger generation doesn't think as you do, sir; does it, Fleur?'

Fleur shrugged her shoulders – the younger generation was just Jon, and she did not know what he was thinking.

'Young people will think as I do when they're my age, Mr Mont. Human nature doesn't change.'

'I admit that, sir; but the forms of thought change with the times. The pursuit of self-interest is a form of thought that's going out.'

'Indeed! To mind one's own business is not a form of thought, Mr Mont, it's an instinct.'

Yes, when Jon was the business!

'But what is one's business, sir? That's the point. *Everybody's* business is going to be one's business. Isn't it, Fleur?'

Fleur only smiled.

'If not,' added young Mont, 'there'll be blood.'

'People have talked like that from time immemorial.'

'But you'll admit, sir, that the sense of property is dying out?'

'I should say increasing among those who have none.'

'Well, look at me! I'm heir to an entailed estate. I don't want the thing; I'd cut the entail to-morrow.'

'You're not married, and you don't know what you're talking about.'

Fleur saw the young man's eyes turn rather piteously upon her.

'Do you really mean that marriage—?' he began.

'Society is built on marriage,' came from between her father's close lips; 'marriage and its consequences. Do you want to do away with it?'

Young Mont made a distracted gesture. Silence brooded over the dinner table, covered with spoons bearing the Forsyte crest – a pheasant proper – under the electric light in an alabaster globe. And outside, the river evening darkened, charged with heavy moisture and sweet scents.

'Monday,' thought Fleur; 'Monday!'

Chapter Six

Desperate

The weeks which followed the death of his father were sad and empty to the only Jolyon Forsyte left. The necessary forms and ceremonies – the reading of the will, valuation of the estate, distribution of the legacies – were enacted over the head, as it were, of one not yet of age. Jolyon was cremated. By his special wish no one attended that ceremony, or wore black for him. The succession of his property, controlled to some extent by old Jolyon's will, left his widow in possession of Robin Hill, with two thousand five hundred pounds a year for life. Apart from this the two wills worked together in some complicated way to insure that each of Jolyon's three children should have an equal share in their grandfather's and father's property in the future as in the present, save only that Jon, by virtue of his sex, would have control of his capital when he was twenty-one, while June and Holly would only have the spirit of theirs, in order that their children might have the body after them. If they had no children, it would all come to Jon if he outlived them; and since June was fifty, and Holly nearly forty, it was considered in Lincoln's Inn Fields that but for the cruelty of income tax, young Jon would be as warm a man as his grandfather when he died. All this was nothing to Jon, and little enough to his mother. It was June who did everything needful for one who had left his affairs in perfect order. When she had gone, and

those two were alone again in the great house, alone with
death drawing them together, and love driving them apart,
Jon passed very painful days secretly disgusted and disap-
pointed with himself. His mother would look at him with
such a patient sadness which yet had in it an instinctive pride,
as if she were reserving her defence. If she smiled he was
angry that his answering smile should be so grudging and
unnatural. He did not judge or condemn her; that was all
too remote – indeed, the idea of doing so had never come
to him. No! he was grudging and unnatural because he
couldn't have what he wanted because of her. There was one
alleviation – much to do in connection with his father's career,
which could not be safely entrusted to June, though she had
offered to undertake it. Both Jon and his mother had felt
that if she took his portfolios, unexhibited drawings and
unfinished matter, away with her, the work would encounter
such icy blasts from Paul Post and other frequenters of her
studio, that it would soon be frozen out even of her warm
heart. On its old-fashioned plane and of its kind the work
was good, and they could not bear the thought of its subjec-
tion to ridicule. A one-man exhib-ition of his work was the
least testimony they could pay to one they had loved; and
on preparation for this they spent many hours together. Jon
came to have a curiously increased respect for his father. The
quiet tenacity with which he had converted a mediocre talent
into something really individual was disclosed by these
researches. There was a great mass of work with a rare continuity of growth in depth and reach of vision. Nothing
certainly went very deep, or reached very high – but such as
the work was, it was thorough, conscientious, and complete.
And, remembering his father's utter absence of 'side' or self-
assertion, the chaffing humility with which he had always
spoken of his own efforts, ever calling himself 'an amateur',
Jon could not help feeling that he had never really known
his father. To take himself seriously, yet never that he did so,

seemed to have been his ruling principle. There was something in this which appealed to the boy, and made him heartily endorse his mother's comment: 'He had true refinement; he couldn't help thinking of others, whatever he did. And when he took a resolution which went counter, he did it with the minimum of defiance – not like the Age, is it? Twice in his life he had to go against everything; and yet it never made him bitter.' Jon saw tears running down her face, which she at once turned away from him. She was so quiet about her loss that sometimes he had thought she didn't feel it much. Now, as he looked at her, he felt how far he fell short of the reserve power and dignity in both his father and his mother. And, stealing up to her, he put his arm round her waist. She kissed him swiftly, but with a sort of passion, and went out of the room.

The studio, where they had been sorting and labelling, had once been Holly's schoolroom, devoted to her silkworms, dried lavender, music, and other forms of instruction. Now, at the end of July, despite its northern and eastern aspects, a warm and slumberous air came in between the long-faded lilac linen curtains. To redeem a little the departed glory, as of a field that is golden and gone, clinging to a room which its master has left, Irene had placed on the paint-stained table a bowl of red roses. This, and Jolyon's favourite cat, who still clung to the deserted habitat, were the pleasant spots in that dishevelled, sad workroom. Jon, at the north window, sniffing air mysteriously scented with warm strawberries, heard a car drive up. The lawyers again about some nonsense! Why did that scent so make one ache? And where did it come from – there were no strawberry beds on this side of the house. Instinctively he took a crumpled sheet of paper from his pocket, and wrote down some broken words. A warmth began spreading in his chest; he rubbed the palms of his hands together. Presently he had jotted this:

If I could make a little song –
A little song to soothe my heart!
I'd make it all of little things –
The plash of water, rub of wings,
The puffing-off of dandie's crown,
The hiss of raindrop spilling down,
The purr of cat, the trill of bird,
And ev'ry whispering I've heard
From willy wind in leaves and grass
And all the distant drones that pass
A song as tender and as light
As flower, or butterfly in flight;
And when I saw it opening,
I'd let it fly and sing!

He was still muttering it over to himself at the window, when he heard his name called, and, turning round, saw Fleur. At that amazing apparition, he made at first no movement and no sound, while her clear vivid glance ravished his heart. Then he went forward to the table, saying, 'How nice of you to come!' and saw her flinch as if he had thrown something at her.

'I asked for you,' she said, 'and they showed me up here. But I can go away again.'

Jon clutched the paint-stained table. Her face and figure in its frilly frock photographed itself with such startling vividness upon his eyes, that if she had sunk through the floor he must still have seen her.

'I know I told you a lie, Jon. But I told it out of love.'

'Yes, oh! yes! That's nothing!'

'I didn't answer your letter. What was the use – there wasn't anything to answer. I wanted to see you instead.' She held out both her hands, and Jon grasped them across the table. He tried to say something, but all his attention was given to trying not to hurt her hands. His own felt so hard and hers so soft. She said almost defiantly:

'That old story – was it so very dreadful?'

'Yes.' In his voice, too, there was a note of defiance.

She dragged her hands away. 'I didn't think in these days boys were tied to their mothers' apron-strings.'

Jon's chin went up as if he had been struck.

'Oh! I didn't mean it, Jon. What a horrible thing to say!' Swiftly she came close to him. 'Jon, dear; I didn't mean it.'

'All right.'

She had put her two hands on his shoulder, and her forehead down on them; the brim of her hat touched his neck, and he felt it quivering. But, in a sort of paralysis, he made no response. She let go of his shoulder and drew away.

'Well, I'll go, if you don't want me. But I never thought you'd have given me up.'

'*I haven't*,' cried Jon, coming suddenly to life. 'I can't. I'll try again.'

Her eyes gleamed, she swayed toward him. 'Jon – I love you! Don't give me up! If you do, I don't know what – I feel so desperate. What does it matter – all that past – compared with *this*?'

She clung to him. He kissed her eyes, her cheeks, her lips. But while he kissed her he saw the sheets of that letter fallen down on the floor of his bedroom – his father's white dead face – his mother kneeling before it. Fleur's whispered, 'Make her! Promise! Oh! Jon, try!' seemed childish in his ear. He felt curiously old.

'I promise!' he muttered. 'Only, you don't understand.'

'She wants to spoil our lives, just because—'

'Yes, of what?'

Again that challenge in his voice, and she did not answer. Her arms tightened round him, and he returned her kisses; but even while he yielded, the poison worked in him, the poison of the letter. Fleur did not know, she did not understand – she misjudged his mother; she came from the enemy's camp! So lovely, and he loved her so – yet, even in her embrace, he could not help the memory of Holly's words: 'I think she has a "having" nature,' and his mother's 'My darling boy, don't think of me – think of yourself!'

When she was gone like a passionate dream, leaving her image on his eyes, her kisses on his lips, such an ache in his heart, Jon leaned in the window, listening to the car bearing her away. Still the scent as of warm strawberries, still the little summer sounds that should make his song; still all the promise of youth and happiness in sighing, floating, fluttering July – and his heart torn; yearning strong in him; hope high in him yet with its eyes cast down, as if ashamed. The miserable task before him! If Fleur was desperate, so was he – watching the poplars swaying, the white clouds passing, the sunlight on the grass.

He waited till evening, till after their almost silent dinner, till his mother had played to him and still he waited, feeling that she knew what he was waiting to say. She kissed him and went upstairs, and still he lingered, watching the moonlight and the moths, and that unreality of colouring which steals along and stains a summer night. And he would have given anything to be back again in the past – barely three months back; or away forward, years, in the future. The present with this dark cruelty of a decision, one way or the other, seemed impossible. He realised now so much more keenly what his mother felt than he had at first; as if the story in that letter had been a poisonous germ producing a kind of fever of partisanship, so that he really felt there were two camps, his mother's and his – Fleur's and her father's. It might be a dead thing, that old tragic ownership and enmity, but dead things were poisonous till time had cleaned them away. Even his love felt tainted, less illusioned, more of the earth, and with a treacherous lurking doubt lest Fleur, like her father, might want to *own*; not articulate, just a stealing haunt, horribly unworthy, which crept in and about the ardour of his memories, touched with its tarnishing breath the vividness and grace of that charmed face and figure – a doubt, not real enough to convince him of its presence, just real enough to deflower a perfect faith. And perfect faith, to Jon, not yet twenty, was essential. He still had Youth's eagerness to give with both hands, to take with neither – to give lovingly to one who had his own impulsive generosity. Surely she had! He got up from the window-seat and roamed in the big grey ghostly room, whose walls were hung with silvered canvas. This house – his father said in that death-bed letter – had been built for his mother to live in – with Fleur's father! He put out his hand in the half-dark, as if to grasp the shadowy hand of the dead. He clenched, trying to feel the thin vanished fingers of his father; to squeeze them, and reassure him that he – he was on his father's side. Tears, prisoned within him, made his eyes feel dry and hot. He went back to the window. It was warmer, not so eerie, more comforting outside, where the moon hung golden, three days off full; the freedom of the night was comforting. If only Fleur and he had met on some desert island without a past – and Nature for their house! Jon had still his high regard for desert islands, where breadfruit grew, and the water was blue above the coral. The night was deep, was free – there was entice-ment in it; a lure, a promise, a refuge from entanglement, and love! Milksop tied to his mother's—! His cheeks burned. He shut the window, drew curtains over it, switched off the lighted sconce, and went upstairs.

The door of his room was open, the light turned up; his mother, still in her evening gown, was standing at the window. She turned and said:

'Sit down, Jon; let's talk.' She sat down on the window-seat, Jon on his bed. She had her profile turned to him, and the beauty and grace of her figure, the delicate line of the brow, the nose, the neck, the strange and as it were remote refinement of her, moved him. His mother never belonged to her surroundings. She came into them from somewhere – as it were! What was she going to say to him, who had in his heart such things to say to her?

'I know Fleur came to-day. I'm not surprised.' It was as though she had added: 'She is her father's daughter!' And Jon's heart hardened. Irene went on quietly:

'I have Father's letter. I picked it up that night and kept it. Would you like it back, dear?'

Jon shook his head.

'I had read it, of course, before he gave it to you. It didn't quite do justice to my criminality.'

'Mother!' burst from Jon's lips.

'He put it very sweetly, but I know that in marrying Fleur's father without love I did a dreadful thing. An unhappy marriage, Jon, can play such havoc with other lives besides one's own. You are fearfully young, my darling, and fearfully loving. Do you think you can possibly be happy with this girl?'

Staring at her dark eyes, darker now from pain, Jon answered:

'Yes; oh! yes – if *you* could be.'

Irene smiled.

'Admiration of beauty and longing for possession are not love. If yours were another case like mine, Jon – where the deepest things are stifled; the flesh joined, and the spirit at war!'

'Why should it, Mother? You think she must be like her father, but she's not. I've seen him.'

Again the smile came on Irene's lips, and in Jon something wavered; there was such irony and experience in that smile.

'You are a giver, Jon; she is a taker.'

That unworthy doubt, that haunting uncertainty again! He said with vehemence:

'She isn't – she isn't. It's only because I can't bear to make you unhappy, Mother, now that Father—' He thrust his fists against his forehead.

Irene got up.

'I told you that night, dear, not to mind me. I meant it. Think of yourself and your own happiness! I can stand what's left – I've brought it on myself.'

Again the word 'Mother!' burst from Jon's lips.

She came over to him and put her hands over his.

'Do you feel your head, darling?'

Jon shook it. What he felt was in his chest – a sort of tearing asunder of the tissue there, by the two loves.

'I shall always love you the same, Jon, whatever you do. You won't lose anything.' She smoothed his hair gently, and walked away.

He heard the door shut; and, rolling over on the bed, lay, stifling his breath, with an awful held-up feeling within him.

Chapter Seven

Embassy

*E*nquiring for her at tea time Soames learned that Fleur had been out in the car since two. Three hours! Where had she gone? Up to London without a word to him? He had never become quite reconciled with cars. He had embraced them in principle – like the born empiricist, or Forsyte, that he was – adopting each symptom of progress as it came along with: 'Well, we couldn't do without them now.' But in fact he found them tearing, great, smelly things. Obliged by Annette to have one – a Rollhard with pearl-grey cushions, electric light, little mirrors, trays for the ashes of cigarettes, flower vases – all smelling of petrol and stephanotis – he regarded it much as he used to regard his brother-in-law, Montague Dartie. The thing typified all that was fast, insecure, and subcutaneously oily in modern life. As modern life became faster, looser, younger, Soames was becoming older, slower, tighter, more and more in thought and language like his father James before him. He was almost aware of it himself. Pace and progress pleased him less and less; there was an ostentation, too, about a car which he considered provocative in the prevailing mood of Labour. On one occasion that fellow Sims had driven over the only vested interest of a working man. Soames had not forgotten the behaviour of its master, when not many people would have stopped to put up with it. He had been sorry for the dog, and quite prepared to take its part against the car, if that ruffian hadn't been so outrageous. With four hours fast becoming five, and still no Fleur, all the old car-wise feelings he had experienced in person and by proxy balled within him, and shaking sensations troubled the pit of his stomach. At seven he telephoned to Winifred by trunk call. No! Fleur had not been to Green Street. Then where was she? Visions of his beloved daughter rolled up in her pretty frills, all blood and dust-stained, in some hideous catastrophe, began to haunt him. He went to her room and spied among her things. She had taken nothing – no dressing-case, no jewellery. And this, a relief in one sense, increased his fears of an acci-dent. Terrible to be helpless when his loved one was missing, especially when he couldn't bear fuss or publicity of any kind! What should he do if she were not back by nightfall?

At a quarter to eight he heard the car. A great weight lifted from off his heart; he hurried down. She was getting out – pale and tired-looking, but nothing wrong. He met her in the hall.

'You've frightened me. Where have you been?'

'To Robin Hill. I'm sorry, dear. I had to go; I'll tell you afterward.' And, with a flying kiss, she ran upstairs.

Soames waited in the drawing-room. To Robin Hill! What did that portend?

It was not a subject they could discuss at dinner – conse-crated to the susceptibilities of the butler. The agony of nerves Soames had been through, the relief he felt at her safety, soft-ened his power to condemn what she had done, or resist what she was going to do; he waited in a relaxed stupor for her revelation. Life was a queer business. There he was at sixty-five and no more in command of things than if he had not spent forty years in building up security – always something one couldn't get on terms with! In the pocket of his dinner-jacket was a letter from Annette. She was coming back in a fortnight. He knew nothing of what she had been doing out there. And he was glad that he did not. Her absence had been a relief. Out of sight was out of mind! And now she was coming back. Another worry! And the Bolderby Old Crome was gone – Dumetrius had got it – all because that anonymous letter had put it out of his thoughts. He furtively remarked the strained look on his daughter's face, as if she too were gazing at a picture that she couldn't buy.

He almost wished the War back. Worries didn't seem, then, quite so worrying. From the caress in her voice, the look on her face, he became certain that she wanted something from him, uncertain whether it would be wise of him to give it her. He pushed his savoury away uneaten, and even joined her in a cigarette.

After dinner she set the electric piano-player going. And he augured the worst when she sat down on a cushion footstool at his knee, and put her hand on his.

'Darling, be nice to me. I had to see Jon – he wrote to me. He's going to try what he can do with his mother. But I've been thinking. It's really in your hands, Father. If you'd persuade her that it doesn't mean renewing the past in any way! That I shall stay yours, and Jon will stay hers; that you need never see him or her, and she need never see you or me! Only you could persuade her, dear, because only you could promise. One can't promise for other people. Surely it wouldn't be too awkward for you to see her just this once now that Jon's father is dead?'

'Too awkward?' Soames repeated. 'The whole thing's preposterous.'

'You know,' said Fleur, without looking up, 'you wouldn't mind seeing her, really.'

Soames was silent. Her words had expressed a truth too deep for him to admit. She slipped her fingers between his own – hot, slim, eager, they clung there. This child of his would corkscrew her way into a brick wall!

'What am I to do if you won't, Father?' she said very softly.

'I'll do anything for your happiness,' said Soames; 'but this isn't for your happiness.'

'Oh! it is; it is!'

'It'll only stir things up,' he said grimly.

'But they are stirred up. The thing is to quiet them. To make her feel that this is just *our* lives, and has nothing to do with yours or hers. You can do it, Father, I know you can.'

'You know a great deal, then,' was Soames's glum answer.

'If you will, Jon and I will wait a year – two years if you like.'

'It seems to me,' murmured Soames, 'that you care nothing about what *I* feel.'

Fleur pressed his hand against her cheek.

'I do, darling. But you wouldn't like me to be awfully miserable.'

How she wheedled to get her ends! And trying with all his might to think she really cared for him – he was not sure – not sure. All she cared for was this boy! Why should he help her to get this boy, who was killing her affection for himself? Why should he? By the laws of the Forsytes it was foolish! There was nothing to be had out of it – nothing! To give her to that boy! To pass her into the enemy's camp, under the influence of the woman who had injured him so deeply! Slowly – inevitably – he would lose this flower of his life! And suddenly he was conscious that his hand was wet. His heart gave a little painful jump. He couldn't bear her to cry. He put his other hand quickly over hers, and a tear dropped on that, too. He couldn't go on like this! 'Well, well,' he said, 'I'll think it over, and do what I can. Come, come!' If she must have it for her happiness – she must; he couldn't refuse to help her. And lest she should begin to thank him he got out of his chair and went up to the piano-player – making that noise! It ran down, as he reached it, with a faint buzz. That musical box of his nursery days: 'The Harmonious Blacksmith', 'Glorious Port' – the thing had always made him miserable when his mother set it going on Sunday afternoons. Here it was again – the same thing, only larger, more expensive, and now it played

'The Wild, Wild Women', and 'The Policeman's Holiday', and
he was no longer in black velvet with a sky blue collar.
'Profond's right,' he thought, 'there's nothing in it! We're all
progressing to the grave!' And with that surprising mental
comment he walked out.

He did not see Fleur again that night. But, at breakfast, her
eyes followed him about with an appeal he could not escape
– not that he intended to try. No! He had made up his mind
to the nerve-racking business. He would go to Robin Hill –
to that house of memories. Pleasant memory – the last! Of
going down to keep that boy's father and Irene apart by threat-
ening divorce. He had often thought, since, that it had clinched
their union. And, now, he was going to clinch the union of
that boy with his girl. 'I don't know what I've done,' he
thought, 'to have such things thrust on me!' He went up by
train and down by train, and from the station walked by the
long rising lane, still very much as he remembered it over thirty
years ago. Funny – so near London! Someone evidently was
holding on to the land there. This speculation soothed him,
moving between the high hedges slowly, so as not to get overheated, though the day was chill enough. After all was said
and done there was something real about land, it didn't shift.
Land, and good pictures! The values might fluctuate a bit, but
on the whole they were always going up – worth holding on
to, in a world where there was such a lot of unreality, cheap
building, changing fashions, such a 'Here to-day and gone to-
morrow' spirit. The French were right, perhaps, with their
peasant proprietorship, though he had no opinion of the
French. One's bit of land! Something solid in it! He had heard
peasant proprietors described as a pig-headed lot; had heard
young Mont call his father a pig-headed *Morning Poster* –
disrespectful young devil. Well, there were worse things than
being pig-headed or reading the *Morning Post*. There was
Profond and his tribe, and all these Labour chaps, and loud-
mouthed politicians and 'wild, wild women'! A lot of worse

things! And suddenly Soames became conscious of feeling weak, and hot, and shaky. Sheer nerves at the meeting before him! As Aunt Juley might have said – quoting 'Superior Dosset' – his nerves were 'in a proper fantigue'. He could see the house now among its trees, the house he had watched being built, intending it for himself and this woman, who, by such strange fate, had lived in it with another after all! He began to think of Dumetrius, Local Loans, and other forms of investment. He could not afford to meet her with his nerves all shaking; he who represented the Day of Judgment for her on earth as it was in heaven; he, legal ownership, personified, meeting lawless beauty, incarnate. His dignity demanded impassivity during this embassy designed to link their offspring, who, if she had behaved herself, would have been brother and sister. That wretched tune, 'The Wild, Wild Women', kept running in his head, perversely, for tunes did not run there as a rule. Passing the poplars in front of the house, he thought: 'How they've grown; I had them planted!'

A maid answered his ring.

'Will you say – Mr Forsyte, on a very special matter.'

If she realised who he was, quite probably she would not see him. 'By George!' he thought, hardening as the tug came. 'It's a topsy-turvy affair!'

The maid came back. 'Would the gentleman state his business, please?'

'Say it concerns Mr Jon,' said Soames.

And once more he was alone in that hall with the pool of grey-white marble designed by her first lover. Ah! she had been a bad lot – had loved two men, and not himself! He must remember that when he came face to face with her once more. And suddenly he saw her in the opening chink between the long heavy purple curtains, swaying, as if in hesitation; the old perfect poise and line, the old startled dark-eyed gravity, the old calm defensive voice: 'Will you come in, please?'

He passed through that opening. As in the picture-gallery and the confectioner's shop, she seemed to him still beautiful.

And this was the first time – the very first – since he married her seven-and-thirty years ago, that he was speaking to her without the legal right to call her his. She was not wearing black – one of that fellow's radical notions, he supposed.

'I apologise for coming,' he said glumly; 'but this business must be settled one way or the other.'

'Won't you sit down?'

'No, thank you.'

Anger at his false position, impatience of ceremony between them, mastered him, and words came tumbling out:

'It's an infernal mischance; I've done my best to discourage it. I consider my daughter crazy, but I've got into the habit of indulging her; that's why I'm here. I suppose you're fond of your son.'

'Devotedly.'

'Well?'

'It rests with him.'

He had a sense of being met and baffled. Always – always she had baffled him, even in those old first married days.

'It's a mad notion,' he said.

'It is.'

'If you had only—! Well – they might have been –' he did not finish that sentence 'brother and sister and all this saved', but he saw her shudder as if he had, and stung by the sight he crossed over to the window. Out *there* the trees had not grown – they couldn't, they were old!

'So far as I'm concerned,' he said, 'you may make your mind easy. I desire to see neither you nor your son if this marriage comes about. Young people in these days are – are unaccountable. But I can't bear to see my daughter unhappy. What am I to say to her when I go back?'

'Please say to her as I said to you, that it rests with Jon.'

'You don't oppose it?'

'With all my heart; not with my lips.'

Soames stood, biting his finger.

'I remember an evening—' he said suddenly; and was silent. What was there – what was there in this woman that would not fit into the four corners of his hate or condemnation? 'Where is he – your son?'

'Up in his father's studio, I think.'

'Perhaps you'd have him down.'

He watched her ring the bell, he watched the maid come in. 'Please tell Mr Jon that I want him.'

'If it rests with him,' said Soames hurriedly, when the maid was gone, 'I suppose I may take it for granted that this unnatural marriage will take place; in that case there'll be formalities. Whom do I deal with – Herring's?'

Irene nodded.

'You don't propose to live with them?'

Irene shook her head.

'What happens to this house?'

'It will be as Jon wishes.'

'This house,' said Soames suddenly: 'I had hopes when I began it. If *they* live in it – their children! They say there's such a thing as Nemesis. Do you believe in it?'

'Yes.'

'Oh! You do!'

He had come back from the window, and was standing close to her, who, in the curve of her grand piano, was, as it were, embayed.

'I'm not likely to see you again,' he said slowly. 'Will you shake hands' – his lip quivered, the words came out jerkily – 'and let the past die.' He held out his hand. Her pale face grew paler, her eyes so dark, rested immovably on his, her hands remained clasped in front of her. He heard a sound and turned. That boy was standing in the opening of the curtains. Very queer he looked, hardly recognisable as the young fellow he had seen in the Gallery off Cork Street – very queer; much older, no youth in the face at all – haggard, rigid, his hair ruffled, his eyes deep in his head. Soames made an effort, and said with a lift of his lip, not quite a smile nor quite a sneer:

'Well, young man! I'm here for my daughter; it rests with you, it seems – this matter. Your mother leaves it in your hands.'

The boy continued staring at his mother's face, and made no answer.

'For my daughter's sake I've brought myself to come,' said Soames. 'What am I to say to her when I go back?'

Still looking at his mother, the boy said, quietly:

'Tell Fleur that it's no good, please; I must do as my father wished before he died.'

'Jon!'

'It's all right, Mother.'

In a kind of stupefaction Soames looked from one to the other; then, taking up hat and umbrella which he had put down on a chair, he walked toward the curtains. The boy stood aside for him to go by. He passed through and heard the grate of the rings as the curtains were drawn behind him. The sound liberated something in his chest.

'So that's that!' he thought, and passed out of the front door.

Chapter Eight

The Dark Tune

*A*s Soames walked away from the house at Robin Hill the sun broke through the grey of that chill afternoon, in smoky radiance. So absorbed in landscape painting that he seldom looked seriously for effects of Nature out of doors – he was struck by that moody effulgence – it mounted with a triumph suited to his own feeling. Victory in defeat. His embassy had come to naught. But he was rid of those people, had regained his daughter at the expense of – her happiness. What would Fleur say to him? Would she believe he had done his best? And under that sunlight faring on the elms, hazels, hollies of the lane and those unexploited fields, Soames felt dread. She would be terribly upset! He must appeal to her pride. That boy had given her up, declared part and lot with the woman who so long ago had given her father up! Soames clenched his hands. Given him up, and why? What had been wrong with him? And once more he felt the *malaise* of one who contemplates himself as seen by another – like a dog who chances on his reflection in a mirror and is intrigued and anxious at the unseizable thing.

Not in a hurry to get home, he dined in town at the Connoisseurs. While eating a pear it suddenly occurred to him that, if he had not gone down to Robin Hill, the boy might not have so decided. He remembered the expression on his face while his mother was refusing the hand he had held out.

A strange, an awkward thought! Had Fleur cooked her own goose by trying to make too sure?

He reached home at half-past nine. While the car was passing in at one drive gate he heard the grinding sputter of a motor-cycle passing out by the other. Young Mont, no doubt, so Fleur had not been lonely. But he went in with a sinking heart. In the cream-panelled drawing-room she was sitting with her elbows on her knees, and her chin on her clasped hands, in front of a white camellia plant which filled the fireplace. That glance at her before she saw him renewed his dread. What was she seeing among those white camellias?

'Well, Father!'

Soames shook his head. His tongue failed him. This was murderous work! He saw her eyes dilate, her lips quivering.

'What? What? Quick, Father!'

'My dear,' said Soames, 'I – I did my best, but—' And again he shook his head.

Fleur ran to him, and put a hand on each of his shoulders. 'She?'

'No,' muttered Soames; 'he. I was to tell you that it was no use; he must do what his father wished before he died.' He caught her by the waist. 'Come, child, don't let them hurt you. They're not worth your little finger.'

Fleur tore herself from his grasp.

'You didn't – you – couldn't have tried. You – you betrayed me, Father!'

Bitterly wounded, Soames gazed at her passionate figure writhing there in front of him.

'You didn't try – you didn't – I was a fool! I won't believe he could – he ever could! Only yesterday he—! Oh! why did I ask you?'

'Yes,' said Soames, quietly, 'why did you? I swallowed my feelings; I did my best for you, against my judgment – and this is my reward. Good-night!'

With every nerve in his body twitching he went toward the door.

Fleur darted after him.

'He gives me up? You mean that? Father!'

Soames turned and forced himself to answer:

'Yes.'

'Oh!' cried Fleur. 'What did you – what could you have done in those old days?'

The breathless sense of really monstrous injustice cut the power of speech in Soames's throat. What had *he* done! What had they done to him! And with quite unconscious dignity he put his hand on his breast, and looked at her.

'It's a shame!' cried Fleur passionately.

Soames went out. He mounted, slow and icy, to his picture-gallery, and paced among his treasures. Outrageous! Oh! Outrageous! She was spoiled! Ah! and who had spoiled her? He stood still before the Goya copy. Accustomed to her own way in everything. Flower of his life! And now that she couldn't have it! He turned to the window for some air. Daylight was dying, the moon rising, gold behind the poplars! What sound was that? Why! That piano thing! A dark tune, with a thrum and a throb! She had set it going – what comfort could she get from that? His eyes caught movement down there beyond the lawn, under the trellis of rambler roses and young acacia-trees, where the moonlight fell. There she was, roaming up and down. His heart gave a little sickening jump. What would she do under this blow? How could he tell? What did he know of her – he had only loved her all his life – looked on her as the apple of his eye! He knew nothing – had no notion. There she was – and that dark tune – and the river gleaming in the moonlight!

'I must go out,' he thought.

He hastened down to the drawing-room, lighted just as he had left it, with the piano thrumming out that waltz, or fox-trot, or whatever they called it in these days, and passed through on to the verandah.

Where could he watch, without her seeing him? And he stole down through the fruit garden to the boat-house. He was between her and the river now, and his heart felt lighter. She was his daughter, and Annette's – she wouldn't do anything foolish; but there it was – he didn't know! From the boat-house window he could see the last acacia and the spin of her skirt when she turned in her restless march. That tune had run down at last – thank goodness! He crossed the floor and looked through the farther window at the water slow-flowing past the lilies. It made little bubbles against them, bright where a moon-streak fell. He remembered suddenly that early morning when he had slept on the house-boat after his father died, and she had just been born – nearly nineteen years ago! Even now he recalled the unaccustomed world when he woke up, the strange feeling it had given him. That day the second passion of his life began – for this girl of his, roaming under the acacias. What a comfort she had been to him! And all the soreness and sense of outrage left him. If he could make her happy again, he didn't care! An owl flew, queeking, queeking; a bat flitted by; the moonlight brightened and broadened on the water. How long was she going to roam about like this! He went back to the window, and suddenly saw her coming down to the bank. She stood quite close, on the landing-stage. And Soames watched, clenching his hands. Should he speak to her? His excitement was intense. The stillness of her figure, its youth, its absorption in despair, in longing, in – itself. He would always remember it, moonlit like that; and the faint sweet reek of the river and the shivering of the willow leaves. She had everything in the world that he could give her, except the one thing that she could not have because of him! The perversity of things hurt him at that moment, as might a fish-bone in his throat.

Then, with an infinite relief, he saw her turn back toward

the house. What could he give her to make amends? Pearls, travel, horses, other young men – anything she wanted – that he might lose the memory of her young figure lonely by the water! There! She had set that tune going again! Why – it was a mania! Dark, thrumming, faint, travelling from the house. It was as though she had said: 'If I can't have something to keep me going, I shall die of this!' Soames dimly understood. Well, if it helped her, let her keep it thrumming on all night! And, mousing back through the fruit garden, he regained the verandah. Though he meant to go in and speak to her now, he still hesitated, not knowing what to say, trying hard to recall how it felt to be thwarted in love. He ought to know, ought to remember – and he could not! Gone – all real recollection; except that it had hurt him horribly. In this blankness he stood passing his handkerchief over hands and lips, which were very dry. By craning his head he could just see Fleur, standing with her back to that piano still grinding out its tune, her arms tight crossed on her breast, a lighted cigarette between her lips, whose smoke half veiled her face. The expression on it was strange to Soames, the eyes shone and stared, and every feature was alive with a sort of wretched scorn and anger. Once or twice he had seen Annette look like that – the face was too vivid, too naked, not *his* daughter's at that moment. And he dared not go in, realising the futility of any attempt at consolation. He sat down in the shadow of the ingle-nook.

Monstrous trick, that Fate had played him! Nemesis! That old unhappy marriage! And in God's name – why? How was he to know, when he wanted Irene so violently, and she consented to be his, that she would never love him? The tune died and was renewed, and died again, and still Soames sat in the shadow, waiting for he knew not what. The fag of Fleur's cigarette, flung through the window, fell on the grass; he watched it glowing, burning itself out. The moon had freed herself above the poplars, and poured her unreality on the garden. Comfortless light, mysterious, withdrawn – like the beauty of that woman who had never loved him – dappling the nemesias and the stocks with a vesture not of earth. Flowers! And his flower so unhappy! Ah! Why could one not put happiness into Local Loans, gild its edges, insure it against going down?

Light had ceased to flow out now from the drawing-room window. All was silent and dark in there. Had she gone up? He rose, and, tiptoeing, peered in. It seemed so! He entered. The verandah kept the moonlight out; and at first he could see nothing but the outlines of furniture blacker than the darkness. He groped toward the farther window to shut it. His foot struck a chair, and he heard a gasp. There she was, curled and crushed into the corner of the sofa! His hand hovered. Did she want his consolation? He stood, gazing at that ball of crushed frills and hair and graceful youth, trying to burrow its way out of sorrow. How leave her there? At last he touched her hair, and said:

'Come, darling, better go to bed. I'll make it up to you, somehow.' How fatuous! But what could he have said?

Chapter Nine

Under the Oak-Tree

When their visitor had disappeared Jon and his mother stood without speaking, till he said suddenly:

'I ought to have seen him out.'

But Soames was already walking down the drive, and Jon went upstairs to his father's studio, not trusting himself to go back.

The expression on his mother's face confronting the man she had once been married to, had sealed a resolution growing within him ever since she left him the night before. It had put the finishing touch of reality. To marry Fleur would be to hit his mother in the face; to betray his dead father! It was no good! Jon had the least resentful of natures. He bore his parents no grudge in this hour of his distress. For one so young there was a rather strange power in him of seeing things in some sort of proportion. It was worse for Fleur, worse for his mother even, than it was for him. Harder than to give up was to be given up, or to be the cause of someone you loved giving up for you.

He must not, would not behave grudgingly! While he stood watching the tardy sunlight, he had again that sudden vision of the world which had come to him the night before. Sea on sea, country on country, millions on millions of people, all with their own lives, energies, joys, griefs, and suffering – all with things they had to give up, and separate struggles for existence. Even though he might be willing to give up all else for the one thing he couldn't have, he would be a fool to think his feelings mattered much in so vast a world, and to behave like a cry-baby or a cad. He pictured the people who had nothing – the millions who had given up life in the War, the millions whom the War had left with life and little else; the hungry children he had read of, the shattered men; people in prison, every kind of unfortunate. And – they did not help him much. If one had to miss a meal, what comfort in the knowledge that many others had to miss it too? There was more distraction in the thought of getting away out into this vast world of which he knew nothing yet. He could not go on staying here, walled in and sheltered, with everything so slick and comfortable, and nothing to do but brood and think what might have been. He could not go back to Wansdon, and the memories of Fleur. If he saw her again he could not trust himself; and if he stayed here or went back there, he would surely see her. While they were within reach of each other that must happen. To go far away and quickly was the only thing to do. But, however much he loved his mother, he did not want to go away with her. Then feeling that he was brutal, he made up his mind desperately to propose that they should go to Italy. For two hours in that melancholy room he tried to master himself, then dressed solemnly for dinner.

His mother had done the same. They ate little, at some length, and talked of his father's catalogue. The show was arranged for October, and beyond clerical detail there was nothing more to do.

After dinner she put on a cloak and they went out; walked a little, talked a little, till they were standing silent at last beneath the oak-tree. Ruled by the thought: 'If I show anything, I show all,' Jon put his arm through hers and said quite casually:

'Mother, let's go to Italy.'

Irene pressed his arm, and said as casually:

'It would be very nice; but I've been thinking you ought to see and do more than you would if I were with you.'

'But then you'd be alone.'

'I was once alone for more than twelve years. Besides, I should like to be here for the opening of Father's show.'

Jon's grip tightened round her arm; he was not deceived.

'You couldn't stay here all by yourself; it's too big.'

'Not here, perhaps. In London, and I might go to Paris, after the show opens. You ought to have a year at least, Jon, and see the world.'

'Yes, I'd like to see the world and rough it. But I don't want to leave you all alone.'

'My dear, I owe you that at least. If it's for your good, it'll be for mine. Why not start tomorrow? You've got your passport.'

'Yes; if I'm going it had better be at once. Only – Mother – if – if I wanted to stay out somewhere – America or anywhere, would you mind coming presently?'

'Wherever and whenever you send for me. But don't send until you really want me.'

Jon drew a deep breath.

'I feel England's choky.'

They stood a few minutes longer under the oak-tree – looking out to where the grand stand at Epsom was veiled in evening. The branches kept the moonlight from them, so that it only fell everywhere else – over the fields and far away, and on the windows of the creepered house behind, which soon would be to let.

Chapter Ten

Fleur's Wedding

The October paragraphs describing the wedding of Fleur Forsyte to Michael Mont hardly conveyed the symbolic significance of this event. In the union of the great-granddaughter of 'Superior Dosset' with the heir of a ninth baronet was the outward and visible sign of that merger of class in class which buttresses the political stability of a realm. The time had come when the Forsytes might resign their natural resentment against a 'flummery' not theirs by birth, and accept it as the still more natural due of their possessive instincts. Besides, they had to mount to make room for all those so much more newly rich. In that quiet but tasteful ceremony in Hanover Square, and afterward among the furniture in Green Street, it had been impossible for those not in the know to distinguish the Forsyte troop from the Mont contingent – so far away was 'Superior Dosset' now. Was there, in the crease of his trousers, the expression of his moustache, his accent, or the shine on his top hat, a pin to choose between Soames and the ninth baronet himself? Was not Fleur as self-possessed, quick, glancing, pretty, and hard as the likeliest Muskham, Mont, or Charwell filly present? If anything, the Forsytes had it in dress and looks and manners. They had become 'upper class' and now their name would be formally recorded in the Stud Book, their money joined to land. Whether this was a little late in the day, and those rewards of the possessive instinct, lands and money, destined for the melting-pot – was still a question so moot that it was not mooted. After all, Timothy had said Consols were goin' up. Timothy, the last, the missing link; Timothy, *in extremis* on the Bayswater Road – so Francie had reported. It was whispered, too, that this young Mont was a sort of socialist – strangely wise of him, and in the nature of insurance, considering the days they lived in. There was no uneasiness on that score. The landed classes produced that sort of amiable foolishness at times, turned to safe uses and confined to theory. As George remarked to his sister Francie: 'They'll soon be having puppies – that'll give him pause.'

The church with white flowers and something blue in the middle of the East window looked extremely chaste, as though endeavouring to counteract the somewhat lurid phraseology of a Service calculated to keep the thoughts of all on puppies. Forsytes, Haymans, Tweetymans, sat in the left aisle; Monts, Charwells, Muskhams in the right; while a sprinkling of Fleur's fellow-sufferers at school, and of Mont's fellow-sufferers in the War, gaped indiscriminately from either side, and three maiden ladies, who had dropped in on their way from Skyward's, brought up the rear, together with two Mont retainers and Fleur's old nurse. In the unsettled state of the country as full a house as could be expected.

Mrs Val Dartie, who sat with her husband in the third row, squeezed his hand more than once during the performance. To her, who knew the plot of this tragi-comedy, its most dramatic moment was well-nigh painful. 'I wonder if Jon knows by instinct,' she thought – Jon, out in British Columbia. She had received a letter from him only that morning which had made her smile and say:

'Jon's in British Columbia, Val, because he wants to be in California. He thinks it's too nice there.'

'Oh!' said Val, 'so he's beginning to see a joke again.'

'He's bought some land and sent for his mother.'

'What on earth will she do out there?'

'All she cares about is Jon. Do you still think it a happy release?'

Val's shrewd eyes narrowed to grey pin-points between their dark lashes.

'Fleur wouldn't have suited him a bit. She's not bred right.'

'Poor little Fleur!' sighed Holly. Ah! it was strange – this marriage. The young man, Mont, had caught her on the rebound, of course, in the reckless mood of one whose ship has just gone down. Such a plunge could not but be – as Val put it – an outside chance. There was little to be told from the back view of her young cousin's veil, and Holly's eyes reviewed the general aspect of this Christian wedding. She, who had made a love-match which had been successful, had a horror of unhappy marriages. This might not be one in the end – but it was clearly a toss-up; and to consecrate a toss-up in this fashion with manufactured unction before a crowd of fashionable free-thinkers – for who thought otherwise than freely, or not at all, when they were 'dolled' up – seemed to her as near a sin as one could find in an age which had abolished them. Her eyes wandered from the prelate in his robes (a Charwell – the Forsytes had not as yet produced a prelate) to Val, beside her, thinking – she was certain – of the Mayfly filly at fifteen to one for the Cambridgeshire. They passed on and caught the profile of the ninth baronet, in counterfeitment of the kneeling process. She could just see the neat ruck above his knees where he had pulled his trousers up, and thought: 'Val's forgotten to pull up his!' Her eyes passed to the pew in front of her, where Winifred's substantial form was gowned with passion, and on again to Soames and Annette kneeling side by side. A little smile came on her lips – Prosper Profond, back from the South Seas of the Channel, would be kneeling too, about six rows behind. Yes! This was a funny 'small' business, however it turned out; still it was in a proper church and would be in the proper papers to-morrow morning.

They had begun a hymn; she could hear the ninth baronet across the aisle, singing of the hosts of Midian. Her little finger touched Val's thumb – they were holding the same hymn-book – and a tiny thrill passed through her, preserved from twenty years ago. He stooped and whispered:

'I say, d'you remember the rat?' The rat at their wedding in Cape Colony, which had cleaned its whiskers behind the table at the Registrar's! And between her little and third finger she squeezed his thumb hard.

The hymn was over, the prelate had begun to deliver his discourse. He told them of the dangerous times they lived in, and the awful conduct of the House of Lords in connection with divorce. They were all soldiers – he said – in the trenches under the poisonous gas of the Prince of Darkness, and must be manful. The purpose of marriage was children, not mere sinful happiness.

An imp danced in Holly's eyes – Val's eyelashes were meeting. Whatever happened; he must *not* snore. Her finger and thumb closed on his thigh till he stirred uneasily.

The discourse was over, the danger past. They were signing in the vestry; and general relaxation had set in.

A voice behind her said:

'Will she stay the course?'

'Who's that?' she whispered.

'Old George Forsyte!'

Holly demurely scrutinised one of whom she had often heard. Fresh from South Africa, and ignorant of her kith and kin, she never saw one without an almost childish curiosity. He was very big, and very dapper; his eyes gave her a funny feeling of having no particular clothes.

'They're off!' she heard him say.

They came, stepping from the chancel. Holly looked first in young Mont's face. His lips and ears were twitching, his eyes, shifting from his feet to the hand within his arm, stared suddenly before them as if to face a firing party. He gave Holly

the feeling that he was spiritually intoxicated. But Fleur! Ah!
That was different. The girl was perfectly composed, prettier
than ever, in her white robes and veil over her banged dark
chestnut hair; her eyelids hovered demure over her dark hazel
eyes. Outwardly, she seemed all there. But inwardly, where
was she? As those two passed, Fleur raised her eyelids – the
restless glint of those clear whites remained on Holly's vision
as might the flutter of caged bird's wings.

In Green Street Winifred stood to receive, just a little less
composed than usual. Soames's request for the use of her house
had come on her at a deeply psychological moment. Under the
influence of a remark of Prosper Profond, she had begun to
exchange her Empire for Expressionistic furniture. There were
the most amusing arrangements, with violet, green, and orange
blobs and scriggles, to be had at Mealard's. Another month and
the change would have been complete. Just now, the very
'intriguing' recruits she had enlisted, did not march too well with
the old guard. It was as if her regiment were half in khaki, half
in scarlet and bearskins. But her strong and comfortable character made the best of it in a drawing-room which typified,
perhaps, more perfectly than she imagined, the semi-bolshevised
imperialism of her country. After all, this was a day of merger,
and you couldn't have too much of it! Her eyes travelled indul-
gently among her guests. Soames had gripped the back of a buhl
chair; young Mont was behind that 'awfully amusing' screen,
which no one as yet had been able to explain to her. The ninth
baronet had shied violently at a round scarlet table, inlaid under
glass with blue Australian butterflies' wings, and was clinging to
her Louis-Quinze cabinet; Francie Forsyte had seized the new
mantel-board, finely carved with little purple grotesques on an
ebony ground; George, over by the old spinet, was holding a
little sky-blue book as if about to enter bets; Prosper Profond
was twiddling the knob of the open door, black with peacock-
blue panels; and Annette's hands, close by, were grasping her

own waist; two Muskhams clung to the balcony among the plants, as if feeling ill; Lady Mont, thin and brave-looking, had taken up her long-handled glasses and was gazing at the central light shade, of ivory and orange dashed with deep magenta, as if the heavens had opened. Everybody, in fact, seemed holding on to something. Only Fleur, still in her bridal dress, was detached from all support, flinging her words and glances to left and right.

The room was full of the bubble and the squeak of conversation. Nobody could hear anything that anybody said; which seemed of little consequence, since no one waited for anything so slow as an answer. Modern conversation seemed to Winifred so different from the days of her prime, when a drawl was all the vogue. Still it was 'amusing', which, of course, was all that mattered. Even the Forsytes were talking with extreme rapidity – Fleur and Christopher, and Imogen, and young Nicholas's youngest, Patrick. Soames, of course, was silent; but George, by the spinet, kept up a running commentary, and Francie, by her mantel-shelf. Winifred drew nearer to the ninth baronet. He seemed to promise a certain repose; his nose was fine and drooped a little, his grey moustaches too; and she said, drawling through her smile:

'It's rather nice, isn't it?'

His reply shot out of his smile like a snipped bread pellet: 'D'you remember, in Frazer, the tribe that buries the bride up to the waist?'

He spoke as fast as anybody! He had dark lively little eyes, too, all crinkled round like a Catholic priest's. Winifred felt suddenly he might say things she would regret.

'They're always so amusing – weddings,' she murmured, and moved on to Soames. He was curiously still, and Winifred saw at once what was dictating his immobility. To his right was George Forsyte, to his left Annette and Prosper Profond. He could not move without either seeing those two together, or the reflection of them in George Forsyte's japing eyes. He was quite right not to be taking notice.

'They say Timothy's sinking,' he said glumly.

'Where will you put him, Soames?'

'Highgate.' He counted on his fingers. 'It'll make twelve of them there, including wives. How do you think Fleur looks?'

'Remarkably well.'

Soames nodded. He had never seen her look prettier, yet he could not rid himself of the impression that this business was unnatural – remembering still that crushed figure burrowing into the corner of the sofa. From that night to this day he had received from her no confidences. He knew from his chauffeur that she had made one more attempt on Robin Hill and drawn blank – an empty house, no one at home. He knew that she had received a letter, but not what was in it, except that it had made her hide herself and cry. He had remarked that she looked at him sometimes when she thought he wasn't noticing, as if she were wondering still what he had done – forsooth – to make those people hate him so. Well, there it was! Annette had come back, and things had worn on through the summer – very miserable, till suddenly Fleur had said she was going to marry young Mont. She had shown him a little more affection when she told him that. And he had yielded – what was the good of opposing it? God knew that he had never wished to thwart her in anything! And the young man seemed quite delirious about her. No doubt she was in a reckless mood, and she was young, absurdly young. But if he opposed her, he didn't know what she would do; for all he could tell she might want to take up a profession, become a doctor or solicitor, some nonsense. She had no aptitude for painting, writing, music, in his view the legitimate occupations of unmarried women, if they must do something in these days. On the whole, she was safer married, for he could see too well how feverish and restless she was at home. Annette, too, had been in favour of it – Annette, from behind the veil of his refusal to know what she was about, if she was about anything. Annette had said: 'Let her marry this young man. He is a nice boy – not so highty-flighty as he seems.' Where she got her expressions, he didn't know – but her opinion soothed his doubts. His wife, whatever her conduct, had clear eyes and an almost depressing amount of common sense. He had settled fifty thousand on Fleur, taking care that there was no cross settlement in case it didn't turn out well. Could it turn out well? She had not got over that other boy – he knew. They were to go to Spain for the honeymoon. He would be even lonelier when she was gone. But later, perhaps, she would forget, and turn to him again! Winifred's voice broke on his reverie.

'Why! Of all wonders – June!'

There, in a djibbah – what things she wore! – with her hair straying from under a fillet, Soames saw his cousin, and Fleur going forward to greet her. The two passed from their view out on to the stairway.

'Really,' said Winifred, 'she does the most impossible things! Fancy *her* coming!'

'What made you ask her?' muttered Soames.

'Because I thought she wouldn't accept, of course.'

Winifred had forgotten that behind conduct lies the main trend of character; or, in other words, omitted to remember that Fleur was now a 'lame duck'.

On receiving her invitation, June had first thought, 'I wouldn't go near them for the world!' and then, one morning, had awakened from a dream of Fleur waving to her from a boat with a wild unhappy gesture. And she had changed her mind.

When Fleur came forward and said to her, 'Do come up while I'm changing my dress,' she had followed up the stairs. The girl led the way into Imogen's old bedroom, set ready for her toilet.

June sat down on the bed, thin and upright, like a little spirit in the sear and yellow. Fleur locked the door.

The girl stood before her divested of her wedding dress. What a pretty thing she was!

'I suppose you think me a fool,' she said, with quivering lips, 'when it was to have been Jon. But what does it matter? Michael wants me, and I don't care. It'll get me away from home.' Diving her hand into the frills on her breast, she brought out a letter. 'Jon wrote me this.'

June read: 'Lake Okanagen, British Columbia. I'm not coming back to England. Bless you always. Jon.'

'She's made safe, you see,' said Fleur.

June handed back the letter.

'That's not fair to Irene,' she said, 'she always told Jon he could do as he wished.'

Fleur smiled bitterly. 'Tell me, didn't she spoil your life too?'

June looked up. 'Nobody can spoil a life, my dear. That's nonsense. Things happen, but we bob up.'

With a sort of terror she saw the girl sink on her knees and bury her face in the djibbah. A strangled sob mounted to June's ears.

'It's all right – all right,' she murmured. 'Don't! There, there!'

But the point of the girl's chin was pressed ever closer into her thigh, and the sound was dreadful of her sobbing.

Well, well! It had to come. She would feel better afterward! June stroked the short hair of that shapely head; and all the scattered mother-sense in her focused itself and passed through the tips of her fingers into the girl's brain.

'Don't sit down under it, my dear,' she said at last. 'We can't control life, but we can fight it. Make the best of things. I've had to. I held on, like you; and I cried, as you're crying now. And look at me!'

Fleur raised her head; a sob merged suddenly into a little choked laugh. In truth it was a thin and rather wild and wasted spirit she was looking at, but it had brave eyes.

'All right!' she said. 'I'm sorry. I shall forget him, I suppose, if I fly fast and far enough.'

And, scrambling to her feet, she went over to the wash-stand.

June watched her removing with cold water the traces of emotion. Save for a little becoming pinkness there was nothing left when she stood before the mirror. June got off the bed and took a pin-cushion in her hand. To put two pins into the wrong places was all the vent she found for sympathy.

'Give me a kiss,' she said when Fleur was ready, and dug her chin into the girl's warm cheek.

'I want a whiff,' said Fleur; 'don't wait.'

June left her, sitting on the bed with a cigarette between her lips and her eyes half closed, and went downstairs. In the doorway of the drawing-room stood Soames as if unquiet at his daughter's tardiness. June tossed her head and passed down on to the half-landing. Her cousin Francie was standing there.

'Look!' said June, pointing with her chin at Soames. 'That man's fatal!'

'How do you mean,' said Francie, 'fatal?'

June did not answer her. 'I shan't wait to see them off,' she said. 'Good-bye!'

'Good-bye!' said Francie, and her eyes, of a Celtic grey, goggled. That old feud! Really, it was quite romantic!

Soames, moving to the well of the staircase, saw June go, and drew a breath of satisfaction. Why didn't Fleur come? They would miss their train. That train would bear her away from him, yet he could not help fidgeting at the thought that they would lose it. And then she did come, running down in her tan-coloured frock and black velvet cap, and passed him into the drawing-room. He saw her kiss her mother, her aunt, Val's wife, Imogen, and then come forth, quick and pretty as ever. How would she treat him at this last moment of her girlhood? He couldn't hope for much!

Her lips pressed the middle of his cheek.

'Daddy!' she said, and was past and gone! Daddy! She hadn't called him that for years. He drew a long breath and followed slowly down. There was all the folly with that confetti stuff and the rest of it to go through with yet. But he would like just to catch her smile, if she leaned out, though they would hit her in the eye with the shoe, if they didn't take care. Young Mont's voice said fervently in his ear:

'Good-bye, sir; and thank you! I'm so fearfully bucked.'

'Good-bye,' he said; 'don't miss your train.'

He stood on the bottom step but three, whence he could see above the heads – the silly hats and heads. They were in the car now; and there was that stuff, showering, and there went the shoe. A flood of something welled up in Soames, and – he didn't know – he couldn't see!

Chapter Eleven

The Last of the Old Forsytes

*W*hen they came to prepare that terrific symbol Timothy Forsyte – the one pure individualist left, the only man who hadn't heard of the Great War – they found him wonderful – not even death had undermined his soundness.

To Smither and Cook that preparation came like final evidence of what they had never believed possible – the end of the old Forsyte family on earth. Poor Mr Timothy must now take a harp and sing in the company of Miss Forsyte, Mrs Julia, Miss Hester; with Mr Jolyon, Mr Swithin, Mr James, Mr Roger, and Mr Nicholas of the party. Whether Mrs Hayman would be there was more doubtful, seeing that she had been cremated. Secretly Cook thought that Mr Timothy would be upset – he had always been so set against barrel organs. How many times had she not said: 'Drat the thing! There it is again! Smither, you'd better run up and see what you can do.' And in her heart she would so have enjoyed the tunes, if she hadn't known that Mr Timothy would ring the bell in a minute and say: 'Here, take him a halfpenny and tell him to move on.' Often they had been obliged to add three-pence of their own before the man would go – Timothy had ever underrated the value of emotion. Luckily he had taken the organs for blue-bottles in his last years, which had been a comfort, and they had been able to enjoy the tunes. But a harp! Cook wondered. It *was* a change! And Mr Timothy had never liked change. But she did not speak of this to Smither, who did so take a line of her own in regard to heaven that it quite put one about sometimes.

She cried while Timothy was being prepared, and they all had sherry afterward out of the yearly Christmas bottle, which would not be needed now. Ah! dear! She had been there five-and-forty years and Smither three-and-forty! And now they would be going to a tiny house in Tooting, to live on their savings and what Miss Hester had so kindly left them – for to take fresh service after the glorious past – No! But they would like just to see Mr Soames again, and Mrs Dartie, and Miss Francie, and Miss Euphemia. And even if they had to take their own cab, they felt they must go to the funeral. For six years Mr Timothy had been their baby, getting younger and younger every day, till at last he had been too young to live.

They spent the regulation hours of waiting in polishing and dusting, in catching the one mouse left, and asphyxiating the last beetle so as to leave it nice, discussing with each other what they would buy at the sale. Miss Ann's workbox; Miss Juley's (that is Mrs Julia's) seaweed album; the fire-screen Miss Hester had crewelled; and Mr Timothy's hair – little golden curls, glued into a black frame. Oh! they must have those – only the price of things had gone up so!

It fell to Soames to issue invitations for the funeral. He had them drawn up by Gradman in his office – only blood relations, and no flowers. Six carriages were ordered. The will would be read afterward at the house.

He arrived at eleven o'clock to see that all was ready. At a quarter past old Gradman came in black gloves and crape on his hat. He and Soames stood in the drawing-room waiting. At half-past eleven the carriages drew up in a long row. But no one else appeared. Gradman said:

'It surprises me, Mr Soames. I posted them myself.'

'I don't know,' said Soames; 'he'd lost touch with the family.'

Soames had often noticed in old days how much more neighbourly his family were to the dead than to the living. But, now, the way they had flocked to Fleur's wedding and abstained from Timothy's funeral, seemed to show some vital change. There might, of course, be another reason; for Soames felt that if he had not known the contents of Timothy's will, he might have stayed away himself through delicacy. Timothy had left a lot of money, with nobody in particular to leave it to. They mightn't like to seem to expect something.

At twelve o'clock the procession left the door; Timothy alone in the first carriage under glass. Then Soames alone; then Gradman alone; then Cook and Smither together. They started at a walk, but were soon trotting under a bright sky. At the entrance to Highgate Cemetery they were delayed by service in the Chapel. Soames would have liked to stay outside in the sunshine. He didn't believe a word of it; on the other hand, it was a form of insurance which could not safely be neglected, in case there might be something in it after all.

They walked up two and two – he and Gradman, Cook and Smither – to the family vault. It was not very distinguished for the funeral of the last old Forsyte.

He took Gradman into his carriage on the way back to the Bayswater Road with a certain glow in his heart. He had a surprise in pickle for the old chap who had served the Forsytes four-and-fifty years – a treat that was entirely his doing. How well he remembered saying to Timothy the day after Aunt Hester's funeral: 'Well, Uncle Timothy, there's Gradman. He's taken a lot of trouble for the family. What do you say to leaving him five thousand?' and his surprise, seeing the difficulty there had been in getting Timothy to leave anything, when Timothy had nodded. And now the old chap would be as pleased as Punch, for Mrs Gradman, he knew, had a weak heart, and their son had lost a leg in the War. It was extraordinarily gratifying to Soames to have left him five thousand pounds of Timothy's money. They sat down together in the

little drawing-room, whose walls – like a vision of heaven –
were sky-blue and gold with every picture-frame unnaturally
bright, and every speck of dust removed from every piece of
furniture, to read that little masterpiece – the will of Timothy.
With his back to the light in Aunt Hester's chair, Soames faced
Gradman with his face to the light, on Aunt Ann's sofa; and,
crossing his legs, began:

'This is the last Will and Testament of me Timothy Forsyte
of The Bower, Bayswater Road, London. I appoint my nephew
Soames Forsyte of The Shelter Mapledurham and Thomas
Gradman of 159 Folly Road Highgate (hereinafter called my
Trustees) to be the trustees and executors of this my Will. To
the said Soames Forsyte I leave the sum of one thousand
pounds free of legacy duty and to the said Thomas Gradman
I leave the sum of five thousand pounds free of legacy duty.'

Soames paused. Old Gradman was leaning forward, convul-
sively gripping a stout black knee with each of his thick hands;
his mouth had fallen open so that the gold fillings of three
teeth gleamed; his eyes were blinking, two tears rolled slowly
out of them. Soames read hastily on.

'All the rest of my property of whatsoever description I
bequeath to my Trustees upon Trust to convert and hold the
same upon the following trusts namely. To pay thereout all
my debts funeral expenses and outgoings of any kind in connection with my Will and to hold the residue thereof in trust for
that male lineal descendant of my father Jolyon Forsyte by his
marriage with Ann Pierce who after the decease of all lineal
descendants whether male or female of my said father by his
said marriage in being at the time of my death shall last attain
the age of twenty-one years absolutely it being my desire that
my property shall be nursed to the extreme limit permitted by
the laws of England for the benefit of such male lineal descendant as aforesaid.'

Soames read the investment and attestation clauses, and,
ceasing, looked at Gradman. The old fellow was wiping his

brow with a large handkerchief, whose brilliant colour supplied a sudden festive tinge to the proceedings.

'My word, Mr Soames!' he said, and it was clear that the lawyer in him had utterly wiped out the man: 'My word! Why, there are two babies now, and some quite young children – if one of them lives to be eighty – it's not a great age – and add twenty-one – that's a hundred years; and Mr Timothy worth a hundred and fifty thousand pound net if he's worth a penny. Compound interest at five per cent doubles you in fourteen years. In fourteen years three hundred thousand – six hundred thousand in twenty-eight – twelve hundred thousand in forty-two – twenty-four hundred thousand in fifty-six – four million eight hundred thousand in seventy – nine million six hundred thousand in eighty-four – Why, in a hundred years it'll be twenty million! And we shan't live to use it! It *is* a will!'

Soames said drily: 'Anything may happen. The State might take the lot; they're capable of anything in these days.'

'And carry five,' said Gradman to himself. 'I forgot – Mr Timothy's in Consols; we shan't get more than two per cent, with this income tax. To be on the safe side, say eight millions. Still, that's a pretty penny.'

Soames rose and handed him the will. 'You're going into the City. Take care of that, and do what's necessary. Advertise; but there are no debts. When's the sale?'

'Tuesday week,' said Gradman. 'Life or lives in bein' and twenty-one years afterward – it's a long way off. But I'm glad he's left it in the family . . .'

The sale – not at Jobson's, in view of the Victorian nature of the effects – was far more freely attended than the funeral, though not by Cook and Smither, for Soames had taken it on himself to give them their heart's desires. Winifred was present, Euphemia, and Francie, and Eustace had come in his car. The miniatures, Barbizons, and J. R. drawings had been bought in by Soames; and relics of no marketable value were set aside in an off-room for members of the family who cared to have mementoes. These were the only restrictions upon bidding characterised by an almost tragic languor. Not one piece of furniture, no picture or porcelain figure appealed to modern taste. The humming birds had fallen like autumn leaves when taken from where they had not hummed for sixty years. It was painful to Soames to see the chairs his aunts had sat on, the little grand piano they had practically never played, the books whose outsides they had gazed at, the china they had dusted, the curtains they had drawn, the hearth-rug which had warmed their feet; above all, the beds they had lain and died in – sold to little dealers, and the housewives of Fulham. And yet – what could one do? Buy them and stick them in a lumber-room? No; they had to go the way of all flesh and furniture, and be worn out. But when they put up Aunt Ann's sofa and were going to knock it down for thirty shillings, he cried out, suddenly: 'Five pounds!' The sensation was considerable, and the sofa his.

When that little sale was over in the fusty saleroom, and those Victorian ashes scattered, he went out into the misty October sunshine feeling as if cosiness had died out of the world, and the board 'To Let' was up, indeed. Revolutions on the horizon; Fleur in Spain; no comfort in Annette; no Timothy's on the Bayswater Road. In the irritable desolation of his soul he went into the Goupenor Gallery. That chap Jolyon's water-colours were on view there. He went in to look down his nose at them – it might give him some faint satisfaction. The news had trickled through from June to Val's wife, from her to Val, from Val to his mother, from her to Soames, that the house – the fatal house at Robin Hill – was for sale, and Irene going to join her boy out in British Columbia, or some such place. For one wild moment the thought had come to Soames: 'Why shouldn't I buy it back? I meant it for my—!' No sooner come than gone. Too lugubrious a triumph; with too many humiliating memories for himself and Fleur. She would never live there after what had happened. No, the place must go its way to some peer or profiteer. It had been a bone of contention from the first, the shell of the feud; and with the woman gone, it was an empty shell. 'For Sale or To Let.' With his mind's eye he could see that board raised high above the ivied wall which he had built.

He passed through the first of the two rooms in the Gallery. There was certainly a body of work! And now that the fellow was dead it did not seem so trivial. The drawings were pleasing enough, with quite a sense of atmosphere, and something individual in the brush work. 'His father and my father; he and I; his child and mine!' thought Soames. So it had gone on! And all about that woman! Softened by the events of the past week, affected by the melancholy beauty of the autumn day, Soames came nearer than he had ever been to realisation of that truth – passing the understanding of a Forsyte pure – that the body of Beauty has a spiritual essence, uncapturable save by a devotion which thinks not of self. After all, he was near that truth in his devotion to his daughter; perhaps that made him understand a little how he had missed the prize. And there, among the drawings of his kinsman, who had attained to that which he had found beyond his reach, he thought of him and her with a tolerance which surprised him. But he did not buy a drawing.

Just as he passed the seat of custom on his return to the outer air he met with a contingency which had not been entirely absent from his mind when he went into the Gallery – Irene, herself, coming in. So she had not gone yet, and was still paying farewell visits to that fellow's remains! He subdued the little involuntary leap of his subconsciousness, the mechanical reaction of his senses to the charm of this once-owned woman, and passed her with averted eyes. But when he had gone by he could not for the life of him help looking back. This, then, was finality – the heat and stress of his life, the madness and the longing thereof, the only defeat he had known, would be over when she faded from his view this time; even such memories had their own queer aching value. She, too, was looking back. Suddenly she lifted her gloved hand, her lips smiled faintly, her dark eyes seemed to speak. It was the turn of Soames to make no answer to that smile and that little farewell wave; he went out into the fashionable street quivering from head to foot. He knew what she had meant to say: 'Now that I am going for ever out of the reach of you and yours – forgive me; I wish you well.' That was the meaning; last sign of that terrible reality – passing morality, duty, common sense – her aversion from him who had owned her body, but had never touched her spirit or her heart. It hurt; yes – more than if she had kept her mask unmoved, her hand unlifted.

Three days later, in that fast-yellowing October, Soames took a taxi-cab to Highgate Cemetery and mounted through its white forest to the Forsyte vault. Close to the cedar, above catacombs and columbaria, tall, ugly, and individual, it looked like an apex of the competitive system. He could remember a discussion wherein Swithin had advocated the addition to its face of the pheasant proper. The proposal had been rejected in favour of a wreath in stone, above the stark words: 'The family vault of Jolyon Forsyte: 1850.' It was in good order. All trace of the recent interment had been removed, and its sober grey gloomed reposefully in the sunshine. The whole family lay there now, except old Jolyon's wife, who had gone back under a contract to her own family vault in Suffolk; old Jolyon himself lying at Robin Hill; and Susan Hayman, cremated so that none knew where she might be. Soames gazed at it with satisfaction – massive, needing little attention; and this was important, for he was well aware that no one would attend to it when he himself was gone, and he would have to be looking out for lodgings soon. He might have twenty years before him, but one never knew. Twenty years without an aunt or uncle, with a wife of whom one had better not know anything, with a daughter gone from home. His mood inclined to melancholy and retrospection.

This cemetery was full, they said – of people with extraordinary names, buried in extraordinary taste. Still, they had a fine view up here, right over London. Annette had once given him a story to read by that Frenchman, Maupassant, a most lugubrious concern, where all the skeletons emerged from their graves one night, and all the pious inscriptions on the stones were altered to descriptions of their sins. Not a true story at all. He didn't know about the French, but there was not much real harm in English people except their teeth and their taste, which was certainly deplorable. 'The family vault of Jolyon Forsyte: 1850.' A lot of people had been buried here since then – a lot of English life crumbled to mould and dust! The boom of an airplane passing under the gold-tinted clouds caused him to lift his eyes. The deuce of a lot of expansion had gone on. But it all came back to a cemetery – to a name and a date on a tomb. And he thought with a curious pride that he and his family had done little or nothing to help this feverish expansion. Good solid middlemen, they had gone to work with dignity to manage and possess. 'Superior Dosset', indeed, had built in a dreadful, and Jolyon painted in a doubtful, period, but so far as he remembered not another of them all had soiled his hands by creating anything – unless you counted Val Dartie and his horse-breeding. Collectors, solicitors, barristers, merchants, publishers, accountants, directors, land agents, even soldiers – there they had been! The country had expanded, as it were, in spite of them. They had checked, controlled, defended, and taken advantage of the process and when you considered how 'Superior Dosset' had begun life with next to nothing, and his lineal descendants already owned what old Gradman estimated at between a million and a million and a half, it was not so bad! And yet he sometimes felt as if the family bolt was shot, their possessive instinct dying out. They seemed unable to make money – this fourth generation; they were going into art, literature, farming, or the army; or just living on what was left them –

they had no push and no tenacity. They would die out if they didn't take care.

Soames turned from the vault and faced toward the breeze. The air up here would be delicious if only he could rid his nerves of the feeling that mortality was in it. He gazed restlessly at the crosses and the urns, the angels, the 'immortelles', the flowers, gaudy or withering; and suddenly he noticed a spot which seemed so different from anything else up there that he was obliged to walk the few necessary yards and look at it. A sober corner, with a massive queer-shaped cross of grey rough-hewn granite, guarded by four dark yew-trees. The spot was free from the pressure of the other graves, having a little box-hedged garden on the far side, and in front a goldening birch-tree. This oasis in the desert of conventional graves appealed to the aesthetic sense of Soames, and he sat down there in the sunshine. Through those trembling gold birch leaves he gazed out at London, and yielded to the waves of memory. He thought of Irene in Montpelier Square, when her hair was rusty-golden and her white shoulders his – Irene, the prize of his love-passion, resistant to his ownership. He saw Bosinney's body lying in that white mortuary, and Irene sitting on the sofa looking at space with the eyes of a dying bird. Again he thought of her by the little green Niobe in the Bois de Boulogne, once more rejecting him. His fancy took him on beside his drifting river on the November day when Fleur was to be born, took him to the dead leaves floating on the green-tinged water and the snake-headed weed forever swaying and nosing, sinuous, blind, tethered. And on again to the window opened to the cold starry night above Hyde Park, with his father lying dead. His fancy darted to that picture of 'the future town', to that boy's and Fleur's first meeting; to the bluish trail of Prosper Profond's cigar, and Fleur in the window pointing down to where the fellow prowled. To the sight of Irene and that dead fellow sitting side by side in the stand at Lord's. To her and that boy at Robin Hill. To the sofa, where

Fleur lay crushed up in the corner; to her lips pressed into his cheek, and her farewell 'Daddy'. And suddenly he saw again Irene's grey-gloved hand waving its last gesture of release.

He sat there a long time dreaming his career, faithful to the scut of his possessive instinct, warming himself even with its failures.

'To Let' – the Forsyte age and way of life, when a man owned his soul, his investments, and his woman, without check or question. And now the State had, or would have, his investments, his woman had herself, and God knew who had his soul. 'To Let' – that sane and simple creed!

The waters of change were foaming in, carrying the promise of new forms only when their destructive flood should have passed its full. He sat there, subconscious of them, but with his thoughts resolutely set on the past – as a man might ride into a wild night with his face to the tail of his galloping horse. Athwart the Victorian dykes the waters were rolling on property, manners, and morals, on melody and the old forms of art – waters bringing to his mouth a salt taste as of blood, lapping to the foot of this Highgate Hill where Victorianism lay buried. And sitting there, high up on its most individual spot, Soames – like a figure of Investment – refused their restless sounds. Instinctively he would not fight them – there was in him too much primeval wisdom, of Man the possessive animal. They would quiet down when they had fulfilled their tidal fever of dispossessing and destroying; when the creations and the properties of others were sufficiently broken and defected – they would lapse and ebb, and fresh forms would rise based on an instinct older than the fever of change – the instinct of Home. '*Je m'en fiche*,' said Prosper Profond. Soames did not say '*Je m'en fiche*' – it was French, and the fellow was a thorn in his side – but deep down he knew that change was only the interval of death between two forms of life, destruction necessary to make room for fresher property. What though the board was up, and cosiness to let? – someone would come along and take it again some day.

And only one thing really troubled him, sitting there – the melancholy craving in his heart – because the sun was like enchantment on his face and on the clouds and on the golden birch leaves, and the wind's rustle was so gentle, and the yew tree green so dark, and the sickle of a moon pale in the sky.

He might wish and wish and never get it – the beauty and the loving in the world!

To Let:
Additional material

Preface to
The Man of Property, In Chancery
and *To Let*

The Forsyte Saga was the title originally destined for that part of it which is called *The Man of Property*; and to adopt it for the collected chronicles of the Forsyte family has indulged the Forsytean tenacity that is in all of us. The word Saga might be objected to on the ground that it connotes the heroic and that there is little heroism in these pages. But it is used with a suitable irony; and, after all, this long tale, though it may deal with folk in frock coats, furbelows, and a gilt-edged period, is not devoid of the essential heat of conflict. Discounting for the gigantic stature and blood-thirstiness of old days, as they have come down to us in fairy-tale and legend, the folk of the old sagas were Forsytes, assuredly, in their possessive instincts, and as little proof against the inroads of beauty and passion as Swithin, Soames, or even young Jolyon. And if heroic figures, in days that never were, seem to startle out from their surroundings in fashion unbecoming to a Forsyte of the Victorian era, we may be sure that tribal instinct was even then the prime force, and that 'family' and the sense of home and property counted as they do to this day, for all the recent efforts to 'talk them out'.

So many people have written and claimed that their families were the originals of the Forsytes that one has been almost encouraged to believe in the typicality of an imagined species. Manners change and modes evolve, and 'Timothy's on the

Bayswater Road' becomes a nest of the unbelievable in all except essentials; we shall not look upon its like again, nor perhaps on such a one as James or old Jolyon. And yet the figures of Insurance Societies and the utterances of Judges reassure us daily that our earthly paradise is still a rich preserve, where the wild raiders, Beauty and Passion, come stealing in, filching security from beneath our noses. As surely as a dog will bark at a brass band, so will the essential Soames in human nature ever rise up uneasily against the dissolution which hovers round the folds of ownership.

'Let the dead Past bury its dead' would be a better saying if the Past ever died. The persistence of the Past is one of those tragi-comic blessings which each new age denies, coming cocksure on to the stage to mouth its claim to a perfect novelty.

But no Age is so new as that! Human Nature, under its changing pretensions and clothes, is and ever will be very much of a Forsyte, and might, after all, be a much worse animal.

Looking back on the Victorian era, whose ripeness, decline, and 'fall-of' is in some sort pictured in *The Forsyte Saga*, we see now that we have but jumped out of a frying-pan into a fire. It would be difficult to substantiate a claim that the case of England was better in 1913 than it was in 1886, when the Forsytes assembled at old Jolyon's to celebrate the engagement of June to Philip Bosinney. And in 1920, when again the clan gathered to bless the marriage of Fleur with Michael Mont, the state of England is as surely too molten and bankrupt as in the eighties it was too congealed and low-percented. If these chronicles had been a really scientific study of transition one would have dwelt probably on such factors as the invention of bicycle, motor-car, and flying-machine; the arrival of a cheap Press; the decline of country life and increase of the towns; the birth of the Cinema. Men are, in fact, quite unable to control their own inventions; they at best develop adaptability to the new conditions those inventions create.

But this long tale is no scientific study of a period; it is rather an intimate incarnation of the disturbance that Beauty effects in the lives of men.

The figure of Irene, never, as the reader may possibly have observed, present, except through the senses of other characters, is a concretion of disturbing Beauty impinging on a possessive world.

One has noticed that readers, as they wade on through the salt waters of the Saga, are inclined more and more to pity Soames, and to think that in doing so they are in revolt against the mood of his creator. Far from it! He, too, pities Soames, the tragedy of whose life is the very simple, uncontrollable tragedy of being unlovable, without quite a thick enough skin to be thoroughly unconscious of the fact. Not even Fleur loves Soames as he feels he ought to be loved. But in pitying Soames, readers incline, perhaps, to animus against Irene: After all, they think, he wasn't a bad fellow, it wasn't his fault; she ought to have forgiven him, and so on!

And, taking sides, they lose perception of the simple truth, which underlies the whole story, that where sex attraction is utterly and definitely lacking in one partner to a union, no amount of pity, or reason, or duty, or what not, can overcome a repulsion implicit in Nature. Whether it ought to, or no, is beside the point; because in fact it never does. And where Irene seems hard and cruel, as in the Bois de Boulogne, or the Goupenor Gallery, she is but wisely realistic – knowing that the least concession is the inch which precedes the impossible, the repulsive ell.

A criticism one might pass on the last phase of the Saga is the complaint that Irene and Jolyon, those rebels against property, claim spiritual property in their son Jon. But it would be hypercriticism, as the tale is told. No father and mother could have let the boy marry Fleur without knowledge of the facts; and the facts determine Jon, not the persuasion of his parents. Moreover, Jolyon's persuasion is not on his own account, but on Irene's, and Irene's persuasion becomes a reiterated: 'Don't think of me, think of yourself!' That Jon, knowing the facts, can realise his mother's feelings, will hardly with justice be held proof that she is, after all, a Forsyte.

But though the impingement of Beauty and the claims of Freedom on a possessive world are the main prepossessions of *The Forsyte Saga*, it cannot be absolved from the charge of embalming the upper-middle class. As the old Egyptians placed around their mummies the necessaries of a future existence, so I have endeavoured to lay beside the figures of Aunts Ann and Juley and Hester, of Timothy and Swithin, of old Jolyon and James, and of their sons, that which shall guarantee them a little life here-after, a little balm in the hurried Gilead of a dissolving 'Progress'.

If the upper-middle class, with other classes, is destined to 'move on' into amorphism, here, pickled in these pages, it lies under glass for strollers in the wide and ill-arranged museum of Letters. Here it rests, preserved in its own juice: The Sense of Property.

1922   John Galsworthy

Reading-group questions

- The character of Soames has sparked much discussion. How does your perception of him change as the story progresses? Do you sympathise with him? Whereas it is often said that young Jolyon embodies the opposite values to Soames. Do you agree? Whom do you like more and why?

- The clash of family loyalty and lovers' passion is the basic force dividing the Forsytes. Do you think the characters make the right choices?

- John Galsworthy commented, 'So many people have written and claimed that their families were the originals of the Forsytes'. How do the Forsytes compare with modern families? In what ways have family values changed since the age of the Forsytes? Are 'tribal instinct' and a 'sense of property' as significant today?

- John Galsworthy described Irene as 'a concretion of disturbing Beauty impinging on a possessive world.' Discuss the character of Irene. Is she merely a literary device? Do you feel sympathy for her?

- John Galsworthy has often been criticised for embodying the repressive Victorian values he was supposedly satirising in *The Forsyte Saga*. How do you think he viewed the Forsytes?

THE FORSYTE SAGA

THE MAN OF PROPERTY

John Galsworthy

'"Soames will have trouble with her; you mark my words."'

London, 1880s: The Forsyte family is gathered – gloves, waistcoats, feathers and frocks – to celebrate the engagement of young June Forstye to an architect, Philip Bosinney. They are intrigued but wary of this stranger in their midst, whom they nickname 'The Buccaneer'. Also present is Soames Forsyte and his beautiful wife Irene – his most prized possession. With that meeting a chain of heartbreaking and tragic events is set in motion that will split the family to its very core . . .

In *The Man of Property*, John Galsworthy's stunning first instalment of *The Forsyte Saga*, the stage is set for one of the most absorbing family dramas ever written.

Since it first appeared in 1906, *The Forsyte Saga* has enthralled generations of readers, and been adapted with huge success for both film and television. These sumptuous new editions of each individual novel include reading-group questions and exciting, exclusive material to introduce them to a whole new audience.

'An immortal achievement . . . it is, at all levels, **readability itself**' *Financial Times*

978 0 7553 4085 9

headline
review

THE FORSYTE SAGA

IN CHANCERY

John Galsworthy

'He had never thought that the sight of this woman whom he once so passionately desired . . . could affect him in this way.'

Separated from his wife Irene, Soames Forsyte has almost accepted that she's never coming back. But he yearns for an heir. When he confronts Irene, the raw wounds of his past passion are exposed and he will do anything to claim back what is his. Then his cousin Jolyon Forsyte moves in to protect Irene and the old family rift splinters into new jealousy, hatred and fear. But this time it runs too deeply for forgiveness . . .

Love, infatuation and dishonour – *In Chancery*, the second episode of John Galsworthy's gripping family drama, sees the Forsytes heartbreakingly divided.

Since it first appeared in 1906, *The Forsyte Saga* has enthralled generations of readers, and been adapted with huge success for both film and television. These sumptuous new editions of each individual novel include reading-group questions and exciting, exclusive material to introduce them to a whole new audience.

'Such a **cracking good story** . . . compulsive, as well as very **modern and outrageous**' *The Sunday Times*

978 0 7553 4086 6

headline
review

THE FORSYTE SAGA

THE WHITE MONKEY

John Galsworthy

'Tomorrow! Second anniversary of her wedding-day! Still an ache when she thought of what it had not been.'

It's 1922 and Fleur Forsyte is now married to Michael Mont. The young couple throw themselves into the social whirlwind of the roaring twenties and seem to be enjoying life, entertaining friends in their smart Westminster house. But their marriage is haunted by the ghost of a past love affair. However vibrant Fleur appears, those closest to her sense a veiled sadness. Michael, devoted to his wife, but not blind to her faults, is determined to stand by her through anything. But just how much can he really forgive?

The hedonism and confusion of post-war London are beautifully captured in *The White Monkey*, drawing us into a new engrossing chapter for Galsworthy's indomitable Forsytes.

Since it first appeared in 1906, *The Forsyte Saga* has enthralled generations of readers, and been adapted with huge success for both film and television. These sumptuous new editions of each individual novel include reading-group questions and exciting, exclusive material to introduce them to a whole new audience.

'Such a **cracking good story** . . . compulsive, as well as very **modern and outrageous**' *The Sunday Times*

978 0 7553 4088 0

headline
review

THE FORSYTE SAGA

THE SILVER SPOON

John Galsworthy

'He was staring at a silver spoon. He himself had put it in her mouth at birth.'

Soames Forsyte, the man of property, has every worldly possession he could wish for. But his daughter Fleur is all he really cares about. Fleur at last seems to be content alongside her husband Michael Mont – with the birth of their son, Michael's move into politics and their glittering social circle, they have much to be happy about. But for old Soames, the carefree, 'live for today' attitudes of London in the twenties are alarming and baffling. And in an attempt to protect his daughter, Soames triggers a major society scandal – a scandal that could destroy his beloved Fleur's happiness, for ever . . .

Shocking lawsuits and passionate affairs threaten the Forsytes' world – *The Silver Spoon* is the fifth thrilling episode in John Galsworthy's compulsive family saga.

Since it first appeared in 1906, *The Forsyte Saga* has enthralled generations of readers, and been adapted with huge success for both film and television. These sumptuous new editions of each individual novel include reading-group questions and exciting, exclusive material to introduce them to a whole new audience.

'Soames Forsyte is one of the best-drawn anti-heroes in English fiction' *Scotsman*

978 0 7553 4089 7

headline
review

THE FORSYTE SAGA

SWAN SONG

John Galsworthy

'When, looking down the row of faces at her canteen table, Fleur saw Jon Forsyte's, it was within her heart as if, in winter, she had met with honeysuckle.'

Jon Forsyte is back. After years living in America, he is thrilled to be home and eager to show off his roots to his new bride Anne. When Fleur Mont, Jon's first love, hears of his arrival, she doesn't know what to feel. She's older now, more worldly, and married too with a young son – looking back can only bring pain. But feelings such as theirs are not easily buried. And when their passion is rekindled, no one can halt the devastating events that follow . . .

Swan Song, the sixth mesmerising instalment of *The Forsyte Saga*, marks the end of an era for the Forsytes, the dramatic culmination of an old family rift that has coloured their lives for decades.

Since it first appeared in 1906, *The Forsyte Saga* has enthralled generations of readers, and been adapted with huge success for both film and television. These sumptuous new editions of each individual novel include reading-group questions and exciting, exclusive material to introduce them to a whole new audience.

'The satire is sharp, the dialogue, **elegant and witty**, and the characterisation – **dazzling**' *Scotsman*

978 0 7553 4090 3

headline
review

THE FORSYTE SAGA

MAID IN WAITING

John Galsworthy

'In this family, the troubles of one were the troubles of all.'

As the 1930s bring dramatic change, so Galsworthy's sweeping family saga turns to the Cherrells, cousins of the Forsytes. Young Dinny Cherrell, seemingly fragile, but strong and determined, is a bright and vivid character who breathes life into all those she encounters. To her, family is everything. So when her brother faces extradition to South America, falsely accused of murder, and her cousin is threatened by her unstable husband, Dinny will do anything she can to shield them from harm.

The heartbreak and scandal continues with another branch of the family – *Maid in Waiting* opens a thrilling new phase in *The Forsyte Saga*.

Since it first appeared in 1906, *The Forsyte Saga* has enthralled generations of readers, and been adapted with huge success for both film and television. These sumptuous new editions of each individual novel include reading-group questions and exciting, exclusive material to introduce them to a whole new audience.

'An immortal achievement . . . it is, at all levels, readability itself' *Financial Times*

978 0 7553 4091 0

headline
review

THE FORSYTE SAGA

FLOWERING WILDERNESS

John Galsworthy

'It was like no other hour she had ever spent, and at the end of it she knew she was in love.'

Dinny Cherrell has been proposed to numerous times. But no one has ever come close to capturing her independent spirit – until she encounters Wilfred Desert. They had met briefly at Fleur Forsyte and Michael Mont's wedding and the spark of attraction felt all those years ago flowers into a deep, all-consuming passion. But Wilfred, made cynical by the war, is a complicated and tortured soul. When his past actions come back to haunt him, and the disapproval of Dinny's family work against them, their love is tested to the very limit . . .

Honour, family loyalty and a heart-wrenching love story – *Flowering Wilderness* is the poignant, utterly engrossing penultimate episode in *The Forsyte Saga*.

Since it first appeared in 1906, *The Forsyte Saga* has enthralled generations of readers, and been adapted with huge success for both film and television. These sumptuous new editions of each individual novel include reading-group questions and exciting, exclusive material to introduce them to a whole new audience.

'Such a cracking good story . . . compulsive, as well as very modern and outrageous' *The Sunday Times*

978 0 7553 4092 7

headline
review

THE FORSYTE SAGA

OVER THE RIVER

John Galsworthy

'Every memory she had of him came to life with an intensity that seemed to take all strength from her limbs.'

As *The Forsyte Saga* draws to a close, the future of the Cherrell family, cousins to the Forsytes, seems uncertain. Clare Cherrell has come home, fleeing the clutches of her violent, abusive husband. When he pursues her she vows she will never return and sets about fighting him in vicious divorce proceedings. Dinny supports her sister all the way, but she has her own heartache to conquer, a grief which threatens to embitter her life for ever. Will the sisters make it safely over the river, or is the stream of painful memories destined to engulf their lives?

Over the River is the dramatic, moving and stunning conclusion to John Galsworthy's unforgettable masterpiece, *The Forsyte Saga*.

Since it first appeared in 1906, *The Forsyte Saga* has enthralled generations of readers, and been adapted with huge success for both film and television. These sumptuous new editions of each individual novel include reading-group questions and exciting, exclusive material to introduce them to a whole new audience.

'The satire is sharp, the dialogue, elegant and witty, and the characterisation – dazzling' *Scotsman*

978 0 7553 4093 4

headline
review